John Timbs

The Year-Book of Facts in Science and Art

John Timbs

The Year-Book of Facts in Science and Art

ISBN/EAN: 9783337235499

Printed in Europe, USA, Canada, Australia, Japan

Cover: Foto ©Andreas Hilbeck / pixelio.de

More available books at **www.hansebooks.com**

THE

YEAR-BOOK OF FACTS

IN

Science and Art:

EXHIBITING

THE MOST IMPORTANT DISCOVERIES AND IMPROVEMENTS OF THE PAST YEAR;

IN MECHANICS AND THE USEFUL ARTS; NATURAL PHILOSOPHY;
ELECTRICITY; CHEMISTRY; ZOOLOGY AND BOTANY; GEOLOGY
AND MINERALOGY; METEOROLOGY AND ASTRONOMY.

By JOHN TIMBS, F.S.A.

AUTHOR OF "CURIOSITIES OF SCIENCE," ETC.

"Marvels, indeed, they are; but they are also mysteries, the unravelling of
which tasks to the utmost the highest order of human intelligence."—*Address
of Lord Wrottesley, President of the British Association, at Oxford*, 1860.

The University New Museum, Oxford.—(See page 13.)

LONDON:
W. KENT AND CO., PATERNOSTER ROW.
MDCCCLXI.

HENRY, LORD BROUGHAM, LL.D., F.R.S., &c.

(*With a Portrait.*)

THIRTY years have rolled away since the hand which sketches this outline of the scientific and literary labours of Lord Brougham was devoted to a similarly pleasurable and not unserviceable purpose. The "man of the people" had just then received from his Sovereign the Great Seal; and Henry Brougham, who had never before been in office, took his seat as Lord High Chancellor of Great Britain. Jubilant were the liberal organs of that day upon this signal elevation of their illustrious leader. "We have had," says the foremost of these writers, "learned Chancellors and political, or, we would rather say, politic Chancellors, but never before Lord Brougham (with, perhaps, the exception of Lord Erskine) have we had what may be justly called a popular Chancellor. . . . . We speak the plain and simple truth when we say, that at no period of our history since the era of the Commonwealth, has any one Englishman contrived to fix so many eyes upon him as Lord Brougham has for the last few years." This was, indeed, a proud moment for the son of the Cumberland gentleman, who, however, is of noble blood, for his lordship is heir general and representative of the ancient and noble house of Vaux.

His tenure of office was short: he retired with his party in 1834; and has since—more than a quarter of a century—principally devoted his great mind to the reform of our Laws, and to the diffusion of Science and Literature, more especially as they relate to the welfare of the masses—

Oblectamento non sui solum, sed populorum.

It is to these peaceful phases of the long and honourable career of Lord Brougham—before and since his elevation to the peerage—as a man of science, a critic, and man of letters, that we shall devote these few pages; the leading events of his Lordship's public life being merely glanced at, in order to preserve the continuity of the biographical narrative.

Henry, Lord Brougham, was born in St. Andrew's-square, Edinburgh, on the 19th of September, 1779. His father, Henry Brougham, Esq., of Scales Hall, Cumberland, and Brougham Hall, Westmoreland, was descended from the ancient family of Brougham, or De Burghams. He married Eleanor Syme, eldest daughter of the Rev. Dr. James Syme, niece, through her mother, of Robertson, the historian. Of six children by this marriage—five sons and one daughter—Henry is the eldest. (Two of the other sons, James and William, were members of Parliament, and took some part in public life during the brilliant career of their brother.) The family seems to have resided for the most part in Edinburgh, though sometimes at Brougham Hall, where Dr. Robertson visited them occasionally, and used to walk about with his grandnephew. The elder Brougham was no extraordinary man, but the mother is described as a woman of talent, and delightful character.

Henry Brougham was educated in Edinburgh, which, in 1857, he declared in public he looked upon as a very great benefit conferred on him by Providence. It was at the famous High School that he received his earliest classical tuition, under Mr. Luke Fraser, one of the under-masters, mentioned by Lord Cockburn in his *Life of Jeffrey*, as having had the distinguished honour of sending forth from three successive classes, three pupils no less celebrated than Scott, Jeffrey, and Brougham; and next under the head master or rector, Dr. Adam, the learned author of the *Roman Antiquities*, and a man of much weight and impressiveness of character, whose memory is not yet locally extinct. From the High School, Brougham passed, at the age of fifteen, to the University of Edinburgh, then so illustrious by having such men as Dugald Stewart, Robison, and Black among its professors, that English youths and youths from the colonies were sent to it to complete their education.

At the opening of the Session of the University of Edinburgh, in 1857, Principal Lee, in his introductory address, gave the following interesting account of the school-days of Lord Brougham:—

"Though descended (he said) from an ancient English family, he was born in Edinburgh, and his mother was a niece of Principal Robertson. In 1786, when seven years old, he entered the High School, in a class of 164 boys; and he had the advantage of being instructed by Mr. Luke Fraser, who was forty years a favourite teacher, under whom Sir Walter Scott commenced his classical studies along with the late Lord Melville, in the year 1777. The late Lord Jeffrey became a pupil of the same master in 1781. Among the schoolfellows of Henry Brougham (amounting, as I have said, to 164) were several youths afterwards highly eminent, of whom I make special mention of James Abercromby, afterwards Speaker of the House of Commons, and Lord Dunfermline; and Joseph Muter, subsequently recognised by the title of Sir Joseph Straton, one of the greatest benefactors of this University.

"Lord Brougham was *dux* of the Rector's class in 1791. I personally know how pre-eminently conspicuous at this University his attainments were, not in one or two branches of study, but in all to which his attention was directed; and particularly in mathematics and natural philosophy, as well as in law, in metaphysics, and in political science. Some of these shreds of information may not be familiarly known to every one."

In a later portion of his Address, the Principal, who himself entered the University as a pupil in 1794, enumerated the following as having been educated there, contemporaneously with, or subsequently to, Lord Brougham: — Thomas M'Crie, the historian; George Cranstoun; Lord Corehouse; Mountstewart Elphinstone; Peter Roget; George Birkbeck; Sir David Brewster; Francis Horner; Henry Cockburn; Henry Petty, (now Marquess of Lansdowne); John Leyden; Henry Temple, (now Lord Palmerston); the Earl of Haddington; Lord Webb Seymour; Lord Dudley; the Earl of Minto; Lord Glenelg; Lord Langdale; and Lord John Russell.

About a year after his matriculation, when not more than seventeen, young Brougham wrote a paper which he forwarded to the Royal Society, entitled "An Essay on the Inflection and Reflection of Light," which was printed in the *Philosophical Transactions* for 1796. In the following year he contributed another paper on the same subject; and in 1798, "General Theorems, chiefly Porisms, in the Higher Geometry," which the author thus introduces :—"The following are a few propositions that have occurred to me in the course of a considerable degree of attention which I have happened to bestow on that interesting, though difficult branch of speculative mathematics, the higher geometry. They are all, in some degree, connected; the greater part refer to the conic hyperbola, as related to a variety of other causes. Almost the whole are of that kind called porisms, whose nature and origin is now well known : and if that mathematician to whom we owe the first distinct and popular account of this formerly mysterious, but most interesting subject,* should chance to peruse these pages, he will find in them additional proofs of the accuracy which characterizes his inquiry into the discovery of this singularly-beautiful species of proposition."

These papers, though the fact of their author's extreme youth was unknown, attracted some notice among scientific men both at home and abroad.

Having chosen the Scottish Bar as his profession, and completed his legal studies at Edinburgh, Mr. Brougham, after a tour in Prussia and Holland in the company of Mr. Stuart, afterwards Lord Stuart de Rothsay, was admitted a member of the Edinburgh Society of Advocates in 1800. His acquaintance with Horner, Jeffrey, and other rising young men of the Scottish Whig party began about this time : and he was one of the most prominent members of the renowned Speculative Society, in which these and other Scotchmen, afterwards known to fame in various capacities, first cultivated their habits of extemporaneous debate. In the year 1802, when the *Edinburgh Review* was started, Mr. Brougham soon became one of the chief contributors. "After the third number," says Jeffrey, "he was admitted, and did more for us than anybody." They were all young men. Allen was thirty-two years of age; Sydney Smith was thirty-one; Jeffrey was twenty-nine; Thomas Brown, the metaphysician, was twenty-four; Horner was twenty-four; and Brougham was twenty-three. Brougham, though the youngest, had the greatest share of literary ambition. While writing his first articles for the *Review*, he was preparing for the press a more elaborate work in his own name, entitled *An Enquiry into the Colonial Policy of the European Powers*, which was published in two volumes at Edinburgh in 1803, and was considered an extraordinary work for so young a man, both in respect of knowledge and in respect of boldness of opinion. After this work had been published, he concentrated his literary efforts on the *Review*. The early numbers had been so immediately and largely successful that Con-

---

* See Mr. Playfair's Paper in vol. ii. of the *Edinburgh Transactions.*

stable, the publisher, had cheerfully acquiesced in the proposal that the articles, at first gratuitous, should be paid for at the rate of 10*l.* a sheet. Of all the contributors during Jeffrey's long editorship, which began in 1803, and closed in 1829, and during which the rate of payment was more than doubled, Brougham was the most industrious and versatile.*

In the second number, Brougham wrote a paper on Kepler's celebrated Problem, which he was led to after the discovery of the law which bears his name.

In 1807, Brougham removed from Edinburgh to London, where he qualified himself for the English bar. The reasons of this change were various. For one thing, as may be learnt from Lord Cockburn's account of the discouragements under which Scottish Whiggism then laboured in Edinburgh, and particularly within the precincts of the 'Parliament House' or Supreme Courts of Law, the prospects of a young Whig lawyer in Scotland cannot have been very brilliant. It is said, however, that a visit to London in 1807, in order to plead before the House of Lords in a case respecting the succession to the Scottish dukedom of Roxburghe, was the immediate cause of his resolution to come permanently to England. At all events, in 1808, when he was in his twenty-ninth year, he was called to the bar at Lincoln's Inn, and began to practise as an English barrister at the Court of King's Bench and on the northern circuit.

Mr. Brougham entered Parliament in 1810, and first sat for Camelford, at once ranging himself with the Whig opposition. He next sat for Winchester, then for Knaresborough; and lastly for the West Riding of Yorkshire, having in the intervals strongly contested Liverpool, the Inverkeithing burghs, and Westmoreland. He entered with spirit, energy, and consummate ability on the discussion of all the great questions of the day. Slavery and the Slave Trade, Agricultural Distress, Parliamentary Reform, Catholic Emancipation, the Holy Alliance, Reduction of the Army, and the Corn Law monopoly, were all supported by his most fervid oratory. His support of Queen Caroline to claim her rights as Queen Consort and wife of George IV., brought Mr. Brougham an immense accession of popularity; and men of all parties and opinions as to the guilt of the Queen, acknowledged the intrepidity and splendid talents of Mr. Brougham on this memorable but painful occasion.

That acute observer and critic, William Hazlitt, has left this portrait-sketch, taken about 1825:—"Mr. Brougham writes almost as well as he speaks. In the midst of an election contest, he comes out to address the populace, and goes back to his study to finish an article for the *Edinburgh Review*, sometimes, indeed, wedging three or four articles in the shape of *refucciamentis* of his own pamphlets or speeches in Parliament in a single number. Such, indeed, is the activity of his mind, that it appears to require neither repose nor any other stimulus than a delight in its own exercise. He can turn his hand to anything, but he cannot be idle. There are few intellectual accomplishments which he does not possess, and possess in a very high degree. He speaks French (and, we believe, several other modern languages), is a capital mathematician, and obtained an introduction to the celebrated Carnot in this latter character, when the conversation turned on squaring the circle, and not on the propriety of confining France within the natural boundaries of the Rhine. Mr. Brougham is, in fact, a striking instance of the versatility and strength of the human mind, and also, in one sense, of the length of human life; if we make good use of our time, there is room enough to crowd almost every art and science into it."

The year 1828 was a memorable one in Mr. Brougham's parliamentary life. Early in the session, in the debate upon the battle of Navarino, he expressed his readiness to support the ministry as long as the members who composed it showed a determination to retrench the expenditure of the country, to improve its domestic arrangements, and to adopt a truly British system of foreign policy. It was on this occasion that Mr. Brougham used the expression, since become so familiar, "The schoolmaster is abroad." He next brought forward a motion on the state of the Law, in a speech of six hours' delivery; when the motion, in an amended shape, was carried, requesting the King to cause "due inquiry to

* Brougham was the predecessor of Lord Jeffrey in the editorship of the *Edinburgh Review*—a fact which is not generally known, but which is certain. Brougham was not the first editor, having filled that office for a short time after Sydney Smith withdrew from the situation.—(*Metropolitan*, edited by Thomas Campbell.)

be made into the origin, progress, and termination of actions in the superior courts of common law in this country," and "into the state of the law regarding the transfer of real property." In the same month, Mr. Brougham eloquently advocated the repeal of the Test and Corporation Acts, and, in the next month, Catholic Emancipation. In 1829 he had the satisfaction of explaining to the House the proceedings of the great Charities Commission, the appointment of which he had procured eleven years before; and which during that interval had investigated into the condition and history of no fewer than 19,000 of the charitable foundations of Great Britain.

Mr. Brougham wrote, in aid of this great labour, a memorable tract, of which the following anecdote is related :—Hallam's *History of the Middle Ages* was the last book of any importance read by Sir Samuel Romilly; and he recommended its immediate perusal to Mr. Brougham, as a contrast to his dry *Letter on the Abuse of Charities*, the tract above referred to. Yet Sir Samuel undervalued the *Letter*, for it ran through eight editions in one month.

In 1830 Mr. Brougham supported Parliamentary Reform, the Abolition of Punishment of Forgery by Death, Local Jurisdictions (Local Courts) in England, and the Abolition of West India Slavery. We have now reached the period of Mr. Brougham's elevation to the House of Lords as Lord Chancellor.

His great exertions in aid of Public Education date from 1824, when he co-operated with Dr. Birkbeck, Mr. W. Tooke, and Mr. Robertson, in the establishment of the London Mechanics' Institution in London; for whose advantage were republished, from the *Edinburgh Review*, Mr. Brougham's excellent *Practical Observations upon the Education of the People*, addressed to the working classes and their employers.

In the following year Mr. Brougham was elected Lord Rector of the University of Glasgow; his opponent was Sir Walter Scott, who lost the election by the casting vote of Sir James Mackintosh in favour of Brougham.

His next good work was his valuable aid, in conjunction with the poet Campbell and Dr. Birkbeck, in founding University College, "for affording literary and scientific education at a moderate expense;" and, greatly by aid of Mr. Brougham's indefatigable exertions, this establishment was opened in 1828, within seventeen months from the day on which the first stone was laid. Lord Brougham is to this day President of the College.

Three years previously, in 1825, Mr. Brougham, associated with Lords Auckland, Althorp, John Russell, and Nugent, and other statesmen and leading members of the Whig aristocracy, established the Society for the Diffusion of Useful Knowledge,[*] with the view of circulating a series of treatises on the exact sciences, and on various branches of useful knowledge; Mr. Brougham being chairman. In the original prospectus we find it stated, "The object of the Society is strictly limited to what its title imports, namely, the imparting useful information to all classes of the community, particularly to such as are unable to avail themselves of experienced teachers, or may prefer learning by themselves." The first publication was in March, 1827, being "A Discourse on the Objects, Pleasures, and Advantages of Science," from the pen of Mr. Brougham; and for attractiveness this treatise has rarely been equalled. Lord Brougham continued to be chairman of the Society until its good work having been accomplished by its own enlightening industry, and by stimulating others in the same course, the Society was dissolved. The scientific and other treatises published at the onset, are considered to have emanated directly from Mr. Brougham; while the later and more popular works were the result of new accessions of intellectual talent and taste.[†] Here we may record as an instance of Mr. Brougham's liberality in his educational philanthropy, that he worked heartily with every labourer in the same field, however humble he might be.

---

[*] The name and title "The Society for the Diffusion of Useful Knowledge," was, however, first employed in the year 1824, when the Editor of the *Year-Book of Facts* wrote, at Brighton, in conjunction with Sir Richard Phillips and Dr. Birkbeck, the prospectus of a series of cheap treatises to be published " under the Superintendence of the Society for the Diffusion of Useful Knowledge."

[†] Among these later works should be mentioned the *Penny Cyclopædia*, the most valuable work of its class, the completion of which was celebrated by a public dinner to Mr. Charles Knight, the originator and publisher; Lord Brougham taking the chair at this intellectual festival.

We especially refer to Mr. Brougham's pamphlet addressed to the Working Classes and their Employers, in which, referring to a cheap series of standard works, then in course of publication by John Limbird, of the Strand, Mr. Brougham thus generously characterized the same publisher's cheap periodical :—

" The *Mirror*, a weekly publication, containing much matter of harmless and even improving amusement, and edited with very considerable taste, has besides, in almost every number, information of a most instructive kind. Its great circulation must prove highly beneficial to the bulk of the people."

It may be as well here to refer to Lord Brougham's other leading exertions in the cause of Public Education. During his Chancellorship (in 1833), greatly through his influence upon the Report of a Parliamentary Committee, the first annual grant for Education Purposes was made by the Government. Five years later, we find Lord Brougham under " sore discouragement," lamenting what he considered as the final and hopeless failure of his life-long efforts in the cause of education of the people. But early in the subsequent year, a Committee of Council was appointed to dispense the annual Government grant for education, and the amount was increased to 30,000*l.* a-year. The next step was the establishment of Normal Schools under Government inspection. This was followed by the formation of Training Schools and Colleges for the education and training of Schoolmasters and Schoolmistresses.

Returning to Lord Brougham's more direct contributions to Science, we come to his able work on Natural Theology, intended as a preliminary discourse to " Paley's Natural Theology, Illustrated." In a dedication to Earl Spencer, Lord Brougham tells us, this work was undertaken in consequence of his having observed that scientific men were apt to regard the study of Natural Religion as little connected with philosophical pursuits ; and many of these persons seemed to regard Natural Theology as a mere speculation. The Society for the Diffusion of Useful Knowledge were urged to publish an edition of Dr. Paley's popular work ; Lord Brougham and Lord Spencer favoured the plan, but some of their colleagues feared it might lead to religious controversy, and the scheme was abandoned. Lord Brougham, however, resolving to carry his plan into execution, associated with the worthy and accomplished Sir Charles Bell. The " Discourse" was mostly written between 1830 and 1833, a portion being added in the autumn of 1834. " In those days (says Lord Brougham) I held the Great Seal of this kingdom ; and it was impossible to finish the work while many cases of another kind pressed upon me. But the first leisure that could be obtained was devoted to this object, and to a careful revision of what had been written in a season less auspicious for such speculations." His dedication of the volume to " honest Lord Althorp " (now Earl Spencer) is touchingly eloquent :—

" I inscribe the fruits of these studies to you, not merely as a token of ancient friendship—for that you do not require ; nor because I have always found you, whether in possession or in resistance of power, a fellow-labourer to maintain our common principles, alike firm, faithful, disinterested—for your known public character wants no testimony from me ; nor yet because a work on such a subject needs the patronage of a great name—for it would be affectation in me to pretend any such motives ; but because you have devoted much of your time to such inquiries—are beyond most men sensible of their importance—concur generally in the opinions which I profess to maintain, and had even formed the design of giving to the world your thoughts upon the subject, as I hope and trust you now will be moved to do all the more for the present address. In this view, your authority will prove of great value to the cause of truth, however superfluous the patronage of even your name might be to recommend the most important of all studies.

" Had our lamented friend Romilly lived, you are aware that not even these considerations would have made me address any one but him, with whom I had oftentimes speculated upon this ground. Both of us have been visited with the most severe afflictions, of a far nearer and more lasting kind than even his removal, and we are now left with few things to care for."

The *Edinburgh Review* says of this work : — " When Lord Brougham's eloquence in the Senate shall have passed away, and his services as a statesman shall exist only in the free institutions which they have helped to secure, his *Discourse on Natural Theology* will continue to inculcate imperishable truths, and fit the mind for the higher revelations which these truths are destined to foreshadow and confirm."

Sir Charles Bell thus gracefully refers to his association in the editorship of *Paley*:—"It was at the desire of the Lord Chancellor Brougham that the author wrote the essay on *Animal Mechanics*; and it was probably from a belief that the author felt the importance of the subjects touched upon in that essay, that his Lordship was led to do him the further honour of asking him to join with him in illustrating the *Natural Theology* of Dr. Paley."

Among the lighter labours of Lord Brougham—recreations they may be termed —are his Sketches of Eminent Statesmen, Men of Letters, and Philosophers, of the time of George III. The philosophers comprise Watt, Priestley, Cavendish, Davy, Simson, Adam Smith, Lavoisier, Banks, and D'Alembert. Although these sketches will scarcely bear the test of historical or biographical accuracy, they are delightful to read, have much of the piquancy of the French *mémoire*, and are full of lively anecdote and pleasantry; although they are varied with graver matter, as in an abstruse mathematical paper to be found in the Life of D'Alembert; and a long paper on Greek Geometry in the Life of Simson. On the other hand, how familiarly are Franklin's characteristics summed up in these few lines:—"Of all this great man's scientific excellencies, the most remarkable is the smallness, the simplicity, the apparent inadequacy, of the means which he employed in his experimental researches. His discoveries were all made with scarcely any apparatus at all; and if, at any time, he had been led to employ instruments of a somewhat less ordinary description, he never rested satisfied until he had, as it were, afterwards translated the process, by resolving the problem with such simple machinery, that you might say he had done it wholly unaided by apparatus. The experiments by which the identity of lightning and electricity was demonstrated were all made with a sheet of brown paper, a bit of twine or silk thread, and an iron key!"

Lord Brougham's contributions to the *Edinburgh Review* fill three large library volumes: they are rhetorical and historical; upon foreign policy, constitutional questions, political economy and finance, and criminal law: and, what is more to our purpose, in physical science. An able critic in the *Examiner* has observed of the entire work:—its great charm is, that it does not merely extend over a range of subjects singularly wide, but that every topic along the range is discussed with a mastery of its essential features, rendering the extent and the versatility alike astonishing.

Great men are, however, liable to great mistakes; and one of Lord Brougham's early criticisms is an instance of this fallibility. The first reception of Dr. Thomas Young's investigations on Light was very unfavourable. In 1801 he made his grand discovery of the principle of interferences in the undulatory theory of Light; and in that and the two following years, he read to the Royal Society memoirs which established the theory on grounds that have since been almost universally recognised as irrefragable. But they were attacked by Mr. Brougham, in the *Edinburgh Review*, with great acerbity, of which the following is a specimen:—

"We demand, if the world of science which Newton once illuminated, is to be as changeable in its modes as the world of fashion which is directed by the nod of a silly woman or a pampered fop? Has the Royal Society degraded its publications into bulletins of new and fashionable theories for the ladies of the Royal Institution? *Proh pudor!* Let the professor continue to amuse his audience with an endless variety of such harmless trifles, but in the name of science, let them not find admittance into that venerable repository which contains the works of Newton, and Boyle, and Cavendish, and Maskelyne, and Herschel."

Further on, the reviewer impugns the account of an experiment made by Young, the deductions from which were of themselves almost sufficient to establish the correctness of the undulatory theory: it was, indeed, a crucial experiment. Dr. Young replied in these triumphant words:—"Conscious of inability to explain the experiment, too ungenerous to confess that inability, and too idle to repeat the experiment, he is compelled to advance the supposition that it was incorrect." This reply was printed by Dr. Young in a pamphlet, of which only one copy was sold! The *Edinburgh Review* had the effect of checking the advance of the undulatory theory. Justice, however, came at length; and the discovery which Brougham had levelled with all his powers of sarcasm, has, in the words of Sir John Herschel, "proved the key to all the more abstruse and puzzling properties of light, and which would alone have sufficed to place the author in the highest rank of scientific immortality, even were his other almost innumerable claims to such a distinction disregarded." The late Dean of Ely (Dr. Peacock) has also nobly vindicated the fame of Dr. Young; and the undulatory theory is now generally received in place of the molecular or emanatory theory.*

However, retribution came: the noble reviewer himself has, in his turn, been treated "very martyrly," as all must remember who read many years ago in *Blackwood's Edinburgh Magazine*, a most severe and lengthy attack upon one of the law reforms of that day, entitled "Lords Brougham, Lyndhurst, and Local Courts." Throughout the volumes of Maga we do not remember a more stinging or fierce assault than this paper, which was strongly overcharged with professional jealousy.

A better estimate has recently appeared. In the *Saturday Review*, Nov. 5, 1860, it is justly said:—"The mass of the legislative reforms which we owe to Lord Brougham, more especially in the various departments of the law, is so surprising, that one can scarcely credit the extent to which the present system of jurisprudence bears the impress of his hand. From the day when Henry Brougham passed his first memorable bill through Parliament, by which the slave trade was declared to be felony, down to the last movement for legal reform, his assiduity has never flagged. Professional demands upon his energies, and excursions of greater or less depth into every department of science and literature, have always seemed to leave him ample time for pursuing the great work of his life —the improvement of the principles and practice of the administration of justice. Of all the important changes which have been made in our legal system during the last half century, there are very few in which the name of Lord Brougham is not in some measure associated; and the number of reforms which he may justly call his own form a progeny such as no other statesman can boast." .... "There is scarcely a branch of law reform to which Lord Brougham has not contributed something of actual legislation; but his great glory is to have been a law reformer when almost all lawyers were obstinately conservative, and to have done more than any one else, by his exertions in and out of Parliament, to set the stone rolling which has crushed a multitude of abuses, and promises to dispose of all that remain."

Lord Brougham has been for several years a member of the National Institute of France; and among the papers which he has read there is one "On certain Paradoxes, real or supposed, in the Integral Calculus," June, 1857;* also, an elaborate memoir, the "Architecture of Cells of Bees," read May, 1858; a tract of "Inquiries, Analytical and Experimental, on Light," in the memoirs of the Institute, 1854. These papers have been reprinted in a volume of *Tracts, Mathematical and Physical*,† published last autumn. The first tract, and two others on Light, were written in 1794, 5, 6, and 7, when the author was a student at the University under Professors Playfair and Robinson. In the preface to this volume, Lord Brougham relates an interesting reminiscence of the University, showing how Professor Playfair's expression of an opinion of his pupil's good fortune in hitting upon the Binomial Theorem, at once fixed his inclination for mathematical studies.

Lord Brougham is Chancellor of the University of Edinburgh, to whom the above tracts, "begun while its pupil, finished when its head, are inscribed by the author, in grateful remembrance of benefits conferred of old, and honour of late bestowed."

Our next record is that of the very interesting inauguration of a statue to Sir Isaac Newton, at his native town, Grantham, in Lincolnshire, Sept. 21, 1858, at which Lord Brougham delivered an eloquent address. His Lordship, after some preliminary observations, said:—The remark is common and is obvious that the genius of Newton did not manifest itself at a very early age. His faculties were not, like those of some great and many ordinary individuals, precociously developed. Among the former, Clairaut stands pre-eminent, who, at

---

* We refrain from dwelling upon this error in judgment; at the same time we feel it to be too important a fact in the history of scientific discovery to be omitted even in the present brief sketch.

† This volume, together with Lord Brougham's *Historical and Miscellaneous Works*, 10 vols.; *Contributions to the Edinburgh Review*, 3 vols.; and *Paley's Natural Philosophy*, 3 vols., have lately been published, in handsome but economical forms, by Griffin, Bohn, and Co.

nineteen years of age, presented to the Royal Academy a memoir of great originality upon a difficult subject in the higher geometry; and at eighteen, published his great work on curves of double curvature, composed during the two preceding years. Pascal, too, at sixteen, wrote an excellent treatise on conic sections. That Newton cannot be ranked in this respect with those extraordinary persons is owing to the accidents which prevented him from entering upon mathematical study before his eighteenth year; and then a much greater marvel was wrought than even the Clairauts and the Pascals displayed. His earliest history is involved in some obscurity, and the most celebrated of men has, in this particular, been compared to the most celebrated of rivers (the Nile), as if the course of both in its feeble state had been concealed from mortal eyes. We have it, however, well ascertained that within four years, between the age of eighteen and twenty-two, he had begun to study mathematic science, and had taken his place among the greatest masters; learnt for the first time the elements of geometry and analysis, and discovered a calculus which entirely changed the face of the science, effecting a complete revolution in that and in every branch of philosophy connected with it. Before 1661 he had not read Euclid; in 1665 he had committed to writing the method of fluxions. At twenty-five years of age he had discovered the law of gravitation, and laid the foundation of celestial dynamics, the sciences created by him. Before ten years had elapsed, he added to his discoveries that of the fundamental properties of light. So brilliant a course of discovery in so short a time, changing and reconstructing analytical, astronomical, and optical science, almost defies belief. The statement could only be deemed possible by an appeal to the incontestable evidence that proves it strictly true. By a rare felicity these doctrines gained the universal assent of mankind as soon as they were clearly understood; and their originality has never been seriously called in question. Some doubts having been raised respecting his inventing the calculus—doubts raised in consequence of his so long withholding the publication of his method—no sooner was the inquiry instituted than the evidence produced proved so decisive that all men, in all countries, acknowledged him to have been by several years the earliest inventor, and Leibnitz, at the utmost, the first publisher. [The noble and learned Lord traced the history of Newton, as far as it is known, namely, from the year 1665, when that great genius first turned his attention to the method of fluxions, touching on his great discoveries in optics, gravitation, the differential calculus, &c., but diverging considerably from the main issue, so as to exhibit the noble lord's own learning quite as much as to glorify the transcendent genius of the deceased philosopher.] Leibnitz, continued the noble and learned Lord, when asked at the royal table in Berlin his opinion of Newton, said that " taking mathematicians from the beginning of the world to the time when Newton lived, what he had done was much the better half." " The *Principia* will ever remain a monument of the profound genius which revealed to us the greatest laws of the universe" are the words of Laplace. " That work stands pre-eminent above all the other productions of the human mind." " The discovery of that simple and general law, by the greatness and variety of the objects which it embraces, confers honour upon the intellect of man.' Lagrange, we are told by D'Alembert, was wont to describe Newton as the greatest genius that ever existed; but to add how fortunate he was also, "because there can only once be found a system of the universe to establish." " Never," says the Father of the Institute of France—one filling a high place among the most eminent of its members—" never," says M. Biot, " was the supremacy of intellect so justly established, and so fully confessed." " In mathematical and in experimental science without an equal, and without an example; combining the genius for both in its highest degree." The *Principia*[*] he terms the greatest work ever produced by the mind of man; adding, in the words of Haller, that a nearer approach to the Divine nature has not been permitted to mortals. " In first giving to the world Newton's method of fluxions," says Fontenelle, "Leibnitz did like Prometheus—he stole fire from heaven to teach men the secret." " Does Newton," L'Hopital asked, "sleep and wake like other men? I figure him to myself as of a celestial kind, wholly severed from mortality."

In the autumn of 1857, Lord Brougham (on Oct. 13) inaugurated at Birmingham the Association for the Promotion of Social Science, intended " to bear as

---

[*] Lord Brougham edited and annotated the *Principia*.

wide a relation to social and political science as the British Association does to mathematical and physical science."* The Association met at Liverpool in 1858, Lord John Russell presiding. In 1859 the Association assembled at Bradford, under the presidency of Lord Brougham; and last year, 1860, his Lordship again presided, the meeting being held at Glasgow. The elaborate address of the noble and learned Lord is far beyond the compass of these pages ; he touched upon almost every public question of importance—political as well as social. Education, parliamentary and law reform, the great "privilege question," pauperism, intemperance, the policy of foreign governments, the volunteer movement, and a host of other subjects, were discussed by the veteran orator. The over-talk in the House of Commons, and the rejection of the Paper Duty Repeal Bill by the House of Lords were anathematized ; despotism was shown to have its uses as well as abuses ; while Bomba II. was alluded to in these terms:—"Young in years to have perpetrated such crimes ! But Caligula died at eight-and-twenty, and Heliogabulus at eighteen." In conclusion, the noble and learned Lord expressed his warm approval of the volunteer movement. The delivery of the address occupied two hours ; and at the close a vote of thanks, moved by Sir J. Pakington and seconded by Lord Ardmillan, was awarded with acclamation to the venerable president.

A journalist of the event pleasantly remarked :—" Lord Brougham has been engaged, if not in throwing any new light upon science itself, at least in showing that age has as yet done nothing towards dimming his own faculties. His power of marshalling facts, and his marvellous resources of language, have seldom been more finely exhibited than at the Glasgow meeting. The warm and cordial tributes which the leading men of Scotland, of all parties, have borne to Lord Brougham's unequalled gifts, do honour to those who have uttered them so ungrudgingly. We say this, claiming Lord Brougham as an Englishman and an English lord."

Another contemporary says :—"The English nation owes a debt of profound gratitude and veneration to this extraordinary man, who now, in his eighty-second year, is labouring steadily and efficiently in the cause which he advocated in evil days—now sixty years ago. When the day comes—may it be a distant one !—when Henry Brougham is summoned away from amongst us, let it never be forgotten that, at a period when to advocate such a doctrine was almost supposed to savour of treason and sedition, Brougham was the steady advocate for the *Education of the People !*"

Lord Brougham's love of science has, for many years, led him from time to time to several interesting investigations of the properties of Light, which have been chronicled in our *Year-Book*. Thus, in 1849, his lordship made several experiments in his delightful retreat at Cannes, in Provence, by an apparatus executed by M. Soleil, of Paris, and with the aid of a heliostate for fixing the sunbeam in one position during the day. The results were communicated by Sir David Brewster to the British Association in 1849.†

In the following year Lord Brougham read to the Royal Society the above experiments and observations, which he described as conducted under most favourable circumstances, arising from the climate of Provence, where they were commenced, being peculiarly adapted to such studies. He referred also to Soleil's most excellent set of instruments and delicate apparatus, only required for experiments depending upon nice measurements. The results of these experiments are thrown into the form of definitions and propositions, in order to subject his doctrines to a fuller scrutiny.‡

In 1853, Lord Brougham communicated to the Royal Society "Further Experiments and Observations on the Properties of Light," wherein the author con-

---

* The reader will find an able paper by Mr. Charles Knight, on the objects of the Association, in the *Companion to the Almanack for* 1858. In his address at Birmingham, Lord Brougham gave some interesting facts and results of the working of the Useful Knowledge Society.

Lord Brougham's services as chairman of the Useful Knowledge Society were such, that notwithstanding he had to preside in the House of Lords and the Court of Chancery, and was at the head of eight or ten public associations, he was most punctual in his attendance, always contriving to be in the chair at the hour of meeting.

† *Year-Book of Facts*, 1849, p. 145.   ‡ Ibid. 1851, p. 147.

siders that Sir Isaac Newton's experiments to prove that the fringes formed by the inflexion and bordering the shadows of all bodies, are of different breadths when formed by the homogeneous rays of different kinds, are the foundation of his theory, and would be perfectly conclusive if the different rays were equally bent out of their course by inflexion; for in that case the line joining the centres of the fringes of the shadow being, as he found them, of different lengths, the fringes must be of different breadths. Experiments are adduced in the paper to show that this property of different flexibility exists, which Sir Isaac Newton had not remarked.*

With the record of the publication of his Lordship's comprehensive work, entitled *The British Constitution; its History, Structure, and Functions*, our sketch must close. This volume has appeared within the present month (January), with an admirable dedication to Her Majesty, in which graceful allusion is made to the course adopted with respect to the second patent of the Brougham peerage, giving him the same title, but with limitation, in default of heirs male, to his brother, William Brougham, Esq., and his heirs male.

" TO THE QUEEN.

" Madame,—I presume to lay at your Majesty's feet a work, the result of many years' diligent study, much calm reflection, and a long life's experience. It professes to record facts, institute comparisons, draw conclusions, and expound principles, often too little considered in this country by those who enjoy the inestimable blessings of our political system; and little understood in other countries by those who are endeavouring to naturalize it among themselves, and for whose success the wishes of all must be more hearty than their hopes can be sanguine.

" The subject of the book, *The British Constitution*, has a natural connexion with your Majesty's auspicious reign, which is not more adorned by the domestic virtues of the Sovereign than by the strictly constitutional exercise of her high office, redounding to the security of the Crown, the true glory of the monarch, and the happiness of the people. Entirely joining with all my fellow-citizens in feelings of gratitude towards such a ruler, I have individually a deep sense of the kindness with which your Majesty has graciously extended the honours formerly bestowed, the reasons assigned for that favour, and the precedents followed in granting it.

" With these sentiments of humble attachment and respect, I am, your Majesty's most faithful and most dutiful servant,

" BROUGHAM.

" Brougham Hall, 11th December, 1860."

The accompanying portrait, which represents Lord Brougham addressing the House of Lords, is from a remarkably fine photograph by Mayall.

* *Year-Book of Facts*, 1854, p. 171.

CONTENTS.

YEAR-BOOK OF FACTS.

Mechanical and Useful Arts.

GREAT WORKS OF 1860.

THE *Great Eastern* steam-ship left Southampton on June 17th, for New York, which she reached on the 28th, after a passage of 11¼ days. Her average rate of speed was about 300 miles per day; the maximum attained was 14½ knots an hour. Her return voyage is thus described in the *London Review:*—"With all the disadvantages of improper trim, with the drawback of the long rank vegetation clinging to her keel, with engines stiff and new to their work, with engineers to a great extent unacquainted with the powers and working of the machinery, the great ship made a run from New York to Milford of 2980 knots, after allowing for difference of time of the longitude, at an average speed of 13·9, or within a mere fraction of 14 knots an hour. The total consumption of coals was 2744 tons, or rather less than one ton per knot run,—a remarkably small quantity when the enormous tonnage of the vessel is taken into account."

The Warrior, the first iron-plated steam-frigate in the possession of Great Britain, was launched on Dec. 29, 1860; this is the largest man-of-war ever built, and more than 1500 tons larger than the largest vessel in the world, after the *Great Eastern*. *The Warrior* was minutely described in the *Year-Book of Facts*, 1860, pp. 11—13. (See also pp. 33—36 of the present volume.)

The French iron-plated steam-ship *La Gloire* is afloat, and an excellent description, with a faithful sketch of her, conveying a correct idea of the profile of the ship, will be found in the *Mechanics' Magazine*, Dec. 28, 1860. (See also pp. 36—40 of the present *Year-Book*.)

The Great Victoria Railway Bridge, Canada, has been opened by the Prince of Wales. An admirable description of this stupendous work, based upon Mr. James Hodges's published account of its construction, will be found in the *Builder*, Oct. 20, 1860.

THE OXFORD UNIVERSITY MUSEUM.
(See the Vignette.)

THIS picturesque edifice has been opened, and was appropriated to a grand *soirée* during the meeting of the British Association at Oxford in July last. The purpose of the Museum is to supply, "for mutual aid and easy interchange of reference and comparison, a common habitation under one roof" of the natural and experimental sciences. The architects were Deane and Woodward ; and the style is mediæval, especially fitted for Oxford. As the group of buildings is entirely isolated, their picturesqueness and variety can be fully appreciated. The principal (or west) front is shown in the vignette, and contains sitting, apparatus, and lecture rooms; the northern wing is devoted to the departments of anatomy, medicine, physiology, and zoology ; the south wing to those of chemistry, experimental philosophy, mineralogy, and geology, with a great lecture-room, &c.; and the large inner quadrangle, called the Museum Court, to the collections. The octagonal building on the south-west (right hand of the engraving) is the large laboratory, and is modelled after the kitchen of Glastonbury Abbey.

One of the happiest ideas of the design was to make the building itself serve to illustrate the studies of the place. The shafts have been selected, under the direction of the Professor of Geology, from quarries which furnish examples of many of the most important rocks of the British Islands. On the lower and upper arcades are placed, west, the granitic series ; east, the metamorphic ; north, calcareous rocks, chiefly from Ireland ; south, the marbles of England. The capitals and bases represent groups of plants and animals, illustrating different climates and various epochs.

THE SOUTH KENSINGTON MUSEUM.

The Art-collections (the nucleus of this Museum) originated in the School of Design in Somerset House, which commenced its proceedings in 1837. The total cost to the public of the Collections of Ornamental Art now deposited in the South Kensington Museum, amounts to 38,269*l.* The value of gifts and loans liberally contributed by the public, were estimated at 460,000*l.* Including the cost of land, buildings, and the other collections, the South Kensington Museum has cost the public 167,805*l.* This great central Museum of " fine art applied to manufactures" contains more than 7000 specimens of ornamental art ; a large collection of British pictures ; a circulating art library ; architectural examples, and various useful collections ; besides which there is a normal school for training art teachers, and the various local schools of art receive substantial aid. The character of this museum is essentially practical. It includes an educational collection of the most approved school buildings, furniture, maps, and books. There is a " Food Collection," which shows the nutritive powers of different substances, a curator supplying the necessary explanation of the cases exhibited. There is also an exhibition of animal products, which is obviously useful. A Collection of Patents forms another class of the contents of the museum : it is of remarkable interest as an historical exhibition, including, for instance, the parent engine of steam navigation by Symington, by which he navigated a boat in 1787, with (it is said) Lord Brougham and the poet Burns for his companions. But Ornamental Art is the main feature in the museum.—*Evidence before Select Committee, House of Commons.*

CONSTRUCTION OF ARTILLERY.

THIS important subject will be found noticed in other portions of the present section of the *Year-Book*, by several inventors. Early in the Session of the Institution of Civil Engineers, a paper was read "On the Construction of Artillery, and other Vessels, to resist great internal pressure," by Mr. T. A. Longridge, C.E.; the inquiry being limited to the question, how to make a gun of sufficient strength to enable the artillerist to obtain the full effect of the explosive compound used in it.

The attention of the author was drawn to the subject early in the year 1855. Following up the reasoning of Professor Barlow, on hydraulic-press cylinders, he was led to consider how the internal defect of any homogeneous cylinder could be remedied. Professor Barlow had shown, that in every such cylinder the increase of strength was not in proportion to the increase of thickness, and that a vessel of infinite thickness could not, ultimately, resist an internal pressure greater than the tensile forces of the material of which it was composed. The material at the internal circumference might, in fact, be strained to its utmost, when that at the outside was scarcely strained at all. To remedy this, it was necessary that each concentric layer of the gun, or cylinder, should be in an initial state of stress, such that when the pressure was applied, the sum of the initial and the induced stresses should be a constant quantity, throughout the whole thickness of the cylinder. It occurred to the author that this could be accomplished by forming the gun, or cylinder, of a thin internal shell, or case, and coiling round it successive series of wires, each coil being laid on with the tension due to its position.

The principle of building up a gun in successive layers, with increasing initial tension, was, therefore, that which it was intended to bring forward in this paper. The author claimed no exclusive merit for this idea. Although then unknown to him, it was being followed up by Captain Blakeley, Mr. Mallet, and others, who, however, sought for its practical outcome in rings, or hoops, contracted, or forced on to the central core. Captain Blakeley had, equally with the author, the idea of making use of wire, although his experiments were entirely confined to hoops. It was in complete ignorance of what others were doing, that the author undertook the experiments recorded, and described in detail in the present paper. The results were so striking, that he lost no time in bringing them before the War Department. The usual reference was made to the Select Committee at Woolwich, with the usual result. The principle was pronounced to be defective, and not such as to warrant any trials at the public expense. The author, however, continued his experiments, and the results were such as entirely to confirm his confidence in the practical utility of the invention.

It was stated that these cylinders could be made at one-fourth the weight, and at about one-half the cost, of the ordinary hydraulic-press cylinders; and that their lightness was of great importance, when intended for export to South America and other countries, where the means of transport for heavy machinery did not exist.

The discussion upon this paper extended over five evenings; and an abstract of the whole, with an account of Mr. Longridge's experiments, has been reprinted, by permission of the Institution, from their Proceedings; extending in the whole to 172 octavo pages, illustrated with diagrams. The pamphlet, with the advantage of the editorship of Mr. Charles Manby, F.R.S., Hon. Sec., and Mr. J. Forrest, Sec., is a most valuable contribution to the science of the subject, which now commands so large a share of public attention, at home and abroad.

INSTITUTION OF CIVIL ENGINEERS—BEQUESTS AND PREMIUMS.

On April 17th, the President of the Institution of Civil Engineers announced to the members, that the late Mr. Joseph Miller, for many years a Member of Council, had kindly bequeathed to the Institution the sum of five thousand pounds, of which three thousand pounds would be receivable immediately, and two thousand pounds on the demise of a gentleman resident in the West Indies. The funds of the Institution would thus be materially augmented, as there would also be soon receivable the bequest of two thousand pounds from the late Mr. Robert Stephenson. To these amounts must be added the sum of nearly five thousand pounds bequeathed by the first President, Mr. Telford ; of two hundred pounds presented by Mr. Charles Manby ; and of one thousand pounds which had recently been invested out of income : total, 13,094l. 12s. 4d.

At a meeting of the Council of the Institution, held on the 23rd of October, the following premiums were awarded :—A Telford Medal, and a Council premium of Books, to James John Berkley, for his paper "On Indian Railways, with a Description of the Great Indian Peninsular Railway ;" a Telford Medal to Richard Boxall Grantham, for his paper "On Arterial Drainage and Outfalls ;" a Watt Medal, and the Manby Premium, in Books, to James Atkinson Longridge, for his paper "On the Construction of Artillery, and other Vessels, to resist great internal Pressure ;" Council Premiums of Books to Edward Leader Williams, for his "Account of the Works recently constructed upon the river Severn, at the Upper Lode, near Tewkesbury ;" to Edward Brainerd Webb, for his paper "Upon the Means of Communication in the Empire of Brazil, chiefly in reference to the Works of the Mangaratiba Serra Road, and to those of the Maná, the first Brazilian Railway ;" to Francis Croughton Stileman, for his "Description of the Works and Mode of Execution adopted in the construction and Enlargement of the Lindal Tunnel, on the Furness Railway ;" to James Ralph Walker, for his "Description of the Netherton Tunnel Branch of the Birmingham Canal ;" and to Daniel Kinnear Clark, for his paper "On Coal-burning and Feed-water Heating in Locomotive Engines."

In the President's Annual Report, December 18, the principal feature was an account of the state of engineering in a few distant countries, and particularly in some of the British Colonies.

The new subjects for premiums on which the Council of the Institution of Civil Engineers invite communications (session 1861) are the following :—"On the Effect of Sluicing, in Removing and Preventing Deposits, at the Entrances of Docks on the Coast and Tidal Rivers ;" "On the Measure of Resistance to Steam Vessels at high Velocities ;" "On the Form and Materials for Floating Batteries and Iron-plated Ships ('frégates blindées'), and the points requiring attention in their construction ;" "On the Initial Velocity, Range, and Penetration of Rifled Projectiles, and the Influence of Atmospheric Resistance ;" "Description of Street Railways and Carriages, as used in the United States of America, in Paris, and at Birkenhead, with the results."

COMBINED STEAM.

, THERE has been read to the Institution of Civil Engineers a paper "On Combined Steam," by the Hon. John Wethered, U. S. The author remarked that, at the present day, the great desideratum in marine engines appeared to be, to obtain increased power, or economy in the consumption of fuel, without the commercial disadvantage of occupying more space, by the enlargement of the boilers and machinery. This object, it was believed, had been attained by the application of ordinary and superheated steam mixed. The mode adopted in carrying out this system was to attach another steam pipe to the boiler, for conveying the steam to be superheated to pipes, or other contrivances, placed in any convenient form near the fire, or in the uptake, or chimney of the boiler, or in a separate furnace; the superheated steam being added to the ordinary steam at, or before its entrance into, the cylinder. In its passage through the superheating apparatus, that portion of the steam was raised, by the waste heat, to a temperature of 500° or 600° Fahrenheit. The heat, thus arrested, was conveyed to and utilized in the cylinder by its action on the other portion of steam from the boiler, which was more or less saturated, according to circumstances. The combined steam was used in the cylinder at from 300° to 450° Fahrenheit, instead of at the low temperature at which steam was generally employed. The effect of using the two kinds of steam was, that the superheated steam yielded a portion of its excess of temperature to the ordinary steam, converting the vesicular water, which it always contained, into steam, and expanding it several hundredfold; whilst, at the same time, the ordinary steam yielded a portion of its excess of moisture, converting the steam gas into a highly rarefied elastic vapour—in other words, into pure steam at a high temperature.

When steam was merely superheated or dried, it was converted into steam gas. It consequently partook of the nature of gas, was a bad conductor of heat, and gave out with difficulty the heat necessary to transform it into mechanical power. On the other hand, mixed steam participated in the qualities of steam proper and of superheated steam, and being a pure, highly rarefied vapour, which readily parted with its heat, thus produced greater mechanical effect.

By the application of combined steam the following advantages, among others, were said to be obtained :—1°. An economy of fuel of from 30 to 50 per cent. 2°. A diminution of one-third in the feed water. 3°. The employment of smaller boilers to produce the same power. 4°. Facility of maintaining any desired pressure, or of increasing it at will in cases of emergency. 5°. A steamer would make a voyage one-third further with the same weight of coals, or one-third the space now occupied by the fuel might be used for freight. 6°. Less risk of explosion. 7°. Boilers would last one-third longer. 8°. A better vacuum was obtained. And 9°. One-third less injection water was required.

The discussion upon this subject occupied the whole of the next evening's meeting. At the close, it was stated that the general opinion appeared to be that the practical introduction of the system of super-heating steam was greatly owing to the exertions of Mr. Wethered. He had succeeded in moving the British Board of Admiralty, when, perhaps, an English engineer might not have been so successful ; but this should be a subject of congratulation, as it was desirable at all times to give the greatest encouragement to foreigners, so as always to attract the best talent from other countries. The case did not, however, seem to be clearly established in favour of combined steam. It rested upon the facts which had been stated, and not upon any scientific explanation of the rationale of the principle, such as would account for the results claimed for it. When more than ordinary attention was given to any machine in daily use, that of itself would often lead to economy. This attention was invariably given when any new invention was being tried, and the whole improvement or economy was supposed to arise from the particular modification then being tested.

IMPROVEMENTS IN APPARATUS FOR REFRIGERATING AND CONDENSING.

Mr. J. P. JOULE, F.R.S., of Manchester, has patented an invention which consists in a method of applying a stream of water or other liquid to the surface of tubes or other receptacles of liquids or elastic fluids, so as to occasion an increased and more rapid interchange and equalization of temperatures. This he effects by placing spirals or spiral coils in the pipes or channels, by means of which spiral coils the stream of water or other liquid is made to acquire a progressive and spirally rotatory motion ; or the same effect may be obtained by placing plates or vanes, so as to divert the stream from its original course into a spiral direction. In the instance of the "Surface Condenser" of a steam-engine of that description, in which the exhaust steam is passed through tubes placed within tubes of a larger diameter, the concentric space between the tubes being used for the transmission of a stream of cold water, he places a spiral coil upon the outside of the inner tube, by means of which the water is compelled to follow the direction of the convolutions of the spirally-formed coil instead of going straight along the space between the tubes. If the surface condenser, on the other hand, be of the kind in which the exhaust steam is made to enter a receiver through which the refrigerating water is transmitted by means of metallic tubes, he places spiral coils within the tubes, and thus causes the water to follow the direction of the coils. In the instance of a refrigerator or other apparatus for cooling hot liquids by a stream of water carried through pipes, he places in each pipe a metallic or other spirally-formed coil ; or when one pipe is placed within another of larger dimensions, the space between the two conveying the liquids to be cooled or heated, and the inner tube conveying the liquid in the process of heating or cooling, he places spiral coils in the space between the tubes, and also within the inner tube : the spiral coils may be constructed of copper or other suitable material, and if of small size, may be made by bending or coiling wire around a mandril or cylinder, and then pulling or extending the coil, so as to separate, conveying a liquid. Mr. Joule remarks that his object in the novel use or employment of these spiral coils is for the purpose of imparting a rotatory motion to the liquid employed for the purpose of refrigeration or condensation ; such motion producing a beneficial effect by causing each particle of the said liquid to pass over a greater surface, thus necessitating a higher velocity, which prevents the adhesion of a film or layer of liquid to the tube, and promotes a more thorough mixture of the liquid as it circulates, and consequently quicker condensation of steam, or vapour, or refrigeration of liquid. He also remarks that the spiral coils may be constructed of any suitable material, and their transverse section may be either square, round, or other convenient form.—*Mechanics' Magazine.* .

Mr. T. Howard has patented an improvement in Condensing Steam in Engines where Superheated Steam is used. This consists in condensing steam which is generated in boilers having attached to or combined with them, or with the cylinders or other parts or adjuncts of steam engines, any apparatus or means for superheating the dense steam. The patentee admits such superheated steam, after it has done its duty in the cylinder or otherwise, into a vessel to be condensed ; but instead of subjecting it to the contact of external cold water, he subjects it to the contact of the same water repeatedly, which is cooled by circulating it, together with that resulting from the condensed steam, through metallic tubes, vessels, or channels, having their opposite surfaces presented in any suitable manner to a current of external cold water, and which, when the supply is limited, should pass in an opposite direction to the water within. The circulation of this condensing water is effected by withdrawing it by the ordinary air-pump into the hot cistern, and passing it thence by the atmospheric pressure through the cooling channels again into the condenser, where it is injected amidst the steam continuously, or it may be intermittently, by actuating a valve or injection cock accordingly. The boiler will now be fed by the ordinary means, with the circulating water constantly replenished by that resulting from the condensation of the steam.—*Ibid.*

MARINE STEAM-ENGINES.

Mr. E. Humphrys has patented certain Improvements in Marine Steam-engines. The object here is the arrangement of these steam-engines on what is well known as Wolfe's system, in a more compact and convenient form than heretofore. The patentee employs in combination with each low pressure cylinder two high pressure cylinders, which are placed between the end of the low pressure cylinder and the crank shaft. The two high pressure cylinders are mounted on the cover of the low pressure cylinder, one on each side of its piston rod, and the pistons of the high pressure cylinders are connected with the piston of the low pressure cylinder by rods passing directly from one to the other through the cover of the low pressure cylinder ; thus the power generated by the pressure of the steam on the pistons in the high pressure cylinders is transmitted to the piston of the low pressure cylinder, and the piston-rod of this cylinder transmits the power of the whole to the crank shaft. By this arrangement a compound engine is obtained which does not occupy more space than an engine having a single cylinder of the size of the low pressure cylinder of the compound engine, with the further advantage that the power generated both in the high and low pressure cylinders is communicated to one crank by a single connecting-rod. The slide valves of the high pressure cylinders, and the slide valves of the low pressure cylinders are connected together, and are actuated by one pair of eccentrics and the link motion, as described in the specification of a previous patent of the present patentee, dated Nov. 10, 1858.—*Ibid.*

INCRUSTATIONS IN BOILERS.

Mr. L. M. BOULARD has patented an "Improved Apparatus for Preventing or Destroying Incrustations in Steam Boilers." This consists in the substitution of a mechanical arrangement to the chemical reagents at present in general use for the prevention of calcareous deposits in steam boilers, or their destruction when formed. This arrangement is composed of a case or bag of pierced steel metal, metallic gauze, or even non-metallic tissue, corresponding in shape with the boiler, in which it is enclosed, and forming as it were an open worked lining, kept at a slight distance from the inner surfaces by means of brackets. If so required, this lining, the meshes or perforations of which should be finer at the bottom than at the top, may be made in several sections, which are passed separately into the boiler, by the main hole, and afterwards connected in any suitable way. In many cases the metallic or other tissue may be replaced by a simple recipient in a sheet metal, or even iron metallic material without perforations inserted in the boiler, and secured by brackets as above. In this case the apparatus, instead of being completely tubular, should be of a gutter form open at the top, the ends being either left open or closed with pierced metal or gauze. Or again, the same results may be obtained by the insertion in the boiler of any required number of wire gauze or other perforated shelves, superposed at equal distances, and so arranged as to be easily withdrawn from time to time for the removal of the calcareous matters deposited.—*Mechanics' Magazine.*

Mr. James R. Napier, shipbuilder and engineer, of Glasgow, has submitted to the Philosophical Society of that city a paper on the Incrustation of Boilers using sea-water. We have only space to quote the following remarks from the conclusion of Mr. Napier's elaborate paper :—

"From the foregoing example," he says, "of a vessel worked at a temperature of 270°, it is also seen that a quantity of fuel, equal to 15¼ per cent. of that which produces evaporation, is consumed by the ordinary blowing-off method, in order to prevent crust, and this amount increases with the temperature. Brine chests have been frequently used for the recovery of this notable loss; but apparently from a misapprehension of the quantity of water necessary to be discharged, and a want of knowledge of the amount of service required to absorb the discharged heat, of a capacity greatly too small for their purpose. If Peclet's formula for calculating this surface is to be trusted, those chests on board the West India mail steamship *La Plata*, and some of the British and North American Company's packets, are $\frac{1}{15}$th to $\frac{1}{20}$th of the size that would be efficient. When these brine chests, regenerators, or heat economizers, therefore, are made with a sufficient amount of surface, so that abundance of water can be supplied to and discharged from the boilers, with little loss of heat, then there will be no incrustation of boilers, and a probable saving of from 12 to 13 per cent. of their fuel. Peclet's formula, or Professor Rankine's reduction of it, which gives the probable amount of surface required for a difference of temperature of 140° between the feed and the discharged water, at $\frac{1}{10}$th square foot per lb. of brine discharged per hour, becomes under the same circumstances, and when the quantity of brine discharged is equal to the quantity of water evaporated, $\frac{1}{10}$th square foot of surface per lb. of water evaporated per hour. The introduction of Dr. Joule's spiral wires to the system will probably render less surface efficient. This amount of discharge and surface, it is expected, will prevent incrustation, and save ninetenths of the heat at present lost."

GREAT CHIMNEY AT GLASGOW.

MR. DUNCAN MACFARLANE, of Glasgow, C.E. and architect, has published a description of the colossal Chimney recently completed at Messrs. Townsend's Chemical Works, Crawford-street, Port Dundas. It is described as being not only the largest structure of the kind, but the loftiest building in the world, excepting the Great Pyramid of Ghizeh, the spire of Strasburg Cathedral, and that of St. Stephen's, Vienna. This chimney is circular on plan.

Total height from foundation	469 feet.
Height above ground	454 ,,
Outside diameter at level of ground	32 ,,
Outside diameter at top	14 ,,
Thickness at level of ground	7 bricks.
Thickness at top	1½ ,,

In a report made on its probable stability, Professor Rankine says—"From previous experiments on the strength of the bricks used in the chimney, I consider that their average resistance to crushing is 90 tons per square foot. I calculate that, at the level of the ground, the pressure on the bricks arising from the weight of the chimney, will be about 9 tons per square foot, or $\frac{1}{10}$th of the crushing pressure. I consider that, in violent storms, the pressure on the bricks at the leeward side of the chimney may sometimes be increased to about 15 tons per square foot, or $\frac{1}{6}$th of the crushing force. On these grounds, I am of opinion that the chimney, if executed as designed, will be safe against injury by crushing of the bricks." On the 9th September, 1859, however, after a hurried construction, a violent storm swayed it from the perpendicular, the deflection produced extending to 7 feet 9 inches. On the 21st of the same month, and subsequent days, it was restored to the perpendicular by twelve separate sawcuts, as recommended by Mr. D. Macfarlane, architect, who afterwards reported, as did Mr. Rankine, that it was then perfectly safe. The highest cut was 128 feet from the top, and the least distance between any two cuts was 12 feet.—*Builder.*

COAL-BURNING AND FEED-WATER HEATING IN LOCOMOTIVES.

Mr. D. K. Clark has described to the Institution of Civil Engineers his Steam-jet System for improving the combustion. He also described a new form of heater introduced by him, in which the steam from the blast-pipe is projected into a short tube in conjunction with the feed-water, which is delivered in a thin annular sheet around the steam nozzle. The water is broken into spray by the steam; the steam is instantly condensed, and the water is raised nearly to the boiling point.

WATER-BLAST FOR STEAM BOILERS.

A PAPER has been read to the Institution of Mechanical Engineers, at Birmingham, "On some Hot-blast Stoves, working at a temperature of 1300° Fahrenheit," by Mr. Edward A. Cowper, of London. These new stoves are constructed on an entirely different plan from the present; the cold blast is heated by being passed amongst a large quantity of fire-bricks, which have been previously heated by passing the heat from the fire in the opposite direction. This arrangement is called a "regenerator" for heat, and is on the same principle in this respect as Mr. Siemens's regenerative furnace for puddling and heating iron and steel, &c., being modified to suit the circumstances of the hot-blast stoves. The whole of the stove is enclosed in an airtight casing, or skin of wrought iron, to keep the blast in, whilst the fire-brick lining of the casing withstands the heat. It is found by experience of the working of a pair of these hot-blast stoves, which have been in regular work for more than two months at Messrs. Cochrane's iron-works, Middlesborough, that they can be conveniently worked for two hours before reversing the currents of cold blast and heat through them; and the variation in temperature of blast during the two hours is only about 100° or 150°. The economy of fuel is very great; for instead of the heat passing away to the chimney at 1200° or 1300°, it does not escape until lowered to 150° or 250°, only about the temperature of boiling water; so that, practically, the whole of the heat given out by the fuel is absorbed in the stoves, and made use of for heating the blast.—*Mechanics' Magazine.*

STEAM TRAFFIC ON CANALS.

AT a meeting of the Royal Scottish Society of Arts, a communication "On Steam Traffic on Canals," by Mr. Thomas Lampray, F.R.S., has been read by the secretary. After premising that it will, he believes, be readily conceded that the future success of canals, and the value consequently of canal property, are dependent entirely upon the possibility or impossibility of the substitution of steam power for the haulage of boats, the author compares the relative advantages of canal and railway conveyance as regards the transmission of merchandise, and expresses an opinion that if steam haulage could be successfully applied to canal navigation, canals would, in a pecuniary sense, become as valuable as they have ever been. The author proposes to remove the difficulty hitherto existing to the introduction of steam-boats on canals, viz., the washing away of the banks by the swell, by lining the upper part of each side with coarse rubble stone; and states that this may be effected by a simple apparatus, without stoppage of the traffic. Presuming the canals to have been prepared for their reception, the author proposes to use steam tugs of horse-power determined by the traffic, and of light draught of water, each of which would haul a flotilla of canal boats dependent in number on the traffic and the power of the engines.

THE EARL OF CAITHNESS' STEAM CARRIAGE.

THE success attending Lord Caithness' experiment with his Steam Carriage for common roads has drawn general attention to the invention.

The front view is that of a phaeton placed on three wheels and made a little wider than ordinary, so as to have room for three or even four abreast. The driver sits on the right-hand side, resting his left hand on a handle at the end of a bent iron bar fixed, below the front spring, to the fork in which the front wheel runs, and guiding with ease the direction of the carriage. Placed horizontally before him is a small fly-wheel fixed on an iron rod, which, passing downward, works at the lower end by a screw through one end of a lever attached at the other end to a strong iron bar that passes across the carriage, and has fitted on it a drag for each of the hind wheels. By giving the fly-wheel in front a slight turn with his right hand, the driver can apply a drag of sufficient power to lock the hind wheels and stop the carriage on the deepest declivities of common roads. Inside the carriage, in a line backward from his right hand, is placed a handle, by which the steam is let on, regulated, and shut off at pleasure.

The tank, holding about 170 gallons, forms the bottom of the carriage, and extends as far back as the rear of the boiler, where the water is conveyed from it into the boiler by a small force pump worked by the engine. There are two cylinders, one on each side, 6 inches diameter and 7 inches stroke. These, and all that is necessary to apply the power to the axle, are well arranged and fitted in so as to occupy the smallest possible space between the tank and the boiler, and appear at first sight insufficient to exert nine-horse power. The coal, 1 cwt. of which is sufficient for twenty miles on ordinary road, is held in a box in front of the stoker, whose duty it is to keep up the fire, see that there is always sufficient water in the boiler, and that the steam is up to the required pressure, as seen by the gauge on the top of the boiler.

The power of the engine, and the perfect control his lordship has over it, have enabled him, on several occasions, to make long

journeys over rough and mountainous roads at the rate of eight miles
an hour ; there can, therefore, be no doubt that carriages propelled
by steam can be used for the purpose of traffic on common roads.
A journey of 140 miles made in two days, at a cost of less than 1d.
per mile for fuel, proves this ; and the fact that no accident to man
or beast was caused by the steam-carriage during the whole journey,
answers the objections as to frightening horses.—*Mechanics' Magazine.*

NEW AND UNLIMITED MOTIVE POWER.

MR. S. D. ROGERS, in a letter to the *Mining Journal*, proposes a
new application of gas, or gases, by which the power of one man may
be augmented to that of more than 26 6-10ths horses or 133 times the
initial force originally put in action. This invention or application
of a new element of force will not only equal the gigantic power of
steam, but actually surpass it in the effect produced more than
twenty-fold. The cost of machines for originating the new power
will be considerably less, in both weight and value, than an equal
power derived from steam. There will be no boilers required in this
case, and consequently explosions could never take place, neither
would engine-houses and stacks be necessary. The power will be
originated from the atmosphere, to the extent of ten pounds
pressure on a square inch of surface (the usual available power of
Boulton and Watt's condensing steam-engine), and limited only by
the capacity of the machine employed, and the motive element made
use of, the cost of which "element" will be, in a manner, nothing, or
at most one penny per horse-power per day of 24 hours.

In the year 1823-4 an engine was contrived by Mr. Samuel
Brown, not Sir Samuel Brown, the chain-cable and chain-pier
inventor, but a contemporary engineer of great renown. These
machines were worked in several shapes, as stationary and marine
engines ; and one of the first screw propellers was a small boat belonging to "Brown's Gas Engine Company," which was worked on
the Thames. The Gas Engine Company fell to the ground in the
dreary times which succeeded the great panic in 1825, when many
valuable undertakings were lost, but Brown to the day of his death
laboured at his engine. The Croydon Canal was drained by one of
these machines, on its conversion into a railway, and Mr. Brown's
propositions were seriously entertained for draining the Haarlem
Meer, but death put a stop to his proceedings, and his engine
(pregnant with almost inexhaustible powers) seems to have died with
him out of the recognition of the scientific world. This engine
was worked by means of the creation of a vacuum in a cylinder by the
combustion of hydrogen or coal gas. Mr. Brown's own description
of his invention is as follows:—"Inflammable gas is introduced
along a pipe into an open cylinder, or vessel, whilst a flame placed
on the outside of, but near to, the cylinder is constantly kept
burning, and at times comes in contact with and ignites the gas
therein : the cylinder is then closed air-tight, and the outside flame
is prevented from communicating with the gas in the cylinder. The
gas continues to flow into the cylinder for a short space of time, when

it is stopped off; during that time it acts by its combustion upon the air within the cylinder, and at the same time a part of the rarefied air escapes through one or more valves, and thus a vacuum is effected. The vessel, or cylinder, is kept cool by water. Several mechanical means may be contrived to bring the above combinations into use in effecting the vacuum with inflammable gas, and on the same principle it may be done in one, two, or more cylinders, or vessels. Having a vacuum effected by the above combinations, and some mechanical contrivance, powers are produced by its application to machinery in several ways." Now, Mr. Brown's engine was worked by means of coal gas, the cost of which, at 1s. 6d. per 1000 cubic feet, would be 3s. per horse-power per day of 24 hours (*i.e.*, 2000 feet of gas); this, in London, would be considered an economical power, but (says Mr. Rogers) the gases to which I invite attention are those flowing from the top of blast-furnaces, the cost of which may be said to be *nil*. A furnace taking 5000 cubical feet of blast per minute will yield at least 7,200,000 feet of gases per day, which gases may be applied to work a gas or vacuum-engine with similar effect to the gas from coal. Brown estimated that 1½ foot of coal gas per minute, applied in his machine, was equivalent to a horse-power, so that it would, by his mode of working, raise 1 ton of water 22½ feet high; but, in my estimate, I put 3 cubical feet of the blast-furnace gases to effect the same power; on this calculation the 7,200,000 feet of furnace-gases, just referred to, would originate a power equal to 1666 6-10ths horses working the entire 24 hours of the day.

Here, then, may be generated a truly gigantic power, from a comparatively waste material at iron-smelting establishments; it is termed a "waste," because the present arrangement of blast engines, their boilers, &c., may be superseded by water-power machines, that would never be in want of a regular and full supply of water; and not only may steam-power be dispensed with for generating blast, but also for rolling, hammering, pumping, winding, lifting, stamping, grinding, sawing, crushing, twisting, and pressing operations of all kinds and degrees: the substituted power being waterfalls of 15, 30, 45, 60, or more feet, *ad libitum*, with never-ending supplies of water, both in the summer and winter seasons of the year. There are about 120 blast-furnaces in constant operation in Monmouthshire, Breconshire, and the eastern parts of Glamorganshire; and the quantity of blast driven into these furnaces may be fairly estimated to average 5000 cubical feet per minute, or an aggregate quantity of 864,000,000 feet per day, then, by estimating 3 cubical feet of these gases per minute, or 4320 feet per day, to be the equivalent of a horse-power (Mr. Brown reckoned one foot of coal gas per minute equal to lifting, with his machine, 250 gallons of water 15 feet high), we have from the 864,000,000 feet of gases the tremendous power of 200,000 horses working constantly for the 24 hours of the day, and that in the district of country alone above mentioned. It perhaps may be said that the gases above referred to are at present used under the blast-engine boilers; this is true to a

certain extent, but the gases flowing from a furnace receiving 5000
cubical feet of blast per minute will yield (not reckoning anything
for the expansion of the blast, or the carbonic oxide and hydrogen
proceeding from the decomposition of the moisture in the atmospheric air, or in the other materials used) will amount to full
7,000,000 feet per day, which gases, as now applied to steam-boilers,
will scarcely raise steam enough to work two engines of 100-horse power
each; but if the same amount of gas were made in a vacuum engine
they would generate a power equal to 1666 horses, according to the
calculations here referred to, or more than eight times the effect now
obtained from them. Hence the proposed new application of such
gases would be a saving of 1400-horse power—a power more than
sufficient to accomplish all the mechanical processes of an iron-works
(the blasting, rolling, pumping, hammering, &c.) capable of turning
out 1000 tons of iron per week.

PROGRESS AND PROFIT OF THE STEAM PLOUGH.

In the *Times* has appeared a most comprehensive paper with this
title, the evidence and arguments of which manifest the writer's
extensive acquaintance with this important subject. To quote the
details of this article would occupy several pages of our volume, and
we have only space for the close of this very able and thoroughly
practical paper:—

"In conclusion, let it not be supposed that one description of
steam-tilling machinery is specially adapted for extensive, and
another only for small farms. The cost price of a Steam Plough
ranges from nearly 800*l.* down to almost half this sum; and a considerable number of engines are at work on farms of all sizes, both
with Mr. Fowler's and Mr. Smith's apparatus. Mr. Fowler has
published thirteen reports from purchasers in ten counties, and
Messrs. Howard, of Bedford (manufacturers of the Woolston imple-
ment), have printed thirty-four reports from employers in twenty
counties,—the two publications alike embracing the experience of
large and other occupiers, on light, medium, and heavy land. The
testimony in every case is remarkable as to the quantity of work
got forward in each season, the economy and advantage in very
many respects, and the proportion of horses dispensed with. These
testimonials, however, do not include anything like all the instances
of machinery supplied and working in this country.

"Then the Continent, the West Indies, and Australia have become customers; and if in the south of France the steam plough
might effect a saving of two-thirds in outlay while doing doubly
better tillage, in our dear-labour colonies the sugar-grounds and
vineyards will show a still greater profit,—the machinery being now
able to cope with the obstacles of wild lands, seeing that its powerful subsoilers prize up stones and crack tree-roots, which master the
common horse-plough. But whatever immense fields are lying open
to the steam plough abroad, we are rapidly progressing with its
adoption at home; and should the rotary cultivation, so accordant
with theory, never reward the inventors who are seeking it, we

are still in a fair way to banish more than a third of, at least, 800,000 farm-horses in Great Britain. With the saved produce of a million and a half acres (which these hungry teams now consume), added to the eight bushels additional yield on 4,000,000 acres of wheat—to say nothing of the augmented production of vegetable food and butchers' meat, from the yet unforeseen revolution in clay-land management, and on other soils from the interpolation of more than a single crop in one year, and the entire remodelling of our system of rotations,—we may be able before long to feed our population, independent of American prairies, and no longer import supplies equal to a fourth of our harvest."

NEW HYDRAULIC CEMENT.

CAPTAIN HUNT has read to the American Association a paper on Hydraulic Cement, prepared by Lieut. Q. A. Gilmore. His deductions from a long series of observations are :—1. In cold weather, when it is necessary that the cement should harden quickly, warm water should be used for mixing the mortar and wetting the solid materials with which it is to be used. In warm weather, on the contrary, cool water should be used for the same purpose, in order to delay the setting until the mortar is laid in position. 2. The time required by the cement to set (if within the ordinary limits of 1·10 of an hour to $1\frac{1}{2}$ hour) furnishes no means of judging of the ultimate strength and hardness which it is likely to attain. 3. It is not probable that while the present method of manufacturing cement is pursued in this country, we can produce an article equal to Parker's Roman cement, or the artificial Portland cement from abroad. 4. The stone furnishing what is generally termed *intermediate* lime, now rejected by our manufacturers as worthless, on account of its containing an excess of caustic lime, may be used with entire safety if combined with five or eight per cent. of an alkaline silicate : "soluble glass" is a good silicate for that purpose. 5. The maximum adhesion to stone is secured by mixing the cement paste,' or mortar, very thin (*en coulis*) rather than very stiff. The maximum density, cohesion, and hardness, on the contrary, are all incompatible with this condition. 6. Cement should be ground to an impalpable powder, when it is intended to give mortar its full dose of sand, the coarse particles of sand being a poor substitute for that article. Finally, all the stone which does not effloresce with dilute hydrochloric acid, or which, during calcination, has been carried beyond the point of complete expulsion of carbonic acid gas, should be rejected.

NEW PORTABLE COFFER-DAM.

CAPTAIN HUNT has also read to the American Association a description of a New Portable Coffer-dam, the idea 'of which occurred to him and was put in practice while he was superintending certain constructions at Fort Taylor, Key West. The novel feature of this coffer-dam is this : — Make a strong canvas case for the whole coffer, using two thicknesses of canvas, and interposing a complete coating of mineral tar, to act both as an adhesive and an impervious agent. Along the line corresponding to the bottom of the coffer must be joined a flap, to spread over the bottom as far as may be necessary, according to the nature of the bed of the stream. This bed should be raked clear of sticks and stones. Then the usual process with coffer-dams may be followed. The facility with which the coffer may be taken up and re-established constitutes its great recommendation.

FLOATING HARBOURS AND BATTERIES.

A CHEAP mode of constructing Wooden Floating Breakwaters has been submitted to the consideration of Lord Clanricarde's committee of the House of Lords. From printed particulars it appears that the design is that of Captain Adderley Sleigh. The system proposed consists of the use of floating structures, built according to the method adopted in the construction of ships, hollow, water-tight, drawing about three feet of water, their bottom broad and flat, and the seaward side of them presenting to the sea a decked plane inclined inwards at an angle of from 12° to 15° from the sea level, and rising upwards from the line of floatation at the same angle to the height of about twelve feet; and the decked plane descending in like manner at the same angle below the water to a depth of about ten feet, the whole being moored from that extremity. It is in principle a *wedge*, of which the point is moored seaward, and it resembles an artificial beach. The cost, it is said, would only be 60l. per yard, instead of 1000l., as the cost of stonework. As outer defences, such wedge-shaped floats, it is conceived, would be useful, as shot would glance off them as they do off the surface of the ocean itself. Coir cables are recommended for anchoring the structures. Wind, it is urged, would be deflected as well as waves by the inclined planes presented to seaward, thus securing quiet harbours to landward by means of such breakwaters. No difficulty as to security in mooring is anticipated.—*Builder.*

IRON NAILS IN WOODEN SHIPS.

M. KUHLMAN asserts that the use of Iron Nails in building Wooden Ships is one of the chief causes of their decay. The rotting by decay of wood is a process of slow combustion or oxidation; and M. Kuhlman considers that the iron nails act as carriers for oxygen, and introduce it into the substance of the timber. By contact with water and air the iron is rapidly converted into a sesquioxide. In this state it yields a portion of its oxygen to the wood, and is reduced to the state of protoxide, which further action of air and moisture converts it to the sesquioxide, and so the process goes on, by a sort of catalysis.

IMPROVED GUN-BOATS.

MR. J. D. HINSCH has patented certain improvements in the construction of Gun-boats. The object of this invention is so constructing gun-boats, as that the floating or buoyant part thereof shall be capable of being submerged in water, so as to either partially or entirely conceal it; and also in forming the battery thereof, or that part in which guns are fixed or mounted, so that it shall resist the force of heavy shot or balls. The patentee employs two long hollow cylinders of metal, each formed conical at one end, which constitute the head of the boat or turn-boat; the other and opposite end of one or both of such said cylinders, constituting the stem, is fitted with a screw propeller actuated by suitable machinery inside one or both of such said cylinders; or one cylinder may be appropriated for carrying the mechanism to the engine-boiler and fuel necessary for working the propelling-screw, and the other cylinder may be appropriated for ammunition, and also for the hands or crew of the boat.—*Mechanics' Magazine.*

LAND BATTERIES AND GUN-BOATS.

Mr. J. Arrowsmith has patented a new or improved method of constructing Land Batteries and Gun-boats. In the construction of a land battery the patentee rolls bars of iron having a groove running their whole length on one side, and a projection running their whole length on the other side, the said projection and groove being of nearly the same size. When bars of the kind described are placed upon one another, the grooved sides being all turned in the same direction, the groove on one engages with the projection on the next one. The bars are curved to the required curvature. The walls of the battery are formed of two thicknesses of the iron described, the outer and inner walls formed by the said iron being separated, and the enclosed space filled with oak. The structure is secured vertically by bolts passing between the walls, and the parts are bound together horizontally by girders, which are secured at one end to rings in the middle of the battery, and at the other end to vertical girders fixed in the foundation. The upper of these rings is supported by bars of wrought iron. The roof may be formed of iron similar to that employed for the walls, and the whole structure may be formed internally with oak. The portholes are closed by plates of hammered steel iron sliding between the walls, and supported by a lever and weight, so that by moving a catch the porthole is closed immediately. The guns may be mounted on a turn-table. An underground magazine may be constructed behind the battery, covered with the same sort of iron, and connected with a tunnel leading to the centre of the battery. A steam-engine may be fixed at a distance, having an exhaust cylinder connected by pipes with the batteries, and having a valve to each battery, the said valves being opened as soon as the guns are fired. The smoke is thereby immediately exhausted from the battery.—*Mechanics' Magazine.*

MARTIN'S ANCHOR.

A series of experiments has been made in the presence of the Master and Brethren of the Honourable Trinity House, Newcastle-upon-Tyne, and a large number of gentlemen interested in shipping matters, for the purpose of testing the comparative holding-power of

Rodger's and Trotman's Anchors, with those made on Martin's principle. The experiments were made on the sands, by the south side of the Tyne, near to the works of Messrs. Hawks, Crawshay, and Sons, the manufacturers of Martin's anchors. One of Rodger's anchor's, one of Trotman's, and one of Martin's were chosen to be tested. They were placed upon level ground, and in pairs, drawn together by means of a tackle composed of two triple blocks and a chain paul, having a winch with fly-wheels upon each end, and set in motion by men. The relative weights of the anchors were as follows:—Rodger's, anchor, 5¾ cwt.; stock, 1¾ cwt.; anchor and stock, 7¼ cwt. Trotman's, anchor, 4¾ cwt. (nearly) ; stock, ¾ cwt. ; anchor and stock, 5½ cwt. Martin's, anchor complete, 5¼ cwt. The relative lengths of the shank, stock, and arms of Rodger's and Trotman's were nearly the same ; Martin's differing from them owing to the nature of its construction. The first trial was made with Rodger's and Martin's, and the result in this case was, that while Rodger's anchor dragged 55 feet nearly before taking a good hold, Martin's only came home about 12 feet, and then got quite immovable. When the anchors were reversed, a similar effect was produced, and it was only when Rodger's was loaded with a weight of 4 cwt. that it gave results equal to Martin's. The next trials were made with the same anchor of Martin's in comparison with the above-mentioned one of Trotman's ; in this case Trotman's dragged 62 feet before it held firmly, while Martin's ceased moving at 7 feet; the same results were obtained by reversing the positions of the anchors, and even when considerably loaded, both Rodger's and Trotman's anchor continued to cut through the ground, while Martin's remained quite fixed. So completely was the superiority of Martin's anchor proved by these experiments, that immediately after the trial a certificate was presented, signed by the Master and Brethren of the Board, expressing their most complete satisfaction at the results, and declaring their conviction that Martin's patent anchor was vastly superior to any other in use, both in a national and commercial point of view, and that by its general adoption many lives as well as much valuable property would be preserved from destruction.—*The Engineer.*

IRON-CASED SHIPS OF WAR.

MR. JOSEPH WHITWORTH, in a letter to the *Times*, says:—"There is no doubt but that ships may be built which are proof against ordinary shot, but my experience leads me to believe that the penetration of armour-plates is a question of firing against them a projectile under the proper combined conditions ; these are, that it shall be of the proper shape, material, and weight, and have the requisite velocity. A flat-fronted projectile of properly hardened material, and weighing less than an ounce, fired from one of my ordinary rifles, will penetrate wrought-iron plates 6-10ths of an inch thick. Again, plates 4 inches thick are penetrated by the 80 lb. projectiles, and I have no doubt but that 6-inch plates would be penetrated by heavier projectiles, with a more powerful gun. Increased thickness of plate, then, is to be overcome by increased power of gun ; and the question.

is, in which case will the capability of increase sooner reach its limits?

"Ships which are cumbered by the weight of enormous plates are so overburdened, that they are unfit to carry a broadside of guns heavy enough to penetrate the armour of vessels plated similarly to themselves.

"Again, a ship constructed to carry very thick plates, cannot be driven at the high speed which must hereafter give the superiority in naval warfare.

"There yet remains the consideration of cost. It is true that the richest nation can best endure the drain of costly equipments, and therefore cheap warfare would be a disadvantage; but it is also true that naval casualties and mishaps must be calculated upon, and it would be bad policy to concentrate too large an outlay upon a single vessel.

"It will be for naval authorities to consider the position in which the large, heavily-plated, yet still vulnerable ship would be placed if attacked by several smaller and far swifter vessels, each carrying a few powerful guns, and able to choose its distance for striking an enemy which presents so large a target. What would be the result of firing flat-fronted shots at her plates below the water-line, or of their concentrated fire directed upon the axis of her screw—a mark that might be hit at a considerable distance?

"The plan of warding off shot by protecting armour has been often resorted to, but the means of attack have continually proved the vulnerability of the armour, and driven it out of use. It has to be shown whether this will be the case with our ships of war, and I fully concur in the opinion expressed in your paper—that the best and speediest mode of arriving at a right decision is to give full publicity to the results of properly conducted experiments.'

Mr. Lynall Thomas, author of a treatise on "Rifled Ordnance," and the inventor of the great gun which has thrown a shot weighing 174 lbs. nearly six miles, has also addressed a letter on Iron-cased Ships of War to the *Times*, from which we take the following remarks:—

"Those persons who have agreed in favour of the construction of these vessels have done so, I believe, from a limited knowledge of the effect which can be produced by heavy rifled cannon, Mr. Whitworth's 80-pounder, the largest hitherto constructed, showing results little, if at all, superior to those produced by a 68-pounder service gun; while, if we may judge from the letter of an Artillery officer, which recently appeared in the *Mechanics' Magazine*, all Armstrong guns of a larger size than 40-pounders are unsafe. Notwithstanding that my opinion may be opposed to that of many naval officers of great weight and experience in their profession, I am nevertheless convinced that an iron-cased ship (unless her plates were of a thickness utterly to preclude the possibility of her being a sea-going ship) might be destroyed from shore batteries, large frigates, or gun-boats at distances at which she could be hit with any degree of certainty, say two or three thousand yards, and with guns very little, if at all, heavier than the service 68-pounder gun. If Government will find the money, I will engage to furnish them with guns and projectiles which shall penetrate the sides of a vessel cased with iron plates 4½ inches thick at the distance I have named. To show that this is no vain boast, I will explain how it can be done. It has been proved that a 68 lb. shot of wrought iron will penetrate a 4½-inch iron plate with facility within the distance of 100 yards, the initial velocity of the shot being less than 1800 feet a second. Those who know any-thing of the theory of projectile force will be aware that a shot of 170 lb. weight, striking an object with a velocity of 1100 feet a second, would have a penetrating power quite equal to that of the 68 lb. shot, while the general effect of the blow would be enormously greater. That a projectile of 170 lb. weight may, without difficulty, be fired with the above-mentioned velocity has been proved beyond a doubt experimentally at Shoeburyness, when, from a rifled gun, an elongated projectile of 174 lb. weight was fired with a mean velocity of 1200 feet a second to a distance of 2126 yards, the time of flight being 5·31 seconds ; while the mean velocity of flight in a range of more than 10,000 yards was as much as about 1100 feet a second. According to the ordinary method of calculation, therefore, this shot should penetrate an iron plate at almost any distance within its range with the same facility as would a 68 lb. shot at a distance of 100 yards. It would really do so, however, with even greater facility. No iron-cased ship could come within the range of guns similar to the one I have referred to without the risk of destruction, unless, as I remarked, the plates of iron were so thick as to render the vessel an inert floating mass, such as might probably be avail-able for coast defences, but for no other purpose. Vessels of this description, indeed, if armed with the above kind of gun, would probably be the most formidable kind of batteries which could be devised.

"With respect to the angular plates which have lately attracted some notice, I would observe that their efficiency in preventing the penetration of shot must depend upon the relative position of the guns which are brought to bear against them. If a vessel con-structed with angular plates were opposed to a battery high above the level of the water, or to another vessel which carried her guns high, the object of having the plates in a sloping position would be defeated."

———

ARMOUR FOR SHIPS.

Mr. A. M. Rendel has patented certain improvements in the construction and arrangement of ships of war. Here the patentee employs Armour in the form of iron or steel plates, or plates of other material ; or armour in any other form, backed with timber or not, or otherwise protected in-board of the ship, upon longitudinal and transverse bulkheads or girders extending upwards from the ship's bottom, or other convenient place, to the height requisite for the shelter of the gun deck, with or without plating of any thickness, laid upon timber or otherwise protected and strengthened overhead. The armour necessary for the protection of the ship may be placed wholly on the girders, or only so much as is necessary for the protection of the gun deck and deck below it may be placed on the girders, the remainder being placed on the ship's sides, or otherwise connected together.—*Mechanics' Magazine.*

A STEEL TROOP-SHIP.

A REMARKABLE ship has been constructed on the banks of the Tees, at the yards of Messrs. M. Pearse and Co., Stockton-on-Tees. This is a Steam Troop-ship, and the largest river steamer in the world, and is intended for the navigation of the Lower Indus. She is constructed entirely of steel, and exceeds in length all ships hitherto built, except the *Adriatic* and the *Great Eastern*. The following are her principal dimensions :—Length over all, 375 feet ; beam moulded, 46 feet, the paddles projecting 13 feet more on each side, making a total breadth of 72 feet. The extreme depth amidships is only five feet. This is uniform throughout, the vessel being quite flat-bottomed, except at the ends, which are alike, and are spoon-shaped. The paddle-wheels are 23 feet in diameter, and are driven by engines of 200 nominal, but capable of working up to 800 horse-power. She is divided into compartments by twelve water-tight bulkheads : has two decks, containing three ranges of beds, separated by two passages. These latter are built in two houses, each 100 feet long, in a somewhat similar mode to the saloons of the American river steamers, and leaving a clear gangway outside all round the ship. The ventilation is by an apparatus steered by a novel contrivance. Two blades at each end, diverging from each other at an angle of 70°, are made to dip alternately into the water at an angle of 35°, right or left of her course, and the slightest immersion on either side is immediately effective beneath the flat bottom of the enormous vessel. The necessary firmness to this great but apparently frail structure is secured by two girders, fastened to two parallel keelsons at the sides of the vessel. These are formed of steel plates, and the keelsons are 300 feet long, from which the girders spring in a chord, whose curve is 18 feet. To these the whole framework of the vessel is braced and trussed, so as to give it enormous strength. The quantity of steel used in her construction is only 270 tons ; she will accommodate 800 soldiers, besides officers and crew, and draw only 2¼ feet of water ; tonnage only 1000 tons. She was built from the designs of Mr. J. B. Winter, engineer to the Council of India, and was taken to pieces to be shipped for Kurrachee, at the mouth of the Indus.

STEAM RAMS.[*]

ADMIRAL SARTORIUS, in a communication to the *Times*, writes :—

As it is clear the iron walls must supersede wooden ones, let us examine which of the two actual arrangements of the former is the most efficient—the steam frigate iron-cased, with the usual mast, yards, and sails, of a line-of-battle ship, only using her guns ; or the modification of the steam frigate, which also

---

[*] See also *Year-Book of Facts*, 1860, p. 25.

uses artillery, and is expressly built for speed and strength, and weight sufficient to sink by concussion, and with a rig subordinate to that important quality. I give my reasons in the following observations to show why I think the latter (steam ram) is infinitely superior for service, less expensive in construction, and much less in maintenance.

The iron-plated steam ram can make use of guns as the steam frigate, equal in calibre, and, if required, equal in number. She can use more guns from each extremity than the steam frigate from her bow or stern; therefore, whether retreating or pursuing, the steam ram is more formidable, even when she trusts to her guns alone.

A single steam ram can effect with her beak an amount of destruction in a few minutes which would take many steam frigates to effect very imperfectly in as many days, if at all. She could get in among a fleet at night, sink two or three ships, and disperse the rest. She could run into a harbour, such, for example, as Cherbourg, by one entrance, and out by the other, sink some of the ships at anchor in the outer road by her beak, and set fire to others by her incendiary projectiles.

The steam rams should have both extremities the same (I proposed a screw and rudder at each end, and also paddle wheels for Channel service) ; she could run in or out among the enemy's vessels, and advance or back with the same velocity and quickness. If attacking at night, with masts lowered, she could not be seen until felt, could launch out her incendiary projectiles into the town and harbour, and there would be no masts, sails, or rigging, to obstruct their flight in every direction. Guarded by loop-holed and bullet-proof towers to afford refuge to her people when boarded, and boiling water made to be ejected from them, it would be impossible to take the steam ram.

No steam frigate could do all this. A steam ram, when prepared for action (she has, of course, no bowsprit), with her masts lowered, the rigging, the little she has, frapped in amidships, and without any kind of outside projection, can clear instantly any vessel she may fall alongside of, or that she has run into. If boarded, the boarders must be killed or scalded. As no wreck can hang overboard, her screw cannot be fouled. The steam frigate falling alongside of her enemy, and either vessel losing masts and yards, they must get entangled, and their screws fouled by their wreck; there would then be nothing to prevent a fresh ship from running alongside and effecting an easy conquest of the steam frigate.

If the steam ram is constructed with both ends as sterns, she will never require turning in action ; she can, therefore, run up or back in passages or rivers as narrow as the breadth of her own beam, and engage batteries at the closest distances. She has two screws to rely upon (she may in addition have paddle-wheels), and her screws cannot be fouled from her own wreck. If a steam frigate of the rig and dimensions of the *Warrior* were to run up a narrow channel or river to engage a battery at close quarters, any wreck from her own guns would infallibly foul her screw; so circumstanced, her great length would prevent her from having sufficient space to wear in, as she would require at least half a mile for the purpose, and the embarrassed screw would prevent her from tacking. The velocity of a steam ram can only be slightly affected by the wind, her schooner rig and lowering masts presenting no comparative resistance when bringing the wind ahead. This position to a steam frigate, with her heavy masts and yards, might make a difference of several knots an hour, besides much impeding the quickness of her movements.

I have hitherto spoken of the "iron-protected shot-proof steam ram." Now, it must be evident to every man acquainted with maritime matters, that when a steam ram has the superiority in speed and quickness of movement over her enemy, she can make herself equally formidable without shot-proof protection. She can then choose the time and mode of attack most advantageous to her. Such a steam ram could carry six weeks' or two months' fuel (the screw ships of the day do not carry more than from seven to ten days') ; besides, as the aggressive party, she can more easily economize her fuel. She would probably keep out of gunshot during the day, and, making frequent feints at night, obliging the ships to keep up full steam, the time would soon arrive when their fuel would be expended, and they would become mere sailing vessels. In a dark night, when the steam ram has all her masts lowered, she uses fuel that emits little or no smoke, and, turning her beak towards her enemy, she becomes invisible to them at 200 yards; but every movement of the ships, with their high broad hulls, tall masts, and square sails, is easily visible to the steam ram. She selects her victim ; 60 or 70 seconds after the first cry of the look-out man that "the enemy is running down upon us," the five or six bow guns are pouring in their molten iron-shells and liquid fire either into the ship attacked or the one ahead or astern of her, and she crushes in either bow, beam, or quarter of the enemy. Every sailor knows that in so short a time it would be impossible to get a large ship to avoid the blow, still less to man, point, and fire her guns at so rapidly-moving an object as the steam ram, going 8 or 10 knots. What must be the moral effect, also, upon the crew attacked, knowing that no earthly courage or skill can save them from the inevitable destruction awaiting them in a few seconds !

As the two vessels have different movements (the beak of the steam ram is made only to penetrate to a certain distance), and the latter immediately backing, she quickly disengages herself, disappears in the darkness, and returns to repeat the same mode of attack. No steam frigate can do this. The shot-proof steam ram's most effective mode of attack is when she presents her sharp stem to the enemy and uses her front battery. A shot striking her in that position it either must glance off the oblique surface, or, hitting the iron plate obliquely, the shot must have double the quantity to penetrate, which Whitworth's flat-headed bolt shot is not likely to do. The steam ram is safe, therefore, from the artillery of the steam frigate, the only mode of offence or defence of the latter. The steam ram, particularly if she has the superiority in speed and quickness of movement, could knock away the masts or bowsprit of the steam frigate or disable her rudder by shot, so that, screw fouled by wreck, or the rudder useless, the steam frigate must give up or be sunk by the blow of the beak. It is unnecessary to prove that no lateral strength can possibly be given to the steam frigate which would enable her side to resist the blow or concussion of a vessel constructed for the purpose, and running into her with the weight and impetus of 3000 or 4000 tons and speed of 8 or 10 knots, from instantly bursting in her side. I now answer some objections, apparently well founded, which have been made to me against using the principle of the steam ram.

The steam ram cannot possibly foul her screw by the wreck of the vessel she destroys. Her working screw must be the whole length of the vessel from the locality of the wreck or the vessel struck, and every stroke of the screw backing removes her further from that locality. The foremost rudder and screw blades, in preparing for the attack, are placed and fixed fore and aft. I have the opinions of some of our ablest ship constructors that the stern piece can be made so strong as effectually to protect screw and rudder from all harm where the concussion takes place. It has been said also that if the steam ram were going at a high speed against a large vessel the force of the blow or concussion would throw the engine out of gear and render it useless. This opinion is abundantly refuted by innumerable facts. We hear unfortunately almost every day of steamers, some that have run down other vessels, upon rocks, and going at 11 or 12 knots against stone walls, as at Birkenhead, or into a stone pier, mounting up the stones on either side as if it had been an earthquake, as at New York, and in every case the engines have never been injured or inutilized until either the bottom has been beaten in by the rocks or the fires have been extinguished by the water rushing in, but the engines have never, and even the stem of the vessel has but seldom, been much the worse for the shock. We must recollect that all these cases of collision or wreck have occurred with merchant vessels of ordinary construction and strength, and as such, therefore, are far inferior in solidity and strength to what the war steamers would be, expressly built and prepared for purposely effecting what has been so often unintentionally done. The beak of the steam ram rushing upon a large ship with the momentum of 3000 or 4000 tons, can never encounter a sudden check ; it is the gradual crushing blow—the side yielding to it, the vessel struck heels over, and is more or less driven before the blow. I am persuaded a man in the gunroom of the steam ram could hardly know that a collision had taken place. It is again said that the application of the principle of the steam ram has never been tried. I point out as my answer the cases of collision I have alluded to. Every steam vessel that has destroyed another by running into that vessel is to all intents and purposes a steam ram.

The steam frigate has only one apparent advantage over the steam ram, and that will disappear on examination—namely, the line-of-battle ship's masts and sails enable her to make long voyages, but the steam ram has her five or six schooner masts, and, if required for a long voyage, topmasts, gafftop sails, staysails, and square sails, can be added, so that she will spread almost as many yards of canvas as the line-of-battle ship. To resist invasion or protect seaports and harbours the steam ram is tenfold more serviceable than the steam frigate or any other description of vessel or shore battery.

In the *Saturday Review*, Oct. 13, 1860, it is observed, upon the danger to the steam ram from her screw becoming entangled with wreck, that Admiral Sartorius, of course writing with exactly the opposite purpose to that for which we use his words, is arguing that the ram would be all-powerful upon the seas, even against an iron-plated ship not built to act in the same way; and he supposes a combat between the two. "Shot and shell against each other's hulls must be harmless, but the shot and shell from the comparative mastless steam ram could soon knock away the masts or bowsprit of the ship, or disable the rudder, so that, the screw fouled by the wreck of masts and rigging, or the ship helpless from her damaged rudder, a blow from the steam ram sends her to the bottom." Let us observe here the words "comparative mastless steam ram," and consider whether they are not a lame attempt to escape an obvious difficulty. The Admiral does not venture to say that the ram would be mastless, but he calls it, not very elegantly, "comparative mastless;" and yet he must know that an iron-plated ship will equally require masts whether she is fitted to act as a ram or not. But if the ram has masts, they may be shot away by any vessel whose guns can reach them; and then, with "the screw fouled by the wreck of mast and rigging," the ram becomes unmanageable, and falls an easy victim to its enemies.

THE FRENCH STEAM-FRIGATE "GLOIRE."

A CORRESPONDENT of the *Scotsman*, gives the following account of the sea-going qualities of this terrible frigate—the iron-plated, invulnerable *Gloire:*—"Whatever notions may exist in England regarding the strength or sea-going qualities of this vessel, people in this quarter of the globe have no misgivings on the subject. The *Gloire* was admirably tested in the recent Algerian trip of Napoleon III. I have spoken with men who assisted in the working of that ship to the African coast, and they declared that not even the Imperial yacht herself, light and trim cut as she is, behaved so well during the heavy gales which the squadron encountered as soon as it had left the French coast. I know that during those gales the steamers from Cette were unable to leave port in consequence of the frightful state of the sea, and that no fishing squadron in any of the Mediterranean ports durst attempt to leave its moorings. The *Gloire*—heavily charged with her full amount of ammunition, with all her guns, with provisions for some months, with her tremendous engines, and her 4¾-inch coat of mail—the *Gloire* cut through these giant billows with a steadiness little less than the *Great Eastern* herself when she breasted the gale in the English Channel during her first sea voyage. In appearance the *Gloire*, which is far larger than any of the other five *frégates blindées*, does not convey to you the idea of either a very heavy or a very powerful ship. Her lines are so delicate and symmetrical, her three taper masts so slim and yacht-like, that were it not for her short wide funnel, which tells of vast machines below, you might, while cruising round her, imagine that she was a huge pleasure-boat, and not the most formidable of existing war-ships."

Strangely opposed to the *Scotsman* correspondent's laudation is the following professional evidence. In his "Postscript" to *Naval Gunnery*, on "Iron Defences" Sir Howard Douglas says :—"I assert, on information on which the reader may rely, that *La Gloire frégate blindée* is a failure as a sea-going ship—that she is really nothing more than a *batterie flottante* upon a large scale, so burdened with the weight of armament, and loaded with 820 tons of armour plates, that she is not capable of ocean-service."

In a letter addressed to the *Times*, Mr. Scott Russell writes :*—

" In regard to the *Gloire*, I may take this opportunity of correcting some of the information which has been given to the public respecting that vessel. We have been told that the *Gloire* is steel-plated. She is not. Her plating, like that used in this country, is merely good hammered iron 4½ inches thick. The plates are of similar dimensions to those of the *Trusty*, and, like those of the *Trusty*, have been penetrated by steel bolts. The experiments made in France, as well as those made on the *Trusty*, the results of which I have carefully examined, prove that the plates are penetrable, but penetrable under rare and exceptional circumstances, so as to be practically shot-proof, and I believe in all cases perfectly shell-proof, which, after all, as your third naval correspondent says, is the important point. . . . Mr. Whitworth, after stating the ability of his shot and gun to penetrate such plates—a fact which no one who knows both can doubt—proceeds to say that ' ships hampered by the weight of enormous plates must be unfit to carry a broadside of guns heavy enough,' and also, ' cannot be driven at the high speed

* The letter quoted was sent to the *Times* primarily in order to correct the statement of a previous Correspondent to the effect that M. Dupuis de Lome, the chief naval architect of the French Government, had been a pupil of Mr. Scott Russell. Mr. Russell's correction is as follows :—"I should not have ventured to join in a discussion on a subject in which I have been too long and deeply interested to give the evidence of a neutral party, except for the accident of finding my name mixed up with that of my distinguished friend M. Dupuis de Lome." [This remark doubtless refers to the fact, which is now pretty generally understood, that Mr. Scott Russell's designs for ships very much like the *Warrior* have been in the hands of the Admiralty for several years past.] "Your very able correspondent of yesterday, ' N. S. M.,' calls him my ' pupil.' Now, as M. Dupuis de Lome and myself are nearly of the same age and standing in our profession as naval architects, it is unfair to him to call him my ' pupil,' our whole professional intercourse having been one of perfect equality. Some 20 years ago, when I was engaged in my experiments on the theory and practical construction of vessels, which led to the establishment of the wave principle as a scientific method of construction, and subsequently to its general adoption as the best mode of obtaining high speed in union with great capacity and power, M. Dupuis de Lome visited me at Greenock, and threw himself with all the enthusiasm of a young man into this new region of science, and from that day to this we have been on terms of free and open professional intercourse. But in this intercourse I frankly confess that I have received at least as much benefit as I have given, for M. Dupuis de Lome has also carried out original scientific researches on a large scale with the ample means placed at his disposal by the wise liberality of the French Admiralty. These researches have led him to important practical results, which are by me reckoned quite as valuable as anything I may ever have communicated to him. Thus much, justice requires me to state on a personal question."

which must hereafter give the superiority in naval warfare.' On
both points allow me to give an opposite opinion. The *Gloire* has
been built by M. Dupuis de Lome after a most exact calculation
of the effect of such plates both upon the weight and speed of the
vessel ; she is perfectly fit to carry a broadside of guns of as heavy
a calibre as any that can be carried and worked in our own wooden
ships ; and she is driven at as least as high a speed as any vessel of
similar dimensions in our own service. She has, therefore, proved
that an exact scientific calculation can be made beforehand of the
power of a ship to carry such a load, and of the velocity at which
a given power will propel her. I have yet to learn that either a
great weight or a powerful battery is such an enemy to speed and
carrying power as not to be overcome by the judicious application
of well-known principles of naval architecture. I may further add,
in justice to M. Dupuis de Lome, that the *Gloire*, although a great
success, must not be considered her builder's *chef-d'œuvre*. She
was built to meet the peculiarities of the circumstances in which a
builder in France at that date inevitably found himself placed. Had
he lived in an iron country like England he would probably have
adopted an entirely different construction ; but, like a wise man, he
made the best of the material he had at hand, and has been rewarded
with corresponding success. I say this much because I have heard the
question mooted of our proceeding to make imitations of the *Gloire*."

In the *Quarterly Review* it is stated that "as early as 1856
designs for an iron-plated corvette with fine lines, and destined for
high speed, very similar to those now being constructed, were submitted to the Admiralty (by Mr. Scott Russell, we presume), and
year after year the subject was pressed upon them, but in vain. It
was not till the accession of Sir John Pakington to office that any
steps were taken to set this most momentous question at rest. That
energetic and able administrator, aided by his secretary, Mr. Corry,
finding how active the French dockyards were in this department,
determined that at least a beginning should be made here. Before
doing anything, however, he most prudently requested six of the
most eminent iron shipbuilders to send in plans and suggestions,
and as these were found not to differ materially from those already
submitted, a slightly modified plan was adopted. The result is, that
a frigate called the *Warrior* is now being constructed at Black-
wall, which promises when completed to be the finest man-of-war
afloat." This frigate has been launched.

We agree with a contemporary (the *Mechanics' Magazine*) that
"it is impossible to avoid feeling some regret that the Admiralty
authorities should in any way accept the suggestions and services
of eminent private shipbuilders, and then leave the fact to gradually
make itself known in the columns of the *Quarterly Review*, the
Mechanics' Magazine, and other publications. A frank public
avowal of the aid received under such circumstances would, we
think, be more consistent with the reputation of our Government
architects, who, in a matter of iron shipbuilding, need certainly feel
no delicacy in receiving assistance from Mr. Scott Russell."

The promptitude and decision of the Emperor of the French in determining upon the building of the *Gloire,* have been contrasted with the apathy of the English Admiralty authorities. The Emperor had no sooner ascertained from the experiment at Kinburn that the idea of protecting ships of war with an iron sheathing was, to a certain extent, a success, than he set the best engineer he could find to work upon the yet unsolved problem—how to construct a vessel which should be as safe as the iron batteries which defied the Russian guns, and, at the same time, as swift and handy as an ordinary frigate. The design was made, and so confidently was the issue expected, that no less than ten of these costly ships were put upon the stocks at once.

"Contrast," says the writer of an able article in the *Saturday Review,* Oct. 20, 1860, "with the course taken in France the leisurely proceedings of our own Board of Admiralty. After the trial of the clumsy batteries which were built for the Russian war, the two countries had a fair start with equal experience. At Cherbourg and at Portsmouth alike a course of experiments was tried, with the view of determining in the first place the amount of protection which iron sheathing could be made to afford. This was rational enough, and a considerable improvement on the part of the Admiralty upon the precipitation with which they had some years before rushed into the plan of building frigates of thin iron plates without ever attempting to ascertain whether the first ball that struck them might not send them to the bottom. Even a Board learns something from its past failures, and the Admiralty resolved not to expose itself a second time to the charge of reckless and precipitate action. For fully six years experiments upon iron plates have been going on, and to this day the Admiralty seems still to be halting between two opinions. The Frenchmen tried their experiments, found what iron-plates could do, and what they could not do, and, having arrived at the practical conclusion that they would add materially to the security of a ship, lost no time in acting upon the results of their experience. Our Board has had the advantage of more complete trials with artillery of greater power, but at the end of six years it has not ventured to announce or to act upon any more definite opinion on the subject than might have been formed on the day after the attack on Kinburn.

" It may be said that the Admiralty have proved their belief in the efficacy of iron sheathing by ordering four ships about three years ago, and by adding one more to the number since the commotion excited by the trial of the *Gloire.* But this is rather a proof of feebleness of purpose than of anything else. On any view, it must be wrong to commence four or five of the new class of vessels of which Napoleon has ordered twenty, and to allow the first of these to remain unfinished and its qualities untested for years. They are either too many o or to few. When once the experiments had gone so far as to justify the trial of at least one vessel of the class, the obvious course was to get her finished without an hour's unnecessary delay. If she proved a failure, the first loss would be all; if she were successful, a model would be at hand for the fleet which will be needed to cope with that which is so rapidly progressing in the dockyards of France. No time ought to be lost in completing the *Warrior* and *Black Prince*, which, from their superior size, are likely enough to prove more serviceable vessels than the *Gloire* and the *Normandie*. The really difficult problem is not to construct a target which shall repel nine shots out of ten, but to build a ship capable of carrying the formidable load of sheathing, and of working her guns with effect in a heavy sea. Already, without crediting the *Gloire* with all the success which is claimed for her, there are data enough to suggest that it may be possible to build a ship which shall satisfy all the required conditions. How to do this is much more a question of naval architecture than of the power of artillery or the strength of iron. It is not necessary to discuss minutely the effect of every round shot or flat-headed bolt which has been fired against an iron-cased target. We know that no plate of four-and-a-half inches thick has yet been penetrated at a greater range than four hundred yards, and that nothing short of a smooth-bore 68-pounder, or an Armstrong or Whitworth 80-pounder, has been able to injure armour of this description, even at point-blank ranges. More than this, the obvious device of setting the plate so as to receive the blow obliquely, as proposed by Mr. Jones, has been so successful, that a much lighter sheathing has borne repeated shots from the most powerful artillery without suffering any serious damage."

"THE ICHTHYON" NEW STEAM-SHIP.

A NEW Experimental Model Steam-ship, upon a novel system of construction and propulsion, has been invented and patented by Captain Beadon, R.N., of Creechbarrow, Taunton, Somerset. This system consists in forming the under part of a ship of two or more tubular vessels, which are incorporated with, and united by, a superstructure or hull above the surface of the water, somewhat resembling the double war-canoes of Polynesia.

The foremost end of each tubular vessel, and, in some cases, each end, is fitted with a strong fixed axle projecting from its centre. Upon each axle is placed a revolving conical stem, with spiral blades thereon, extending from the base to the apex of the cone, and when turned round by steam or other power, producing the effect of pectoral fins; but the mechanical action is to bore through the water, by which operation the fluid is not raised in front, nor is resistance accumulated before the vessel in motion, however great the speed may be. The displacement of this experimental vessel consists only of two tubular bottoms of 2 feet in diameter, and 18 feet long; her large upper hull deceives as to her real size. Two such tubular bottoms of 20 feet diameter would displace upwards of 6350 tons, which would carry a magnificent upper hull of one, two, or three decks, 60 feet broad, 360 feet long, containing two saloons 50 feet long by 30 feet broad, and upwards of 180 private cabins, of 10 feet square by 8 feet high upon each deck. For example, a tube of 20 feet diameter contains above 314 square feet, which, multiplied by

360, viz., the vessel's assumed length, give 113,040 cubic feet, equal to 3154 tons for each tubular bottom. The speed of the experimental vessel is quite equal to the power, eight men constantly working her by hand as fast before the engines were put in ; the screw which works in undisturbed water ahead advances its length, viz., 4 feet, during each turn or number of revolutions.—See *Mechanics' Magazine* for further details.

STRENGTH OF IRON SHIPS.

MR. JOHN GRANTHAM has read to the Institute of Naval Architects a paper upon this inquiry, which he concludes as follows :—

The effect of experience in iron-ship building should be to remove excessive weight in one part and add more weight to other parts, until uniform strength is attained. At present the author's observation leads him to believe that signs of weakness are now most frequently to be observed at the gunwale and sides amidships, and at the hollow ends below the water-line. In the rules laid down by Lloyd's Committee the strengthening of these parts had not been duly provided for. The *Royal Charter* presented a remarkable example of the defects alluded to, and the author quoted from his published work on *Iron-Ship Building* a passage, bearing upon this subject, which was written after he h 1 examined that vessel in the graving dock some time ago. He then discussed the three following questions, viz. :—1. The form and proportions to which the use of iron in shipbuilding tends ; 2. The important bearing which form and proportion have upon strength ; 3. How these tendencies should be dealt with in iron ships. The tendency which the employment of iron in shipbuilding has given rise to is, to build vessels, especially steamers, much longer and finer than they were before. The author had frequently examined one vessel, that has sailed round the world, whose length is nine times her breadth. A much greater proportion of length to breadth may be ultimately attained, especially in large vessels. But the excess of weight over displacement at the ends will increase in the same ratio unless precautions are taken to reduce the weight there. It is clear, however, that a vessel should be so constructed, and, where possible, so loaded, that when in smooth water the weight should as nearly as possible correspond with the displacement of every portion. The same conditions will also obtain when the circumstances of a ship taking the ground are considered. The construction of the *Royal Charter* was then examined at length, and her weakness attributed, not to badness of material, nor to inferiority of workmanship, but solely to the defective principles upon which she was designed. The author contended for a great diminution in the weight of iron ships at their extremities ; and stated that Lloyd's Rules operated injuriously by narrowing too much the sphere of improvement. He also considered it inconsistent to class iron ships for years, as was at present done. He further held it important to bear in mind that the chief strain which a ship has to sustain is similar to that which is required in an ordinary girder, and that any serious departure from this principle will lead to errors of construction. The *Great Eastern* was, perhaps, the only large vessel in which this principle has been effectually applied; and although the exact form there adopted could only be employed in very large ships, yet the principle is correct, and probably the proportions also. He concluded by a strong appeal to Lloyd's Committee fundamentally to alter their Regulations, and to issue them as Recommendations, and not to make them binding; also to private builders to study good work.

Mr. Fairbairn has also read to the Institute a paper upon this inquiry, in which he proposes the following plan for securing the most effective distribution of the material which is to be added to the upper part of the ship :—"Iron vessels are ordinarily constructed with ribs or frames placed from fifteen to eighteen inches apart. They are about two feet deep at the keel and taper to the width of the angle iron round the bilge on each side. From that point to the top of the deck the angle iron is in some cases considered of sufficient strength for the reception of the sheathing plates. On the top side of the ribs a lighter description of angle iron is riveted, and to this the flooring, whether of wood or iron, is attached. This plan of construction is not objectionable, provided two more longitudinal stringers on each side of the keel are made to run from one end of the ship to the other, and in large ships chain riveted as previously recommended, which will greatly enhance the value of the ship. If this were done so as to give the required midship section necessary for the security of the vessel, it would prove highly advantageous. The *Great Eastern*, which is probably the strongest vessel in proportion to her size ever built, is constructed on this principle, and the designer, the late Mr. Brunel, was too sagacious an engineer to lose sight of the cellular system, developed first in the Britannia Bridge, to neglect its application to the deck as well as the hull of the monster ship. The result of this application, with the longitudinal bulkheads, constitutes the enormous strength of this magnificent vessel, proving the importance of the cellular system for vessels of large tonnage. It combines lightness with strength, and the double sheathing gives immense rigidity to the construction; in fact, the *Great Eastern* is a double ship up to the water-line. With smaller vessels, however, this system is not applicable, but a modification of it may be safely adopted, with advantage to both builder and owner. The exchange from the old system to the one I am urging will not call for any great sacrifice; the change I propose is a new and more scientific distribution of the material, and not any great increase of sectional area, and consequently of weight throughout the construction.

"In the formation of the deck, it is essential for public security that a new principle of construction should be immediately adopted, and that the cross beams forming the upper deck should be covered with iron stringer plates, thickest towards the middle of the vessel, and tapering from $\frac{3}{4}$ to $\frac{1}{8}$ inch thick as they approach the stem and stern. The sectional area thus obtained, however, is short of what would be required for a vessel of the magnitude we have been considering. To secure a proportionate resisting power in the deck, we shall require the arrangement, giving an area of 750 square inches, exclusive of the hatchways, which I have estimated at eight feet wide. This sectional area would be distributed as follows :—

Section of Longitudinal Cells.	Square Inches.
2 plates 25½″ × ¾″	38·0
6 plates 13″ × ¾″	81·0
8 angle irons 3″ × 3″ × ⅝″	26·8
Section of Corner Cells.	
6 angle irons 4″ × 4″ × ⅝	27·6
2 ,, 6½″ × 5½ × ⅝″	15·0
2 plates 31″ × ⅞″	54·0
2 ,, 48″ × ⅞″	84·0
2 ,, 33″ × ⅞″	57·7
2 ,, 72″ × 1″	144·0
4 stringers 24″ × ⅞″	84·0
2 stringers on lower deck	25·0
Deck timbers, say	120·0
Total area of top ...	757

Section of Bottom.	Square Inches.
1 keel 12″ × 3½″	42·0
2 plates 31″ × 1 1/16″	66·0
2 lengths 246″ × 1″	492·0
12 angle irons 6½″ × 5½″ × ⅝″	90·0
2 bulb irons 10½″ × ¾″	18·0
Keelson 18″ × ⅞″	15·75
2 plates 25″ × ¾″	37·5
Total area of bottom ...	761·25

"Thus we should have in the hull and deck a maximum area of security, and the vessel, so far as regards her ultimate strength, would be superior to any tests to which she might be subjected at sea or on shore. Under the most trying circumstances she would never break up, and the passengers and cargo would be secure."

In these recommendations Mr. Fairbairn has not, he states, aspired to teach the experienced shipbuilder the details of his business; all he contends for is greater security for life and property, obtained by adherence to broad principles of construction, of well-ascertained truth. In furtherance of these objects, he also suggests the following improvements and additions to the midship section of iron vessels, viz., the introduction of two cellular rectangular stringers, one on each side of the hatchways, and two triangular stringers, one on each side of the vessel, which run the whole length of the ship, and rest on the watertight bulkheads which divide the ship into eight separate compartments. These cells to be chain riveted, and by the same means to be attached to the angle iron of the bulkheads on which they are supported. "These will diminish," says Mr. Fairbairn, "the span of the cells and lighten the deck beams, which will not exceed fifteen feet in length from the cells to the side of the ship. It will not be necessary to go further into detail, as the cross beams and gusset stays to the lower deck are of much less importance than the corresponding parts in the deck we have considered."

"As respects the quality of the iron used for shipbuilding, the greatest care should be observed," Mr. Fairbairn remarks, "in the selection. Twenty to thirty shillings a ton will make all the difference between good plates and worthless ones, and no plates ought to be used which will not stand an average tensile strain of 20 tons per square inch. The better qualities of plates vary from 22 to 25 tons per square inch, but well-wrought plates, free from dross and equal to an average test of 20 tons per square inch, will give to the vessel, if well constructed, adequate durability and strength."

After the reading of Mr. Fairbairn's paper, a very lengthy and elaborate discussion took place upon it, and also upon that read on the previous day by Mr. Grantham. In the course of this discussion (which will here be given merely in outline), Mr. J. H. Ritchie, one of the chief surveyors of Lloyd's, corrected certain misapprehensions which prevailed in reference to the rules laid down for the guidance of shipbuilders by Lloyd's Committee, and mentioned several important instances in which those rules had been modified so as to favour improvements when such were manifestly based upon sound and scientific principles. He further reminded the authors of the papers that Lloyd's Rules for the building of iron ships were drawn up at the repeated and earnest request of persons interested in the safety of our shipping, and explained that all they pretended to do was to prescribe a minimum in each case, leaving builders to make the ships as much stronger as they might please.

Mr. Scott Russell said that as at former periods he had frequently had occasion to oppose Lloyd's Rules, he was happy to bear testimony to the wisdom of the policy which Lloyd's Committee had for some time past adopted; for while they very properly made rules for the purpose of informing iron-ship builders everywhere how they might build so as to ensure the registration of their ships, they did not stand immovably in the way of changes for the better, but amended their rules from time to time, and had even gone so far as to give some ships which were not built according to their rules as good a classification as if they had been, where it had been clearly proved that the ships were at least as strong and sound as they would have been had the rules been followed. If Lloyd's Committee continued to follow this policy they might take to themselves all the credit of strictly enforcing rules for the public safety, and at the same time might defy any one to say that they stood in the way of the progress of iron ships. Mr. Russell also protested against the present system of loading the fine ends of steam-ships with great weights, such as forecastles over the bows, and engines, &c., aft, as being the most dangerous system that could be adopted. (It was mentioned that the *Royal Charter* had a tank of 3000 gallons at her bows.) He likewise objected *in toto* to Mr. Fairbairn's proposal to make the top of the ship as strong and weighty as the bottom. He pointed out numerous causes which tend to deteriorate the bottoms of ships which do not affect their upper parts: he stated that, for his part, he believed that when from wear, or any other cause, the bottom of a ship had become as weak as the top, we ought to begin to consider her in a dangerous state. He also considered that while it was incumbent upon iron-ship builders to continually improve their systems of construction, it was their duty also to assist in putting down the clamour against iron ships which had lately prevailed, and to protest against the assumption that any ship ought to be, or could be, built so strongly as to stand beating upon rocks in heavy seas, without going to pieces. Mr. Fairbairn would never, he said, get that in this world. The Britannia Bridge itself fell once only six inches, and was materially damaged by the fall. Mr. Russell recommended the adoption of water-tight bulkheads, wherever practicable, and described various improvements in the construction of iron ships, which he had from time to time introduced and found to answer, and which not only attained, he said, all the objects which Mr. Fairbairn had in view, but even went considerably further in the direction indicated by him.

Mr. Grantham expressed his satisfaction at learning that Lloyd's Rules were not so absolutely binding as he had always believed, and as the language in which they were expressed undoubtedly implied. He now felt relieved of a great difficulty. He went all lengths with Mr. Fairbairn.

Mr. James Martin, another of the principal surveyors to Lloyd's, contended that, as Lloyd's Committee were in the first place urged to draw up and enforce rules ; and as they applied in vain to iron-ship builders for assistance in the matter, persons ought not now to find indiscriminate and hasty fault with the rules which the Committee had laid down, and which had confessedly been of very great service to the country. He said that the object of Lloyd's Committee and its surveyors was simply and solely the general good of the public, and they would be perfectly willing to co-operate with the Institution of Naval Architects in considering and carrying out such improvements as they might mutually deem desirable. Mr. Martin likewise spoke warmly against the use of inferior iron in ships.

After remarks had been offered by various other speakers, Mr. Fairbairn explained that he had no objection to give the bottom of the ship a sufficient excess of strength over the top to provide for any extra wear that might occur there, nor did he contend for the adoption of any specific details by way of improvement. He was only advocating general principles. He believed that some of the modes of construction adopted by Mr. Scott Russell were attended by great and manifest advantages. He would be most happy at any time to put himself in communication with Lloyd's surveyors and with the Institution of Naval Architects, to give them whatever information he possessed, and do all in his power to establish sound principles of construction. He believed it highly desirable, and quite possible, to give the public perfect confidence in iron ships ; and this was what he wished to see realized in constructions of such vast importance to the community.—*Abridged and Selected from the Reports in the Mechanics' Magazine.*

THE SCREW-PROPELLER.

HER Majesty's screw vessel *Cygnet* has completed at Portsmouth a series of highly interesting and important experimental trials with the Griffiths Propeller, testing some suggested improvements in its form by the patentee. It has always been a great object with engineers to obtain greater propelling power from the screw, without, at the same time, increasing its size, in order that screw ships with full power might be constructed with a light draught of water, and at the same time have the screw well immersed. The present trial in the *Cygnet* is the nearest approach to this ye tattained; and a fair hope may be now entertained that, after having puzzled scientific men during the past twenty years, the marine screw-propeller may for the future be more fully understood.

It is now upwards of ten years since Mr. Griffiths brought forward his theory of the screw—viz., that the centre part of the screw, equal to one-third its diameter, should be filled up, and the screw-blades should be wide at the root, and tapering towards their extremities, in contradistinction to the generally-received rule, and the form of the Admiralty pattern.

The improvements suggested by Mr. Griffiths in the form of his own screw, and which have now been tested in the *Cygnet* with the greatest success, consist of an addition of an angular surface at the after edges of the screw blades, springing from their widest part, and increasing the width of the angulated portion as it proceeds outwards to the periphery or circumference of the blade. These angular surfaces stand at an inclination to the after-face of the blades: consequently, as they rotate, the water, which has been acted on and put in motion by the fore part of the blade, is again struck by this after, or angulated portion, thus making the blades double-acting; whereby, it is stated by Mr. Griffiths, smaller diameter of screw-propeller may be used without decreasing the power employed or given by the larger diameter in the old form ; the theory of this being that the front of the blade travels at the rate of 3000ft. per minute, while the root, or wider portion of the blade, only moves at the rate of 1500. The water, being struck with the higher rate of velocity at the point of the blade, recedes off, and the after, or angulated portion, catching the same body of water, strikes it a second time. In the first trials the *Cygnet's* screw was 9ft. diameter, with a 12ft. pitch, the engines in this instance making 114 revolutions per minute. With the same screw reduced to 7ft. 6in. diameter, and 12ft. pitch, with the angulated addition made to the blades, the revolutions of the engines were 108, while the speed of the ship was the same on both trials, the 7ft. 6in. screw thus doing an equal amount of work with the 9ft. screw, and with less revolutions. The screw was afterwards reduced to a 7ft. diameter, with the same pitch as before. The result gave 111 revolutions, but the ship lost a quarter knot in speed. The sternposts of the *Cygnet* are 12 inches in width, and, as a matter of course, produced a greater deteriorating influence upon the small screw than upon the larger one. The sphere in the smaller screw was also of the same size as in the larger one. Both these causes, therefore, militated much more against the smaller screw, notwithstanding its success, than is shown by the figures. It is a singular fact, that the recent trials of the French authorities in their endeavours to obtain the same results which have now been achieved by these trials, were conducted on the opposite principle, and have failed.

THE ARMSTRONG AND WHITWORTH RIFLED CANNON.

FOR four weeks in succession, each Tuesday night, the Institution of Civil Engineers, Great George-street, Westminster, was crowded by members, to hear the papers and discussions on Rifled Cannon—on the Armstrong and the Whitworth Rifled Cannon—actual working samples of these rivals (twelve-pounders) having been placed on the

table, open to the inspection of all the persons present. If there
was a secret once, there is no such thing in this case now. On one
evening Sir William Armstrong explained the mode of manufacture,
the make, the method of working, loading, sighting, and firing, in
the simplest and clearest possible language. Few men possess the
enviable gifts of Sir William Armstrong. With a gentlemanly presence, a musical voice, a fluent delivery, a powerful and cultivated
intellect, Sir William Armstrong is a man any nation ought to be
proud of ; and Lord Derby will have the honour conferred on Sir
William long reflected back on himself and on his Government.
But to the rifled cannon subject. The gun invented by Sir William
Armstrong is in appearance light and even elegant : in use it is indestructible, and in its effects tremendous. A dozen such guns at
Sebastopol would have shortened that terrible contest, as every ship
and steamer afloat in the harbour must have been sunk within the
first week of opening fire, and the most distant buildings would
have been rendered untenable. All this, and more, was explained
during this interesting lecture. Sir William Armstrong explained
how his gun was made, the reasons why it was so made, showed its
several parts, manipulated the breech, explained the mode of loading, the several sorts of solid shot, hollow shot (shell), their mode of
bursting, and their effects.

The Armstrong shot is coated with lead, to allow of its passing
the rifle grooves ; and this is, we think, *the* objectionable feature in
this otherwise most admirable cannon. A solid iron shot cannot be
turned, or rather, returned, to any offensive use, unless it happen to
fit the bore of any hostile cannon most exactly. Hundreds of tons
of round shot, and fragments of shell, lay about in front of Sebastopol, and on the plains of Inkermann and Balaclava, perfectly un-
useable ; but if these had been fired from Sir William Armstrong's
rifled cannon, the lead would all have been useable for rifle bullets ;
and, if ever fired against semi-savage nations, the lead from Sir
William's shot will most certainly be so returned to us. The
leaden jacket, or coating, is necessary to Sir William's plan of
rifling, and in this necessity the weakness of his invention lies.

On the Tuesday night following Sir William Armstrong's exposition, Mr. Whitworth had a full meeting, and one of his wonderful
12-pounder field-guns was on the table before him.

Sir William Armstrong makes his guns of flat bars and flat rings
of wrought iron twisted and welded together. Whitworth makes his
guns out of homogeneous iron or steel,—that is, iron run from crucibles into moulds, so as to form one solid, compact, homogeneous
mass. Both guns are breech loaders, both have a direct passage
through, from breech to muzzle, and both breeches open and close
by means of levers and screws. In the Armstrong gun, the breech
piece is small and movable, and there may be any number ready to
replace a lost or damaged one. In the Whitworth gun, the breech
piece is heavy, and opens clumsily on a hinge, so as to be sadly in
the way during loading, and liable to accident. Injury to the
breech would be for the time ruination to the gun. This hinged

breech is a weak point: in all besides, the Whitworth gun has a decided advantage. Homogeneous iron is better than welded iron bars, and the even bore and solid shot are far better than the lead-coated shot of Armstrong. Any enemy must possess Whitworth guns of the exact calibre, to return any of his shot, as each solid shot or shell fits to the 1-50th of an inch. It requires a power of many tons weight to force one of Armstrong's lead-coated shot through from breech to muzzle ; but any child may easily push one of the Whitworth shot through his guns, the fit is so true, even, and easy. The Armstrong gun cannot be used as a muzzle-loader: the Whitworth gun can be so used, if required. The Whitworth material and *form* of bore and mode of rifling, with the Armstrong breech and mode of sighting, would constitute a perfect weapon in every respect. With such guns Great Britain will fight her next great battles, and woe be to whatever may be brought within the range of such terrible weapons ;—wrought-iron plates, the thickest and strongest which can be made for any vessel to carry, as plate-mail, will be punched and perforated as if only of the consistency of cork. Shells and hollow shot of the most destructive character will pierce ships and scatter annihilation around, either above or below the water-line. No material will be able to resist the direct action of such engines. A Whitworth ball will pass through 40 feet of sand, and continue in a direct line at any angle through water. A Whitworth rifle bullet has a range of 2000 yards, and spins on its axis at a rate of 100,000 revolutions per minute. Rope mantlets, sand-bags, or other known means of protection hitherto used, will be of no avail against such a spinning, direct, and insinuating projectile. Gunpowder cannot burst either the Armstrong or the Whitworth guns ; this is about all which need be said on strength, and as to range and accuracy, these have been proved.—*Selected and Abridged from the Builder.*

Sir William Armstrong has proved the deadly nature of his guns and projectiles, but unfortunately his first success was secured at the expense of an *English* soldier's life. Sir William, in giving an account of his shells, in May, 1859, represented that they could not strike even a bag of shavings without exploding ; an unfortunate soldier, who seems to have believed this statement, in meddling with some of the shells fired at the old tower at Eastbourne, paid the penalty of his credulity by losing his life. It appears that they can strike, not only bags of shavings, but granite towers, without exploding. We now leave these competing cannon-makers for a third inventor.

Captain Blakeley has read to the British Association a paper on Rifled Cannon, in which the writer pointed out that to make an efficient rifled gun, no more was needed than to copy any good small rifle in the number and shape of the grooves, degree of twist, and other details, provided one difficulty was overcome, viz., that of making the barrel strong enough. Taking Sir W. Armstrong's 80-pounder as a standard, Captain Blakeley gave several examples of large rifled cannon on the model of successful small ones, which had given satisfactory results in every way, except that they had failed after a short time for want of strength. Mr. J. Lawrence, in 1855, rifled a 6½-inch gun with three shallow broad grooves, like an Enfield, and fired a lead and zinc bullet, like the Enfield. At an elevation of 5°, the range was 2600 yards—150 more than Sir W. Armstrong's; but the gun burst after about 50 rounds. Mr. Whitworth, after making some excellent small arms and nine-pounders, tried a large gun with four inches bore, and sides nine inches thick; but it burst. He then tried another, eleven inches thick, and it, too, burst. He had, however, since made a stronger cannon, whose success was absolute proof that the one thing wanting in the other was strength. Captain Blakeley explained his own method of obtaining strength, which consists simply of building up the gun in concentric tubes, each compressing that within it. By this means the strain is diffused throughout the whole thickness of the metal, and the inside is not unduly strained, as in a hollow cylinder made in one piece. As the whole efficacy of the system depended entirely on the careful adjustment of the size of the layers, Captain Blakeley said he was not astonished that Sir W. Armstrong had lately failed utterly in his attempts to carry it out, because he did not put on the outer layers and rings with any calculated degree of tension: "they were simply applied with a sufficient difference of diameter to secure effectual shrinkage," to quote his own words at the Institution of Civil Engineers. To show that the late failure by Sir W. Armstrong did not disprove his (Captain Blakeley's) theory, he quoted official reports of a trial of a nine-pounder made by himself in 1855, which showed an endurance sevenfold that of an iron service gun, and threefold that of a brass gun; as well as of an 8-inch gun, from which bolts weighing 4 cwt. had been fired; and of a 10-inch gun which had discharged bolts weighing 526 lb. Mr. Whitworth's last new 80-pounder was another instance of the successful application of Captain Blakeley's principle. To quote Mr. Whitworth's own words,—"It was made of homogeneous iron. Upon a tube having an external taper of about one inch, a series of hoops, each about 20 inches long, was forced by hydraulic pressure. Experiments had enabled him to determine accurately what amount of pressure each hoop would bear. All the hoops were put on with the greatest amount of pressure they would withstand without being injured. A second series was forced over those first fixed." This gun was so made at Captain Blakeley's suggestion.

Captain Blakeley's method of rifling cannot be made intelligible without a diagram; but it may be described as a series of grooves of very shallow depth, so arranged as to exert a maximum force in the direction of the rotation of the bullet with a minimum force in a radial or bursting direction. Captain Blakeley exhibited in the court of the building in which the Section met, a 56-pounder, constructed on his own plans, from which he had thrown shells on Mr. Bashley Britton's system to a distance of 2760 yards, with only 5° of elevation, which was stated to be a range 200 yards greater than that of Sir W. Armstrong's 80-pounder.

Mr. Scoffern said, he thought Captain Blakeley had proved his point,—that strength was the important desideratum. He said that a large number of Sir W. Armstrong's large guns had lately burst. Mr. E. Cowper agreed with Captain Blakeley. Sir W. Armstrong's guns that were said to have burst were simply cast-iron guns hooped. For small arms, he was of opinion that the Lancaster rifle was very successful. The bullet was of lead, and did not jam, as was sometimes the case with the iron shot in the larger guns. If Captain Blakeley's plan were adopted, he thought that for 10l. any gun in the service might be made sufficiently strong. Mr. Dennis thought that Captain Blakeley's method of giving strength was right.

IMMENSE AMERICAN CANNON.

THE *Scientific American* publishes the following :—" A Cannon, weighing 35 tons, has been successfully cast at the Fort Pitt Foundry, Pittsburgh, under the superintendence of Lieutenant Rodman, of the Ordnance Department. This is stated to be the largest cannon in the world. The casting is fifty inches in diameter, and nineteen feet five inches long. Seventy-eight thousand pounds of metal were melted for it in three reverberatory air furnaces within four and a half hours after the fires were lit. The furnaces were tapped in succession, and the iron run in separate channels into a common reservoir, from which it passed into the mould—the latter being filled within twenty-one minutes after the first tap. The mould was a ponderous structure, and was placed vertically in a pit prepared for the purpose. The gun has been named the 'Floyd,' in compliment to the Secretary of War, whose zeal for the improvement of artillery prompted this laudable experiment in gunnery. The model of the gun was designed by Lieutenant Rodman, and made under his supervision from a plan of which he is the inventor, for casting guns hollow, and cooling them by circulating a stream of water through the interior of the core. The cold water enters at the top, passes down through a pipe in the centre of the core, and is discharged at the bottom of the hollow part; and then, passing up through the core, becomes heated, and is discharged at the top. It circulates a constant stream at the rate of forty gallons per minute, and is continued until the casting becomes cool. The drawings, patterns, and computations were made by Mr. N. R. Wade, junior member of the firm of Knapp, Rudd, and Co. The moulding and casting were conducted by Mr. J. Kaye, and Joseph Marshall melted the iron. The ease, regularity, and thorough success with which the different processes were conducted were astonishing, and sufficiently manifested the extraordinary practical skill and judgment of all concerned in the operation."

IMMENSE RIFLED CANNON.

MR. LYNALL THOMAS'S Rifled Cannon, the largest rifled weapon ever made, has been tried with complete success at Shoeburyness. This cannon weighs upwards of 6 tons, and fires a shot of 174 lbs. weight, with a charge of powder of no less than a quarter of a hundredweight! We are unable to say what range was attained, but, judging from the initial velocity of the shot and its time of flight, it must have been enormously great, and altogether unprecedented. The gun is made of the Mersey puddled steel by Mr. Clay, and stood the immense strain brought upon it with perfect success, showing no sign of weakness anywhere. The heaviest rifled cannon ever made prior to this of Mr. Thomas's, is the Whitworth 80-pounder ; but the weight of this is but $4\frac{1}{2}$ tons, nearly a third less than that of the new weapon. The heaviest projectile ever before fired from a rifled cannon is Sir William Armstrong's 100 lb. shot from a cannon of considerably less than 4 tons. It will be seen, therefore, that another great advance has been made in the art of gun construction, and one which will bear seriously upon the much-agitated question of iron-cased ships.—*Mechanics' Magazine.*

THE WHITWORTH RIFLE.

THE Whitworth Rifle has now afforded such ample proofs of its superiority to the Enfield arm, that the single adverse consideration of its cost cannot be allowed to operate much longer against its introduction. The costliness of the Armstrong gun, extreme as it was and is, proved no insuperable obstacle to its adoption ; nor can that of the new rifle be allowed to prevail against it. When Colonel Eardley-Wilmot recently reminded Sir William Armstrong (at the Institution of Civil Engineers) that it was unfair to compare the cost of the new rifled cannon with the cost of a brass gun, because after the latter became unserviceable as a gun it was almost as valuable as ever to sell as old brass, Sir William replied that he trusted his guns would prove "almost everlasting." Mr. Whitworth may surely employ the same argument, and with even greater reason. It is fallacious to compare the cost of one of his rifles with that of an ordinary Enfield. Mr. Whitworth uses the best material that can be obtained—material that costs no less than 60*l.* per ton, and which is very hard and tough and difficult to work, but which is also correspondingly strong and durable. That it is so there can be no doubt. In illustration of its great strength, Mr. Whitworth put into a rifle barrel one inch in diameter at the breech, with a bore of ·49 inch, a leaden plug eighteen inches long, as tightly as it could be driven home upon the charge. It was fired with an ordinary charge of powder, and the leaden plug being expanded by the explosion remained in the barrel, the gases generated by the gunpowder all passing out through the touchhole. The same experiment was repeated four times with the same result. It is evident, therefore, that gunpowder cannot burst the Whitworth rifle. With such strength great durability must of necessity co-exist, unless the quick turn of the rifling should tend to its rapid deterioration. But this is not the case ; Mr. Longridge's elaborate investigations having proved that the amount of the force expended upon the rifling of the Whitworth rifle scarcely exceeds two per cent. of the total force of the powder.

Perhaps the most remarkable testimony which has been borne to the merits of this rifle is that of General Hay, the Director of musketry instruction at Hythe. After admitting the superiority of the Whitworth to the Enfield in point of accuracy, General Hay said (at the meeting already mentioned) there was a peculiarity about the Whitworth small-bore rifles which no other similar arms had yet produced—they not only gave greater accuracy of firing, but treble power of penetration. For special purposes, any description of bullet could be used, from lead to steel. The Whitworth rifle with a bullet one-tenth of tin, penetrated thirty-five planks; whereas the Enfield rifle, with which a soft bullet was necessary, only penetrated twelve planks. He had found that at a range of 800 yards the velocity added to the hardened bullet gave a power of penetration in the proportion of 17 to 4 in favour of the Whitworth rifle. This enormous penetration is of the highest importance in a military weapon in firing through gabions, sand-bags, and other artificial defences. General Hay thought the merits of the small-bore had never been sufficiently understood. It has recently been stated that the small-bore Enfield beat the small-bore Whitworth; but nothing of the kind has, General Hay states, taken place. It was also proper to state, he said, that the exact bore of the Whitworth rifle has been adopted at Enfield without acknowledgment; even the same twist has been given to the rifling, one turn in twenty inches, still the penetration of the Whitworth was two-thirds more than that of the Enfield. "Mr. Whitworth has solved," said General Hay, in conclusion, "the problem he undertook, viz., how to project, to the best advantage, a given quantity of lead with a given quantity of gunpowder; and there is no gun in England at this moment which will fulfil that condition to the same extent as the Whitworth rifle." In reply to a question from the president (Mr. Bidder), he said the Whitworth small-bore rifle, fired with common sporting powder, would never foul so as to render loading difficult. He had himself fired one hundred rounds one day, sixty rounds the next, then forty rounds, and so on; and left the gun without being cleaned for ten days, when it fired as well as it did on the first day.

With these facts before us, proceeding from the very highest authority, it will be impossible, we submit, for the War Department to continue the manufacture of the Enfield arm to the exclusion of the Whitworth. Every soldier in the service costs the country from 50l. to 100l. for his education, and 50l. a year for his maintenance; and to hesitate upon a question of five or ten shillings, or even ten pounds, in the cost of the weapon to arm the soldier, certainly appears, as Mr. Bidder remarked, to be carrying economy in the wrong direction.—*Mechanics' Magazine,* May 11, 1860.

GREAT EXPERIMENTS WITH THE WHITWORTH GUN.

In the spring of last year, the following important results were obtained in experiments made on the Southport beach. The spot selected as the site of the guns is known as Ainsdale Point, which is between three and four miles from Southport. Thence, there is a clear and practicable range of 10,000 yards (or nearly six miles) south towards Formby ; and of this distance about 7000 yards had been measured, each 100 being marked by a small stake, with other indications of distance as adopted by the Government in their beach trials of long-range guns. The experiments were in progress, more or less continuously, and with different guns, for between six and seven months.

Mr. Whitworth had five guns at Southport during these trials; but we have now to deal with three only, viz.:—A three-pounder, 6 feet 3 inches long, weighing 1¾ cwt.; a twelve-pounder, 7 feet 9 inches long, weighing 8 cwt.; and an eighty-pounder, 9 feet 10 inches long, weighing four tons. The pitch of the rifling varies, there being one turn in 60 inches for the three-pounder, and one in 100 inches for the sixty-eight pounder. Thus Mr. Whitworth adheres to the sharp pitch characteristic of his musket, each gun having rather more than one complete turn in its rifling.

Mr. Whitworth has issued the following tabular summary of the result of each trial of the 3, 12, and 80-pounders, at different degrees of elevation, which has been carefully prepared :—

SUMMARY OF EXPERIMENTS with Mr. Whitworth's Rifled Cannon, at Southport, showing the Mean Range and Deviation of all the Shots fired at each Experiment.

Date.	Calibre of Gun.	Elevation.	A. No. of Shots Fired.	B. Range.	C. Longitudinal Deviation.	D. Lateral Deviation.
Feb.		Deg.		Yards.	Yards.	Yards.
22	3-pounder	3	10	1579	12	·52
15	,,	10	5	4174	27	1·17
16	,,	,,	5	4190	87	5·5
23	,,	,,	10	3842	43	3·23
15	,,	20	4	6793	58	4·83
16	,,	,,	4	6960	69	8·58
22	,,	,,	5	6647	109	7·4
22	,,	,,	4	6421	94	4·25
23	,,	,,	11	6663	33	3·83
15	,,	35	4	9015	96	10·92
16	,,	,,	5	9580	81	19·33
22	12-pounder	2	5	1247	24	·85
16	,,	5	5	2324	11	1·57
22	,,	,,	10	2336	16	1·08
23	,,	,,	10	2219	22	2·00
21	,,	7	4	3049	17	·5
21	,,	,,	4	3098	9	·54
16	·,	10	5	4027	50	3·31
23	,,	,,	10	3774	37	3·1
15	80-pounder	5	2	2575	36	2·33
	,,	,,	2	2574	30	1·66
23	,,	7	4	3493	8	·58
16	,,	10	2	4700	30	·5
22	,,	,,	4	4409	50	5·17

Column A shows the number of shots fired at each experiment, B shows their average range in yards, C shows their average longitudinal, and D their average lateral, deviation from a central point, according to the system adopted at Hythe.

The following communication from Mr. Whitworth himself (in the *Mechanics' Magazine*) will be read with interest :—

The results of the experiments recently made with my rifled cannons at Southport have elicited notices and comments which I think require me to make some explanation. My rifled guns have not been made expressly with the view of obtaining great range: that is one of the advantages they possess, but it is not obtained at the sacrifice of others. They are all adapted, not only for firing solid shot, but also for hollow shot (which may be filled with molten iron), and for every description of shell. The capacity of the shell is easily increased by adding to its length; and, as my guns are rifled throughout and require no chamber, shells of any length may be fired with any requisite charge of powder. The tables of results published in the newspapers were in some instances arranged by the gentlemen who reported them, in increasing or decreasing order; but the numbers prefixed do not indicate the order in which the shots were fired. This arrangement may have produced an impression that the ranges in certain cases gradually diminished. This was not the case: in some series the longest ranges were attained by the last shots fired, and the piece, as it was warmed by the discharges, became cleaner than it was after the first or second shot. The fact that the ordinary cast-iron service guns which I rifled as an experiment in 1858 proved too weak to be used as rifled pieces has been much dwelt upon; and it was perhaps an error of judgment to apply my system experimentally to the cast-iron blocks without strengthening them. I may mention that the service cast-iron 68-pounder rifled by me, when tried at Portsmouth in 1858, propelled my flat-fronted shot through one of the 4-inch wrought iron plates, and also through the ship's side on which they were firmly bolted, the range being 450 yards. In no other instance, I believe, has a single shot been driven through the 4-inch plate. The experiment was not repeated, as the cast-iron gun burst. All the guns, however, which I have myself made are ready for any proof and any comparison that may be required. Their strength is such that they can be elevated on their carriages, and be fired, if necessary, as mortars, at any angle, with the largest charge of powder that can be consumed in them. The 3-pounder was repeatedly fired at an angle of 35 deg., and attained a range of more than five and a-half miles, without doing the piece or its carriage the slightest injury.

These guns being stronger than is practically necessary, there would be no gain in adding to their strength, though I could do it if requisite. The material of which the cannon is made is the same as that used for my rifled musket barrel—homogeneous iron. To obtain an extreme proof of its strength I loaded one of the barrels with a leaden plug, so long that a full charge of powder was unable to drive it out. On firing the powder, the plug remained in the barrel, and the gases of the explosion all came through the touchhole, leaving the barrel uninjured. This experiment was repeated four times with a similar result. The brass howitzer guns which I rifled for the Government in 1856 stood every proof to which they were subjected. I could not now improve upon them as muzzle-loading guns, and feel confident that they are as efficient as any rifled cannon of like calibre that have been made. In fact, of the rifled cannon, as of the rifled musket, constructed on the principles which I have adopted, it may be said that practically, they must all shoot alike—a result which necessarily follows accurate measurement and workmanship in making them. I had no wish to make a special gun, any more than to choose out special experimental results. Records of all the shots fired during our late experiments were taken by disinterested spectators, and have been published in several journals. The merits of the system have, I believe, been thoroughly tested, and may now be fairly judged. The practice with the smallest gun, the 3-pounder, proved all I wished to establish in point of range; it was, therefore, not requisite to surpass it with the heavier cannon fired at a high elevation. Of the durability of my guns I can speak with the utmost confidence. Being made of the harder and tougher homogeneous iron, they must be more durable than forged guns made of comparatively soft and fibrous wrought iron. From one of them upwards of 1500 shots have been fired, chiefly at high elevations, without the gun exhibiting any injury or sign of wear. The breech-loading arrangements are so simple that they are not easily injured. The guns fired at Southport had all been standing on the open shore exposed to the action of sea air and drifting sands for some weeks, most of them during the whole winter. The relative merits of my own and other systems are best compared by appealing to practical results. These show that the system of construction which enables the simple hard metal pro-

jectile to be fired gives better results, and is capable of a more extended application, than the construction which requires the compound projectile and soft
metal coating. In other words, the system of rifling by mechanical fit is capable
of doing much more than that of rifling by the force of the explosion. The latter
is a construction of which I cannot be said to have approved, otherwise I should
have adopted it. Among other objections to the use of the compound coated
projectile, one of great importance is, that it involves an arrangement which is
complicated, whereas the shaped hard metal projectile is far more simple, and
may be produced at less cost. Simplicity of arrangement and construction is
the special object I sought to obtain, knowing that in this, as in all other improvements based on mechanical principles, that system is the most perfect which
is reduced to its simplest elements. When this is done successfully it may generally be considered that the result cannot be surpassed.

NEW GUN-METAL.

In a discussion on Artillery at the Institution of Civil Engineers,
several facts of interest have been stated incidentally. Mr. F. A.
Abel, chemist to the War Department, for example, replied to
an inquiry,—that he had been induced to make some experiments
upon the combinations of phosphorus with copper, and had found
that by the introduction of a small proportion of that substance, say
from 2 to 4 per cent. of phosphorus into copper, a Gun-metal was produced remarkable for its density and tenacity, and superior in every
respect to ordinary gun-metal (the alloy of copper and tin known by
that name). He believed the average strain borne by gun-metal
might be represented by 31,000 lbs. upon the square inch, whilst
the material obtained by adding phosphorus to copper bore a strain of
from 48,000 lbs. to 50,000 lbs. But the increased tenacity was not
the only beneficial result obtained by this treatment of copper. The
material was uniform throughout, which was scarcely ever the case
with gun-metal. The experiments alluded to were merely preliminary, and had been, to a certain extent, checked by the improvements since introduced in the construction of field-guns, which had
led to a discontinuance of the employment of gun-metal. Sir Charles
Fox also thought the best guns would be made of iron mixed with
some other metals, such as wolfram and titanium, so as to ensure the
greatest strength and density. Mr. Musket had, he said, obtained
great density by mixing with iron a small per-centage of wolfram,
and great strength by the use of titanium.

THE LANCASTER GUN.

Mr. Lancaster has explained to the Institution of Civil Engineers, the causes of the temporary failures which had attended the
use of his oval-bored cannon. It was true, he said, that three were
burst at the muzzle in the Crimea, but it must be understood that
those which failed were the service-guns, bored oval on his system,
and not the guns specially made for the purpose. It was generally
supposed that the action of the shell in passing out of the bore burst
the gun. The fact was simply that the shells were originally made
in two pieces, the base of the shell being welded to the upper portion. In practice this weld was often imperfect. Hence, at the
moment of the explosion of the service charge, the flame penetrated
through the defective weld to the charge within the shell. The

charge, amounting to 12 lbs. of powder, was fully ignited just at the moment the shell was in the act of leaving the muzzle of the gun. It could, therefore, only be a question of time whether the shell burst within or outside the gun. If the shell burst within the muzzle of the gun, the destruction of the gun followed as a matter of course. Directly this failure in the manufacture of the shells was discovered, steps were taken to rectify it. Instead of being made of two pieces, the shells were now constructed of one piece of iron, and the muzzle of the gun had been strengthened by the addition of a ring of wrought iron. Should, therefore, any of the old store of shells be used by any chance, the gun would be strong enough to resist the contingency. It was found that these guns were now thoroughly equal to the requirements of the service.

THE NYCTOSCOPE.

Sir W. Armstrong has described to the Institution of Civil Engineers the principle of the Nyctoscope, an ingenious instrument designed by him for enabling the gunners to maintain a fire upon any given object after nightfall. The principle of the instrument is to render a false object in the rear, or at one side, visible upon a vertical line in a mirror, when the gun is laid upon the true object. A lamp attached at night to the false object becomes visible upon the same mark in the mirror, when the gun is in line with the true object. The vertical adjustment for elevation is effected by a spirit-level clinometer, forming part of the instrument.

KRUPP'S GERMAN CAST-STEEL GUN.

From a Report made to the Prussian Government by Colonel Orges, it appears that this German Cast-steel Gun has given the most satisfactory results, as regards strength. A bar of one inch square of this material has borne a weight of 50 tons, whereas a bar of wrought iron of the same dimensions broke with 33 tons. Mr. Krupp's gun bore five and a-half times the internal pressure of an ordinary cast-iron gun of the same internal and external diameters, and three times the internal pressure which burst a bronze cylinder of the same dimensions. Mr. Krupp is now making three hundred guns for the Prussian Government. The weight of his 12-pounder breech-loading gun was 825 lbs. The cost of the forging was about 93*l*., and that of the gun complete was 150*l*. These statements have been made by Mr. C. W. Siemens, C.E.

BREECH-LOADING RIFLES.

Mr. W. Strode has exhibited and explained to the Institution of Civil Engineers specimens of Messrs. McKenzie and Wentworth's Breech-loading Rifles.

The conditions sought to be fulfilled in these rifles are :—

1st. That they should be able to take the present ammunition.
2nd. That they should have a sound joint at the junction of the breech and the barrel.
3rd. That there should be nothing liable to be discharged against the soldier himself, by his own act, in case of bursting ; and, therefore, no plug or stopper put in from the back, or breech-end of the barrel.

4th. That the strength should not be less, and the weight scarcely more, than in the present guns.

5th. That the moveable breech should be capable of adaptation to any barrel, as well as to any form of ammunition.

It was stated that these rifles only differed from the Enfield pattern in the breech and in the "stocking;" so that if the changes were made which these alterations involved, they could be readily manufactured at the Government establishment at that place. It was thought that such a weapon would be especially useful for Volunteer Rifle Corps, as muzzle-loading would not be necessary.

The United States Secretary of War is in favour of breech-loading fire-arms, saying—

"Immediate steps ought to be taken to arm all our light troops with the most approved of these arms. I hold it to be an inhuman economy which sends a soldier into the field, where his life is constantly in danger, without furnishing him with the best (not the most expensive) arms that are or can be made. It is no answer to say that our troops cannot be taught to use with skill this character of arm as well as another. It is the practice and drill that make the soldier expert in the use of his arm, and while he may attain to great skill with a good weapon, he certainly never can do so with an indifferent one. I think it may be fairly asserted now that the highest efficiency of a body of men with fire-arms can only be secured by putting in their hands the best breech-loading arm. The long habit of using muzzle-loading arms will resist what seems to be so great an innovation, and ignorance may condemn; but as certainly as the percussion-cap has superseded the flint and steel, so surely will the breech-loading gun drive out of use those that load at the muzzle. For cavalry the revolver and breech-loader will supersede the sabre."

His suggestion as to arming the cavalry is, it will be noticed, directly in antagonism with the opinions now alleged to be held at the Horse Guards,—the sabre only being considered the proper weapon for cavalry, and the use of the revolver as being opposed to the thorough efficiency of that arm of the service.

IMPROVED CARTRIDGES AND PROJECTILES.

MR. J. MACINTOSH has patented certain improvements in manufacturing Cartridges, by employing collodion, (which is, as is well known, a solution of gun-cotton or fibre in a solvent,) to form the case of the cartridge. He forms the case by dipping a mandril of suitable form into the collodion, and withdrawing it when the film is sufficiently set; the mandril is then taken out, and the charge and ball are introduced.

SMITH'S PATENT SHOT, SHELLS, AND OTHER PROJECTILES.

MR. GUSTAVUS ADOLPHUS SMITH, C.E., has patented an invention which consists principally in giving to an elongated projectile certain forms hereafter described, the object of which is to cause the projectile to maintain a position in which its longitudinal axis coincides with its line of flight, this result being produced by the resistance or reaction of the air upon the projectile. He has found, he says, that "in general a cylindrical body terminated anteriorly by a flat cone or by any analogous figure whose surface lies at a very wide angle with the axis of the cylinder, tends to assume the required position when moving through the air, and appears to be in a condition of stable equilibrium when in flight in that position; whereas, if the front of the body be formed in an acutely angled cone or any conoid or other figure whose surface lies in general at a very acute angle with the axis of the body, there is no such tendency to assume the required position, and no stability of equilibrium in that position. . . . . By this invention I am," he says, "enabled to construct projectiles of forms suitable for shot, common carcase or shrapnel shells, bullets for small arms, or rockets, and which forms have this property, that the resistance of the air acting in lines perpendicular to the surface on which it strikes, such lines will for the most part be nearly parallel to the longitudinal axis of the projectile, or else will meet the line of the axis in points which lie behind the centre of gravity of the mass, that is to say, further from the apex of the projectile, and the result of this is, that if the projectile should happen to deviate from its correct position so that its axis no longer coincides with its line of flight, the resistance of the air will tend to restore the projectile to its correct position instead of tending to increase the deviation, as is the case with elongated projectiles of the ordinary forms." For details, with illustrations, see *Mechanics' Magazine*, May 18, 1860.

WILSON'S BREECH-LOADER.

IN adopting a Breech-loader for military purposes, the utmost caution is required in making the selection. Now, there are a considerable number of breech-loaders before the public, and most of them distinguished for great ingenuity and variety in their combinations and arrangements. A new weapon of this kind, appearing to possess the real and substantial requisites of an effective military rifle, has been invented and patented by Mr. Thomas Wilson, of Birmingham. The extreme simplicity of its construction, combined with its unquestionable strength and safety of action, point it out as a gun pre-eminently adapted for military purposes. There are several other breech-loaders which have recently attracted much attention; but most of them are quite unequal to the wear and tear of military use, and are, moreover, encumbered with levers, joints, and screws, which of all things are the most objectionable in a military arm, being constantly liable to entanglement with the accoutrements of the soldier, and almost certain to get strained or deranged in use, or by the slightest accident. A military breech-loader, to be of real use, should be of the simplest construction, and entirely free from joints, levers, screws, and, in fact, everything which requires nice adjustment and careful and delicate handling. It is precisely on these grounds that we express ourselves strongly in favour of Mr. Wilson's breech-loader, which is open to none of these objections. It requires no adjusting or delicate handling in use, is in no way liable to derangement, and cannot be wrongly manipulated, even by the clumsiest operator. The action is simply a plug and a cotter, both of which are withdrawn in a second by the thumb and finger, and replaced with equal speed and certainty after charging. It is impossible to devise an action more simple and direct, or less liable to objection than this ; and it is a great relief, after the complicated arrangements of levers, joints, and screws, and the consequent difficult and unnatural twisting and bending motions which have hitherto seemed inseparable from breech-loaders, to find one at least free from these objections, and likely to be of substantial use. In addition to the advantages we have named, we are informed that the action of Mr. Wilson's breech-loader can be readily applied to existing muzzle-loading guns, so that any number of Enfield rifles can be converted into breech-loaders.—*Aris's Birmingham Gazette.*

FOULING GUN-BARRELS.

A CORRESPONDENT of the *Mechanics' Magazine* writes :—To prevent Fouling in Gun-barrels, two very neat and economical processes for preventing rust have been submitted to the War-Office, and the Gunmakers' Society. 1. If nitro-muriate of platina be mixed with a fourth part of its bulk of ether, and the mixture suffered to settle, the ethereal solution of platina will float and may then be poured off. When this is poured into the barrel, its interior surface will be covered instantly with a coat of platina that forms an indestructible coat, not affected by fire, or concentrated acids. 2. If ether be added to a solution of muriate of gold, the gold will leave the acid, and float upon its surface combined with the ether. To such a solution of gold add about a fourth part of ether, shake them together, and wait till the fluids separate ; the upper stratum, or ethereal gold, is then to be carefully poured off into another vessel. If this is poured into the barrel, and when poured out the barrel is *instantly* plunged into a trough of water, its interior surface will have acquired a coat of pure gold.

IMPROVED ORDNANCE AND PROJECTILES.

IN this improvement, patented by J. Spurgin, the inventor applies to muzzle-loading and smooth-bore cannon a tube of steel having rifle grooves formed within it. The tube is made to fit the bore of the cannon, and so that it may be placed and locked therein, and unlocked and withdrawn at pleasure. The tube is chambered or made somewhat larger in the bore at the breech-end for a sufficient length to receive a ball and cartridge. The ball should be furnished with a leaden ring of a slightly larger diameter than the bore of the tube beyond the chamber. The gun is loaded by placing the ball and cartridge into the tube when it is out of the gun, the tube is then put into its place and there locked ; the gun is discharged in the ordinary manner.—*Mechanics' Magazine.*

IMPROVED REVOLVING FIRE-ARMS.

M. F. A. LE MAT has patented certain improvements in the

construction of revolving or repeating Fire-arms, consisting in a construction of parts whereby a repeating fire-arm may be rendered a more convenient and effective weapon than heretofore, without adding to the weight or to the complication of the parts. The invention relates to that description of repeating fire-arm in which a moveable breech piece, pierced for several charges, is made to rotate on a central spindle, in order to bring every charge in succession under the hammer, and opposite to a common barrel, through which every such charge is made to pass. The invention consists principally in mounting such rotating breech on a hollow central spindle or barrel, which will form an additional barrel for the arm, and which additional barrel the patentee prefers to charge with a cartridge containing a number of small bullets instead of a single bullet. This central barrel or hollow spindle may be charged either at the muzzle or the breech.—*Ibid.*

TESTIMONIAL TO MR. ROBERT HUNT—MINERAL STATISTICS.

A SILVER tea and coffee service, value 200 guineas, a silver salver of 200 ounces, and a purse of 200 guineas, have been presented to that very efficient public officer, Mr. Robert Hunt, Keeper of Mining Records, by gentlemen interested in the mineral industries of the kingdom. In acknowledging this handsome and well-merited present, Mr. Hunt thus explained the difficulties with which he had to contend in his office:—"When I commenced the work of collecting the Mineral Statistics of the United Kingdom, in 1848, the whole question was of so uncertain a nature, that I then had little hope of advancing it to that condition which has elicited this substantial approval of my labours. I commenced my work with some compilations showing the state of tin and copper mining in Cornwall. It was then extended to the lead mines of the kingdom, at the suggestion, and by the aid of Mr. John Taylor, and eventually enlarged by the recommendation of a Government commission, consisting of Sir Stafford Northcote and Sir Charles Trevelyan, to embrace the coal mines and the iron manufacture of these important islands. I am bound to acknowledge the great assistance which I have received from all parties who are especially interested in our mineral industries. But for this it would have been quite impossible for me to have published annually, as I have now for some years been enabled to do, a volume embracing returns of all the metalliferous minerals and coal raised in Great Britain and Ireland. This inquiry has extended itself to the earthy minerals; and within a few weeks I shall place in the hands of the public a volume of returns, obtained by the Mining Record Office, of the production of clay, the manufacture of bricks, tiles, &c., and of our building and ornamental stones. I have thus sought to render the Mining Record Office, established upon the recommendation of the British Association, as useful as possible to the public. I can point with satisfaction to the collection of records obtained and preserved, showing the extent of our subterranean explorations in many of our most important mining districts."

REMARKABLE PROPERTY OF IRON.

IN 1856, says a contemporary, Mr. Marsh, an able chemist connected with the Royal Arsenal, discovered that it was an invariable rule with Iron which has remained a considerable time under water, when reduced to small grains or an impalpable powder, to become red-hot. This he found by scraping from a gun some corroded metal, which ignited the paper containing it, and burnt a hole in his pocket. The knowledge of this fact may account for some spontaneous fires and explosions. The tendency of moistened particles of iron to ignite was discovered by the French chemist, Lemery, as far back as 1670.

NASMYTH'S STEAM-HAMMER.

WE find in the *Engineer* the following deserved tribute to the genius of the inventor of the Steam-hammer, a stupendous specimen of which has been manufactured to be employed in forging Armstrong guns, at Woolwich Arsenal.

Without detracting in the smallest degree from the merit of any engineers who have modified or improved this invention from time to time (says the *Engineer*), we should like to see due prominence and just praise given to Mr. Nasmyth, who first introduced the Steam-hammer in a practically efficient form. The invention of this potent and yet pliant tool is one of those affairs which seem exceedingly simple in themselves, after they are accomplished, but which, nevertheless, are of incalculable value to mankind. It is not too much to say that, but for Nasmyth's Steam-hammer, we must have stopped short of many of those gigantic engineering works which, but for the decay of all wonder in us, would be the perpetual wonder of this age, and which have enabled our modern engineers to take rank above the gods of all mythologies.

Writing as we are for the perusal of engineers, we need not dwell upon this subject. But there is one use to which the steam-hammer is now becoming extensively applied by some of our manufacturers, that deserves especial mention, rather for the prospect which it opens to us than for what has already been actually accomplished. We allude to the manufacture of large articles in dies. At one manufactory in the country, railway wheels, for example, are being manufactured with enormous economy by this means. The various parts of the wheels are produced in quantity either by rolling or by dies under the hammer'; these parts are then brought together in their relative position in a mould, heated to a welding heat, and then by a blow of the steam-hammer, furnished with dies, are stamped into a complete and all but finished wheel. It is evident that wherever wrought iron articles of a manageable size have to be produced in considerable quantities, the same process may be adopted, and the saving effected by the substitution of this for the ordinary forging process will doubtless ere long prove incalculable.

For this, as for the many other advantageous uses of the steam-hammer, we are primarily and mainly indebted to Mr. Nasmyth. It is but right, therefore, that we should keep his name in honour. In fact, when we think of the universal service which this machine is rendering us, we feel that some special expression of our indebtedness to him would be a reasonable and grateful service. The benefit which he has conferred upon us is so great, as to justly entitle him to stand side by side with the few men who have gained name and fame as great inventive engineers, and to whom we have testified our gratitude—usually, unhappily, when it was too late for them to enjoy it.*

TO INCREASE THE WEIGHT OF IRON.

AN increase of near 30 per cent. in weight may be given to Iron by heating it red-hot, and passing a continued stream of steam over it when in that state. This increase of weight arises from its de-composing the water, and imbibing its oxygen. Whenever iron becomes oxidized by exposure to the air, it may be known that this is occasioned by the absorption of oxygen, from the increase of weight which the metal acquires during the operation ; and to con-firm the fact, the oxide may be again reduced, and the original quantity of metal left unaltered. If nickel, in a certain proportion, is combined with iron, it gives a degree of whiteness to iron, and diminishes its disposition to rust, and adds to its ductility.— *Mechanics' Magazine.*

NEW PROCESS FOR MAKING MALLEABLE IRON.

A BEAUTIFUL and very simple process for Decarbonizing Iron has been put in successful operation by the inventor, Professor H. K. Eaton, at Elizabethport, New Jersey. It consists in packing the cast metal in the white oxide of zinc, instead of oxide of iron, and heating the whole to redness, whereby the carbon of the iron is ex-tracted, and metallic zinc distils and is condensed in a water-bath. By the method heretofore in use in this country, for making mal-leable iron, the heat is usually kept up for eight or nine days in succession, and it frequently happens that great trouble and expense follow the process of decarbonization in removing the small particles of metal that are reconverted from the oxide of iron, in which the castings are packed, and which adhere to the surface. In Professor Eaton's method, all this trouble and expense are obviated. The oxide of zinc not only effects the decarbonization in about forty hours, but, on account of the comparatively low temperature at which the oxide is converted, and its different constituency, nothing adheres to the surface of the castings, which come from the fire almost ready for finishing. The castings that have as yet been treated by this process are the smaller iron parts of harness hardware—such

* To the genius of James Watt may be traced the first idea of using a hammer in connexion with the power of steam, although it was left for one of our own time practically to carry out the project. In Watt's patent of April 28, 1784, he proposes to apply "the power of steam or fire engines to the moving of heavy hammers, or stampers, for forging or stamping iron, copper, and other metals," without the intervention of rotative motions or wheels, by fixing the hammer either to the piston or piston-rod, or working-beam of the engine.—*Curiosities of Science,* Second Series, p. 210.

as rings, buckles, and links—and several kinds of cutlery, and parts of small machinery. It is claimed for the invention, that it not only makes a far better kind of malleable cast-iron, but can be done at much less expense, as the time of keeping up the heat is greatly reduced, and the product of the packing material is valuable.

The formula of the process is as follows :—Oxide of zinc : zinc, 32 ; oxygen, 8 ; total, 40. So that if a mass of iron, or a number of pieces of castings, containing 6 lb. of carbon, were packed in 40 lb. of oxide of zinc, the 8 lb. of oxygen would separate from the zinc, and combine with the carbon of the iron, producing 14 lb. of carbonic oxide gas, which would be lost in the atmosphere, and leaving 32 lb. of pure metallic zinc, and the castings 6 lb. lighter. So that, if the oxide of zinc costs 4½ cents per lb., and the metal was worth 7 cents, there would be a gain as follows :—40 lb. oxide zinc, 4½ cents, 1 dol. 80 cents ; 32 lb. metallic zinc, 7 cents, 2 dols. 24 cents ; gain, 44 cents. So that one heat, using 40 lb. of oxide of zinc, would cost 44 cents less than the price of the fuel required in the process, and the time of keeping up the heat is not more than one quarter of the old method. Another important fact connected with this way of decarbonizing iron to render it malleable is the certainty with which the manufacture can be carried on. Nothing is left to guess-work, or, what is nearly the same thing, the conjecture of experience ; for when the zinc ceases to distil, if there is an excess of the oxide of zinc present (which can always be provided for), it is certain there is no more carbon to be extracted from the iron and unite with the oxygen, and the process of decarbonization is necessarily perfect. The specimens that have been dealt with by this method are found to be nearly chemically pure iron—silicates and phosphates being removed.—*American Railway Review.*

MALLEABLE IRON CASTINGS.

A NEW method of *"malleableizing"* Iron Castings is announced in the *New York Tribune* to have been discovered by Professor A. R. Eaton, of that city. It consists in exposing the castings to the contact of oxide of zinc, as a substitute for the oxide of iron in the furnace. It is stated that the employment of the oxide of iron which combines with the excess of carbon in iron castings when long exposed to red heat, leaves a spongy residuum on the castings, which is obviated by the zinc oxide, because the zinc is volatile and passes off, leaving the oxygen gas to combine with the carbon in the iron ; although, were both metals equally fixed, the zinc would rather deprive the iron of oxygen than the iron the zinc.

METHOD OF CONVERTING IRON INTO CAST-STEEL.

PLACE layers of small pieces of iron in a crucible, with a mixture of the carbonate of lime. Six parts of the carbonate of lime, being either chalk, marble, limestone, or any other calcareous substance, and six parts of the earth of pounded Hessian crucibles, must be employed for twenty parts of iron : and this mixture is to be so disposed, as that, after fusion, the iron may be completely covered by it, in order to prevent its coming into contact with the atmosphere; when the mixture is to be gradually heated, and at length exposed to a heat capable of melting iron. Where the fire is well kept up, an hour will generally be found a sufficient time to convert two pounds of iron into excellent and exceedingly hard steel, capable of being forged.—*Correspondent of the Mechanics' Magazine.*

SUSPENSION CHAINS AND GIRDERS.

Mr. P. W. Barlow has read to the British Association a paper "On the Mechanical Effects of combining Suspension Chains and Girders, and the Value of the Practical Application of the System," illustrated by a large model. The object of the paper is to. point out that such bridges are adapted for carrying railway traffic, and are less costly than the bridges usually adopted in this country for that purpose.

In the discussion on Mr. Barlow's paper, the chairman, Mr. Fairbairn, Mr. Froude, and Mr. E. Cowper, took part; the latter gentleman pointing out that, in his opinion, danger would result from the rapid wear and tear of the rivets joining the links of the chain; and he suggested and described a bridge, on the suspension principle, formed of boiler-plate of such a curve above, and such a horizontal line below for supporting the platform, and of such depth as to include in it all the curves of distortion which the catenary would undergo when subjected to the varying load of trains passing over a bridge suspended from it. This combines the necessary rigidity with the suspension principle.

STRENGTH OF WROUGHT-IRON GIRDERS.

Mr. Fairbairn has communicated to the British Association certain "Experiments to determine the Effects of Vibratory Action and Long-continued Changes of Load upon Wrought-iron Girders." The paper is entirely of a technical character, and details the results of a set of experiments having for their object the determining matters with which the public are intimately concerned, viz., the efficacy of girders supporting bridges over which railway trains are constantly passing. It is well known that iron, whether in the shapes of railway axles or girders, after undergoing for a length of time a continued vibratory or hammering action, assumes a different molecular structure, and though perfectly efficient in the first instance, becomes brittle and no longer capable of sustaining the loads to which it may be subjected. Mr. Fairbairn stated that the practical conclusion to which his experiments, so far as they had at present gone, would lead was, that a railway girder bridge would, irrespective of other causes, last a hundred and fifty years.

NEW ZEALAND STEEL.

Ever since the settlement of New Zealand by Europeans their attention has been daily called to the peculiarities of a kind of metallic sand along the shores of New Plymouth, in Taranaki. This sand has the appearance of fine steel filings, and if a magnet be dropped upon it, and taken up again, the instrument will be found thickly coated with the iron granules. The place where the sand abounds is along the base of Mount Egmont, an extinct volcano; and the deposit extends several miles along the coast, to the depth of many feet, and having a corresponding breadth. The geological supposition is that this granulated metal has been thrown out of the volcano along the base of which it rests into the sea, and there pulverized. It has been looked upon for a long time as a geological curiosity, even to the extent of trying to smelt some of it; but, although so many years have passed since its discovery, it is only recently that any attempt has been made to turn it to a practical account; in fact, the quantity is so large that people out there looked upon it as utterly valueless. It formed a standing complaint in the letters of all emigrants that when the sea breeze was a little up they were obliged to wear veils to prevent being blinded by the fine sand which stretched for miles along the shore. Captain Morshead, resident in the West of England, was so much impressed with its value that he went to New Zealand to verify the reports made to him in this country, and was fortunate enough to find them all correct. He smelted the ore first in a crucible, and subsequently in a furnace; the results were so satisfactory that he immediately obtained the necessary grant of the sand from the Government, and returned to England with several tons for more conclusive experiments.

It has been carefully analysed in this country by several well-known metallurgists, and has been pronounced to be the purest ore at present known: it contains 88·45 of peroxide of iron, 11·43 of oxide of titanium, with silica, and only 12 of waste in 100 parts. Taking the sand as it lies on the beach and smelting it, the produce is 61 per cent. of iron of the very finest quality; and, again, if this sand be subjected to what is called the cementation process, the result is a tough, first-class steel, which, in its properties, seems to surpass any other description of that metal at present known. The investigations of metallurgical science have found that if titanium is mixed with iron the character of the steel is materially improved; but, titanium being a scarce ore, such a mixture is too expensive for ordinary purposes. Here, however, nature has stepped in, and made free gift of both metals on the largest scale. To give some idea of the fineness of this beautiful sand, it will be enough to say that it passes readily through a gauze sieve of 4900 holes or interstices to the square inch. As soon as it was turned into steel by Mr. Musket, of Coleford, Messrs. Moseley, the eminent cutlers and toolmakers, of New-street, Covent-garden, were requested to see what could be done with the Taranaki steel. They have tested it in every possible way, and have tried its temper to the utmost; and they say the manner in which the metal has passed through their trials goes far beyond anything that they ever worked in steel before. It has been formed into razors, scissors, saws, penknives, table cutlery, surgical instruments, &c.; and the closeness of the grain, the fineness of polish, and keenness of edge, place it in the very foremost rank—almost in the position of a new metal.

E

Some silk-cutting tools have been made, and so admirably have they turned out that one particular firm will in future use no others. In the surgical instruments the edges have been examined by the microscope, and have stood the test in keeping the superiority. This steel is stated to possess peculiar advantages for gun-barrels and boring-cutters for ordnance purposes. As far as is at present known of this extraordinary metal, it bids fair to claim all the finer classes of cutlery and edge-tool instruments to itself, so well has everything made from it turned out. Messrs. Moseley, in whose hands the sole manufacture of cutlery and edge-tools is vested for this country, have placed a case, filled with the metal in all its stages, in the Polytechnic Institution. There is the fine metallic sand, some beautiful specimens of the cutlery made from it, and the intermediate phases of the iron and steel.—*The Australian Mail.*

THE NEW BRONZE COINAGE.

WE need not describe this New Coinage, now in general circulation. Its artistic character is by no means creditable to Her Majesty's Mint, the authorities of which are responsible for strangely misrepresenting the agreeable features and stately contour of our beloved Queen. The Britannia on the obverse is also a very conventional affair, of the insurance-office type. No sooner had the coin been issued than a few precocious critics seized upon the "Britt." of the legend as an error; though, probably, these wiseacres were not born when a similar objection was made to the "Britt." of the legend on the Victoria crown-piece, explained by the customary doubling in abbreviation of the final consonant, to denote the plural, as in the Roman *Coss.* (Consuls). We quote the following details from the *Mechanics' Magazine :*—

The material of which the coins are composed is far more suitable for coinage than pure copper. It resembles in its composition, indeed, very closely the "gun-metal" so well known and largely patronized by engineers, and has, when free from oxidation, a golden hue. The exact composition of the bronze mixture for these coins is as follows : —

Copper	95 parts.
Tin	4 „
Zinc	1 part.

It may not be improper to add that to the pound weight avoirdupois there are of—

Bronze pence	48
„ halfpence	80
„ farthings	160

individual pieces will, therefore, weigh :—

Penny	145·83 grains.
Halfpenny	87·50 „
Farthing	43·75 „

The individual weights of the most recent copper coinage were :—

Penny	291½ grains.
Halfpenny	145½ „
Farthing	72¹¹⁄₁₃ „

And it is a singular fact in relation to the diameters of the new coins, which are respectively :—

Pence ...	...	...	...	...	1·200 inches.
Halfpence	...	...	...	...	1·000 ,,
Farthings	...	...	...	...	·800 ,,

that as twelve halfpence give an exact measurement of one foot, so do four pence, four halfpence, and four farthings placed edge to edge, on a flat surface in single file, give the same result.

As the halfpenny is exactly one inch in diameter, like the Canadian decimal cent, it may be used, if need be, in lieu of the carpenter's rule. As, for example, 12 halfpence = one foot, and 36 halfpence = one yard.

_____

PATENT ENAMEL SURFACING FOR METAL PIPES, &c.

IT has long been noted that ordinary earthenware is not adapted to stand the varied temperature of the oven. It was with the idea, in the first place, of obviating this difficulty that it suggested itself to Mr. Paris to manufacture dishes and basins of sheet iron or other metals, and cover them with a Coating of Enamel, making them, in fact, china with a metallic core ; thus causing them to be free from the destroying properties of oxidization, and at the same time be durable and not liable to break when heated to any moderate temperature. This peculiar manufacture has now become an important feature in the Birmingham hardware trade ; it has been already pretty well brought to perfection, and the manufacture of enamelled pie-dishes, wash-hand and other basins, candlesticks, and other articles is very extensive.

Some slight idea may be conceived of the increasing demand for this kind of article, from the fact that during the last year 60,000 pie-dishes were turned out at Salt's patent enamel works. But the most important use to which this enamelling process has yet been applied, is for securing both the internal and external surfaces of iron pipes from the corroding action of fluids. This improvement is well worthy of the attention of hydraulic engineers, for it has been found, in practice, where pipes so prepared have been laid down, that the water delivered has retained its original purity, nor does it even deteriorate by long standing ; added to this, the pipes themselves are found to last three or four times as long as they otherwise would, so that the extra outlay is soon compensated for. The process of enamelling miscellaneous articles is simply as follows :— Having been stamped out in a most ingenious manner by machinery prepared for that purpose, they are in the first place immersed in a pickling bath for the purpose of freeing their surfaces of extraneous matter ; they are then placed for a short time in a sulphuretted furnace, and, thus prepared, are brushed over with a thick coating of pounded glass, &c. The articles are then placed in a furnace heated to a temperature of between 2000° and 3000°, which causes a liquefaction of the silicious covering, and then a combination of the enamel and iron takes places. This is so perfectly effected that if

the glaze becomes injured, the iron is still found to remain uninflu-
enced by the presence of fluids.—*Mechanics' Magazine.*

DRILLING HOLES IN WROUGHT IRON.

Mr. JOHN COCHRANE, of Woodside Ironworks, Dudley, has described a machine for Drilling instead of Punching Holes in
Wrought-iron Plates, which was designed for the purpose of drilling
a large number of holes in some wrought-iron plates, required for the
erection of the new railway bridge over the Thames at Hungerford,
a piece of work in which the ordinary system of punching was not
sufficiently accurate. The plate to be drilled is placed securely on a
table, and accurately adjusted to the proper position by set screws
at each corner; the table is then raised by water pressure, and
pressed against the drills by an accumulator. There are eighty
drills, which are driven at a speed of from forty to fifty revolutions
per minute, at a pressure of twenty tons on the table, or five cwt.
on each drill; and at this speed the entire eighty holes of one inch
diameter are drilled through a five-eighths of an inch plate within fifteen minutes. The drills last on an average ten hours without grinding.
The power required to drive one machine with eighty drills is about
ten-horse.—*Ibid.*

ZEIODELITE.

Such is the name which has been given to a new composition
which has recently been patented by Mr. Joseph Simon, of Paris,
and intended as a substitute for lead. According to the *Mining
Journal,* he mixes, with about 19 lbs. of sulphur, 42 lbs. of broken
jars or glass finely pulverized; he exposes the mixture to a gentle
heat, which melts the sulphur, and then stirs the mass until it
becomes thoroughly homogeneous, when he runs it into suitable
moulds, and allows it to cool. This preparation is proof against
acids in general. To unite it in slabs no solder is required; a portion of the molten Zeiodelite being run in between the slabs placed
1 inch apart, when, the heat being 208° Cent., the edges of the slabs
will be melted, and a uniform surface will be obtained, the whole
forming but one piece.

FILE-CUTTING MACHINERY.

An efficient, well-working File-cutting Machine has long been a
desirable apparatus; and the operation has hitherto been considered
to be one not admitting of the application of machinery. This difficulty has, however, been overcome, and the requisite machine produced, which Mr. T. Greenwood, of Leeds, has described to the Institution of Mechanical Engineers.

Operations much more difficult than cutting files have been performed by machinery in various manufactures; among which may
be named the combing of wool, in which, by the manipulation of the
machine itself, the long fibres are selected and delivered into one
compartment, and the short fibres into another; an operation
which at first sight would appear to require an intelligent and dis-
criminating power. The actual process of file-cutting is, however,

one of the simplest description. It consists in driving a chisel of suitable form and inclination to a small depth into the prepared surface of the blank, and steadily withdrawing it again ; and cutting a file is merely a repetition of this operation. The difficulties to be surmounted are—to present the blank perfectly parallel to the cutting edge of the chisel ; to withdraw the chisel from the incision made in the blank without damaging the edge of the newly-raised tooth ; to prevent a rebound of the chisel after the blow which drives it into the blank, and before the next blow is struck ; to give a uniform traversing motion to the blank, ensuring regularity in the teeth ; to proportion the intensity of the blow to the varying width of the file, so as to give a uniform depth of cut ; and to perform these operations at such a speed as to make them commercially profitable. In most of the attempts that have been made to accomplish this process by machinery, the idea has been to construct an iron arm and hand to hold the chisel, and an iron hammer to strike the blow ; and by this means to imitate as nearly as possible the operation of cutting by hand. The difference in the material used inevitably led to failure : the flexible and to some extent non-elastic nature of the fingers, wrist and arm, enabled the man to hold the chisel, strike the blow, and then lift the chisel from the tooth, without vibration : not so when the iron hand and hammer are tried to perform the same operation ; the vibration consequent upon the material employed frequently caused irregularity in the work and a ragged and uneven edge on the tooth. The slow speed at which these machines were worked rendered them unable to compete with hand labour.

In the machine forming the subject of the present paper the above objections have been nearly, if not altogether, obviated by an ingenious modification in the mode of action. This machine is the invention of M. Bernot, of Paris, and has been already working successfully for some time both in France and Belgium. The blow is given by the pressure of a flat steel spring pressing upon the top of a vertical slide, at the lower end of which the chisel is firmly fixed ; the slide is actuated by a cam making about one thousand revolutions per minute, and the chisel consequently strikes that number of blows per minute, thus obviating the vibration consequent upon the blow with an iron-mounted hammer, and moving at such a speed as to render any vibration impossible.

In the files cut by this machine the teeth are raised with perfect regularity, and consequently when the file is used each tooth performs its proper share of work ; whereas, in hand cutting, from the varying power of the muscles, especially towards the close of the day, it is impossible to produce such perfectly uniform work.

A manufactory employing twelve of these machines has been established at Douai, in the north of France, and another at Brussels, in both of which the machines have been in successful operation for nearly two years.

In a discussion which followed the reading of the paper, Mr. Greenwood stated that there was no difficulty in cutting round files in the machine as well as flat files ; the machines were of smaller size for this purpose, working at a speed as high as 1500 strokes per minute, and the tang of the file was fixed in a chuck like a lathe head, divided for the several cuts required in a complete revolution, so that the whole process was carried out completely without any difficulty. The Chairman (John Fenn, Esq.) observed that when there was so great a difference as from 32d. to 4d. per dozen in the cost of labour in the manufacture, the expense of the machine would be of little consequence, since it would soon pay for itself if it did as good work. Mr. B. Fothergill said he was acquainted with the working of machine-cut files manufactured at Manchester, and they were found to be quite as good and durable as the best hand-cut files, if not superior; he was satisfied that the best class of files would ultimately be manufactured by machinery.

See the details of the machine, with engravings, in the *Mechanics' Magazine*, Feb. 17, 1860.

PRICE'S PATENT IMPROVEMENTS IN LOCKS.

MR. GEORGE PRICE, of Wolverhampton, has patented an invention which consists of a novel and simplified arrangement and construction of certain parts of Locks, so as to prevent the possibility of picking by what is known as the "tentative process," or feeling the position of the gatings of the levers by applying pressure in any way to the bolt. "Since the Great Exhibition of 1851," says Mr. Price, "it has been universally admitted that the principle on which the picking of locks depends is, that whenever pressure can be applied to the bolt in such a manner as to indicate the points of resistance to its withdrawal, such a lock can be picked. Since this tentative method became generally understood and practised in this country, many inventions of a more or less complicated character have been patented to prevent it; but although most of them show that great ingenuity has been employed in their construction, yet from their complex movements, liability to derangement, unsuitableness for general purposes, and their expensiveness, nearly all have been abandoned by the respective patentees. The security against picking by pressure, obtained in the construction of the locks above referred to, has been by the addition of a number of 'limbs' to the parts (the bolt, levers, and springs) forming the essential mechanism of a lock, and which has added, in corresponding proportion to the complexity, liability to derangement, and cost. My improved lock comprises the case, the bolt, levers and springs of an ordinary lever lock, and the security against picking is mainly obtained by the peculiar arrangement and position of its parts." The peculiarity of the principle of its construction is illustrated in the *Mechanics' Magazine*, June 15, 1860.

These Locks are not only warranted unpickable against every mode of picking, but also proof against repeated charges of gunpowder, as two dwts. are said to be the most that can be hammered into it. "The hardened steel nozzle," says Mr. Price, "prevents the keyhole being enlarged, and the spindle of the knob being case-hardened, and working in a rebate with a shoulder inside, prevents gunpowder being got into the lock-chamber by breaking the spindle." These and other important improvements in locks and safes are secured by his patents of 1855, 1859, and 1860. Mr. Price has published a document with numerous names of military men, engineers, and others, who witnessed the experiments with gunpowder at Burnley in April last, from which it appears that it was not this lock at all into which gunpowder was introduced, so as to explode it on that occasion, the safe produced by his opponent, after every attempt on the right one had failed, being an old one, though of Price's make ; and that Mr. Price and his agent and friends repeatedly protested against its introduction, or any operation on it, as a test of the properties of Price's gunpowder-proof locks and safes.—*Builder.*

PERMANENT WAY OF RAILWAYS.

THE Earl of Caithness has patented the following railway improvement :—

It is proposed to make a portion of one or both of the rails at the points or change of line slide along horizontal parallel slots made at an angle to the rails, the two ends of such sliding rails, and the ends of the stationary abutting rails being inclined or bevilled to correspond to the angle of the slots, whereby an overlap bevil joint is obtained. When one of these sliding rails is used the pointed swivel switch rail remains unaltered in shape, and is coupled with the opposite switch rail in the ordinary manner, but the latter rail end is bevilled in place of being cut square off. To this latter rail is fitted a slide which is connected with that portion of the rail which works in the parallel slots, so that on the slide being moved by the lever which opens or closes the switch, it carries with it the loose rail, and causes it to travel in its parallel slots, and change the points accordingly. When two sliding rails are employed, one for each side of the way, they are coupled together and move in their slots simultaneously, the ordinary swivel switch rails being in this case dispensed with. On the first bevil end meeting the train (the switch being right for the main line), there is a rigid stop for maintaining the rail firmly in a permanent line. It is also proposed to combine by means of rolls a T shaped steel bar, with two wrought iron L shaped or angled bars, so as to produce an I shaped rail with the steel rail in the centre, and forming the wheel-bearing surface. The parts may be further secured by bolts or rivets. The T shaped rail may also be rolled with obtuse angled rails of wrought iron, one on each side, so as to form a rail suitable to the saddled back sleeper, and having a steel wheel-bearing surface. It is further proposed to cover the wheel-bearing surface of the ordinary double headed rail with a layer of steel by rolling the rail in combination with a steel plate, the steel being either made simply to grip or fold over the head of the rail, or let into the same by a longitudinal dove-tailed or other groove or channel formed in the rail head.

Mr. W. B. Adams has also patented certain improvements in the Permanent Way of Railways.

These improved methods of holding chairs to sleepers consist in forming a large-sized conical hole in the chair, and applying thereto a spike or screw, the neck of which may be conical or cylindrical, but with a loose collar of iron or other metal, either coned or flat, placed in the neck of the spike, so that in driving down the spike the elasticity of the collar will ensure a fit against both spike and chair, without risk of splitting the chair; and in case of wear they can easily be tightened by driving. The improvement in fastening rails in chairs consists in the use of keys of iron or steel, either on one or both sides of the rail. The keys are driven with elastic pressure between the rail and chair, thus preventing the splitting of the chairs by rigid pressure, and dispensing with the ordinary wooden keys. The improvement in cast-iron sleepers consists in the extension of the bases of the various improved chairs before described, so as to form a sufficient bearing in the ballast, making every chair its own sleeper also. The improvements in girder rails consist, 1, in a double-headed rail of the ordinary form as regards the tables or running surfaces, but rolled with wide central flanges of sufficient area to bear on the ballast without the aid of sleepers, being an improvement on a previous patent of the present patentee, where similar rails bear on sleepers.

These foregoing two abridged specifications are from the *Mechanics' Magazine.*

At Wormwood Scrubbs, on the Great Western line, has been laid Seaton's Patent Safety Saddle Rail, which has been under trial for upwards of two years and a half. The alleged superiority of the patent safety rail and the sleepers consists in the fact, that the latter is cut diagonally instead of rectangularly from a square balk of wood. The two triangular sleepers which are thus produced from the balk are laid longitudinally with the base downwards, the apex being crowned by a saddle rail, of which the flanges cover a portion of the sides of the triangle. Chairs, fish-plates, and trenails are all done away with by the new system. The first cost per double mile on the London and North-Western Railway, exclusive of wages, is 4146*l.*, while under Seaton's patent the prime cost, it is said, would not be more than 3300*l.* The cost per annum for maintenance on the North-Western Railway is stated to be 317*l.* per mile, whilst the maintenance under the new system is computed at 188*l.* By a scientific inspection of the patent way on the Great Western, the new line was found, it is said, to present a perfect even and level surface; the rails undisturbed, although from fifty to sixty trains pass over them, and the fastenings, both longitudinally and to the "ties," perfectly tight and undisturbed; the line being in exactly the same state as when laid down upwards of two years and a half since.— *Builder.*

ENLARGEMENT OF A RAILWAY TUNNEL.

This very novel engineering operation has been described to the Institution of Civil Engineers, by Mr. F. C. Stileman. This was the Enlargement of the Lindal Tunnel, on the Furness Railway, which, as a single line, was completed and opened in June, 1851. The facilities afforded by this railway having led to a great development of the mineral traffic of the district, an Act of Parliament was obtained for the formation of the Ulverston and Lancaster Railway, thus completing the chain of coast railways between Lancaster and Whitehaven, and so onwards to Carlisle. It then became evident that a single line would be insufficient to accommodate the traffic. Consequently, in August, 1854, it was decided to widen the line, and to enlarge the Lindal tunnel. The tunnel was increased in width equally on each side of the existing single-line tunnel, the level of the rails remaining the same. Before the works of enlargement were commenced, the contractor, Mr. Tredwell, suggested that another single, or twin, tunnel, parallel with the existing one, could be constructed with less risk; and he offered to complete it for the same sum, notwithstanding the additional excavation necessary in the approaches. This proposition had not been favourably entertained, because there was no precedent for such a work, and because it was known that there were many and grave disadvantages in working a single-line tunnel. From its limited area, the atmosphere in such a tunnel after the passing of heavy trains becomes so charged with steam and sulphurous vapour, that the plate-layers cannot work for any length of time continuously, and hence there is a difficulty in properly lifting and packing the permanent way. Again, the condensation of the steam upon the rails in single-line tunnels practically increases the expense of working. From the commencement of the Lindal tunnel works in June, 1855, to their completion in November, 1856, nearly seven thousand five hundred passenger trains, conveying one hundred and twelve thousand passengers, and two thousand one hundred goods trains, carrying two hundred and five thousand tons of minerals, &c., exclusive of light engines, passed through the tunnel, without the slightest casualty to either description of train, or any accident even of the most trivial character to any individual. A special code of rules was arranged for working the traffic, and for watching and signalling every train. The stations at each end of the tunnel were in telegraphic communication, and there were semaphore signals at each entrance, connected by an endless wire. The wire was fastened to wheels at various points, having cranks outside the trough in which it was enclosed. A signalman, whose duty it was to remain in the tunnel, could, by means of a portable lever, lower both semaphore signals simultaneously. As a precautionary measure, the signalman sounded a large gong on being informed by the telegraph that a train was approaching; and it was not until he had satisfied himself that no impediment existed to the passage of the train, that he lowered the signals, and thus sanctioned the engine drivers to proceed.

PREVENTABLE RISK IN FAST RAILWAY TRAVELLING.

In a Report to the Board of Trade, on the accident at Hatfield in the month of April, 1860, when a Great Northern train after passing over a rail that had been turned got off the line, and Mr. Pym, a passenger, lost his life, Colonel Yolland states that the whole weight of the train was about 100 tons, and the total weight on the wheels to which break blocks could be applied was but about 26 tons. Now a train at Hatfield, travelling down an incline of 1 in 200 at the rate of 60 miles an hour (a frequent rate of that train at that point), could not have been stopped by these breaks in less than three-quarters of a mile. Colonel Yolland says this is a very unsatisfactory condition attending fast railway travelling, and that such quick trains ought to be furnished with an amount of break power which will enable them to be stopped in a third of that distance, and that this can be done by means of continuous breaks, which augment the retarding power three or four fold. Two years ago the Board of Trade sent to all railway companies a report of the successful working of such breaks on the East Lancashire Railway, where a train of 90 tons, supplied with 80 per cent. of break power, travelling at the rate of 53 miles an hour down an incline of 1 in 120, was stopped after running 235 yards. The carriage in which Mr. Pym rode was not thrown over on its side until it was 408 yards from the spot where the accident occurred.

ELECTRO-MAGNETIC RAILWAY BREAK.

At the late meeting of the British Association at Oxford, Dr. Richardson read a paper "On an Electro-magnetic Railway Break," which he illustrated with a model. He proposed the application of electro-magnetism to the stoppage of railway carriages when in motion, and suggested that "between the wheels on each side of every railway carriage there should be placed an electro-magnet. The magnet would have a slight movement up and down between two grooved blocks affixed to the carriage, or through a hollow cylinder, if a straight magnet were used. When out of action the two poles of the magnet would be supported either by a buffer spring or by a steelyard weight, so that a distance not exceeding an inch would exist between the poles of the magnet and the tram rail. In the tender of the engine should be carried a voltaic battery, from one pole of which should proceed a series of connectable chains which should link each electro-magnet to the next throughout the whole line, one end of the chains now made continuous being brought to the battery to be connected with the opposite pole whenever desired. Above the battery should be placed an electric dial and connecting handle for the use of the driver, so as to enable him at any moment to close or break the circuit, or so graduate it as to permit him to govern the connection between any number of plates; in other words, so as to enable him to govern the force of the current as well as its connection and disconnection."

Dr. Richardson did not say that his plan should replace the present breaks in use; these might be continued, but they could never perform all the important offices of the electro-magnet placed as above described. Its advantages were—1, It would at all times be at the command of the driver of the engine; 2, its action would be instantaneous; 3, its action would be capable of gradation in arresting the momentum; 4, it would impede the motion of the carriage, not by friction on the rail, but by adhesion with the rail—the arresting force would thus be brought to bear on all points—the carriage being for the under-current made essentially part and parcel of the line; 5, the force of adhesion being exerted through a line of carriages would double with the action of each magnet, and becoming cumulative would increase in proportion to the length of the train, so that within a certain range, which experiment could soon determine, the same battery force would answer for all trains whether long or short; 6, the magnets being brought to their arresture in any given case of accident, the overturn of the carriages by the escape of it from the rail would be to a considerable extent prevented; 7, in cases where from fear of collision or other circumstances, the driver is compelled at all risks to stop in the briefest time, the electro-magnetic break would so act that every carriage would stop with an equal resistance—collision of carriages would thus be prevented, since each carriage would stop itself by a spark communicated from the engine to the whole moving mass. The expense of this would depend upon the kind of battery; and in addition to the uses he had enumerated, Dr. Richardson mentioned several others to which it could be put.—*From the Report of the Meeting in the Oxford University Herald.*

STREET RAILWAYS.

MR. G. F. TRAIN (of Boston, U.S.A.) has read to the Mechanical Section of the British Association a paper descriptive of "Street Railways as used in the United States," illustrated by a model of a tramway and car, or omnibus capable of conveying sixty persons. In America such a car is drawn by a pair of horses. The tramway is laid in the centre of the street, and the rail is so shallow that it offers no obstruction whatever to carriages crossing it. In wide streets two such tracks are laid down, one for the going and the other for the returning traffic.

In America, in the cities of Boston, New York, Philadelphia, Baltimore, St. Louis, and Cincinnati, railways cars are displacing omnibuses in all the large streets. "They have already become a public utility ; and Americans would miss their railway car as much as the English would their penny-postage system. The horse railway is a fixed fact. It has had a fair trial and has met with striking success," says Mr. Train. Mr. Alexander Easton, C.E., of Philadelphia, in a work on the same subject, speaks of the effects already produced by the horse-railway system. "Time is economized by regularity of transit ; the cars being quickly stopped by the application of the brake, the most refractory horses are immediately arrested : while the whole operation becomes so mechanical that the horses, when accustomed to the signals of the bell, stop or start without any action on the part of the driver, by which means a time-table can be effectively used, and business men are not subjected to delays incident to the old—and we trust soon to say obsolete—omnibus system. Space is economized because omnibuses (the most numerous and dangerous portion of the travel), surging from side to side of the streets, are abolished; while the work heretofore inadequately performed by three of those vehicles is easily accomplished by one car, in half the time, notwithstanding it is concentrated and confined to one channel. By the convenience afforded the public by the cars, the side-walks are relieved from pedestrians, and the centre of the streets from vehicles ; a seat can be obtained and vacated without trouble or danger to the occupants of the car, whether invalid or infirm, and the rails present such an even and smooth surface for the wheels of ordinary vehicles, that the drivers avail themselves of their continued use." In addition to all this, the scarcely tolerable nuisance occasioned by omnibuses rattling over rough stones is abolished.

Mr. Train appears to have greatly *amused*, if not invariably convinced, the *savans* met at Oxford in July last, with the details of his " invention," the advantages of which he thus summed up :—

1. Each railway car displaces two omnibuses and four horses, thus relieving the street of one of the main causes of the oft recurring lock-ups.

2. The wear and tear from these omnibuses being transferred to the rail, as well as that of many other vehicles that prefer the smooth surface of the iron to the uneven stone pavement, the ratepayers save a large per centage in taxes.

3. The Gas and Water Commissioners are not inconvenienced when making

repairs, as the rails are laid on longitudinal sleepers which can be diverted in case of need ; and as these cars, as well as the carts and carriages that take the rail, move on a direct line, it is a self-constituted police system, saving confusion without expense to the public.

4. The cars move one-third faster than the omnibus, and so gentle is the motion that the passenger can read his journal without difficulty.

5. The rails are so constructed that no inconvenience arises at crossings from wrenching off carriage wheels, and as the improved rail is nearly flat, even with the surface, and some five inches wide, no grooves impede the general traffic, and the gauge admits all vehicles that prefer the track to the pavement.

6. The facility of getting in and out at each end of the car and on each side, giving the passengers the choice of four places, together with the almost instantaneous stoppage by means of the patent brake, permits passengers to step in or out when in motion without danger, instanced by the fact that nearly seventy millions of passengers passed over the New York, Boston, and Philadelphia roads last year with only twelve accidents. Seventy millions ! being more than the population of the United States and Canada, Great Britain and Australia—one-half the entire number of passengers carried on the railways of the United Kingdom the same year ; or, to make it more striking, six times the number carried in Scotland, and eight times as many as passed over all the Irish railways, and yet only twelve persons met with any accident.

7. In case of necessity, troops can be transported from one part of the city to the other at ten miles an hour.

8. It is a special boon to the working man who, often in America, saves threepence beer-money to buy a ticket from his work in the city to his cottage in the suburbs.

Considerable discussion ensued, and several engineers and other gentlemen present, bore testimony to the success of the street trains in the United States.

Dr. Carpenter remarked that one of the great objections to street railways was that a stoppage in any part would inconvenience the rest ; but a plan had been introduced by Mr. R. Main to obviate that by having an eccentric flange. There was a plain wheel, and at the side an eccentric ring or disc, and by turning a lever it converted it into a railway carriage, and by turning it back it got on the common road.

An engineer of high standing stated that, when he was at Baltimore, he was surprised at the ease with which the street railway cars ascended steep hills, and the facility with which they were checked in descending. From what he had seen in America, and the system being in operation there so extensively, with a perfect freedom from accident or inconvenience of any kind, there was no valid objection to it, either on account of steep ascents, sharp curves, or interference with the general traffic.

The President (Mr. Macquorn Rankine) said that, before Mr. Train replied, he should venture to offer a few remarks. With respect to the system of street railways it would doubtless have been introduced and adopted before now, had it not been that the public attention, and the attention of engineers, had been directed mainly towards perfecting the railway system, which comprehended a wider range, and was not restricted to large towns or to a locality. At the same time he was not insensible of the value of the system of street railways, advocated so ably and so successfully by Mr. Train, for it so happened that he was well acquainted with them, his father and himself having constructed one, where they used to convey 40 passengers with one horse up ascents varying from 1 in 66 to 1 in 40, at the rate of five miles an hour, their average speed on the level being at ten and twelve miles an hour. They had level crossings, but yet met with no accident, and although there were continually trains of coal waggons, no difficulty was found in passing them ; and there was this convenience, that they could stop when they liked, almost instantaneously, and set down a farmer on his own farm, instead of setting him down at a considerable distance from it. That was the Edinburgh and Dalkeith line, but it was afterwards bought up and worked with locomotives, so that the horse-power was discontinued. Horse-rails had, in fact, become to be looked on as an exploded system, and but for that reason they might have been introduced here earlier, and to a great extent. Having had considerable experience in this matter, he was bound to say that he saw no difficulty in carrying on the traffic in our streets on this improved system ; and, so far from its being an obstacle, great facilities would be obtained, for passengers would reach their destination earlier ; and the size of the railway cars, affording increased accommodation, would lessen the number, and thereby lessen the pressure which was now felt in the streets of large and populous places. The rails themselves, constructed as proposed by Mr. Train, presented no obstacle, and would not interfere with the ordinary use of the road, whereas the width of the rails rendered them available by vehicles in general use. As far as his experience went, there was no difficulty whatever in getting round curves of great sharpness or steep ascents; and even on single lines the horses at the end of the journey could be taken from one end and put to the other in very quick time, for nothing but traces were required. By Mr. Train's plan breaks were employed, which could be made use of either by the driver or conductor, or both, so that they could stop the fore or hind wheels, or both, if necessary. With regard to steep ascents, all that was required was an additional horse ; but with respect to Ludgate-hill and Holborn-hill, he was of opinion that the only effectual way of dealing with them was by a viaduct.

Mr. Train said, in answer to Mr. Ryland's remarks, that, as he proposed to make his rail along the centre of the street, it would leave the sides open for general traffic. In reply to Dr. Steadman's observation, as to the stoppages on the line, he did not anticipate any, as the increased accommodation of the cars would so materially lessen the number of vehicles that a stoppage was not likely to be so common as at present, in addition to which the traffic would be more divided, and besides this there might be branches where what might be likely to be impediments could be shunted.

The first public experiment with Mr. Train's railway was made at Birkenhead, on August 30, with great success. The line of rails —which had been laid down under the superintendence of Mr. Palles, of Philadelphia, and Mr. Samuel, of London—extended from the Woodside Ferry, the landing-place at Birkenhead, just opposite the centre of Liverpool, by the Shore-road, through Angle and Conway streets, and so on to the entrance to Birkenhead Park. The whole distance is little more than a mile and a quarter. A junction in Conway-street enabled the carriages to return from the park by Hamilton-street to the point from which they originally started.

Nothing can well be less complicated than the machinery which is employed for the accomplishment of this double journey. The tramway itself consists simply of two iron plates, each being raised about an inch on the outer side, and running parallel to one another, as in the case of the rails on an ordinary railroad. They are fixed upon longitudinal bearers, which rest upon transverse sleepers, and are so let into the street as to run completely on a level with its surface. They do not, therefore, interfere in the slightest degree with the ordinary traffic. To ply on these iron plates carriages capable each of affording abundant accommodation to from 50 to 60 passengers were built by Mr. Main, of Birkenhead. They are more than double the size of an ordinary omnibus, are somewhat similar in shape, and are provided underneath with wheels like those of a railway carriage, but somewhat smaller in size. Each carriage is 24 feet long by 7 feet wide ; 7 feet being also the height of the interior from floor to roof. It furnishes sitting room for 24 persons inside and for as many more outside. A space of two or three feet intervenes between the passengers on each side of the interior. A small platform at each end of each carriage, raised about a foot and a half from the ground, and separated from the horses—which may be yoked to either end—by a contrivance somewhat resembling the splashboard of a Hansom cab, affords the means of ready ingress and egress to the new conveyances. Each has its sliding windows, with louvres, to prevent a draught. Each is provided also with a driver and conductor, both of whom have it in their power to control, by means of a patent break, the machinery by which the progress of the carriages is stopped or retarded.

Shortly before ten o'clock, two of the new carriages were drawn out from the depôt in Canning-street and placed upon the line. At eleven, two horses were yoked to each, and they proceeded on their way well freighted with passengers, gliding along the rails at the rate of about four miles an hour—a rate of speed which might without difficulty be increased to six or seven miles an hour—smoothly and uninterruptedly, turning one or two extremely sharp curves with the utmost facility, and setting down passengers at their several destinations in security. An idea seems to be entertained that 'such a tramway and its adjuncts are unprecedented in Europe ; but, for some years, the very same sort of conveyance (which has been for many years advocated, for London and other towns, in the *Builder*) has existed in Paris. There are also tramways (of granite) even in the streets of London, the last of which were laid along new Westminster Bridge ; but large omnibuses specially adapted to run along such tramways—and, indeed, tramways specially adapted for such omnibuses—have not yet existed in London.

We have another instance of the previous mention of horse railway trains, made nearly 50 years since, and less known than it deserves to be. In Sir Richard Phillips's *Morning's Walk from London to Kew* (the portion written in 1813), he says, at Wandsworth, "I felt renewed delight at witnessing the economy of horse labour on the iron railway. Yet, a heavy sigh escaped me, as I thought of the inconceivable millions which have been spent about Malta, four or five of which might have been the means of extending *double lines of iron railways* from London to Edinburgh, Glasgow, Holyhead, Milford, Falmouth, Yarmouth, Dover, and Portsmouth! A reward of a single thousand would have supplied coaches, and other vehicles of various speed, with the best tackle for readily turning out; and we might, ere this, have witnessed our mail coaches running at the rate of ten miles an hour, drawn by a single horse, or impelled fifteen miles by Blenkinsop's steam engine! Such would have been a legitimate motive for overstepping the income of a nation, and the completion of so great and useful a work would have afforded rational ground for public triumph in general jubilee!"

To this we may add, that the late Herbert Ingram (who lost his life in the terrible steam-boat catastrophe on Lake Michigan, in September last), more than once advocated in his journal, the *Illustrated London News*, the introduction of horse trains in England and its large towns. In the management of this journal also (which Mr. Ingram, by his genius and enterprise, called into existence, and established in world-wide favour), he gave unceasing encouragement to the applications of mechanical science to the improvement of printing machinery, in order to meet the large requirements of his journal, as well as to show his appreciation of genius and enterprise in others, and the interest he took in fostering inventive industry.

Mr. Train has made application to the Westminster district authorities to be allowed to extend his tramways to various streets under their jurisdiction, such as Oxford-street, Regent-street, Piccadilly, Coventry-street, and Pall-mall. Mr. H. Greaves applied to be allowed to submit his plan for combining tramways with gas and other pipes, the pipes to form the sleepers under the rail or train. His gas-pipe sleepers are patented, and form, he says, one continuous structure, so that gas could not escape, and each would bear 30 or 40 tons weight. By laying such pipes, he urges, the breaking up of streets would be obviated, as also the contamination of the subsoil by gas escape. Both projects were referred to the Works Committee of the district for consideration. Mr. Train also applied to the City Sewers Commission for permission to construct railways in some of the principal thoroughfares in the City. (These permissions have not, however, been conceded.)*

An inventor resident in Manchester has patented a plan of what he terms a "perambulating railway," the main features of which are as follows :—He proposes to lay down his line perfectly level with the roadway, each rail not exceeding 3 inches in width; and in the centre he places a grooved rail in which is to run what he terms the peram-

---

* For an able view of the history and economy of this invention, see the Treatise *On the Construction of Horse Railways for Branch Lines and for Street Traffic*, by Charles Burn, C.E.

bulator, which is simply a wheel 9 inches in diameter, centred in a bar hinged to the fore axle of the vehicle, and spurred to it on both sides, so that when the wheel revolves in the groove the axle is always at right angles to the rails. This bar is suspended from the splinter-bar by a strong elastic band, which holds the wheel about 4 or 5 inches clear of the road ; and an upright rod, passing through the footboard, and acting on the perambulator, enables the driver, when he has fairly adjusted his vehicle upon the rails, to depress, by the action of his foot, the wheel into the groove of the centre rail, and to retain it in position as long as he wishes to remain on the metals.

SUBWAYS FOR GAS AND WATER MAINS.

PROFESSOR SPENCER'S Report to the New River Water-works Company, on the corrosion of iron mains from the effects of gas leakage, basing the calculation on a gas waste of 20 per cent. (a standard somewhat below the fact), after making a fair allowance for probable waste from other causes than that of leakage,—such, for instance, as defective meterage, condensation, &c.,—estimates the actual amount of loss from leakage through the joints of the gas mains at 630,000,000, cubic feet per annum, all of which is absorbed into the earth, imparting to the subsoil of the streets the blackened appearance and odour so familiar to the in-dwellers of the metropolis.

As respects the more immediate object of his employment in this instance, viz., the cause of the premature decay of the iron mains that takes place in some of the denser parts of the metropolis, Professor Spencer—by careful observation, and a series of experiments conducted through a period of three years—arrives at the conclusion that such decay is caused by the gas that is always escaping from the joints of the gas mains, not directly by the action of the gas itself —for alone this is harmless in this way on the iron—but by an acrid alkaline fluid, a sort of distillation, as it were, from the gas-charged earth by means of moisture from the rain-fall ; which fluid, coming in contact with the metal of the pipes, produces profuse corrosion, having the effect of converting the iron, in a shorter or longer period, into a sort of plumbago. Numerous specimens of decayed pipage turned up during the progress of the inquiry, showing the action of this destructive agent, so rapid in certain spots where more than usual gas escape had been going on, as to effect that transition in the short space of from seven to ten years ; the ordinary serviceable duration of iron similarly employed in earth in its natural state being about a century.

As respects the injuries sustained by the public from the chronic escape of gas, Professor Spencer affirms, first, that the gas-saturated earth, in combination with certain other chemical properties, which the London street subsoil imbibes from other causes, gives out a sulphurous gaseous matter, which, inhaled, is highly prejudicial to health ; and it is observed that, when it is taken into account that each cubic foot of this enormous quantity of gas, which is continuously passing into the street earth, contains something like one-fifth of a grain of sulphuret of carbon, and one-twentieth of a grain of ammonia, it becomes surprising that the effects, bad as they are, are not more sensibly felt. 2ndly. That the gas-mains and water-mains usually lying side by side, the escaped gas from the former will frequently enter the water-mains at their joints; and at times, when the water but partially fills the pipes, a large quantity of gas in this way gets admitted, and, mingling with the water, imparts to it that nauseous quality so frequently complained of. And hence, too, the cause of the not unfrequent occurrence of partial explosions by the ignition of gas from the presence of a lighted candle on the opening of the water-tap. 3rdly. That the mud banks, the sewage deposits on the tidal banks of the Thames within London, derive their peculiar fœtid and blackened character from the action of gas leakage on the oxide of the corroded street mains, which finds its way by numerous channels into the sewers, and is thence carried to the river, where, retained in the sewage mud, it becomes the direct agent of the too well-known noxious odour the Thames water evolves in the summer months of June and July, when the temperature ranges above 70° Fahrenheit.

The properly constructed accessible *subway*, for the "common" conveyance of the mains through at least the greater trunk lines of the metropolis, offers the medium of extensive mitigation of all these evils, since the facility for a system of daily inspection and immediate repair would admit of the maintenance of the mains gas-tight and water-tight, as in ordinary house fittings.—*Communication to the Builder.*

SUBWAY IN LONDON.

THE Metropolitan Board of Works have published the plans for a Subway in the new street to Covent-garden (commencing at the junction of Long-acre and St. Martin's-lane), which were prepared for them by Mr. Marrable and Mr. Bazalgette, their architect and engineer. The following report accompanies the drawings:—

Having been directed by the Committee on New Streets to prepare a design for a subway under the new street leading from Cranbourne-street to Covent-garden, in which the pipes and mains for gas and water might be laid in such a manner that easy access could be had to them at all times without disturbing the surface or roadway, we now beg to submit the accompanying plans, which we believe to embrace all the desiderata of such an arrangement in the simplest form and at the least possible expense. The plan consists chiefly of a central continuous passage or subway, extending the whole length of the new street, of sufficient dimensions (12 feet by 6 feet 6 inches) to admit of the deposit of any requisite number of gas and water mains, with ample working room for alterations, additions, or repairs. Under the centre of this passage runs the sewer, to which means of access by man-holes are provided at convenient distances, as also ventilating shafts, gullies, &c. Side-arched passages communicating with the central way will be constructed between every two houses, in which the service-pipes will be carried from the mains into the open areas in front of the houses, and open channels will be left in the footings of the walls dividing the house-vaults, through which the service-pipes will be passed, without any interference with the structural arrangement, and these channels, although of small dimensions, (4½ inches by 3 inches), being always left open, will act as drains for the admission of air from the open areas into the central passage, which, in conjunction with ventilating shafts at convenient distances into the roadway, will secure an ample current of air for all the purposes of ventilation. An entrance to the main passage will be provided in Rose-street, similar to the ordinary side entrances, but of such dimensions as will allow of the ready admission of the main pipes for gas and water, which, as all the service pipes will be laid in sunken channels, can be readily carried to any required point on a small truck kept in the subway for the purpose. Provisions have also been made for the hydrants or fire-plugs, and for the service of the street-lamps, but these are matters of detail which would doubtless be subjects for final arrangements with the different companies.

Careful estimates have been prepared, showing the cost of the private vaults to the houses, the paving of the foot and carriage ways, and the cost of the ordinary sewer, including digging, side entrances, ventilating shafts, gullies, &c., by which it appears that the extra cost of constructing the subway as now proposed will not exceed 2l. 0s. 11d. per foot run, or about 1l. per foot frontage on each house, which, together with the cost of the vaults, sewers, and road, might either be charged at once on those taking up the ground-rents, or be added as an annual charge, in addition to the ground-rent, and which would of course form a part of the annual rental to be sold when the Board should think fit to realize the ground-rents. The estimates in all cases are given at so much per foot run on the frontages, so that the charge on each house may be seen more readily.

Premiums were offered by the Board for the best designs for a subway, and we may conclude that the plan adopted was the result of careful consideration of all that were submitted.

(Nearly forty years since, Mr. Williams, of Birchin-lane, published an octavo volume, projecting a system of subways for the metropolis, and otherwise advocated the measure at considerable cost, but without satisfactory results.) ———

REGENERATIVE HOT-BLAST STOVES.

MR. COWPER'S Regenerative Hot-blast Stoves will doubtless introduce great improvements, chiefly of an economical character, in that very important business—the iron manufacture. It is now pretty generally acknowledged that a much hotter blast than the ordinary one would greatly improve and economize the production of pig-iron in the smelting-furnace : ironmasters have often tried how far they could go in obtaining a higher temperature, and have of course soon arrived at a limit from the destruction which ensued of the cast-iron pipes ; and it is obvious that there must always be a wide difference between the temperature of the air heated inside a cast-iron pipe and the fire outside the pipe heating it, as there will be the difference in temperature between the fire and the pipe, together with the difference in temperature between the pipe and the air passing through it. These differences must be considerable, in order to ensure a tolerably rapid conduction of the heat ; so that in no case can the hot-blast approach at all near to the temperature of the fire, nor indeed would the cast-iron stand if anything of the sort were attempted; in fact, it is well known that care is necessary in damping the fires of common hot-blast stoves, when the cooling effect of the air inside the pipes is taken away by the blast being stopped, at tapping time or on any other occasion. The temperature at which the products of combustion pass away from ordinary stoves is from 1250° to 1500°, whilst the blast is heated to about 700° only.

To remedy these evils, and secure a blast of 1400° or 1500°, Mr. Cowper employs Mr. Siemens's regenerative furnace system, in which the hot products of the combustion of the fuel are sent through a large mass of blocks of fire-brick, which extracts the heat from them; the air to be heated being afterwards forced through the same mass, in the reverse direction, in order to withdraw the heat from them, the air thus heated being then sent into the blast furnace.

The economy of heat obtained by the new stoves as compared with the ordinary ones is most striking when using gas as fuel; for it has been found by direct experiment that the heat passing away from the ordinary stoves amounts to more than 1250°, and as the temperature produced by the combustion of the gas is about 2000°, the difference of about 750° is all the heat that is taken up by the ordinary cast-iron pipes; whereas the regenerative stoves do not part with the heat at a higher temperature than about 200°, and as the temperature produced is about 2000°, the difference, or 1800°, is used in place of only about 750°.

As regards utilizing the waste-gas from the top of a blast-furnace, Mr. Cowper has very properly remarked that recent experience, both in this country and abroad, has fully proved that there is no real difficulty in accomplishing this, either on the plan adopted at the Ebbw Vale works, or on that of Mr. Charles Cochrane, and all doubt on the subject is now removed; the regenerative stoves are also particularly well adapted for being heated by gas, as there are no iron pipes to be injured by the gas flame.—*Mechanics' Magazine.*

GAS-MAKING.

Mr. W. Clark has patented certain improvements in the Manufacture of Gas, and in apparatus for the same. These relate, 1, to a new method of distilling matters furnishing gases which are only slightly carbonated; which matters the patentee distils with products furnishing carbonated gas, having very great lighting power, for the purpose of obtaining therewith gas more fit for lighting and heating. 2. To a peculiar apparatus for the distillation of the mixture of these two matters. This improved method is applicable equally for the distillation of peat, which furnishes a gas having like lighting power mixed with carbonate of hydrogen, produced from matters which furnish by distillation a lighting gas; the principle of the said method being to effect at the same time the distillation of gas from the two matters introduced in proper proportions by hastening the distillation of the one and retarding that of the other; thus, the two gases resulting from peat and tar will chemically combine and furnish a rich suitable gas. In order to obtain such simultaneous distillation, he makes use of a distilling apparatus which retards the distillation of the carburets of hydrogen.—*Mechanics' Magazine.*

NEW GAS FOR LIGHTING.

Superheated steam, charged with coal-tar, produces, with marvellous rapidity, and at an exceedingly low price, any quantity of a very rich gas for lighting. Careful analysis is composed of free oxygen, 1·8; oxide of carbon, 3; carbonic acid, 5·8; bicarburetted hydrogen, 17·8; and protocarburetted hydrogen, 17·9. Compared with ordinary coal gas, this artificial gas is found to contain nearly one half less oxide of carbon, and twice as much bicarburetted hydrogen; its intrinsic value is, therefore, twice as great. Besides, its composition proves that it is a very permanent mixture or combination, which remains intact for any distance it may be conducted. The entire absence of sulphuretted hydrogen in this gas is not the least of its recommendations.—*Photographic News.*

SMOKE FROM GAS LIGHTS.

IT is pretty generally imagined that the smoking of ceilings is occasioned by impurity in the gas, whereas, in this case, there is no connexion between the deposition of soot and the quality of the gas. The evil arises either from the flame being raised so high that some of its forked points give out smoke, or more frequently from a careless mode of lighting. If, when lighting the lamps, the stop-cock be opened suddenly, and a burst of gas be permitted to escape before the match be applied to light it, then a strong puff follows the lighting of each burner, and a cloud of black smoke rises to the ceiling. This, in many houses and shops, is repeated daily, and the inevitable consequence is a blackened ceiling. In some well-regulated houses, the glasses are taken off and wiped every day, and before they are put on again the match is applied to the lip of the burner, and the stop-cock cautiously opened, so that no more gas escapes than is sufficient to make a ring of blue flame: the glasses being then put on quite straight, the stop-cocks are gently turned, until the flames stand at three inches high. When this is done, few chimney-glasses will be broken, and the ceilings will not be blackened for years.—*Sir John Robison.*

DISCOVERY OF OIL IN WESTERN NEW YORK.

A NEW product is in course of development in the State of New York, at a place called Union Mills, where has been discovered a tract of land, which, at depths varying from a few feet to 500 feet from the surface, abounds in liquid matter, of which one-third is *oil*, capable of being used as one of the best illuminating agents; and also, when mixed with fish-oil, of being applied as a lubricant in various manufacturing processes. Already the product is found to extend over 100 square miles; and the oil is despatched to New York at the rate of 1500 barrels per day. The distance of Union Mills from New York is about 400 miles, but the country is traversed by the Atlantic and Great Western, and the Erie railways.

An exceedingly plentiful and profitable spring of petroleum, or "rock oil," as it has been called, has been got by artesian boring, as a venture, in Oil Creek, Philadelphia. Under a lease in May last, a Mr. Drake commenced sinking an artesian well for salt, oil, or anything which might turn up. Boring through forty-seven feet of gravel and twenty-two feet of shale rocks, with occasional small apertures in it, he struck, in August, a large opening, not yet explored as to depth or area, but filled with coal oil, somewhat mixed with both water and gas. A small pump on hand brought up from 400 to 500 gallons of oil a day. An explosion soon blew it up. One of three times its size and power was put in its place, and during the first four days threw up 5000 gallons of oil; 1250 gallons per day, or one gallon per minute for twenty hours fifty minutes per day. The oil, as raised, was worth eighty cents a gallon, which produced the large income of 1800 dollars per day for four successive days, and so the matter goes on, yielding about one gallon per minute during working time. A large company, called the "Consolidated Rock Oil Company," with a capital of 1,000,000 dollars, has been formed in New York, to buy and work the oil lands.

WATER-GAS.

THE *American Gaslight Journal* contains a detailed account from *Le Journal de l'Eclairage au Gaz*, of the renewed and apparently successful attempt to introduce Water-Gas into Narbonne, in France. The gas, according to *Le Génie Industriel*, quoted by its French contemporary, is made without retorts. The decomposition of water-steam into gas is effected by passing the steam over a mass of burning coke in a close furnace, and the more rapidly this is done the more effective and economical is the process. The oxygen and hydrogen of the steam are of course separated, and the oxygen forms with the carbon of the coke carbonic acid gas, leaving the hydrogen unattached even to carbon, so that the water-gas is pure or mere hydrogen. The carbonic acid is withdrawn by means of damp quicklime, which, however, rapidly accumulates in quantity: it is proposed to use carbonate of soda instead, as the carbonate of soda will unite with the carbonic acid and form bicarbonate, from which moderate heat will again expel all the gas absorbed, so that the carbonate of soda, it is calculated, may be used over and over again indefinitely. Could not the carbonic acid also be made use of, as in the production of aërated drinks? Bicarbonate of soda itself, too, is of some value. One chief peculiarity in the water-gas is in the mode of burning it. Hydrogen yields a very weak light of itself, but each burner is supplied with the well-known contrivance of a small wirework of platinum, which, by adequate pressure on the main, becomes white-hot, and produces an intense light with the hydrogen, without wasting the rather expensive platinum. The price of the gas, however, is still high, from the limited number of consumers, it is said.—*Builder*. (See *Year-Book of Facts*, 1860, p. 102.)

NEW APPLICATION OF PEAT.

SOME improvements in manufactures from Peat have been patented by Mr. H. Hodgson, of Ballyreine and Merlin Park, and Mr. P. M. Crane, of the Irish Peat Works, Athy. The invention consists in preparing from peat, in its natural state, blocks, slabs, or pieces of any size, form, or thickness, which blocks, slabs, or pieces are said, when so prepared, to be useful and economical in the construction of parts of buildings, and for various other useful purposes. These blocks are placed between cloths of woven or textile fabric, or other suitable material, and the peat is placed between shelves, and submitted to hydraulic or other pressure. The water is entirely forced out and the peat solidified ; and drying is effected either by exposure to the atmosphere or in a room heated artificially, or by any other process. They are then put again between the plates of a hydraulic or other press, and extreme pressure put on them. If the product of this invention be required for use for inside work in building, such as partitions, linings, inside roofing, or for other work, as a non-conducting substance, they do not require other further preparation than shaping, provided they are not to be exposed to wet. But the slabs or pieces used for roofing (instead of slates, tiles, or other things of that nature) they prepare to resist the wet or action of the atmosphere by steeping them in, or saturating or coating them with, some fitting material to resist wet, such, we presume, as pitch.—*Builder.*

ELECTRIC ILLUMINATION FOR LIGHTHOUSES. BY PROFESSOR FARADAY.

THE use of light to guide the mariner as he approaches land, or passes through intricate channels, has, with the advance of society and its ever-increasing interests, caused such a necessity for means more and more perfect, as to tax to the utmost the powers both of the philosopher and the practical man, in the development of the principles concerned, and their efficient application. Formerly the means were simple enough ; and if the light of a lantern or torch was not sufficient to point out a position, a fire had to be made in their place. As the system became developed, it soon appeared that power could be obtained not merely by increasing the light but by directing the issuing rays: and this was in many cases a more powerful and useful means than enlarging the combustion ; leading to the diminution of the volume of the former, with, at the same time, an increase in its intensity. Direction was obtained, either by the use of lenses dependent altogether upon refraction, or of reflectors dependent upon metallic reflexion ; and some ancient specimens of both were shown. In modern times the principle of total reflexion has also been employed, which involves the use of glass, and depends both upon refraction and reflexion. In all these appliances much light is lost. If metal be used for reflexion, a certain proportion is absorbed by the face of the metal ; if glass be used for refraction, light is lost at all the surfaces where the ray passes between the air and the glass ; and also in some degree by absorption in the body of the glass itself. There is, of course, no power of actually increasing the whole amount of light, by any optical arrangement associated with it.

The light which issues forth into space must have a certain amount of divergence. The divergence in the vertical direction must be enough to cover the sea from the horizon to within a certain moderate distance from the shore, so that all ships within that distance may have a view of their luminous guide. If it have less, it may escape observation where it ought to be seen ; if it have more, light

* The abstract of a paper read at the Royal Institution of Great Britain, at the weekly evening meeting, Friday, March 9, 1860.

is thrown away which ought to be directed within the useful degree of divergence ; or if the horizontal divergence be considered, it may be necessary so to construct the optical apparatus, that the light within an angle of 60° or 45° shall be compressed into a beam diverging only 15°, that it may give in the distance a bright flash having a certain duration instead of a continuous light,—or into one diverging only 5° or 6°, which, though of far shorter duration, has greatly increased intensity and penetrating power in hazy weather. The amount of divergence depends in a large degree upon the bulk of the source of light, and cannot be made less than a certain amount with a flame of a given size. If the flame of an argand lamp $\frac{7}{8}$ths of an inch wide, and 1$\frac{1}{2}$ inches high, be placed in the focus of an ordinary Trinity-house parabolic reflector, it will supply a beam having about 15° divergence : if we wish to increase the effect of brightness we cannot properly do it by enlarging the lamp flame ; for though lamps are made for the dioptric arrangement of Fresnel, which have as many as four wicks, flames 3$\frac{1}{2}$ inches wide, and burn like intense furnaces, yet if one be put into the lamp place of the reflector referred to, its effect would chiefly be to give a beam of wider divergence ; and if to correct this the reflector were made with a greater focal distance, then it must be altogether of a much larger size. The same general result occurs with the dioptric apparatus ; and here, where the four-wicked lamps are used, they are placed at times nearly 40 inches distant from the lens, occasioning the necessity of a very large, though very fine, glass apparatus.

On the other hand, if the light could be compressed, the necessity for such large apparatus would cease, and it might be reduced from the size of a room to the size of a hat : and here it is that we seek in the electric spark, and such like concentrated sources of light, for aid in illumination. It is very true, that by adding lamp to lamp, each with its reflector, upon one face or direction, power can be gained ; and in some of the revolving lights ten lamps and reflectors unite to give the required flash. But then not more than three of these faces can be placed in the whole circle ; and if a fixed light be required in all directions round the lighthouse nothing better has been yet established than the four-wicked Fresnel lamp in the centre of its dioptric and catadioptric apparatus. Now the electric light can be raised up easily to an equality with the oil lamp, and if then substituted for the latter, will give all the effect of the latter ; or by expenditure of money it can be raised to a five or tenfold power, or more, and will then give five or tenfold effect. This can be done, not merely without increase of the volume of the light, but whilst the light shall have a volume scarcely the 2000th part of that of the oil flame. Hence the extraordinary assistance we may expect to obtain of diminishing the size of the optical apparatus and perfecting that part of the apparatus.

Many compressed intense lights have been submitted to the Trinity-house ; and that corporation has shown its great desire to advance all such objects and improve the lighting of the coast, by spending, upon various occasions, much money and much time for this end.   It is manifest that the use of a lighthouse must be never-failing, its service ever sure ; and that the latter cannot be interfered with by the introduction of any plan, or proposition, or apparatus, which has not been developed to the fullest possible extent as to the amount of light produced—the expense of such light—the wear and tear of the apparatus employed—the steadiness of the light for 16 hours—its liability to extinction—the amount of necessary night care—the number of attendants—the nature of probable accidents—its fitness for secluded places, and other contingent circumstances, which can as well be ascertained out of a lighthouse as in it.   The electric spark which has been placed in the South Foreland High Light by Professor Holmes to do duty for the six winter months, had to go through all this preparatory education before it could be allowed this practical trial.   It is not obtained from frictional electricity, or from voltaic electricity, but from magnetic action.   The first spark (and even magnetic electricity as a whole) was obtained twenty-eight years ago.   (Faraday, *Philosophical Transactions*, 1832, p. 32.)   If an iron core be surrounded by wire, and then moved in the right direction near the poles of a magnet, a current of electricity passes, or tends to pass, through it.   Many powerful magnets are, therefore, arranged on a wheel, that they may be associated very near to another wheel, on which are fixed many helices with their cores like that described.   Again, a third wheel consists of magnets arranged like the first ; next to this is another wheel of the helices, and next to this again a fifth wheel, carrying magnets.   All the magnet-wheels are fixed to one axle, and all the helix wheels are held immoveable in their place.   The wires of the helices are conjoined and connected with a commutator, which, as the magnet-wheels are moved round, gathers the various electric currents produced in the helices, and sends them up through two insulated wires in one common stream of electricity into the lighthouse lantern.   So it will be seen that nothing more is required to produce the electricity than to revolve the magnet-wheels.   There are two magneto-electric machines at the South Foreland, each being put in motion by a two-horse power steam engine ; and, excepting wear and tear, the whole consumption of material to produce the light is the coke and water required to raise steam for the engines, and carbon points for the lamp in the lantern.

The lamp is a delicate arrangement of machinery, holding the two carbons between which the electric light exists, and regulating their adjustment ; so that whilst they gradually consume away, the place of the light shall not be altered.   The electric wires end in the two bars of a small railway, and upon these the lamp stands.   When the carbons of a lamp are nearly gone, that lamp is lifted off and another instantly pushed into its place.   The machines and lamp have done their duty during the past six months in a real and practical manner. The light has never gone out through any deficiency or cause in the engine and machine house : and when it has become extinguished in the lantern, a single touch of the keeper's hand has set it shining as bright as ever.   The light shone up and down the Channel, and across into France, with a power far surpassing that of any other fixed light within sight, or anywhere existent. The experiment has been a good one. There is still the matter of expense and some other circumstances to be considered ; but it is the hope and desire of the Trinity-house, and all interested in the subject, that it should ultimately justify its full adoption.

GAS LEAKAGE AND ITS EFFECTS. *

AN able Report, made by Mr. Spencer, the analytical chemist, and the acknowledged discoverer of electro-type, has a peculiar bearing upon the question of the purification of the Thames, its summer stench, and its black mud. Now this mud, Mr. Spencer maintains, after investigations for several years past, is not only the legitimate offspring of the stinking black earth of the London street subsoil, but also the special source of the summer stench of the river in the metropolitan bounds.

The origin of this stinking black mud, Mr. Spencer traces, not to the sewage of London, but to the abundant percolations of the black earth of the street subsoil into the sewers, and this black earth he traces back without difficulty to its well-known source in gas leakage. But he does not attribute this abomination merely to impurities in the gas so leaking, but to the gas itself, however pure or impure ; and of this gas the quantity which leaks from London gas-pipes is something enormous,—no less than 9 per cent., or between six and seven million cubic feet per annum. No such leakage occurs in other populous towns, such as Liverpool or Manchester, where the joints of the pipes are bored and turned, and so fitted to each other like glass bottles to their ground stoppers ; whereas, the London gas-pipes are jointed with tow and lead, so that, after a little endurance of changes of temperature in summer and winter, and consequent expansion and contraction, the lead parts from the more expansive iron in summer, and is compressed by the more contractile iron in winter, in such a way as to destroy the joint entirely as a tight fit, especially for gas.

The gas so allowed to leak in enormous and perpetual quantities has been found by Mr. Spencer to react upon the gypsum or sulphate of lime in the London subsoil, and thus to liberate the sulphur from its harmless combination with the lime, and promote its union with the carbon of the gas ; forming a vile sulphuretted carbon, which corrodes not only the gas-pipes but the water-mains also, and converts them almost entirely into a sort of plumbago in ten years ; although in pure London subsoil they will last for a century. The corroded matter crumbles, and is converted into black, foul earth ; and, according to Mr. Spencer's investigations, percolates, with moisture, into the sewers, chiefly from above, and not only subsides into the heavy black "slike" of the Thames banks, but is actually choking up the sewers themselves.

* "Report to the New River Company on the Corrosion of Iron Mains, and the effects of Gas Leakage on the Metropolitan Street Earth." By Thomas Spencer, F.C.S., &c. Printed by J. Hedderwick and Son, printers to Her Majesty. 1860.

As for mere sulphuretted hydrogen, Mr. Spencer, like others, has failed to obtain any really serious, or noxious, or even simply obnoxious, quantity from the Thames water, or even from the London sewage ; and he is quite convinced that the summer stench does not arise from mere sulphuretted hydrogen, but mainly from sulphuretted carbon : other chemists differ.

The importance of Mr. Spencer's conclusions, if correct, is obvious, and so is their novelty. If he be right in these conclusions, a new way opens up for the sweetening of the Thames. The immediate removal of the black mud would be but the initiative : gas companies would require to be compelled, by legislative enactment, to rejoint their pipes, or otherwise abate their nuisance ; and not only Mr. Spencer, but gas engineers whom he has consulted, can see no difficulty, such as may be alleged to be peculiar to London streets, in the matter : the thing has already been done in other populous and busy towns ; why should it not be done in London ? The saving of gas would repay the cost. Only think of 6,000,000 cubic feet of gas adding, every year, with sulphate of lime *ad libitum*, to the accumulative nuisance of the ill-smelling black earth of the street subsoil beneath our feet, even though its connexion with the cognate black mud of the Thames banks could be disproved.

However feasible the result of Mr. Spencer's interesting and important investigations may appear, there is one apparent objection to the idea that it is the black mud alone whence the summer stench issues which we must reiterate. If it were so, why is it that the stench subsides as the black mud becomes exposed to the sun at low water, and increases as this mud becomes covered by the rising tide? We do not mean to say that an ingenious and skilful chemist like Mr. Spencer may not be able easily to explain away such an objection ; but, at all events, it requires explanation ere his final result can be fully admitted, even though he has extracted the stench (or at least the abominable sulphuretted carbon) from this very mud by an artificial summer's heat, and has even simulated the whole process, *ab initio*, in his laboratory.—*Abridged from the Builder, No.* 903.*

* Dr. M'William, of Her Majesty's Customs, has inquired into the effects of the river miasms, and has clearly shown that they have not yet produced the mischief which was anticipated of them. Happily for us, there is evidently some condition wanted to make " this filthy river capable of generating cholera, or of forming a soil fit for the germination of the seeds of that disorder when introduced into it." There is great uncertainty in the proposed plan for deodorizing the river by means of perchloride of iron. Dr. Letheby has ascertained that the perchloride is highly charged with a compound of arsenic, which is exceedingly poisonous. A sample of the liquid furnished to him by the patentee, Mr. Dales, and described by him as the same as that used in the experimental inquiries for the Board of Works, has yielded from 296 to 297 grains of chloride of arsenic per gallon. If, therefore, the sewage of London were deodorized in the way proposed, there would be discharged daily into the Thames as much as 227 pounds of chloride of arsenic. This would be equivalent to the casting into the river about 1½ cwt. of powdered arsenic daily. It is true that the poison would be diluted with a large quantity of water and with many millions of gallons of sewage, but a knowledge of this fact would afford no relief to our apprehension of danger, or to the anxiety which must be felt lest the accumulated effects of the poison might in the course of a very short time be dangerous in the extreme.—*Dr. Letheby's Quarterly Report to the Commissioners of Sewers.*

ROASTING BY GAS.

MR. S. HARRISON has patented an improvement upon that class of Chop Broilers and Meat Roasters which are usually constructed of sheet or cast iron, and are heated by the flame of incandescent carburetted hydrogen gas. The invention consists of an iron frame, having a lid or cover, so as to reserve the heat or vapours arising from the flame of the gas. The frame is made to rest on four legs or feet, two grooves being attached to the legs or feet to admit a pan or tray made to receive the fat or gravy issuing from the meat, &c. The inner part of the apparatus consists of a main or feeding tubing having more or less tubings connected thereto. The tubings have more or less gas burners or jets fixed therein, and supply tap as may be required. There is an iron convex shell, having more or less points fixed horizontally to an iron frame or grating, over each gas burner or jet, for conducting the heat of the gas burner or jet, and also for destroying the smoke or soot arising from the flame of the gas. The interior of the apparatus may be applied to baking, or to heating apartments.—*Mechanics' Magazine.*

DISTILLING AND COOKING APPARATUS.

MESSRS. BATHGATE AND WILSON have patented an improved apparatus for Distilling Water and Cooking on board ship.

This consists of a parallelogramical or other suitably shaped metallic chest, having a small enclosed fireplace and ashpit about the centre of its length, and a baking oven at one side, with a space left between the sides of the oven and the outer casing that the heat may be circulated around the sides thereof, and which may be regulated by a damper or dampers. The top of the outer casing immediately above the fireplace, and the flue above the oven, is perforated with holes to receive the bottoms of the cooking vessels, the said openings being closed by covers when not in use. On the opposite side of the fireplace to that on which the oven is fixed, a small vertical steam-boiler is placed. The patentees form this boiler with flat sides and an arched top, and encompassed by a horizontal metallic flanch which is riveted to the boiler about half-way from the bottom. The lower end of the boiler is inserted through a suitably shaped hole in the upper side of the casing or chest, and forms one side of the fireplace, the flanch serving as a saddle, and resting upon the top of the chest. Space between the boiler and sides of the chest admits of the heat circulating round the lower portion of the boiler, and which can be controlled by a damper or dampers. One side of the upper portion of the boiler is fitted with gauge-cocks, and the reverse is constructed with a manhole. The steam-pipe is carried upwards and connected to a condensing worm placed in a tank which is elevated above the camboose. The worm delivery pipe is carried down to any convenient position, and the distilled water received in a suitable vessel. The boiler is supplied with water from the worm-chest, and the worm-tank is supplied with sea-water by the ordinary ship's force-pumps.—*Ibid.*

NEW STOVE, OR COOKING APPARATUS.

AT the late meeting of the Royal Cornwall Polytechnic Society, Mr. Hearder, of Plymouth, exhibited a new Stove or Cooking Apparatus, which is stated to possess the following advantages:—With the consumption of three-pennyworth of coals a day, it will cook for a family of from twelve to sixteen persons; second, it requires no extra fire for baking, as, so long as the kettle will boil the fire will bake; third, vessels will boil on any part of the hot plate; fourth, the stove being air-tight, the draught is certain, and ashes may be burnt over and over again until reduced to clinkers; fifth, the flues will go two or three months without clearing; sixth, the flues are all complete in the stove, and consequently no masonry is necessary for fixing, except for appearance; seventh, roasting by the open fire does not interfere with the baking of the oven; eighth, direct consumption of fuel is so regulated by the valve in the ashpit door, that the fire may be kept in all the night; ninth, the hot closet below keeps viands hot after being cooked, or warms plates; tenth, boilers can be fixed so as to be moveable without interfering with the fixings of the stove; eleventh, meat baked in this stove cannot be distinguished from roast meat; and twelfth, it is an infallible cure for a smoky chimney.

WIND-ENGINES.

Mr. PEILL, of New Park-street, Southwark, has introduced an arrangement of Engine driven by Wind, which answers many useful purposes on farms and in other situations; as, on a farm where beasts are stall-fed, or in a yard, where it would very soon pay for itself in the labour of pumping water for the supply of the cattle. For cutting chaff, too, it is most useful; the saving effected by cutting hay and straw into chaff is well known, for it prevents a great deal being wasted, and also where sheep are fed on land it is serviceable. The supply for cattle being required in winter, the engine comes into action very frequently, and if placed on a barn, two men can be employed when they can do nothing out of doors, and, in a few hours, cut chaff and roots enough to last for a week. A wind-engine of $\frac{3}{4}$-horse power, with one of Messrs. Warners' pumps attached, erected nearly half a mile from the premises, pumps the water from a spring to the height of 70 feet, supplying the house and farm-yards, and filling a pond that has been dry for years. It requires very little wind, and owing to the sails being self-adjusting, no attention save oiling once a week.—*Abridged from Communications to the Mechanics' Magazine.*

PNEUMATIC DESPATCH COMPANY.

At a recent meeting of shareholders of this Company, held at Westminster, the chairman, Captain Huish, in the course of the proceedings, said they were continuing experiments, not to ascertain the power of propulsion by exhaustion, but to ascertain the means by which they could produce a revenue at the lowest possible cost. The experiments had shown most satisfactory results; and a tabulated statement has been furnished by the engineers to the board. The engineers had already informed him that, by the use of the fan, which was a most elaborate thing, but very economical, they could obtain a speed of thirty or forty miles at a very inexpensive cost. The first pipe it was proposed to lay from St. Martin's-le-Grand to Bloomsbury for post-office purposes.

IMPROVED WATER-METERS.

Mr. D. CHADWICK has read to the British Association a paper

"On Improvements in High-pressure Water-meters." Mr. Chadwick stated, there were at the present time about 10,000 high-pressure water meters in use in Europe, of which about one-half were of the kind known as "inferential meters," Siemens's, Adamson's, Taylor's, Mitchell's, and others; the remainder being "positive meters," working on the principle of the piston and cylinder, such as Kennedy's, Worthington's, Jopling's, Duncan's, and Chadwick and Frost's. If no serious practical objection had hitherto existed to the adoption of water-meters, it is within reasonable probability that the number now in use would have been 100 times greater than it is. After reviewing the progress of invention as regards these meters, Mr. Chadwick showed that from 1824 to 1858, 84 patents had been taken out for water-meters; of that number it might safely be affirmed that not more than six or seven were now in practical use, and only two in extensive use. Of inferential meters only those of Mr. Taylor and Mr. Siemens have been extensively used; and although the latter was admitted to be an ingenious invention, its inventor admitted that under certain circumstances his meter would allow a certain small quantity of water to pass unmeasured. The principle of measuring by inference, however, from the revolution of a wheel, spiral fan, or turbine, did not present to the mind that conclusive evidence of exactitude which we were accustomed to demand in our dealings with other matters; and this feeling of uncertainty was increased when it was known that these meters, even with the most perfect possible workmanship, must allow a leakage varying according to the size of the meter, when used under circumstances in which the velocity of the current was insufficient to overcome the friction of the working parts of the machine.

Having pointed out the defects of some of the meters already in use, Mr. Chadwick said that the new high-pressure piston water-meter of Chadwick and Frost effectually overcame the difficulties and objections he had noticed. It consists of a vertical cylinder and piston with a reciprocating action. The cylinder is lined with brass, and the piston packed with cupped leather. The piston rod passes through a stuffing-box at the top of the measuring cylinder into a separated valve chamber, to which there is no connexion with the measuring cylinder except through the parts of a slide three-way valve, the two ends of the moving part of which form pistons working in small cups or cylinders, and on the top of this valve a second slide valve works. When the main piston has fully completed its stroke, a projecting portion of the rod comes in contact with a catch, which moves the top slide valve and admits the full pressure of the water to one of the cups; whilst it at the same time opens a way for the discharge of water from the opposite cup, and the pressure so exerted moves the main valve by which the flow of water is reversed and directed into the other end of the measuring cylinder until the completion of another stroke, when the like motion is again repeated. The opening of the top valve to admit the water to the small cups at the completion of each stroke entirely prevents all concussion on the change of valve. Mr. Chadwick more minutely explained his invention by a diagram suspended from the wall; but to the general reader the explanation would prove unintelligible unless we could furnish a diagram of a similar nature. Nearly 100 of these meters have been in use for periods varying from one to twelve months, and the result has been to confirm in every respect the anticipations of their correctness under all variations in discharge, and great durability. Those parts which in other meters are generally referred to as liable to great wear, namely the slide-valves, are in this meter scarcely affected in consequence of their working in equilibrium, and subject comparatively to no unequal pressure. The well-known cupped leather packing for pistons which work in cylinders lined with brass tube, has proved to be in every respect the most efficient, satisfactory, and durable of any.

We quote the above from an able report of the meeting of the Association in the *Oxford University Herald*. The reports in the metropolitan journals were unusually meagre, notwithstanding the Association met but 50 miles distant.

THE SEWAGE QUESTION.

DR. DAUBENY, Professor of Rural Economy in the University of Oxford, has delivered in Oxford a lecture "On Sewage, with special reference to Baron Liebig's remarks relative to the system of disposing of sewage adopted in the principal cities of this country."

The lecturer remarked that when a man of Baron Liebig's extended European reputation lifted up his warning voice to the British nation on a subject on which he had a right to speak with authority, and staked, as it were, his character as a man of science, by foretelling the ruinous consequences of a system in which the inhabitants of our large cities are embarked, it seemed to be the duty of all who thought they could either directly or indirectly influence public opinion, to secure, if possible, a calm and impartial hearing to the arguments advanced. He proceeded to point out three methods by which it had been attempted to render the sewage of large cities available for agricultural purposes. The first of these methods was to detain the excrementitious matter in its passage towards its outfall for a sufficient time to allow of the solid matter suspended in it to deposit itself, and then to collect this portion as a manure; the second arrived at the same object by a different expedient, viz., by bringing about a separation of the solid matter from the water, which was its vehicle, through the instrumentality of certain chemical re-agents; and the third was to convey the whole in a liquid state to the very spot where it could be usefully applied, by the aid of pipes and other mechanical contrivances calculated to supersede the necessity for employing cartage and vessels capacious enough to contain so bulky a material. The first of these methods was adopted at Cheltenham, the second at Leicester, and the third at Rugby. It would appear, however, that except in a few small places, like Rugby, which scarcely held out an example which great cities could safely imitate, no successful method had as yet been discovered for combining the sanitary with the economical object sought; accordingly, in London, the public appeared to have acquiesced in a plan which, at a vast expense, was intended to carry off the filth of the city to a distance, and disregarded altogether the agricultural value of the material itself. It was against this procedure that Baron Liebig entered his protest. It might be urged by a practical man, in defence of the metropolitan system, that the valuable constituents of the manure were equally sacrificed under the old *régime* as they will be when the new arrangements are brought into complete operation ; that, although cesspools might exist, their contents were rarely made available for the purposes of agriculture, and that no more use was made of the manure, when poured into the Thames in the immediate proximity to the city, than will be the case now, when it is conveyed to a distance of many miles. Thus, the sanitary object, at least, was provided for, whilst the economical question stood upon the same footing as before. The authority of chemists of great eminence might also be appealed to, who reported, as the result of their investigations, that in their opinion no profitable application of the sewage of London to useful purposes that could be adopted on a large scale has up to the present time been suggested. Those and similar reasons, however, although they might serve by way of apology for embarking in the present system in lieu of a better, left untouched the main argument advanced by Baron Liebig, and could not justify us in a blind acquiescence in the system pursued as one intrinsically good. The transport of the sewage matter to a distance from the metropolis had indeed become, with the present arrangements, a matter of paramount necessity; but the accomplishment of that end ought by no means to stifle the inquiry as to whether some means ought not to be devised for rendering the same material available for useful purposes. If the citizens of London were as fully impressed as they ought to be with the importance of the subject, if they could realize the enormous pecuniary loss they are at present sustaining by the system pursued, they would not quietly acquiesce in the report of those chemists who have expressed doubts as to the practicability of employing their sewage for agricultural purposes, but would persevere in putting both science and capital into requisition until the difficulties had been surmounted.

W find in the *Scientific American,* a suggestion from a Correspondent in Buffalo, who proposes to drain cities by sinking vaults in the bottoms of sewers for the reception of solid matters, which are to be removed from the vaults periodically. This plan was patented and brought to the notice of the London Metropolitan Board of Works a year or two since by His Honour Commissioner Fane, of the Bankruptcy Court. ———

INDURATION OF THE STONEWORK OF THE HOUSES OF PARLIAMENT.

DURING the past year, the full extent of the certainty of the decay of certain portions of the stone used in building the Houses of Parliament has been made patent to the country.

In May last, in the House of Commons, Mr. Wise asked the First Commissioner of Works whether any Report had recently been made on the condition of the Stonework of the Houses of Parliament, and what had been done with the 7280*l.* voted last session for the purpose of Indurating the external stonework. Mr. Wise said the Commission reported that the Bolsover stone combined the requisites of durability, economy of conversion, beauty of colour, and other qualities; but the contract entered into for the supply of the material was cancelled, and a new quarry opened belonging to the late Duke of Leeds, the stone obtained from which was, in the estimation of experienced builders, of an inferior description. He referred to Mr. C. H. Smith's charge, that proper supervision had not been exercised over the delivery of the stone ; and the question was, who was responsible for so serious a neglect? The consequence of this was, that they now found inferior material had been used, and large sums, in addition to the enormous outlay already incurred, would be required to preserve these buildings from a decay which ought to have been foreseen and guarded against. At the bottom of that state of affairs lay, he believed, the modern system of contracts, which gave great profit to the few and inflicted great injury on the many. For some time he had noticed a rapid, constant, and increasing disruption of the surface of the stone, especially on the terrace front. The decomposition was not confined to the plain face of the stone, but extended to the sills, bases, capitals, plinths, and the stonework above and below all these. He should be glad to know from the Chief Commissioner of Works what remedy he proposed to adopt for this state of things.

Mr. W. Cowper, in course of reply, said that what was supposed to be the best stone that England could produce, had been found not to combine those exact proportions of carbonate of lime and carbonate of magnesia, which were expected to make it indestructible. On the contrary, the action of the weather upon it had been such, that on the river front, not merely on the carved portions, but on many of the plain surfaces where the water dripped, the decay was advancing most rapidly. The only thing which could now be done was to find some composition which would render the stone impervious to moisture, and would, in fact, have the same effect upon it as paint had upon wood and iron. There were several patented compositions which professed to attain that object, and two of them, —one patented by Mr. Ransome, and the other by Mr. Szerelmey, —were now being tried upon the river front. As far as ordinary investigation could form a guide, they seemed to promise very fairly; but he had thought it desirable to ask Mr. Faraday and Sir R. Murchison to examine and report upon these experiments, and he trusted that their labours would be more successful than were those of the Commission which sat sixteen years ago, to which the hon. gentleman referred. He did not think it right to expend any of the money which had last year been voted by Parliament, until it had been shown that this operation was successful in excluding moisture and preventing decay of the stone.

Next, let us see what this professional blunder has already cost the nation.

A Return published of all sums paid for indurating or preserving the external stonework and the iron roofs of the Houses of Parliament since the year 1853 shows that 3517*l*. 10*s*. 11*d*. have been devoted to that purpose. The works appear to have been undertaken by Mr. G. B. Daines and Mr. N. C. Szerelmey. The former gentleman received 1*s*. per yard superficial for stonework and 1*s*. 10*d*. per yard for the iron roofing. Mr. Szerelmey was paid 2*s*. 2*d*. and 2*s*. per yard for the roofing, and 1*s*. per yard for the stonework. Referring to the decay of the stone used in the new Houses of Parliament, Sir Charles Barry said :— " The decay which has taken place in the stone employed in the new Palace seems to be confined principally to the parapets, where the stone is exposed on two faces ; also in the water-tables, sills, cappings, bases, and plinths, and the courses of stone above and below them, within the influence of the drippings and splashings of showers of rain (particularly where opposed to the south and south-west winds), and to a very limited extent on the plain faces of the ashlar, owing probably to soft varieties of the stone. A fruitful source of decay is also due to the unusual and extensive use of water externally, for purposes of ventilation, by which a considerable portion of the masonry is constantly rendered alternately wet and dry ; which should be prevented, if possible, as it is the severest test to which any stone can be subjected. Experience has fully satisfied my mind that in proportion as stones are absorbent, so in proportion is the extent of discoloration and decay which ensue in a smoky and impure atmosphere like that of London."

We well remember the costly travelling Commission for collecting specimens of the building-stones for the new Palace ; and it is grievous to find that all such precautionary measures have been frustrated. But, who is to blame ? Mr. C. H. Smith has justified his selection of the Anston stone, as the stone of all others best calculated to withstand the effects of the London atmosphere, *because it has resisted for some centuries the atmosphere of Yorkshire*, its natural element, in several of the old churches in the neighbourhood of the quarries ; and, consequently, it would have stood equally well in London, had greater care and supervision been used in its selection.

Here we must, however, protest against the argument that because stone lasts well in buildings in the locality wherein it is found, it should last equally well in another locality. This was explained not to be the fact, at the time the selection of the stone was made, in a short note to the *Times* journal ; and we recollect the statement to have been received with surprise and even incredulity.*

Mr. Smith, in his defence, maintains that official supervision of the stone was necessary ; upon which Mr. Grissell, the contractor, conceiving an attempt to be made to shift the blame upon him, asks, How comes it that Mr. Smith and the Commissioners did not recommend *at the onset*, that a practical chemist should be resident at the

* The statement to which we refer is in a note appended to Mr. George Godwin's communication of the Commissioners' Report to the *Civil Engineer and Architects' Journal*. The note is as follows :—" The publication of this document has occasioned a Mr. John Mallcott to observe in the *Times*, that ' all stone made use of in the immediate neighbourhood of its own quarries is more likely to endure that atmosphere than if it be removed therefrom, though only thirty or forty miles.' " (See *Year-Book of Facts*, 1840, p. 78.) Twenty years' experience has shown Mr. Mallcott's statement to be correct.

quarries to determine which beds of the stone would resist the London atmosphere, and which would not?   Mr. Grissell denies that any practical mason, even Mr. Smith himself, had he been the party selected for the purpose, could have undertaken to decide this point.

Thereupon Mr. Smith replies that—

He and the other Commissioners *did* strongly recommend, *" at the onset,"* not only that some fit person should occasionally inspect the quarries, but also that a properly-qualified individual should frequently, perhaps two or three times a week, examine the stone at Westminster, with full power to admit or reject any of the blocks. But such recommendation was entirely disregarded by the Government authorities at Whitehall-place. There might have been some difficulty in finding a duly-qualified man to undertake such supervision : no *mere* chemist, *mere* practical stonemason, nor *mere* anybody else, could have performed the duties with credit to himself and advantage to those who employed him : it must have been a man possessing a certain amount of general scientific attainments, conjointly with long practical experience in the selection of different kinds of stone, and actual handling of the mallet and chisel. No doubt many such persons were to be found, had they been sought after.

Mr. Smith continues : By far the greater portion of the stone appears to be of a good and durable quality ; and it is worthy of especial notice that the carvings show scarcely a trace of decay. Along the whole length of the river front there is a series of heraldic sculptures, executed in stones originally weighing perhaps five tons each, with rampant animals as supporters, carved in very bold relief, consequently, more exposed to all the severities of frost and thaw, rain and sunshine than mouldings or plain surfaces; yet all these large stones are as free from decay as when they were just left by the carvers. This may seem to infer that the workmen, or the principal carver, exercised considerable discrimination in the choice of the blocks ; that is, to take such as would cut and work freely, or appear to be of one uniform quality throughout their entire mass : and we now have positive proof that such stones are amongst those of the least perishable quality.

Mr. Smith then refers to the Parliamentary Report of March, 1839, after his first tour of inspection to the newly-discovered quarries in the neighbourhood of Bolsover Moor.

He likewise, in August, 1843, proceeded with Sir H. T. De la Beche to examine and report especially upon the Anston quarries. On each of these occasions, fair average sample blocks were procured, forwarded to London, minutely examined, and mechanically and chemically experimented upon, in order to compare their physical properties with samples from other quarries, and from old buildings in the neighbourhood, in a manner precisely similar to the mode adopted on all former occasions connected with the Parliamentary Commission.

Mr. Grissell then quotes in justification the statement of Professor Ansted that—

To all outward appearance the stone which has failed was, before being fixed in the building, as sound and as suitable as that which remains sound ; and up to the period when he (Mr. Grissell) ceased to be concerned for the Government, about seven years since, the only stone which had showed symptoms of decay was that which had been used in the under surfaces of string-courses and cornices, while that which had been thoroughly exposed to wind and weather, particularly the plain surface, was perfectly sound.

We now return to Mr. Grissell's own defence, in which he states that—

So long as these stones were crystallized they were the best stones that could be taken, and the specimens examined in the churches in the neighbourhood of the quarry selected went to prove this ; but, unfortunately, the quarry from which the stone had been taken was not found to be in such a state as to supply so large a quantity as was required for the Houses of Parliament, and they were obliged to go to another quarry in the same neighbourhood, which was not of the same quality of stone as that which had been experimented upon by the Commissioners, and no doubt this is the correct history of the matter.

With respect to the sound condition of the carved stone in the river front, which Mr. Smith attributes to the judgment shown by the principal carver in the selection of the stone, Mr. Grissell assures us that—

The whole of these large blocks were obtained from various parts of the quarries, where the sizes could best be obtained, and were in no case selected by the talented carver, Mr. John Thomas, who had charge of that portion of the work, but were got invariably more with regard to size than to quality. The result of which goes to prove that the more thoroughly the stone is exposed to the action of the wind, rain, and sunshine, the less liable it is to decay. I may add also that all these stones are fixed the reverse way to the bed, and (adds Mr. Grissell), I believe, had they been used in more sheltered situations, would not so strongly have commended themselves to Mr. Smith's kind notice and consideration.

At a late period (in October) a very interesting letter from "An Architect," appeared in the *Times*, investigating the circumstances under which our Palace of Parliament, which has already cost upwards of two millions of money, notwithstanding the care and science bestowed upon it, is found to be in a state of decay. This very competent correspondent of the *Times* narrates of the Commission as follows :—

" When the Palace of Westminster was to be built, at great expense a Commission, consisting of the architect, two geologists, and a chymist, went all over England to examine stone and buildings, and they believed that in Yorkshire they had found what they wanted in a bed of stone called mineralogically 'dolomite,' or, more generally, magnesian limestone. It is a crystalline stone, composed of sulphate of lime and sulphate of magnesia, and much harder than even Portland stone. The best accounts I can find of its composition are in De la Beche's *Geological Manual*, 1832, or in Van Bach's *Annales des Sciences Naturelles*, 1827, to which De la Beche refers. Let me remark, however, that dolomite is a crystalline rock—that is, a chymical combination of lime and magnesia, some thinking that it was originally limestone, but altered by heat and other circumstances. I believe the Commission were a little misled by their chymistry, but they found in Coningsburgh Castle, in the neighbourhood of the quarries, a building which certainly appears to have braved, with but little loss, the war of the elements for 700 or 800 years. I believe, however, that the outside of York Cathedral is a dolomite; and certainly the various states of decay of that building might have taught us caution in its adoption. From the crystalline composition of this stone, however, all the present mischief arises ; for when the crystallization is complete, and the magnesia and lime in proper proportions, it is indestructible ; but nature does not work quite uniformly on so large a scale, and imperfect crystallization, or an excess of lime or magnesia, would naturally lead to all we see at Westminster. Some beds—nay, very large portions of the external facing, then, look as good as ever ; but others, and unluckily those the best decorated, and the upper portions of this splendid edifice, are already in a state of fearful decomposition. The stone turns to powder, and in some cases, I understand, large masses have fallen down from actual decay.

"I really look upon this accident as a national calamity. If it cannot be stayed, but goes on, there is no alternative whatever but to cut out every decayed stone, carve another, and put the new one in the place of the old. The expense of this process would be enormous ; and with what material is it to be done ? Can we depend on any beds of dolomite, or must we have recourse to Portland stone ? About the choice and durability of the latter there would be no difficulty ; but Portland stone becomes rapidly white, and dolomite turns brown, and so every step of the decay would become marked with colour, and the building become a disgrace.

"A few words will dispose of the present state of the question and the expedients proposed. Buckingham Palace is painted from a similar misfortune to that I have already explained ; and we paint our stucco-fronted houses, and occasionally our stone porticos. Of course all oily coatings, such as paints, rapidly yield to the sun and wind, and the covenant in our leases, ' that we should paint all external work now painted with two or three coats of oil paint every three years,' shows our universal experience on that point. From the nature of things, no oily or fatty mixtures can be permanently exposed to the atmosphere. What then ? Science steps in and shows us that flints, hard, indestructible, and apparently imperishable, are dissolved in nature in hot water containing alkalis, as in Iceland, and may be easily dissolved by art in hot water and caustic alkali ; and it was immediately seen that if we could get decaying stones to imbibe, firstly, this solution, and then chymically to harden it again, the problem was solved. Flint, as our readers know, is technically ' silica,' whence the term invented for this process, ' silicated.'

"Fuchs, in Munich, was the first who turned his attention to this suggestion, followed by Kuhlmann, in Paris ; and about the same time by Mr. Ransome, of Ipswich, who has patented his application, the patent applying to a double decomposition, which he alleges he has discovered. Mr. Szerelmey followed : his process he keeps a secret ; but Professor Faraday states that some bituminous substance is mixed and introduced at some part of the process ; but, with this difference, I believe it to be chymically the same as the ordinary method. There is no doubt of the bitumen ; for, being in attendance at committees of the House last Session, the smell of bitumen was complained of while the workmen were occupied in the second court at the back of the Select Committee-rooms. For this additional process, or composition, Mr. Szerelmey introduces the term ' zopissa,' and calls his process ' silicata zopissa,' and proposes to apply it to bricks, cements, wood, &c. The word ' zopissa' is an unusual one, though Πίσσα, or Πίττα, ' pitch,' is, of course, a well known Greek word. This difficulty sent me to *Liddell and Scott's Dictionary.* They give the word under the authority of *Dioscorides.* I then turned to *Stephens,* and there I found all about it, and extracts from *Dioscorides* and *Pliny* relating to the substance called zopissa by the Greeks. As I write, as I said at the outset, simply to make the question intelligible, I will not quote the Greek. It seems, however, that zopissa was pitch, compounded with wax, scraped from the sides of ships which had been at sea. Sprengel's Latin gives the Greek with great accuracy, and that permit me to quote :— 'Zopissam alii dicunt esse resinam cum cerâ navibus derasam, à nonnullis apochyma vocatum, quæ dissipandi vim habet, quia aquâ marinâ est macerata.' Pliny, according to the quaint old translation of Philemon Holland, gives it thus :—

" ' It would not be forgotten how the Greeks have a certain pitch, scraped, together with waxe, from ships that have laine at sea, which they call zopissa ; so curious are men to make experiments, and try conclusions in everything ; and this is thought to be much more effectuall for all matters that pitch and rosin are good for, by reason of the fast temperature that it hath gotten by the salt water.'

"In *Ducange* the word is spelt 'zupissa,' and in *Donnegan's Lexicon* '$Z\alpha\iota\grave{o}s$' and '$\Pi\iota\sigma\sigma\alpha$' are given as the etymology, as if the compound signified 'living pitch.' Ainsworth derives the whole word from the Hebrew 'Zephth'—pitch or bitumen. All this, however, points distinctly at the distinguishing characteristic of Mr. Szerelmcy's process.

"I wish I could believe he had succeeded. I agree with you in thinking that in the face next the river his specimen looks better than Ransome's ;* but if you go into either of the two courts coated this summer by Mr. Szerelmey, you can scrape the composition off with your nail. In truth, it seems to me that neither one solution nor the other is absorbed into the stone, which is the whole question, and that consequently the stone is not silicated.

" I did hope the distinguished chemist to whom the Chief Commissioner referred the question would have suggested something, but he evidently only answered certain questions, and I fear that the whole difficulty remains exactly where it was ; and we may spend thousands upon thousands in literally doing but little more than whitewashing this magnificent specimen of a national misfortune.

"The only course I can suggest is that the Chief Commissioner should at once remit the question to a commission composed of our best chemists and most experienced architects."

In this letter, the opinion of the writer that the secret of *silicating* stone is still to be discovered, called forth a reply from Sir Henry Rawlinson, stating as follows :—

"The art of indurating stone by the application of a solution of silica to the surface was certainly known to the ancients, and the substance actually employed by them is still to be obtained in sufficient quantities to admit of minute chemical analysis. In a notice of the great cuneiform inscription of Darius Hystaspes on the rock of Behistun, which I published thirteen years ago (*Journal of the Royal Asiatic Society*, Vol. X., part 3, p. 193), I gave a remarkable instance of the successful use of liquid 'silica' by the ancient Persians. The passage is as follows :—

---

* This was in justification of a lengthy account of Szerelmey's process, and its successful results, overstated, according to the showing of Mr. Ransome.

"It would be very hazardous to speculate on the means employed to engrave the work in an age when steel is supposed to have been unknown, but I cannot avoid noticing a very extraordinary device, which has been employed apparently to give a finish and durability to the writing. It was evident to myself, and to those who in company with myself scrutinized the execution of the work, that after the engraving of the rock had been accomplished, a coating of 'silicious varnish' had been laid on to give a clearness of outline to each individual letter, and to protect the surface against the action of the elements. This varnish is of infinitely greater hardness than the limestone rock beneath it. It has been washed down in several places by the trickling of waters for three-and-twenty centuries, and it lies in flakes upon the footledge like thin layers of lava. It adheres in other portions of the tablet to the broken surface, and still shows with sufficient distinctness the forms of the characters, although the rock beneath is entirely honeycombed and destroyed. It is only, indeed, in the great fissures, caused by the outburstings of natural springs, and in the lower part of the tablet, where I suspect artificial mutilation, that the varnish has entirely disappeared.

"I would only correct this description, in so far as to suggest that, the flakes of silicate which lie on the footledge are the original droppings of the varnish when it was first laid on in a liquid state, rather than the effect of the subsequent trickling of water over the surface of the rock. These flakes might be easily detached from the rock with a chisel and hammer, and their analysis would show if any other ingredient were employed in the composition than flint and caustic alkali. The substance looks like opaque glass, but has no perceptible effect on the colouring of the rock. It is certain, moreover, that it was absorbed into the stone, and prevented decomposition, so far as it penetrated. The sculpture, indeed, which extends over several hundreds of square feet, and which was executed about 500 B.C., is, although exposed to the full force of the prevailing storms from the S.E., for the most part in as good a state of preservation as if it had been engraved but yesterday.

"Surely, if a commission be appointed to report on the silicata zopissa question, it would be worth their while to obtain specimens of the flint varnish of the ancients from Persia, and perhaps also from Egypt."

Upon reading this letter, a Correspondent of the *Builder* asks whether the ancients might not have applied the first varnish in a fused or heated state, which would at once render it impervious to the weather, and might in some measure account for the deposit, so desirable to obtain.

Mr. Szerelmey has published a pamphlet on his process, which he terms "The Encaustic and Zopissa of the Ancients;" but, whatever time may prove as to the value of his process, we are not prepossessed by his arguments as to the cause of the decay. We therefore await further report.

One of the consequences of the question of the preservation of the stonework being thus publicly mooted was an erroneous view of the comparative merits of the processes of Mr. Szerelmey and Mr. Ransome, greatly to the disadvantage of the latter; this erroneous impression being, doubtless, increased by the minute account of Szerelmey's process filling a column of the *Times*.

Mr. Ransome has, however, in a communication to that journal dated Ipswich, Dec. 23, 1860, set the matter right by the publication of a letter from Dr. Faraday, and Sir Roderick Murchison, both showing that two bays on the river front of the Houses of Parliament have been prepared, one by the Szerelmey process, and the other by Ransome's; and agreeing that at the time the bays were examined (soon after their preparation), the Szerelmey stone was less absorbent of water than the Ransome, and had then the most perfect and uninjured surface; but that, 2. "the result looked for is eminently practical, and in either case can only be obtained by the lapse of time."

IMPROVED PRINTING MACHINERY.

Mr. A. Applegath has patented certain improvements in Machinery for Printing and for cutting printed paper into sheets. In combining a machine for these purposes, two surface-printing rollers are used between two pairs of cylinders, each covered with blanketing; to prevent as much as may be the effect of set-off on such cylinder, where the already printed paper comes in contact with the cylinders, they are each made of two or more times the circumference of the printing surface rollers; and further, to prevent the effects of set-off, each cylinder may be provided with moveable blanketing on the inside capable of being moved a short distance over the exterior surface of the cylinders from time to time, in order to bring up fresh quantities of the blanketing. The combination of the surface-printing rollers, then, and the cylinders is so arranged as to admit of two webs or lengths of paper being simultaneously printed on both sides; the paper, after receiving an impression on one side, passes over or against rollers with endless or other blanketing or absorbing material, so as to have any superfluous ink or colour removed from the impression before the paper is printed on the other side; and after such second impression it is also subjected to the action of like absorbing apparatus before passing to the cutting apparatus. The cutting apparatus consists of a cylinder coated with a material into which puncturing or cutting points or blades may penetrate; such puncturing cutters are so set on rollers that the puncturing of one roller shall be intermediate of the other or others, so that when the paper has passed the rollers it shall be divided across. The printed paper thus divided is delivered at several different places by carrying tapes or aprons on rollers, in such manner that one pair of delivering tapes or aprons may (by one pair of the rollers by which the tapes or aprons are carried) be arranged so as to move from and to two or more sets of carrying tapes.—*Mechanics' Magazine.*

TYPE-COMPOSING MACHINERY.

Mr. G. Davis has patented an improvement consisting principally in the use in Typographic, Lithographic, and Copper and other plate Printing Presses of endless paper in place of separate sheets; also, in damping the paper by automatic apparatus. The endless paper is passed around rollers which keep it at the requisite tension, being prevented from unrolling too fast by a break and weighted lever, and it is drawn forward by two feeding rollers covered with cloth. The paper is then cut transversely by a pair of automatic scissors, and passed to the printing cylinder. To cut the paper into two or more sheets longitudinally after being printed, it passes between pairs of revolving circular cutters. The damping apparatus consists, principally, of two hollow perforated metal rollers containing water, and covered with cloth or flannel, round which the endless paper passes in its progress from one roller on to another.

NEW PRINTING MACHINE.

At Vienna, a printing machine has been brought out, dispensing with the use of all other assistance save that of mechanical apparatus. No persons are required to feed it with paper, or to remove the printed sheets, both processes being accomplished through the instrumentality of the machine itself. The paper for this purpose is supplied in rolls many hundred yards in length. The machine first cuts a sheet off the requisite size, then prints, and finally throws it off—a newspaper ready for the reader. All that manual labour is required to do is to bring forward fresh rolls, and to take away the printed sheets.

PROCESS FOR ENLARGING AND REDUCING ENGRAVINGS.

The Editor of the *Builder* thus describes a very simple and ingenious Process for the Enlargement and Reduction of Prints, at the Electro-printing Block Company's premises, in Burleigh-street, Strand:—"A sheet of vulcanized rubber, prepared in some special way, it was said, and coated with an elastic composition on which had been printed a copy of an engraving, was fixed to an iron framework with hooks and rings attached to small iron bars, crossing so as to form a square; and by means of screws the rubber sheet was stretched, according to a graduated scale, until the inked impression had attained certain increased dimensions. The whole being fixed, was then taken to a lithographic press, and the rubber laid with the inked side on a clean lithographic stone, and passed repeatedly through the press. The inked impression was thus completely transferred to the stone, and from that in a few minutes an impression of the enlarged engraving was worked off. This impression we examined with a magnifying-glass, comparing it also with an unenlarged copy, and certainly it displayed not the least rottenness or comparative imperfection, but was, on the contrary, quite as good as the unenlarged one in every way: nor did it seem to be anywise distorted, although it does seem clear that minute differences in the amount of the stretching, from the central point of rest outwards towards the squared circumference, must exist, and must hence produce minute, though it would appear inappreciable, distortion in the enlarged impressions taken by such means. However this may be, a pair of compasses seemed to show that round the circumference at least of the rubber, which was marked with equidistant lines, the enlargement was equable in all its parts. Moreover, the sheet of rubber was thin, and very elastic, and easily stretched, and seemed to be of uniform thickness. Another process exhibited was the converse of the first, namely, reduction: but in this case it happened to be the reduction of a portion of a page of the *Times* of that day. The rubber sheet in this case had to be stretched beforehand, and relaxed after the impression was stamped on its elastic coating. The diminished copy was quite as vivid as the original. In this case another process, which we did not witness, was said to have been used in obtaining the first impression: of course it was not from the *Times* types. A piece of a copy of the *Times* had been cut out and submitted to a simple process of maceration in a bath; an impression was then taken off it on to a lithographic stone, and thence it was impressed upon the stretched rubber sheet for the reduction. This process is, however, not quite new."

PAPER-MAKING.

Mr. T. ROUTLEDGE has patented certain improvements in the manufacture of Paper. These consist in the preparation of half stuff (paper pulp) and paper from esparto or Spanish grass (comprising the plants Spartum Tigeum, Stipa Tenecissima, Dis or Alpha), commercially so denominated, by an improved and economical process of manufacture, the same being applicable to straw and other raw fibrous substances. On the 31st of July, 1856, a patent was granted to the present patentee for the treatment of the above, and other raw fibres, by a process consisting of boiling the same in a caustic ley composed of soda, with more lime added than was necessary to render the same caustic; and secondly, by a subsequent boiling in carbonate or bicarbonate soda solution. He has found that not only does the excess of lime in the ley so prepared, but even the use of lime beyond a certain point in caustic ley, as ordinarily employed, set or regulate the silicious, albuminous, glutinous, and gummy resinous compounds or matters; but it fixes or dyes the colouring and extractive matters combined more or less with all raw fibres, and which it is necessary to render soluble before the fibres can be efficiently separated from each other, and so constitute a finely-divided fibrous half stuff. He finds that by employing a ley in which the lime is not, as it were, so prominent, he obtains a better practical result.— *Mechanics' Magazine.*

Mr. Richard Herring, the author of several works on the paper manufacture, has published an important letter on the supply of paper-making materials. He says there are more rags wasted, burnt, or left to rot, than would make our paper manufacturers independent of all assistance from abroad. A regular communication ought to be formed by country carriage, and by railways for the conveyance of the rags to London, or to those paper-mills in the country which enter largely into the trade. A plan is proposed which will place the whole subject plainly before the public, offer proper pledges, establish proper means, and give the whole movement the degree of activity and regularity which may render it profitable to individuals and the country.

COLLODION IN WATERPROOFING.

MR. J. MACINTOSH has patented certain improvements in the manufacture of Waterproof and other fabrics, and of moulded or formed articles. The patentee takes a batt, or fleece, or thin and loose layer of cotton or other fibre, and spreads over the surface of the same a thin coating of collodion, which, in hardening, cements the fibres firmly together, and produces a fabric more or less waterproof, according to the quantity of collodion employed. The cotton or fibre which he employs is not chemically prepared, and therefore is not acted on by the solvent of the collodion as it hardens. Articles may in this manner be made of any desired shape : as, for instance, tubes may be produced by lapping the batt, or fleece, or layer of loose fibre around a form, and then applying the collodion ; in this way gloves, shoes and boots may be produced.—*Mechanics' Magazine.*

IMPROVED DISINFECTANT.

M. D. S. AGATA has patented the process of this preparation. He collects the common cockle and other shells found on the seashore, and calcines them in a furnace until they are reduced to a friable condition, and readily broken and powdered. To this powder he adds, first, half the quantity of sulphate of iron, thus producing a fine yellow inodorous powder resembling ochre. The material is inexpensive, and it is quick and economic in its action, as it requires but about one part of the Disinfectant to one hundred of the matter to be treated. It is more especially intended for all kinds of feculent matter, &c. ; when used as a disinfectant for urine, about two per cent. of common tar is to be added.—*Ibid.*

THE WARMING OF ST. PAUL'S CATHEDRAL.

DURING the past winter, the Cathedral has been successfully warmed by the London Warming and Ventilating Company, with the assistance of the architect, Mr. F. C. Penrose.

The cubic contents of this vast building are, in round numbers, 5,000,000 feet, the dome itself containing 2,000,000 feet, about equal to the whole capacity of Westminster Abbey. By means of the present plan of warming, there has seldom been a variation of temperature in any part of the interior of the Cathedral greater than 2° Fahrenheit, the average temperature being about 54°.

As a proof of the efficacy of the present plan, it may be mentioned that on one occasion the temperature was raised, in ten hours, from 40° to 58°, or 18°, and this without relatively increasing by more than 2° the heat of the upper portion of the dome. The whole apparatus is under easy control, and the hygrometric condition of the air is always maintained in a healthy state.

This is effected by the use of the well-known "Gurney stoves," 13 of which are placed in the crypt, and have large gratings over them, through which the warm air ascends ; while others are provided with downcasts for the cold descending current to be warmed.

The cost of the fuel is about 1d. per hour for each stove ; the whole of them, however, are not used at one time, except in very severe weather. The average cost of the whole fuel consumed during the three winter months is not more than 5l. per week.

A witty canon (the Rev. Sydney Smith) is said to have given his opinion that Middlesex itself might be as easily warmed as St. Paul's Cathedral. Sir Christopher Wren appears, however, to have actually provided ample flues for the warming, which are used in the present operations, and the existence of which has greatly assisted the engineers in carrying out their plans.—*Times.*

LONDON SMOKE AND FOG.

WHAT is often called fog, which darkens the metropolis in winter, is, in reality, the smoke of millions of coal fires, which are much increased in very cold weather. To prevent this, a Correspondent of the *Times* recommends this simple plan :—Before you throw on coals, pull all the fire to the front of the grate towards the bars, fill up the cavity at the back with the cinders or ashes which will be found under the grate, and then throw on the coals. The gas evolved in the process of roasting the coals will then be absorbed by the cinders, and will render them in an incredible degree combustible ; the smoke will thus be burnt, and a fine, glowing, smokeless fire will be the result. This rule should be enforced from the kitchen upwards.

THE SEWING-MACHINE.

THE manufacture of clothing may be regarded as divisible into the three stages of spinning, weaving, and sewing. Each of these operations may now be performed almost entirely without manual labour ; but whilst the two former are entrusted to machines, the latter, though a simple operation, is executed to a great degree by hand. No country in the world approaches our own in the excellence of its spinning and weaving machinery, or in the number and magnitude of its factories ; but in sewing machinery, and in the number of our factories of ready-made clothing, we are far behind the United States. We have given the Americans the spinning-mule and the power-loom ; they have sent us the sewing-machine. The two former are of native growth ; the latter is an importation, and hence may be partly attributed its comparatively slow progress in this country.

Whether the sewing-machine will add as largely to the wealth and prosperity of this country as the spinning-jenny or the power-loom, is a question which we shall not attempt to decide. We expect, however, that the United States will maintain for many years her present superiority over Great Britain in the manufacture and use of sewing-machines. At the present time there are *ten* times as many workmen, and *ten* times the amount of capital employed in the manufacture of sewing-machines in the United States as in Great Britain. The number of machines in use in the United States cannot be less than 100,000 ; the number in use in Great Britain does not exceed 10,000, and even of these a large proportion are of American manufacture. This may be accounted for by the fact that machines made in America are much superior in workmanship and finish to those made in this country. Our mechanics do not seem to have yet learned to manufacture sewing-machines. Even the needles made in England are not equal to American-made needles. Our needle-makers have yet to learn this branch of their trade.

At the late meeting of the Royal Cornwall Polytechnic Society, Messrs. Newton, Wilson, and Co., of High Holborn, London, exhibited eleven of their very elegant-looking Sewing-machines, including two highly ornamental and beautiful lady's boudoir machines; eight of the handsome machines invented by Grover and Baker, Boston, United States; and a cottage machine. In addition to these, they also exhibited a binding machine, which puts on the binding without the necessity of previously tacking it. To one of Grover and Baker's machines is attached Newton and Wilson's patent hammer, and as this turns down the head or seam, the double process of folding the hem and stitching is carried on at the same time. This machine is calculated to work comfortably at the rate of 1500 stitches per minute, but it can be worked up to 1800 a minute. The prices of the machines vary from five to thirty-five guineas. The machines were exhibited in operation by an agent of Messrs. Newton and Wilson, and formed objects of general interest and curiosity. The process of working the machine is very light and simple, consisting merely of the pressure of the foot upon a board or plate at rapid intervals, something very like the motion of the foot in turning the spinning wheel in former times.

Mr. W. Tillie has patented an invention, the first part of which is intended to be applied to a number of sewing-machines driven by hand, steam, or other power, and has for its object the stopping of any of the machines upon a thread breaking either accidentally, or on the work any of the machines have to do being completed. The invention applies, secondly, to the use of a clamping guide, which directs the cloth to the needle, and which is capable of adjustment in one direction in order that the stitching may take place at the desired distance from the edge, and in another direction according to the thickness of the fabric.—*Selected and Abridged from the Mechanics' Magazine.*

WEAVING BY MAGNETO-ELECTRICITY.

M. BONELLI, of Milan, director of the Sardinian telegraphs, by means of his Electric Loom, has set aside the complicated and costly appliances necessary to the Jacquard looms, by the use of electricity. The little bobbins or bars which hold up the thread of the warp in the Jacquard loom he makes into electro-magnets in the usual way. The design is painted on a sheet of tinfoil, with the portions not used in the pattern covered with a non-conducting varnish. The pattern passes slowly over a roller under an immense number of brass teeth, communicating by fine insulated wires with the bobbins, the pattern, of course, being in connexion with one pole of a battery, and the bobbins or magnets with the other. Thus, as the tinfoil slowly moves round, the parts which are not to be worked, being covered with a non-conducting varnish, transmit no current through the brass teeth to the bobbins. The pattern, or exposed portion of the tinfoil, on the contrary, does so, and transforms the bobbins into electro-magnets, which attract and hold the bars opposite their points attached to the threads of the warp, which, as the lever descends, the bars are thus held up for the instant, and, of course, raising their threads below, and allowing the shuttle to be passed between. The first machine, constructed at Turin, was afterwards modified by M. Hipp, at Berne; and though it demonstrated the possibility of weaving by means of electro-magnetism, it nevertheless left much to be desired with respect to the success of its practical application. It was not until 1859 that success in perfecting the machinery, and in rendering it available for either hand or power-loom weaving, was attained.

M. Bonelli has patented his improvements, the abridged specification of which is thus given in the *Mechanics' Magazine*—

By a novel construction and arrangement of mechanism, the patentee is enabled to dispense with the use of Jacquard cards, and of all the apparatus or operations required for the reading and preparing of these cards from an original pattern or design. For this purpose, instead of these cards, a single plate of the same dimensions as one of these cards is employed. This plate has openings or perforations made in it corresponding in number to the horizontal needles of the Jacquard apparatus. These openings or perforations are stopped or closed when required by small iron rods, which are drawn forward at suitable times by electro-magnets, but when these small rods are not drawn by the electromagnets, the openings or perforations in the plate will be left open. The insulated wires of the coils of the electro-magnets are connected respectively to one of a series of thin metallic plates which come in contact with the pattern, the said pattern being for that purpose painted or drawn upon a flexible metallic sheet with an insulating varnish; or the design may be composed of a sheet-metal pattern fixed upon an insulating layer or surface. In order to prevent induction he winds the insulated wire of the coils of neighbouring electro-magnets in opposite directions, and arranges the magnets so that the positive pole of one magnet shall be next to the negative pole of its neighbour.

APPARATUS FOR TESTING SILK.

THIS apparatus has been invented by M. Froment, for testing the tenacity and elasticity of Silks of different sorts. The dynamometric portion of the apparatus is composed of a small thin and very flexible lamina of steel horizontally fixed in its centre. Its extremities are connected by two small rods to a single shaft rising to some height, and having its upper extremity finely split for the purpose of fixing the thread to be tested. When this thread is subjected to traction, it causes the lamina or spring above described to bend, and this motion is communicated to the hand of a dial-plate. When the thread snaps, this hand remains at the point to which it had been brought by the effect of the traction. The other portion of the apparatus by which the traction is effected, is a piece of clock-work which descends by its own weight. It is provided with a pair of pincers, into which the other end of the thread is inserted. By means of this apparatus M. Persoz has been enabled to make experiments on the tenacity of various silks, the results of which he has communicated to the Société Impériale d'Acclimatation. Thus, the threads tested being all of the length of half a metre, M. Persoz shows that the tenacity of the Calcutta cocoon is represented by 5·3, that of Teneriffe 5·2, while those from Avignon and Prussia were 12 and 12·9 respectively; that of Neuilly marked 8. The elasticity of these sorts per metre was respectively 9·9, 12·8, 14·4, 13·4, and 12·9. The following general conclusions derived from these experiments are interesting:—1. The male cocoon yields a finer and more tenacious silk than the female one. 2. The same species reared on different soil and in different climates does not yield threads of the same tenacity. The latter fact, M. Persoz thinks, should induce the Société d'Acclimatation to undertake experiments for the sake of determining with precision the effects which soil and climate, as well as the kind of food, produce on the silk worm.—*Galignani's Messenger.*

BITUMENIZED PAPER PIPES.

EXPERIMENTS have been made for testing a new kind of Pipe or Tube made of Paper and Bitumen, and intended to serve many of the purposes for which metal pipes and tubes have hitherto been employed. The ingenious idea of hardening paper by means of an admixture of bitumen under the influence of hydraulic pressure, so as to convert it into a substitute for iron, is due to M. Jaloureau, of Paris, who was present, and explained his process. The world has already become familiar with the universal utility and value of papier mâché, with the beautiful application of paper as a substitute, equal in appearance to stone or marble, for moulding, architectural castings, busts, and statues; it has also heard recently that the Chinese constructed their cannon of prepared paper lined with copper—that an eccentric character at Norwood has built himself a house of paper, and that our American friends have invented a veritable paper brick —but nothing probably has lately come before the British public in the way of paper so curious, and yet so commercially practicable and useful, as these bituminous paper pipes. The process of fabrication was fully explained, and the testing experiments, which were conducted under the great clock-tower at the Houses of Parliament, proved, to the surprise and satisfaction of all present, that the material, while it possessed all the tenacity of iron, with one-half its specific gravity, had double the strength of stoneware tubes, without, moreover, being liable to breakage, as in the case of other material, and which frequently causes a loss to the conductor of some 20 or 25 per cent. on the supply. In order to test their strength, two of these bituminous paper pipes of 5 inch bore and ½ inch thick, were subjected to hydraulic power, and they sustained, without breaking or bursting, the enormous pressure of 220 lb. to the square inch, or equivalent to 506 feet head of water, being double the actual pressure that the present London water-pipes of iron have to bear. In another experiment, to test the transverse strength of the material

of a pipe of 2 inch bore, it required a breaking weight to be applied
of 4 cwt. 1 qr. 13 lb. before the fracture was effected.—*Engineer.*

PATENT WATER PURIFIER.

THE Reports of Mr. Arthur Aikin, F.G.S., and, in 1849, Dr.
Alfred S. Taylor, Professor of Chemistry in Guy's Hospital, went to
show that only one-fifth of a grain, or a sixteenth part of the whole
amount of organic matter, was arrested by the then best known
process. Since then chemists both at home and abroad have applied
their energies to find a remedy, but they almost one and all agree in
the admission that science has been, if not wholly baffled, very considerably frustrated, in its attempts to arrive at a successful result.
But recently, however, "D. N.," a Correspondent in the *Times*,
inquired, "How water which is impregnated with lead could be
made wholesome?" This elicited a reply from, as we understand, a
chemist of repute in Berlin, who wrote: "Fortunately this can be
easily accomplished by means of well-burnt animal charcoal, which
may be used either in the manner of the whiting recommended by
Dr. Faraday, namely, by stirring up the charcoal in the water and
allowing it to subside, or by filtering the water through a vessel
containing the charcoal in coarse powder. An apparatus in a very
portable form has been recently invented for the purpose of applying
charcoal to the purification of water from both lead and organic
matter. Dr. Letheby has tested it very severely for the Drinking
Fountain Association, and has reported very favourably of its action.
It can be easily attached to the supply pipe of a cistern, and thus
used at the time of drawing the water."

The composition thus used as a purifying medium is a mixture of
animal charcoal, silica, and iron; and although it is sufficiently
porous to permit water passing through it as rapidly as by any known
method of filtration, it does not allow of the impurities penetrating
below its extreme surface, from which they can be removed at any
period by a brush or cloth. The solidity and indestructibility of this
purifying medium is a guarantee against its becoming deteriorated or
out of order.

It is but justice further to state, that it is the invention of a Mr.
Dahlke, a native of Berlin, who has further got the testimony of
Dr. Lankester to its entire efficiency; and that the low price at which
it is about to be publicly introduced as a portable apparatus for
domestic use, for travellers and for emigrants and others, places the
fact of the ingenious inventor's desire to give the utmost circulation
to its beneficial objects in the most favourable light.—*Mechanics'
Magazine.*

NEW WASHING MACHINES.

THE Board of Guardians of the parish of Hampstead, together
with the medical officer of health, the master of the workhouse,
and its matron, have been employed in a series of experiments to
test the relative merits of certain Washing Machines, with a view to
the selection of the most effective. The one upon which their choice

has fallen was only introduced into this country during the previous month, and as its powers are somewhat extraordinary as compared with others, we have purposely visited the workhouse at Hampstead to see it in operation. The construction of the machine is very simple, but this simplicity could not have been arrived at without a profound knowledge of the mechanical requirements necessary to fulfil the entire course of manipulations involved in washing every description of cloth. In this respect, the machine and its workings will present to those who are interested in mechanics a great deal that is new and well worthy their attention. Its mode of action is to press the linen between two ridged or beaded boards, then to slightly rub and turn it over, in such manner that the position of the linen is changed about fifty times every minute, and the soap and hot water are forced through it as often. The Board of Guardians certify that it is used by two of the inmates of the workhouse under the superintendence of the matron, and that it has been found to work to the entire satisfaction of the board; no hand rubbing whatever being requisite. The medical officer of health states that "it is calculated to promote economy, cleanliness, and public health;" and the master that "it has been used in washing all articles of wearing apparel, sheets, blankets, rugs, &c., in this house, and that upwards of one thousand articles have been washed weekly in twenty-five hours; the cost of fuel, soap, and soda not exceeding five shillings," and he adds, "every article washed as above has greatly improved in colour and sweetness when dry." It is certainly somewhat curious that the two most successful washing machines of late years have been from America. The American floating-ball machine was a most ingenious and useful contrivance, and had an enormous success in this country in opposition to the strenuous exertions of the whole body of laundresses to stay its progress. This machine, however, it is said, leaves that far behind; whether the economy in labour and cost to work it or its results be considered. It is but fair to state that the bulk of the things at the workhouse are of a coarse nature, such as house linens, blankets, and bed-ticks, but the more delicate muslins, cambrics, and lawns were submitted to it and were washed without the slightest injury; nor was hand-rubbing required to get the creased dirt out of the collars and the wristbands of shirts.—*Mechanics' Magazine.*

There has also been described to the British Association, an Atmospheric Washing Machine, by Mr. J. Fisher. The action of this machine was derived from streams of air forced through the water from below. The author in his paper observed, that for effectual use the water must never be of a higher temperature than 140° of Fahrenheit. It was stated that machines on this principle, driven by steam-power, had been for some time past in successful operation for cleansing the soiled laces at Messrs. Fisher's manufactory at Nottingham.

_____

BREAD-MAKING AND BAKING.

Dr. Lankester, F.R.S., has read to the Royal Institution a paper, of which the following is an abstract:—

The speaker stated that the principal object he had in view in delivering the discourse was to answer the question so often put as to what was "Aërated Bread." Bread, as used at table, assumed two forms dependent on its preparation, *vesiculated* and *unvesiculated*. The latter is known under the name of unleavened bread, and consists of such preparations of flour as biscuits, passover cakes, &c. Vesiculated bread is prepared in two ways, either by fermentation or aëration. In all cases fermented bread is made from the flour of wheat, or a mixture of this with the meal or flour of other grain. Barley, oats, maize, rye, will not alone make fermented bread. The meal of these grains is added to wheaten flour when they are made into bread.

Wheaten flour is made from the grains of wheat, which are the fruit of the plant. Six layers of cellular tissue were described between the albumen or perisperm of the seed and the outside of the grain:—1, the epicarp; 2, the sarcocarp; 3, the endocarp (these belong to the fruit); 4, the testa of the seed; 5, a secondary membrane; 6, the covering of the perisperm. These layers constitute the bran, which is separated from the fine flour. They contain the same chemical constituents as the flour, and so far from being objectionable, are a desirable addition to the flour. The gluten of the flour is represented in the bran by a principle, called by its discoverer cerealin. Like gluten it acts as a ferment, but its power in this respect is said to be destroyed at a temperature of 150° Fahr. It is soluble in cold water, and in that state acts as a ferment. Bran tea accelerates the changes of fermentation. It is this agent which, during the fermentation of bread, gives the brown colour to meal bread. Twenty-one ounces of wheat yield five ounces of bread, and sixteen ounces of fine flour. One pound of flour contains—

Water	...	...	2¼ ozs.	Gum	...	...	¼ oz.
Gluten	...	...	2 ,,	Fat ...	...	...	⅛ ,,
Albumen	...	...	¼ ,,	Cellulose	...	...	¼ ,,
Starch	...	...	9½ ,,	Ashes	...	...	¼ ,,
Sugar	...	...	1 ,,				

The gluten and albumen are flesh-forming substances, sugar and starch heat-giving. In the making of fermented bread yeast is added to the flour, and the gluten is put into a state of change, but not decomposed. A small portion of the starch is converted into glucose, which is decomposed, and alcohol formed, and carbonic acid produced. The carbonic acid gas escaping from the mass vesiculates the bread. The quantity of starch changed in this process is very small. It is expressed by the quantity of carbonic acid gas necessary for the vesiculation of the bread, as little or none of this gas escapes in the rising of the bread. The conversion of starch into glucose during the fermentation of the bread does not appear to be greater than is necessary to form the carbonic acid for vesiculation. The starch during fermentation acquires the power of being more quickly converted into glucose and its subsequent products than when heated and not exposed to this process. This is probably the great peculiarity of fermented bread, that the starch more rapidly passes into a state of change.

When the starch of wheat has already acquired this tendency to

H

change from the sprouting of the wheat, the flour forms a sweet, heavy, and sticky bread. In order to prevent this, alum is employed. Alum is not necessary to the making of palatable bread from "sound flour," but it is necessary for the making of saleable bread from unsound flour made from sprouted grain.

Bread is vesiculated without being fermented by two processes :— 1. By the addition of substances which during their decomposition give out carbonic acid, as carbonate of soda and hydrochloric acid. 2. By making the bread with water charged with carbonic acid. The first is the process recommended by the late Dr. Whiting, and sold in London under the name of Dodson's Unfermented Bread. The second process consists in mixing intimately water containing carbonic acid with flour, so that when the dough is baked the escape of the carbonic acid gas vesiculates the bread. This process is worked in London under Dr. Dauglish's patent,* and extensive machinery for making this bread has been erected by Messrs. Peek, Frean, and Co., at Dockhead. This is the "Aërated Bread." The process of making fermented bread is tedious ; the time employed for making the bread varying from three to twelve hours. By the aërating process the whole time taken, from the mixing flour and carbonated water to putting the loaves into the oven, is only 26 minutes. The necessity of handling the dough in kneading is also avoided by the use of machinery. Other advantages of this process are the saving of the starch destroyed in fermenting bread, and the absence of yeast and other substances—as potatoes—employed for facilitating the process of fermentation.

The baking of the bread is the same in all processes. At the same time the healthy digestion of bread depends much on the way in which this process is conducted. The regularity of the temperature and the condition of the atmosphere in the oven exert a considerable influence on the wholesome character of the bread. An oven has been recently constructed by Mr. Bonthron, of Regent-street, by which steam can be turned into the atmosphere of the oven. The action of the steam prevents the charring of the crust of the bread, allows of the interior expansion of the bread by preventing the hardening of the crust, and produces a natural varnish on the outside by reducing the sugar and gum on the outside to a liquid state.

With regard to the action of the two breads on the system, there can be no doubt that either, when properly prepared and baked, is adapted for general use. The question of flavour or appearance every one will decide for himself. In certain morbid conditions of the stomach fermented bread undergoes rapid changes, which are productive of inconvenience, and which is prevented by the use of unfermented bread.

ARTIFICIAL LEATHER.

At Ipswich has been realized an idea suggested in the *Builder*, of gathering up heaps of rubbish in the shape of leather cuttings, parings,

* Since the delivery of the lecture, my attention has been called to the fact that a patent was obtained by Mr. Luke Herbert for making bread with carbonic acid gas.—E. L.

and shavings ; and, by a peculiar process, partly chemical and partly mechanical, reducing them to a pulpy mass, and moulding them to any desired form for useful and ornamental purposes. The goods manufactured are more durable, and 20 to 30 per cent. cheaper than all other leather goods. The leather may be made as pliant as India-rubber, or as hard as board, and becomes adapted to an endless variety of uses, as bands for machinery, buckets for pumps (having all the suction of leather, with tenfold durability), and rubber for pencil-marks. It is adapted for all kinds of architectural ornamentation, indoor or out, and is an excellent material for picture-frames. Mr. R. Seager is stated, in the *Suffolk Chronicle*, to be the originator of this useful invention. The gathering of the shavings and scraps of leather reminds one of scraping the posted bills from the walls of Paris, many years since, to serve as a material for the celebrated *papier-mâché*, the French name for an English invention.

The Patent Painted and Gilded Leather Cloth has long been used extensively in France, supplied by the company in Cannon-street, London ; but here, as yet, it has only been occasionally used. In the New Westminster Palace Hotel, for example, it is hung in the smoking-room ; and, at the Royal Hotel, Bridge-street, Blackfriars, in the billiard and reading-rooms. Many of the designs already produced are very elegant ; and it may be made to present all the elegance of gilded leather, the *cuir doré* and the *cuir argenté* of the Middle Ages ; while its cost is but trifling as compared with those hangings with which, as we know, in the sixteenth and seventeenth centuries, all the houses of the Venetian nobles and gentry were hung. In England, too, it was greatly used, and examples may still be found in old houses. The cost of the painted and gilded leather-cloth may be called about 2s. 6d. a yard square, being enamelled by a patent process, which preserves the original beauty of the gilding, and allows it to be washed without injury. It is very durable, and it could be hung on new walls, on which it would not be safe to paint or put paper.

The above Company, who have manufactories also in France and Belgium, have large works at West Ham, where they employ about 150 men.—*Builder*.

_____

PROTECTION OF TEXTILE MATERIAL FROM FIRE.

Mr. F. A. ABEL, the chemist of the Royal Arsenal, Woolwich, has patented the means of affording Protection against Fire to Textile Materials in the raw or in the manufactured state, by impregnating such materials with insoluble metallic silicates within the fibre of the material. The process by which he effects this is as follows :—"I take," he says, "a solution of lead, of zinc, or, practically speaking, of any other metallic base capable of forming, by its action upon a soluble silicate, a double silicate, insoluble in water. For this purpose I prefer the use of a basic acetate of lead prepared, as is well known, by boiling sugar of lead and litharge with water ; and although I have found that solutions of various strengths will answer the purpose, yet that which I prefer is prepared by boiling together, or according to the following proportions—twenty-five pounds of sugar of lead, fifteen pounds of litharge, and forty gallons of water, for about half an hour, allowing to stand for about a couple of hours ; the decanted clear solution forms a liquor well adapted to my said purpose. When I want to use the liquor so prepared, and which, in the present instance, is a solution of basic acetate of lead, I take such a quantity of it as will be at least sufficient to cover completely the fabric or material which I intend to render unin-flammable ; or else the said fabric or material may in many cases be simply passed through the said liquid, raised to nearly the boiling point ; the object being simply to saturate or impregnate it thoroughly with the said liquor. This having been done, the fabric or material so saturated or impregnated with the said liquor is to be removed, and spread out for about twelve hours to the contact of the air. This hanging or spreading out of the fabric or material to the air may be dispensed with ; but I prefer to do so, the subsequent operation now to be described yielding then a better result. The material or fabric, after having been subjected to the first operation just described, should now be immersed for a period of from one to two hours, or thereabouts, into a hot and moderately strong solution of an alkaline silicate, by preference in silicate of soda. The material or fabric should then be withdrawn from the said bath of alkaline silicate, allowed to drain, washed thoroughly in soft water, and dried, when it will be found to have acquired the properties claimed for it."—*Mechanics' Magazine.*

NEW PATENT FIRE-ESCAPE.

DR. R. GARDINER HILL, of Inverness Lodge, Brentford, has in-troduced a Fire-Escape which consists of a rectangular framing of wood, bound together by means of tie rods. The bottom part of this frame is formed of a lattice-work of thin iron. One side of the frame is made with a half door, to afford facility for getting out of the escape. The frame is covered at the bottom and round the sides with non-inflammable canvas. A ring is securely fastened to the floor or window-sill of the house, and to this ring is simply hooked the end of a chain carrying a block through which the tackle of the escape is rove. The whole of the tackle and block are kept inside the frame when the escape is not in use, the hooking of the block-chain to the ring being the only thing to be done when the escape is required to be brought into use. The lowering rope is thrown to the persons below, or the occupant of the escape may lower himself by its means. The escape is then hauled up to bring down other persons, or for removing property from the upper part of a dwelling. The frame of the escape is fitted with castors on the inner side, and when not in use it stands upon them, and is covered with an ornamental drapery, which converts the escape into a con-venient ottoman. It can be used also as a dressing-table ; for which purpose it is placed on its side, and fitted with a loose deal top and muslin hangings in place of the cushion. In this way the fire-escape may at all times be kept near the window, from whence it would be used if required.—*Builder.*

PATENT PORTABLE BUILDINGS.

MESSRS. CALVERT, YORK, AND LIGHT, Parliament-street, London, the patentees, first form foundation shoes, consisting of a screw having a gaining thread, or thread of variable angle, cast or wrought upon it; and above the screw a sole-plate or loose plate, which supports either an iron standard or a socket; and one or more pockets for receiving the horizontal beams and upright posts or standards of the building. They prefer to commence the thread at the point of the screw, where they make it very narrow, and to increase the breadth of it, and increase also the angle which it makes with the axis of the screw as it rises from the point towards the sole or base-plate, the greatest diameter of the screw being equal to two-thirds of the diameter of the base-plate. The principal standards are supported directly by the screwed foundation shoes; and the intermediate standards are tenoned into mortises formed in horizontal beams, which extend from one foundation shoe to the next, and which are held at either end by the pockets before mentioned. Framed panels form the wall, and are dropped down from above between the standards, being held in position by tongues or fillets of hard wood or other suitable material. These framed panels are formed hollow, and are composed, by preference (although not necessarily) of Bielefeld's fibrous slab, which secures the interior of the building from extremities of temperature. The edges of the fibrous panels are received in rabbets formed in the wooden framing of the panel. The roofing is composed of grooved rafters, the grooves of which hold canvassed slabs of the aforesaid fibrous material, or a roofing of any other suitable material. The whole of the fibrous slabs are waterproofed with a suitable composition. Buildings constructed in the aforesaid manner are said to be exceedingly light and portable, and easily put together without the aid of skilled labour. The invention also consists in the employment of a gaining screw for fencing posts, gate-posts, and other purposes.—*Builder.*

DE TIVOLI'S NEW PATENT OMNIBUS.

THIS new Omnibus is divided into separate, well-ventilated compartments, disposed in two rows, back to back, the passengers sitting alone, each in one compartment, facing the pavement on their respective sides. A small window, with a shutter on each side, puts in communication the contiguous compartments, if agreeable to both parties to converse. The compartments are fitted like first-class railway-carriages. A portion at the back of the omnibus is left undivided to contain four persons, just as a four-wheel cab or a private carriage, and constitutes a second-class carriage. Palmer's patent signal or a bell puts each passenger in communication with the conductor. Access to, and egress from, the compartments is obtained by two steps (as in private carriages) leading to a kind of landing or railed platform, upon which open the doors of the compartments. This platform runs round the forepart of the carriage, to give to all the passengers on each side the advantage of entering or leaving the carriage always on the near-side pavement. The doors may be kept open or shut by means of well-adapted self-acting springs.

This omnibus runs as lightly as any other on the metropolitan roads. It has been weighed at the General Post, and certified to be only twenty-two hundredweight and three-quarters; while twenty-five and even twenty-seven hundredweight is not an uncommon range for omnibuses now plying on the London thoroughfares.

JAPANESE MANUFACTURES.

PROFESSOR DOWSON has exhibited to the Royal Asiatic Society a variety of specimens of the Arts and Manufactures of Japan, brought from Jeddo by Captain Creagh, of the 86th Regiment. These articles excited a great deal of interest, not only by their excellence and novelty, but by the surprisingly low prices at which they were purchased. Captain Creagh, having been one of the first who visited Jeddo, made his purchases at something like the real price, before it was unduly raised by the demands and ignorance of foreigners. Among the articles exhibited was a cabinet, beautifully inlaid with different woods; a very good telescope, which cost about 1s. 6d.; a very neat little clock, worked by a weight, the index being a small pin, which, as it descends, marks the time upon a scale forming the front of the clock. As the length of the Japanese hour differs in various seasons, the clock is furnished with a series of scales, or figure plates, for accommodating it to these changes. The cost of this clock was 9s. There were also several specimens of illustrated books, the woodcuts of which were very neatly executed, and exhibited a good knowledge of perspective, as well as of drawing; also a large number of prints in colours, somewhat roughly executed, but spirited. These are sold at an exceedingly low rate, and show that the art of printing in colours is well known in Japan. The paper used for pocket-handkerchiefs, and various other kinds of paper, attracted a great deal of notice for their fineness and extreme tenacity of fibre. There was also a very showy fabric, the woof of which was of silk and the warp of gilded and coloured paper, forming an excellent material for the decoration of rooms, tents, &c.

THE MIRACULOUS CABINET.

UNDER this title an extraordinary work of art, invented and produced by H. Nadolsky, has been exhibited in the Dudley Gallery, Egyptian Hall. This Cabinet, measuring only 5 feet high, 3 feet wide, and 18 inches deep, contains 150 pieces of furniture, of the same size as in ordinary use, as—a judge's large table, with ornaments, books, and six chairs; four large card-tables, two Chinese tables, a smoking-table, a lady's work-table, two beautiful large Chinese toilet-tables, a large chess-table, four work-boxes, four flower-pots with flowers, a what-not, a large candelabra, a full-sized bed with hangings, and a baby's swing cot; a round toilet table, an embroidery frame, a large flower-table, five small Chinese lamps, two large ditto, two Chinese toilet candlesticks, twelve fancy boxes, a footstool, a painter's easel, four music-stands, a dining-table with twenty-four covers laid complete; four large dishes, twenty-eight plates, thirty cups, saltcellars, &c.; a large chandelier containing twelve wax lights; nine garden chairs, four parlour candlesticks, a Chinese writing-desk, a fancy inkstand with wax tapers, rulers, and bell; a tea-tray, a drawing-room table, a throne, a throne-chair, four small flower-tables, a large table, inlaid with specimens of shells, glass top, &c., &c. It certainly is a most ingenious work of mechanical skill. When the various articles are put together and spread over the apartment, the notion of putting them all back again into the snug little cabinet seems scarcely less than absurd.

PATENT CERAMIC WOOD.

MR. J. C. MARTIN, of Barnes, has patented a Plastic Material, resembling Wood in its finished state. It may readily be moulded by pressure into moulds of any form: it admits of carving or cutting to any extent required; may with facility be glass-papered; and will receive the highest French polish.

The material is in great part composed of fibrous pulp of as long a description as possible (to which it owes its strength), which is worked together with resinous and gelatinous gums, acted upon chemically, and as nearly to imitate the nature of wood as possible.

The inventor says:—"It is unlike all the ordinary descriptions of moulded papier-mâché or carton pierre, as it contains no earthy or non-fibrous substance in order that it may be made to take a fine impression: to this it in a great measure owes its strength and the facility with which it may be carved and finished, and renders it suitable for the manufacture of many articles to which other descriptions of plastic materials could not be applied; and, at the same time, from articles made from it being homogeneous throughout, they do not chip with a blow, as is the case with ordinary moulded ornamented papier mâché articles, which are faced over with a weak, readily-moulded material, in order to take an impression."

It was while engaged in experimenting with various woods, with a view to their conversion into pulp for the manufacture of paper, that it occurred to Mr. Martin to replace the pulp and the gums of which the wood had been deprived, varying the proportions to meet the circumstances, and upon this the invention is based.—*Builder.*

PATENT COMPOSITE BLOCKS FOR PAVEMENT.

THE novelty of the invention consists in the combination together of both wood and stone; and the cement by which both materials are thus united together is described as being impervious to water; whilst the materials themselves are rendered less liable to abrasion by ordinary traffic. It is notorious to all persons living in London, that wood and stone pavements are liable to two great objections— the wood in wet weather being dangerous to horses, and the stone causing great annoyance from the incessant noise of carriages rolling over granite blocks. It is supposed that a combination of wood and stone—such as has been effected in the construction of "the Composite Blocks" will present these three advantages—"cleanliness, safety to horses, and comparative freedom from noise." An experiment has been already made with the "composite blocks." Three years ago a specimen was laid down at the Holborn end of Little Queen street, the great thoroughfare from Holborn to Covent Garden. This specimen has been examined by Mr. Braithwaite, the civil engineer, and Mr. Trehearne, surveyor to the Board of Works in the district; and both express the opinion, that having withstood the traffic to which it was exposed for thirty-three months without requiring repair, its general adoption would be advantageous to the public.—*London Review.*

KILN-DRYING GRAIN.

Mr. W. Norton has patented certain improvements in Kilns for Drying Grain. This drying-kiln the patentee forms with a rotating circular head or platform, mounted on a vertical shaft, and driven by suitable gearing. To the centre of this rotating kiln-head or platform (which is to be heated by fire placed underneath, or by means of heated air) the grain is supplied by an adjustable leading spout, fitted at its lower end with a sliding or telescope tube, which is intended to lengthen or contract the spout, and thus increase or decrease at pleasure the supply of grain to the kiln-head or rotating platform, the spout forming a channel for leading down the grain direct from the grain store. Extending from the centre of the circular rotating head or platform to its circumference is a rotating brush, formed of wire and hair, or other suitable elastic material set helically around a horizontal axle. This brush receives a slow rotatory motion, and is for the purpose of distributing the grain over the surface of the kiln-head or rotating platform, and of discharging it over that edge thereupon after it has, by being exposed on the rotating heating surface, been sufficiently dried. The apparatus may be driven by steam or other power, and regulated by a pendulum.—*Mechanics' Magazine.*

MANUFACTURE OF GLASS.

Mr. Balmain, St. Helen's, has provisionally specified certain improvements in the Manufacture of Glass and other vitrified substances. The object of the invention is to ensure the removal, from the furnace or pot in which the raw materials for forming glass are placed, of each portion of the glass mixture immediately it is vitrified, and thus to separate it from the unvitrified mass. This object is attained in an open furnace by constructing it with the two beds, one horizontal or nearly so, on which the raw material is introduced, and the other joining it (with an inclination of about 1 foot in 6 feet, more or less), which removes the material as fast as it fluxes, and perfectly vitrifies it by the time it has run from 6 to 8 feet. The advantages gained, it is said, are an economy of fuel and labour, and an improvement in the quality of the glass.—*Builder.*

BOOT AND SHOEMAKING MACHINERY.

Mr. C. H. Southall has patented an improved apparatus for

Making and Finishing Boots and Shoes. This relates to that description of boots and shoes in which the soles and heels are fixed to the upper-leathers or welts by screwed pins. The machinery consists of self-acting movements by which the wire is screwed or forced into the boot or shoe, and afterwards cut off by shears, for moving the boot or shoe the distance required, and giving continuous rotary motion to the cutters and glazing wheels. By means of a wheel with teeth upon a portion of its periphery a revolving motion is given at certain intervals to the wire for forming the screwed pins, the threads of which are made by a screwplate or dies, the entrance of the pins into the sole and welt or upper-leather going on at the same time. During the stopping of the revolving motion of the wire, the pins are cut off by shears or cutters put in motion by a cam driven in any suitable manner, the boot or shoe being moved by dividing wheels according to the required distance between the screwed pins. After the sole has been screwed on, the boot or shoe is removed to another part of the apparatus, the table of which is moved so as to press the edge of the sole against a circular cutter put in motion by wheels and pulleys in the usual manner, a guard being employed to maintain the correct action of the cutter. After the sole is cut, it is pressed against circular polished surfaces and a brush, so as to give it the desired finish. The patentee uses an intermediate shaft, in which he places wheels, cams, or tappets, which produce the required operations.

Mr. C. Stannet has also patented certain improvements in apparatus used in the manufacture of Boots and Shoes, or other coverings for the feet. The patentee claims a resilient, or spring bed or table, disengaged and fixed at intervals, accordingly as the piercing and pegging or movement of the article under operation takes place. Also a construction of carriage for the support of the article under operation, mounted on castors or other contrivances to admit of motion on the table in any direction required. Likewise an arrangement of escapement for delivering the pegs one by one as required ; and a certain construction of reciprocating knife. Also blocking or forming the soles and other parts of boots and shoes by a bag filled with shot or sand. Also a hammer arranged and actuated for the hammering of leather ; and certain moulds mounted on suitable tongs or levers, for partially moulding parts of boots and shoes ; all as described with reference to the drawings. — *Mechanics' Magazine.*

CIVIL ENGINEERING AND MATHEMATICS.

SIR DAVID BREWSTER, in his Address on opening the Winter Session of the University of Edinburgh, of which he is Principal, made the following admirable remarks on the necessity of mathematical attainments to Civil Engineers :—" Great Britain has always been distinguished among civilized nations for the magnitude and splendour of her public works ; but it is a remarkable circumstance that the engineers who executed them were neither mathematicians, chemists, nor natural philosophers, but, generally speaking, persons of humble station, who, by habits of observation almost innate, by powers of discrimination almost intuitive, and by practical know-ledge gathered in the workshop or acquired in manual labour, gradu-ally rose to professional celebrity. Mr. Watt himself informed me that he never attended Dr. Black's lectures on chemistry, as has been alleged; that he had been unfortunately prevented, by the necessary avocations of his business, from attending any other lec-tures, and that he had a natural inaptitude for mathematics; and yet there was no one among the chemical and mechanical philoso-phers of his day whose knowledge of these subjects, within certain limits, was so varied and correct, and who had treasured up with equal care those irrefragable results which could be safely applied in the construction of great works. Mr. Telford, also, had not only an inaptitude, but a singular distaste for mathematical studies, and he never even made himself acquainted with the elements of geo-metry. So remarkable, indeed, was this peculiarity, that when we had occasion to recommend a young friend as a neophyte in his office, and founded our recommendation on his having distinguished himself in mathematics, he did not hesitate to say that he consi-dered such acquirements as rather disqualifying than fitting him for the situation. That this opinion, which is far from being an uncommon one among engineers, is not utterly groundless, may be inferred from a comparison of the labours of some foreign engineers who were great mathematicians with those of Watt, Smeaton, Brindley, Rennie, Telford, and Isambard Brunel; but we are clearly of opinion that such a doctrine cannot be gravely maintained by any person who has viewed the subject in all its phases. If sound practical knowledge and habits of accurate observation should be found incompatible with mathematical and physical attainments, we would at once pronounce in favour of 'science' as the distin-guishing quality of the engineer; but we hold both to be essentially requisite in the construction of works in which the materials are exposed to the disintegrations of chemical and atmospherical agents; to the superincumbent pressure of solid and fluid bodies; to the action of complicated mechanical forces; to the direct assaults of the lightning and the tempest, and to various contingent pressures which require to be foreseen and resisted."

THE DEBUSSCOPE.

A SMALL instrument has lately made its appearance, which seems to be of the greatest utility to designers, draughtsmen, painters, and other trades engaged in the ornamental and decorative arts. It is of French origin, called a Debusscope, we presume from the name of its inventor. It consists of two silvered plates of great reflective power, placed together in a framework of cardboard or wood, at the angle of 70°. On being placed over a small picture or design of any kind, no matter how rough, or whether good or bad, the debusscope will reflect the portion immediately under the eye, on all sides, forming the most beautiful and elaborate designs; and, by being slowly moved over the picture, will multiply new designs to any extent. No matter what the subject is on which the instrument is placed, the result is marvellous : there is produced from the most unlikely objects, such as scraps of paper-hangings, blots of ink, leaves, flowers, bits of lace, &c., an endless series of new and really beautiful designs. The debusscope, although of the same species, possesses an advantage over the kaleidoscope. The latter is merely suggestive of any effect likely to prove useful to a designer ; there are no means of retaining any particular pattern which may literally "turn up" until it can be transferred to paper. The debusscope gives the design, and that in such a manner that it can be made stationary at pleasure until copied ; it therefore recommends itself at once as an inexhaustible source of new patterns to draughtsmen, calico printers, dyers, paperhangers, painters, and others ; and as it is produced and sold at a price which brings it easily within the reach of all such trades, we have no doubt that it will soon be extensively used.

_____

MACHINERY FOR TEACHING.

Mr. Smalley, of King's College, has constructed two very efficient aids to teachers of elementary science, which are manufactured by Messrs. Elliott, in the Strand. The first is a machine demonstrative of the composition of forces, in which the pressure equivalent to two other pressures is shown to be represented by the diagonal, when the component pressures are represented by the sides. The second is a very simple revolving radius, which carries with it a pendulous perpendicular, both graduated, as also is the line of the base. The character and the approximate values of the trigonomical functions are exhibited, in all parts of the revolution, in a manner singularly clear and free from the confusion which attends a diagram of several instances. There are also some illustrations of the disused linear definitions.

_____

THE TROCHEIDOSCOPE.

This beautiful instrument has been constructed by Messrs. Horne and Thornthwaite, of Newgate-street, and is the invention of Mr. Thomas Goodchild, architect, of Guildford, designed for displaying . various effects of the combination of colours upon a novel principle—some of them in a most brilliant manner. The Trocheidoscope is a train of wheelwork, so arranged that by gently turning the handle the horizontal disc table is made to revolve at varying speeds, at the will of the operator, from fifty to two thousand revolutions per minute. In the centre of the disc table is a carefully-fitted spindle, with a screw and flange at the lower end, and a shoulder at the upper end, just under which is a universal joint for adjusting the position of the topmost portion, upon which the patterns or devices are to be hung when exhibited. Proceeding from the side of the instrument is an arm of brass, with a small appendage or hook at the top for receiving the strings of the patterns, and a spring to act as a check upon the discs used in the Protean experiments. The spindle is jointed near the top to give a peculiar vibratory motion to the pattern when fitted. As the spindle revolves it strikes the sides of the circular hole by which the pattern is suspended, and so imparts to it a shaking motion just sufficient to fill up the pattern with all the colours on the disc below, but then lost to the eye by its rapid revolution. If the pattern were perfectly still, the colours would not appear; but if allowed slight motion as above described, the colours are reproduced upon the principle—that of images being retained upon the eye, which is thus elucidated in a very beautiful manner.—*Described and Figured in the Mechanics' Magazine.*

CRYPTOGRAPHY.

MR. R. A. BROOMAN has patented a Crytographic Machine, or apparatus for carrying on secret correspondence.

The object of this invention is to provide a machine or apparatus, by means of which secret correspondence, for diplomatic and other purposes, may be carried on conveniently and so as effectually to prevent the deciphering of the despatches by any person not in possession of the key to the same. The main feature of the invention consists in the employment of several pairs of alphabets, one alphabet of each pair being capable of longitudinal motion along the other, so as to bring different letters of the two alphabets opposite each other. By arranging the several pairs of alphabets according to positions indicated by means of a "key-word" and a standard pair of alphabets, and transmitting in succession the letters found on one of the two alphabets opposite to the proper letters of the despatch on the other, the several pairs of alphabets being successively used, a despatch in cipher may be sent, which despatch may be readily interpreted by reading the letters of one of the sets of alphabets found opposite to the received letters on the other set—or, in other words, by reversing the sending process. In the machine or apparatus devised by the inventor for these purposes, the moveable alphabets are printed or written on endless bands or tapes, which pass round rollers, and may be driven by pinions or otherwise. All the pairs of alphabets are mounted on an axle, which is caused to rotate by a crank handle or otherwise, so as to bring successive pairs of alphabets into view.— *Mechanics' Magazine.*

IMPROVED HARMONIUMS.

IN this improvement, patented by Professor Wheatstone, the wind chest is placed above the somnier, and the somnier itself is inverted, having its note frames and vibratory above, and its palettes or valves below, and opening downwards; so that by causing one of their ends to project beyond the front board of the somnier, the plungers of the finger keys can be made to act directly upon the palettes, and open the valves required. The wind apparatus is placed vertically in the instrument, and consists of three cuckoo bellows, two of which serve as feeders, and the third as a reservoir. The feeders are actuated by two pedals or treadles, to which they are connected by bands or straps passing over small pulleys secured to the back board of the reservoir, thus dispensing with the lever spindle and short arm of the ordinary instrument. The wind which enters the feeders in these instruments when distended by their internal springs is forced by the descent of the treadles through valves in the middle board of the bellows into the reservoir, from whence it passes through wind passages at the back of the reservoir, and through the somnier into the wind chest.—*Ibid.*

SCHEUTZ'S CALCULATING MACHINE.

THE inventors of this ingenious and complicated engine are the two Messrs. Scheutz, father and son, Swedes, who were stimulated with the ambition of rivalling Mr. Babbage by reading, so long ago as 1834, an account of his invention, published in the *Edinburgh Review*. For twenty years they toiled unremittingly, and at last produced an engine which seemed absolutely capable of thinking. With the costly result of their patient labour, packed up in a box, six feet by two feet, they came to England, and about the year 1855 took out a patent for it in this country. Mr. Babbage warmly espoused the invention, and gave his cordial co-operation to the ingenious Swedes, who had succeeded in overcoming all the mechanical impediments which had prevented him from realizing his fondest expectations. The machine was taken to Paris, and shown there at the Great Exhibition. A gold medal was unanimously awarded to the inventors. For some reasons or other, unexplained, both the English and the French Governments—Governments who have so often, not wastefully, but with the greatest advantage to their people, lavished large sums of money to secure accurate astronomical and other tables—let this marvellous machine pass away from them. An enlightened and public-spirited merchant of the United States, John F. Rathbone, Esq., bought the machine and presented it to the Dudley Observatory, at Albany, where he resides. The apathy of the French and English Governments, or their want of appreciation of the valuable instrument offered them, has been the theme of regret to all who can appreciate its national importance and value. The Registrar-General and Dr. Farr have, however, succeeded in wiping away the reproach from the English Government. They obtained the requisite funds, some 1200*l.*, for procuring a copy of the machine now in America. It has been constructed in admirable style, with some admirable improvements, by Messrs. Donkin, the civil engineers, from working drawings by the Messrs. Scheutz. It has for some time commenced its labours by printing some tables relating to life assurance, of considerable importance. It is almost hopeless to describe the operation of a machine of this kind without the aid of diagrams.—*American Paper.*

Our Transatlantic contemporary omits to state that to our eminent engineer, Mr. W. Gravatt, F.R.S., is due the honour of having greatly assisted the Messrs. Scheutz in their great labour, more especially during their stay in England, when Mr. Gravatt generously accommodated the Messrs. Scheutz in his house at Westminster, in order that they might complete the engine for the British Government. An interesting narrative of the circumstances will be found in *Stories of Inventors and Discoverers in Science and the Useful Arts*, by the Editor of the present work ; and the former volume contains a large engraving of Mr. Babbage's engine (the only one ever published), now in the museum of King's College, London.

SCHOOL OF ART AND SCIENCE AT THE CRYSTAL PALACE.

IT was a leading purpose in the first foundation of the Crystal Palace that its courts and collections should be a means of education by the eye; and that the treasures of art and beauty, collected and stored up from every part where greatness and civilization had left them, should here present a new and advanced starting-point for the student. With lavish means the Directors have been enabled to bring together the most complete collections of their kind in the world; and now what formerly occupied years of study, and difficult and costly travel, may be judged of in almost as many hours. This bringing together and into series the great examples of art, so that comparison may enlarge and amend our judgment, is, perhaps, the greatest aim achieved by the Crystal Palace. We have often pointed out the the value of the collections, and urged making use of them. In the Crystal Palace has been collected such a complete representation of the schools of antique sculpture as no academy or single collection in the world can show. The same may also be said of architecture; and other arts and sciences could be particularized. It is especially with a view to utilize all these particular advantages for purposes of education that the Directors have organized the School of Art, Science, and Literature; while at the same time they have borne in mind the necessity of making the system pursued as complete as possible in all its branches, and capable of every practical development. The Directors have also extended many privileges to the pupils, such as the free admission to the Palace on all days when the classes are attended; and the purchase-right to a full season-ticket, admitting to the Palace on every occasion when open to the public, with some other rights, for 10s. 6d. Professorships have been arranged to utilize the whole eastern range of Fine Art Courts, and also the series on the western side. The magnificent collection stored in the Industrial and Technological Museum, arranged by Dr. Price, in the galleries at the end of the central transept, and described by us in some detail, may also be particularized as thus available. For the use of these and other collections every practical facility is given.

We quote from the *Builder* this merited tribute to the well-directed energies of the management of the Crystal Palace.

THE PATENT "ECLIPSE" SPUR-BOX.

MESSRS. GULLICK AND Co., of Pall Mall, have patented an improvement in Spur-boxes, which removes the well-known objections to the spur-box hitherto in use; and in which, in consequence of the door opening below, it places the spur too near the ground, renders it inconvenient in walking, especially on soft ground; while the spur is liable to break, in the wearer coming down stairs, or in dancing: the box is also liable to get filled with dirt, the boot-heels are very unsightly, and it is inconvenient to insert and take out the spur.

The Patent "Eclipse" Spur-box at once removes these several objections. The spur is elevated to the top of the heel, by placing the door of the box above instead of below. The space hitherto lost is therefore gained, and thus the spur sets more elegantly.

This Eclipse spur-box may be inserted in low heels, and the spurs can be more easily used. It will fit all kinds of spurs at present in use; but the patentees call attention to their registered spurs, which have the plugs reversed, to suit more perfectly the action of the improved spur-box.

_____

IMPROVED IRON MANUFACTURE.

THE President (Mr. Bidder) of the Institution of Civil Engineers, in his annual address, referred to the recent great changes in the Iron Manufacture, and stated that—

The result has been that whereas the annual "make" of a blast furnace in the year 1750 was only about 300 tons, now it ranges from 5000 to 10,000 tons per annum, and in a few cases amounted even to 15,000 tons per annum. In reference to wrought iron it was said that the plan of reversing the rolls has been considerably extended, and occasionally a second pair of rolls is placed close to the first, running continuously in the opposite direction, so that the iron can be rolled either in coming forward or in going back. Plates 1¼ inches thick by 3 feet wide and 20 feet long, and plates 4½ inches thick by 3 feet wide and 15 feet long, have been rolled, as well as bars up to 72 feet long. Most of the improvements in the manufacture of steel have been introduced within the last half century. Cast-steel bells, weighing 53 cwt. each, have been made in this country, and castings of steel weighing 100 cwt. in Austria. Large plates and very heavy bars have also been made of puddled steel produced direct from cast-iron; and, lastly, steel wire, when hardened to about a deep blue temper, is found capable of carrying 130 tons per square inch. More than one process has been used in the production of cheap steel, which has been found by recent experiments to possess nearly double the strength of ordinary iron, accompanied by other valuable properties. With regard to the applications of iron, a new era commenced with the construction of the Conway and Britannia Bridges, as the elaborate experiments made prior to their construction tended to prove that previously received theories were in some respects erroneous. Again, the building erected for the Great Exhibition in 1851, from its lightness and security, called attention to the hitherto undeveloped capabilities of the combined use of cast and wrought iron for such purposes.

The improvements in the artillery and projectiles of the present day, which had resulted from the efforts of civil engineers, are calculated to lead to important changes in modern warfare. Simultaneous with the rapid advance in the destructiveness of weapons of offence in attack, there was a necessity for a corresponding alteration in the means of resistance. These subjects have led to elaborate researches and experiments for ascertaining the best qualities of metals to resist the enormous strains and concussions which have to be encountered, and the best dispositions in which to employ them. Iron-coated ships were for some years regarded as a probable coming necessity; but it was not until about the end of the year 1858, that the Admiralty for the first time seriously considered the subject. This resulted in the designs on which the _Warrior_ and _Black Prince_ are now being constructed. The problem is one of great difficulty. An enormous weight of armour has to be added to the weights hitherto carried. At the same time greater speed is demanded, and that involves increased weight of engines and a larger supply of fuel. Then, again, the weight is top-weight and wing-weight, which has to be carried on fine lines for speed. To reconcile these conditions with the practical points in a war vessel, and to give such a ship good seafaring qualities, to make her a good cruiser, and also well suited for a voyage, and for the probable conditions that would attach to a European war, is a problem which may well employ the professional skill of naval architects, and of every member of the Institution.

Natural Philosophy.

THE President, Sir Benjamin Brodie, in his Address on St. Andrew's Day, thus comprehensively sketched the foundation and history of the Royal Society :—

It was on the 28th of November, just two hundred years ago, that several eminent individuals, who had previously been in the habit of meeting for the purpose of communicating with each other on subjects of common interest, assembled in Gresham College, and agreed to form themselves into a Society, having for its object the promoting of physico-mathematical experimental learning. When they reassembled in the following week, it was reported to them that what they proposed was highly approved by the reigning Monarch, who intimated at the same time his desire to do what lay in his power towards promoting so useful an undertaking. Accordingly, steps were taken for the incorporation of the Society under Royal Charter, that charter being conferred on them, in due form, two years afterwards. Such was the origin of the institution, to which the world is indebted for the long series of scientific memoirs contained in the 150 volumes of the *Philosophical Transactions*. The publication of these *Transactions*, however, was not begun until the year 1665, and then only in the form of a few pages, produced at uncertain intervals, which, being collected, made a thin volume at the end of the year. Many years elapsed before the *Transactions* became of larger dimensions. But we must not, therefore, suppose because so little was done in the way of publication, that little was really done for the promotion of the objects which the founders of the Royal Society had in view. At this time, Lord Bacon had already pointed out the right method to be pursued for the advancement of learning ; and the abstract science of Geometry, inherited from an ancient nation, had been partially applied in the investigation of the physical sciences. Nevertheless, it cannot be said that any of these sciences were otherwise than in an infant state ; and some of those which are now the greatest subjects of attention, for instance Chemistry, and Geology, had scarcely been called into existence. There was, indeed, as yet, no sufficient number of facts collected on which the super-structure of science could be raised. The founders of the Royal Society well comprehended what was required. They had the good sense to begin at the beginning, and their first endeavours were to collect a large number of facts by a course of experimental inquiry. The early records of the Society furnish us with valuable information as to this part of their labours, and give us a more just notion of what the society accomplished in those days than can be obtained from the *Philosophical Transactions* themselves. The famous Hooke was appointed experimentalist ; and an account of the various experiments made during the above period would of itself form an instructive volume. It might not, indeed, add much to our knowledge, but it would show us in what manner much of that knowledge with which we are now familiar had its origin; at the same time furnishing a grand example of the caution and circumspection with which all experimental inquiries should be conducted. With the gradual extension of knowledge, the method of inquiry necessarily became modified. The *Transactions* gradually increased in size, and longer and more elaborate investigations superseded the brief memoirs of which the earlier volumes were composed.

It is not, observed Sir Benjamin, in conclusion, for the Fellows of the Royal Society to form an opinion of what the society has done during the last few years; but we are at liberty to refer to what has been done by their predecessors, and with regard to them we are justified in the conclusion that they have well performed the task which they have undertaken. In adding to human knowledge, they have added to human happiness. Standing apart from politics, they have pursued an independent course, having no selfish objects in view, but acting harmoniously with the Government of the day whatever it might be. Every existing Fellow of the Society will, assuredly, join in the desire that this course may be pursued so as to maintain the dignity of Science, and do honour to our country—

Alterum in lustrum meliusque semper
Proroget ævum.

EDUCATIONAL SCIENCE.

SIR DAVID BREWSTER, Principal of the University of Edinburgh, in his Address on the opening of the Winter Session of 1860, thus eloquently characterized the scientific requirements of the times :—

The advances which have recently been made in the mechanical and useful arts have already begun to influence our social condition, and must affect still more deeply our systems of education. The knowledge which used to constitute a scholar and fit him for social and intellectual intercourse will not avail him under the present ascendancy of practical science. New and gigantic inventions mark almost every passing year—the colossal tubular bridge, conveying the monster train over an arm of the sea; the submarine cable, carrying the pulse of speech beneath 2000 miles of ocean; the monster ship, freighted with thousands of lives; and the huge rifle gun, throwing its fatal, but unchristian, charge across miles of earth or of ocean. New arts, too, useful and ornamental, have sprung up luxuriantly around us. New powers of nature have been evoked, and man communicates with man across seas and continents, with more certainty and speed than if he had been endowed with the velocity of the racehorse or provided with the pinions of the eagle. Wherever we are, in short, art and science surround us. They have given birth to new and lucrative professions. Whatever we purpose to do they help us. In our houses they greet us with light and heat. When we travel we find them at every stage on land, and at every harbour on our shores. They stand beside our board by day, and beside our couch by night. To our thoughts they give the speed of lightning, and to our timepieces the punctuality of the sun; and, though they cannot provide us with the boasted lever of Archimedes to move the earth, or indicate the spot upon which we must stand could we do it, they have put into our hands tools of matchless power by which we can study the remotest worlds; and they have furnished us with an intellectual plummet by which we can sound the depths of the earth and count the cycles of its endurance. In his hour of presumption and ignorance man has tried to do more than this; but though he was not per-

I

mitted to reach the heavens with his cloud-capt tower of stone, and has tried in vain to navigate the aërial ocean, it was given him to ascend into Empyrean by chains of thought which no lightning could face and no comet strike; and though he has not been allowed to grasp with an arm of flesh the products of other worlds, or tread upon the pavement of gigantic planets, he has been enabled to scan, with more than an eagle's eye, the mighty creations in the bosom of space—to march intellectually over the mosaics of sidereal systems, and to follow the adventurous Phaëton in a chariot which can never be overturned.

MAGNETIC PHENOMENON.

M. Ruhmkorff has the following notice in the *Comptes Rendus*, vol. i. p. 166 :—" If a stay (*bride*) of soft iron be pressed against one of the poles of an artificial magnet, the soft iron is observed to become hard, it is more difficult to file. If the stay be removed, it loses its hardness and resumes all the properties of soft iron."

FIXATION OF THE MAGNETIC IMAGE.

The name of Magnetic Image is given to the appearance observed when iron filings are placed on a paper screen over the poles of a powerful magnet. It may be fixed in the following manner :—A sheet of waxed paper is placed over the poles of a powerful magnet, and kept in its position by means of a screen interposed between the paper and the poles. The image is then developed in the usual way; and when this is effected, a hot brick or crucible cover is brought near enough to melt the wax. The melted wax by capillarity penetrates the agglomeration of filings, just as water penetrates a mass of sand. It is necessary that the layer of wax have a considerable thickness, in order to be sufficient for the action of capillarity. On cooling, the wax retains the filings in their place, and they present the same appearance as if still under the influence of the magnet.—*M. J. Nickles; Comptes Rendus.*

THE MAGNET AND EARTHQUAKE.

The Japanese have discovered that a few seconds previous to an Earthquake the Magnet temporarily loses its power, and have ingeniously constructed a light frame supporting a horse-shoe magnet, beneath which is a cup of bell metal. To the armature is attached a weight, so that upon the magnet becoming paralysed the weight drops, and, striking the cup, gives the alarm. Every one in the house then seeks the open air for safety.

SPOTS ON THE SUN AND MAGNETISM.

On the 1st of September, 1859, at 11h. 18m. a.m., a distinguished astronomer, Mr. Carrington, had directed his telescope to the Sun, and was engaged in observing its spots, when suddenly two intensely luminous bodies burst into view on its surface. They moved side by side through a space of about 35,000 miles, first increasing in brightness, then fading away; in five minutes they had vanished. They did not alter the shape of a group of large black spots which lay directly in their paths. Momentary as this remarkable phenomenon was, it was fortunately witnessed and confirmed, as to one of the bright lights, by another observer, Mr. Hodgson, at Highgate, who, by a happy coincidence, had also his telescope directed to the great luminary at the same instant. It may be, therefore, that these two gentlemen have actually witnessed the process of feeding the sun, by the fall of meteoric matter ; but however this may be, it is a remarkable circumstance, that the observations at Kew show that on the very day, and at the very hour and minute of this unexpected and curious phenomenon, a moderate but marked magnetic disturbance took place ; and a storm or great disturbance of the magnetic elements occurred four hours after midnight, extending to the southern hemisphere. Thus is exhibited a seeming connexion between magnetic phenomena and certain actions taking place on the sun's disc— a connexion, which the observations of Schwabe, compared with the magnetical records of our Colonial Observatories, had already rendered nearly certain. The remarkable results derived from the comparison of the magnetical observations of Captain Maguire on the shores of the Polar Sea, with the contemporaneous records of these Observatories, have been described on a former occasion. The delay of the Government in re-establishing the Colonial Observatories has hitherto retarded that further development of the magnetic laws, which would doubtless have resulted from the prosecution of such researches.—*Lord Wrottesley's Address to the British Association.*

PHYSICAL CONSTITUTION OF THE SUN.

The Rev. Professor Walker, at the late meeting of the British Association at Oxford, delivered a " Discourse on the Physical Constitution of the Sun" to a numerous audience in the Theatre of the University. The topics embraced the sun's spots, its heat, light, and magnetism. Upon each of these the rev. Professor successively enlarged, and laid before his audience a copious account of the present state of our knowledge of the great central body of our system. The learned Professor also noticed many theories regarding this branch of study which have been given to the world, and replied to such as he dissented from in an able and lucid manner. In his concluding remarks he said we had yet much to learn, perhaps more than would be given to man to learn in this state of his existence, concerning the great luminary of our world. We were as yet ignorant of the way in which its perpetual fountains of heat and light were so continuously supplied, of the effects which those streams were producing as they quivered in the apparently barren fields through which the bodies of our system described their circuits, or in the wider regions of space. We were ignorant of these and of many other unceasing operations ; but as we exercised our faculties upon them, this truth seemed to come out more and more strongly that the Creator had made nothing in vain. At the conclusion of the lecture a vote of thanks, moved by the Bishop of Oxford, and seconded by Professor Lloyd, of Dublin, was awarded to Professor Walker for his valuable paper. (This very interesting discourse has been published *in extenso.*)

SOLAR SPOTS AND AURORÆ BOREALES.

MR. R. P. GREG, in the *Philosophical Magazine*, No. 132, remarks :—M. Rudolph Wolf, of Berne, has shown that those years remarkable for abundance of Solar Spots have also been more than commonly rich in Auroræ Boreales. The great auroral display at the commencement of September, 1859, occurring about the time for the return of sun-spot maximum, and which seems to have been visible over the greater portion of both hemispheres, appears to have been the precursor of a great meteorological disturbance : in England and Northern Europe more than an average amount of cold, wind, and rain, have prevailed ever since ; in North America and India more than an average amount of drought and heat. The opinions of philosophers differ respecting the influence of a paucity or an abundance of solar spots upon the temperature and seasons of the earth ; the probability is, there is simply a general disturbance, arising from increase of (solar) magnetic influence, which may produce greater heat and dryness in one part of the globe, and more cold and rain in other parts.

SCIENTIFIC BALLOON ASCENTS.

PROFESSOR WALKER has presented to the British Association, the Report of the Committee requested "to report to the Meeting at Oxford as to the Scientific Objects to be sought for by continuing the Balloon Ascents formerly undertaken to Great Altitudes." The Committee would observe at the onset that the main object for which the former Committee, in 1858, was appointed, remains yet unaccomplished ; and this is the verification of that remarkable result derived from the observations of Mr. Welsh in his four ascents in 1852 ; viz., "the sudden arrest of the decrease in the temperature of the atmosphere at an elevation varying on different days, and this to such an extent that for the space of 2000 or 3000 feet the temperature remains nearly constant or even increases to a small amount." It is obviously important to determine whether this arrest represents the normal condition of the atmosphere at all seasons of the year. The ascents of Mr. Welsh were made between the 17th of August and the 10th of November. The question remains whether this "arrest" would be observed before the summer solstice as well as after, and whether there were any variations at different seasons. The changes in the temperature of the dew-point, consequent upon this interruption in the law of decrease of temperature, would extend our knowledge of the condition of the atmosphere at such altitudes. To accomplish thus much would not require ascents to very great altitudes, although there are many objects to be attained by ascending as high as possible. The liberal offers that have been made by Mr. Coxwell and Mr. Langley, of Newcastle, would enable observations to be made at a very moderate cost, and Mr. Langley appears fully competent to accomplish the task.

There are also many other observations which may be made in balloon ascents which may prove of very great value. Prof. W. Thompson is anxious that observations should be made on the electrical condition of the atmosphere. He has described in the article on the Electricity of the Atmosphere in Nichol's *Cyclopædia*, a portable electrometer, and also a mode of collecting electricity by that which he styles the water-dropping system, which would, in his opinion, be easily applicable. The observations might be carried on, first, by ascending to very moderate heights, and then going as high as possible. Dr. Lloyd desires that observations should be made for "the determination of the decrease of the earth's magnetic force with the distance from the surface." The failure of Gay-Lussac to detect any sensible change ought not to deter future observers. His methods were wholly inadequate ; but Dr. Lloyd is of opinion that if attention be confined to the determination of the total force on its vertical component (instead of the horizontal) it would be easy to arrive at satisfactory conclusions.

Sir David Brewster suggests that further information may be obtained as to the polarization of the atmosphere and the heights of the neutral point. And, lastly, Dr. Edward Smith and Professor Sharpey are desirous that experiments should be made as to "the quantitative determination of the products of respiration at different high elevations." Dr. Smith has, as it is well known, been for the last two or three years engaged in experimental inquiries on inspiration ; and he is so satisfied of the value and importance of the investigation, that he is not only willing, but desirous, to make the requisite experiments himself. Dr. Smith has furnished directions as to the points to be observed and the mode of observation.

ATMOTIC SHIP.

THE Hon. W. Bland, N. S. Wales, has proposed to the British Association the construction of a light keel and ship-formed body, buoyed up by an elongated balloon, by two heavy weights guided by a rope slung from stem to stern, so to alter the centre of gravity of the machine as to direct its motion upwards or downwards at pleasure ; and to cause it to move onwards in any assigned direction by the aid of large but light and strong vanes, driven round and acting like the screw-propeller of a ship.

IMPROVED AIR-PUMP.

MR. W. LADD has described to the British Association an Improved Form of Air-Pump for Philosophical Experiments. This pump consisted of an ordinary pump with two barrels to exhaust rapidly at the early stage, then a horizontal barrel, worked by a rack and handle ; the piston-rod passing through a stuffing-box and cistern of oil, the top of the barrel forming the side of the cistern, and having a valve opening outwards. In the bottom of this barrel was also a valve, opening outwards, to let out any oil which might, in working, pass the piston. The piston of this third barrel, when it passed a hole in the barrel, communicated the vacuum above its piston through a tube connecting it with the receiver. When this barrel worked, a cock shut off the two large barrels from the receiver. The author stated that he could exhaust to the $\frac{1}{10}$th of an inch by this pump. Mr. Yeates, of Dublin, explained a simple pump nearly similar in construction to that now shown by Mr. Ladd, which he had executed several years ago. _____

CURRENTS OF THE AIR AND THE OCEAN.

MR. THOMAS HOPKINS has read to the Royal Society a paper " On the Forces that produce the great Currents of the Air and of the Ocean." In this paper the writer pointed out the fact that we have at present no satisfactory evidence in books of what are the·immediate causes of the great currents of the air and of the ocean ; and he maintained that the liberated heat of condensing vapour is the cause of these currents. He then proceeded to show that all the great winds terminate in comparative vacua created in particular localities where much vapour has been condensed ; and contended that such vacua enable and cause heavier air to press and flow towards the parts which have been rendered light,—to re-establish the equili-brium of atmospheric pressure,—thus making heat the disturbing power in the aërial ocean, and leaving gravitation to act to restore an equilibrium. The great primary currents of the ocean were also described, and they were shown to be so situated as to be under the influence of the principal winds, which, in their passage over the waters, press on them, and force them forward as currents. These currents were maintained to be of a velocity, extent, and depth proportioned to the strength and continuity of the wind, showing that the pressure of the air on the water, whilst moving over it, is capable of producing the movement which takes place. When, how-ever, water is put into motion, it may be obstructed by land, and turned from its direct course, and in that way be made to form secondary currents. But it was contended that heat of vapour, set free in the atmosphere, is the force which disturbs the equilibrium of pressure, and either directly or indirectly produces all the great continuous movements that take place both in the atmosphere and the ocean.

VERTICAL AND OBLIQUE CURRENTS OF THE ATMOSPHERE.

PROFESSOR HENNESSY, in the *Atlantis*, No. 5, remarks : " The influence of Vertical and Oblique Currents in the Atmosphere is not only manifest in the comparative limited and local phe-nomena of sea- and land-breezes, mountain-winds, and whirlwinds, but it has also been appealed to in order to explain the circulation of the great winds of the earth. Thus Maury, in his attempt to exhibit the general laws of the great winds, presents a diagram in which ascending and descending currents are distinctly indicated over different regions of the globe. Their agency is also appealed to by other inquirers ; and their principal seats of action seem to be indicated as the calm regions, that is to say, the regions where hori-zontal winds blow with least intensity. Observations with the aid of the anemoscope in the regions of equatorial and tropical calms would therefore probably serve to test the accuracy of the general views here alluded to. The systematic study of the non-horizontal movements of the atmosphere has scarcely been commenced ; but what little knowledge we possess of such movements shows that they are so closely connected with some of the most important phenomena of the weather, that their further investigation is certain to be attended with interesting and valuable results."

BRITISH STORMS.

A VALUABLE communication has been received by the British Association from Admiral Fitzroy, on British Storms, in which he entered into many details of recent storms, and concluded with the following interesting intelligence :—"The British Association has made application to Her Majesty's Government to authorize arrangements for communicating warning of storms from one part of the country to the other ; and, in conclusion, I will read to you the details of that arrangement which promises to be so beneficial. Arrangements have been authorized by the Board of Trade (under a minute from the President, dated June 6), in consequence of which a daily and mutual interchange of certain limited meteorological information will be transmitted between London and Paris, the results of five subsidiary communications to the central stations of Paris and London. Authority being thus given to collect and communicate, by the telegraph, particular meteorological intelligence, a commencement may be made on the 1st of September, as the plan proposed is simple and the machinery is ready. Once a day, at about nine a.m., barometer and thermometer heights, state of weather, and direction of wind, will be telegraphed to London from the most distant ends of our longest wires, namely, Aberdeen, Berwick, Hull, Yarmouth, Dover, Portsmouth, Jersey, Plymouth, Penzance, Cork, Galway, Londonderry, and Greenock. Facts sent thus from five of these places will be put into one telegram and sent to Paris immediately, when a corresponding communication will be made from the Atlantic coasts southward. When threatening signs are not apparent, no further notice will be transmitted to or from London on that day, respecting weather. But when indications are such as to warrant some cautionary signal at a certain part of, or along all our coasts, the words 'Caution,—North' (or 'South') will be sent to some of the thirteen places specified, or to all of them ; on the receipt of which a cone (or triangle) will be hoisted at a staff (point up for north, down for south), indicating the side whence wind may be expected. This signal will be repeated along any part of the coast by the coast-guard, at such of their stations as may be authorized (at most of their stations, flagstaffs are visible to coasters). Danger will be implied by a drum (or square), a cone, and perhaps, in addition, very great danger by a cone, a drum, and a second cone. (The cones and drums may be made with hoops and black canvas, to collapse, without top or bottom. They will be the same shape from all points of view, and unlike any other signal, such as a time-ball, used ordinarily.) As the coast-guard extends all along the frequented parts of our shores, and as the telegraph companies are liberally willing to have instruments and signals placed at their extreme stations, in charge of and used by their officials, only the necessary materials and instructions will be required, all of which are ready or in progress. By vigilance at the central station, and by taking great care to avoid signalling too frequently, much may be done towards diminishing the losses of life on our increasingly crowded coasts."

OPEN SEA OF THE ARCTIC REGIONS.

MR. W. W. WHEILDON, of Charleston, in a paper read to the American Association, considers that the arguments in favour of the Open Sea at the Pole being caused by the action of the Gulf-stream, are inadequate; and that while the influence of the Gulf-stream has been exaggerated, that of the air has been overlooked. He concludes that the open sea is due largely, if not entirely, to the currents of air from the equatorial region, which move in the higher strata of the earth's atmosphere, bearing heat and moisture with them. He cites the well-known fact that in the high polar regions the winds blowing from the north and north-east are warm.

PENDULUM EXPERIMENTS.

PROFESSOR PIERCE has read to the British Association a paper "On the Motion of a Pendulum in a Vertical Plane when the Point of Suspension moves uniformly on a Circumference in the same Plane." The author wrote down the mathematical formulæ which gave the laws which govern such motions. He then exhibited beautifully-executed diagrams on transparent cloth, which showed by curves, some most regular and some most fantastic in their forms, the behaviour of such a pendulum under various conditions, and at several periods of its course. He pointed out cases in which these curves exhibited all the symmetry and regularity of exact mathematical forms; and others, in which these forms were complicated and irregular almost beyond conception. He showed that in some of these cases the state of the pendulum was that of a stable equilibrium, whilst in others the equilibrium was unstable, and the pendulum went off into the most rapid motions. By another series of curves, something like Contour lines, he showed how the succession of these motions could all be tracked; and he concluded by showing how a similar method was applicable to the tracing of matter through its several varieties of form. Inorganic matter being analogous to the changes and varieties observed in the state of stable equilibrium, while the various states of unstable equilibrium gave many of the surprising and irregular transitions observed in the vegetable or animal kingdom, or in organized matters.

STUDY OF THE EARTH.

PROFESSOR HENNESSY has read to the British Association a paper "On the Possibility of Studying the Earth's Internal Structure from Phenomena observed at its Surface." This the author showed to result from the comparison of the level surface, usually called the earth's surface by astronomers and mathematicians, with the geological surface which would be presented if the earth were stripped of its fluid coating. At present the number of unknown quantities in an inquiry as to the earth's internal structure was greater than the number of conditions; but by knowing the true surface, and adopting the results of established physical and hydrostatical laws relative to the supposed internal fluid mass, we should be able to establish as many equations as we have unknown quantities, and thus obtain a solution. Professor Stevelly stated, that the exact spheroidal form of the earth and the direction of gravity at each part of its surface were not so completely determined as the remarks of Professor Hennessy would lead a person to suppose. Very interesting papers printed in the last volume of the *Transactions* of the Royal Society, by Colonel Sir Henry James and Captain Clarke, had shown conclusively that not only did the spheroidal form of the earth, as deduced from the great Ordnance Survey of the British Islands, differ somewhat from that considered as most suitable to the form of the earth as derived from a comparison of all observations; but even particular localities had the plumb-line so affected by local circumstances, that the form, as deduced from particular portions of the Survey, differed sensibly from one another. Thus, the plumb-line near Edinburgh was found to be affected not only by the proximity of Arthur's Seat and the Calton Hill, but even in the defect of matter in the Frith of Forth, and the excess in the distant Pentland Hills, were shown to exercise important influences. Colonel Sir H. James showed by various examples that the method of grouping the measurements of different countries proposed by Mr. Hennessy would not, in the present state of these measurements, lead to the exact results he supposed. He then pointed out circumstances not only respecting the Russian measurements, but even the French, which would make a re-examination of them not only desirable, but necessary.

ICE PHENOMENA.

Mr. B. F. Harrison has read to the American Association a paper on the Solution of Ice in Inland Waters, accounting for the sudden disappearance of ice by a theory based upon observations upon a small lake in Connecticut, so hedged in that only the south and south-west winds blow upon it. No large stream feeds it, and its outlet is small. January 23, 1860, the ice was ten or eleven inches thick: the temperature of the ice varied from $34°$ just below the ice to $43\frac{1}{2}°$ at the bottom; average $38\frac{3}{4}°$. March 6, the ice disappeared very rapidly, about one-third disappearing during two hours. The mean temperature of the water was then $41\frac{1}{2}°$. He concludes, therefore, that the solution of the ice is caused by heating the water upward from the bottom, since the temperature of the air was less than that of the water.

Prof. Elias Loomis has read to the above Association a paper on Natural Ice-Houses and Frozen Wells. These occur in places where the ice accumulates in the cold season, and remains during the summer months, or even the entire year, although the mean temperature of the neighbourhood may be $10°$ or $15°$ above the freezing point of water. Four such ice caverns are found in Switzerland and the neighbouring portion of France ; one being near Besançon. The bottom of the latter cave is covered with ice about a hundred feet square and about a foot thick. There is but one opening to the cave, and so no chance for the circulation of air. The water trickles from the roof or flows in at the mouth, and the cold air which settles in the cave, and freezes all its moisture, maintains its place through the summer by reason of its greater specific gravity, so that the ice wastes very slowly even in the hottest weather. Professor Loomis gave a list of eight such "ice-houses" in different parts of Europe. Similar cases exist in America. On the western bank of Lake Champlain, near the village of Port Henry, is an ice mine which has been extensively worked for many years. There are fifteen such places in the United States. The phenomenon of frozen wells is explained in the same way ; but to secure a frozen well, it is necessary that the water should not be changed. It is only the fact that the water in most wells is constantly changing, that prevents all of them from presenting this phenomenon. Professor Loomis produced a list of about thirty frozen wells, the most remarkable of which are, one in Tioga, New York, 77 feet deep ; one in Ware, Massachusetts, 38 feet deep; one in Brandon, Vermont, 34 feet deep ; six in Oswego, New York, from 16 to 30 feet ; and one in Prattsburg, New York, 25 feet.

TRANSMISSION OF RADIANT HEAT THROUGH GASEOUS BODIES.

PROFESSOR TYNDALL, in a note communicated to the Royal Society, states that he has experimented with several Gases and Vapours, and has, in all cases, obtained abundant proof of calorific absorption. Gases vary considerably in their absorptive power— probably as much as liquids and solids. Some of them allow the heat to pass through them with comparative facility, while other gases bear the same relation to the latter that alum does to other diathermanous bodies.

Different gases are thus shown to intercept radiant heat in different degres. Dr. Tyndall has made other experiments, which prove that the self-same gas exercises a different action upon different qualities of radiant heat.—(See the paper by Professor Tyndall, in Year-Book of Facts, 1860, p. 139.)

CONDUCTION OF HEAT BY GASES.

PROFESSOR MAGNUS, in a paper on this subject, observes :—The simplest mode of ascertaining whether a gas conducts heat, consists in warming it from above, and observing the action of a thermometer placed within. It might be objected to this method, that even with heating from above, currents in the gas might be formed, and that thereby the temperature indicated by the thermometer in various gases might be different without any difference in conductibility.

There is one method of testing this objection. For if, in fact, a gas can conduct heat, the temperature assumed by a thermometer in a space heated from above must be lower when the conducting substance is wanting than when it is present ; that is, it must be lower *in vacuo* than in a space filled with air.

In order to ascertain whether this was the case, a glass apparatus was used, in which a thermometer, observable from without, was firmly fixed. It could be filled with different gases, and these could be variously dilated. The upper part of this apparatus was maintained at the same temperature, namely that of boiling water, and the temperature was observed which a thermometer introduced into the interior ultimately assumed. It was necessary that the space surrounding the apparatus should always be at the same temperature. In these experiments the temperature of the surrounding space was 15°. In this way the following results were obtained :—

1. The temperature which a thermometer ultimately assumes in a space heated from above, differs when this space is filled with different gases.

2. In hydrogen the temperature is higher than in any other gas.

3. In this gas the temperature is higher than *in vacuo;* and the denser the gas is, the higher is the temperature.

4. Hence hydrogen conducts heat like metals.

5. In all other gases the temperature is lower than *in vacuo;* and the denser they are, the lower is the temperature.

6. It cannot hence be concluded that gases do not conduct heat, but only that they do this in so small a degree that the action of conduction is cancelled by their diathermancy.

7. This remarkable property of hydrogen is evinced not only when it moves freely, but also when it is contained between eider down, or any loose substance which hinders its motion.

8. The great conductibility of this gas is a further confirmation of its analogy with metals.

9. Hydrogen conducts not only heat, but also electricity, better than other gases.

PERCEPTION OF COLOURS.

Dr. Gladstone has read to the British Association a paper "On his own Perception of Colours." The author described himself as in an intermediate position between those who have a normal vision of colours, and those who are termed "colour-blind." These latter are usually unacquainted with the sensations of either red or green, and it becomes a desideratum to have good observations on those who are capable of acting somewhat as interpreters between them and those who perceive every colour. By means of Chevreul's chromatic circles and scales, Maxwell's colour-top, coloured beads, &c., the author was able to determine the following points in respect to his own vision. He sees red, in all probability, like other people, but it requires a larger quantity of the colour to give the sensation than is usually the case ; hence a purple appears to him more blue, and an orange more yellow, than to the generality of observers. He is perfectly sensible of green, or rather of two distinct greens—the one yellowish, the other bluish — but between them there lies a particular shade of green, to which his eyes are insensible as a colour. This modifies his perception of many greens that approximate to what is to him invisible. The shade occurs in Nature on the back of the leaf of the variegated holly, and it may be produced in Maxwell's top by certain combinations of the coloured disc ; the simplest being—

94·5 Brunswick Green (Blue Shade) + 5·5 Ultramarine = 94 Black + 6 White.

While able perfectly to distinguish between red and green, the contrast does not readily catch his eye, especially at a distance ; in fact, he is somewhat short-sighted in respect to these colours. He has reason to believe that, in his case, there has been a gradual improvement in his actual perception of colours, independently of his greater knowledge of them ; though this is in opposition to the general experience of those whose vision is in any way abnormal, and no other instance was known to. the late Professor George Wilson, whose book is the standard one on the subject of colour-blindness.*

THEORY OF COLOURS.

In the *Philosophical Transactions* has appeared a paper by Professor J. Clerk Maxwell, of King's College, on the Theory of Compound Colours, and the Relations of the Colours of the Spectrum. The professor gives, first, a history of the theory, with especial reference to the researches of Newton, Young, Brewster, Grassman, and Helmholtz ; an account of his own experiments follows, with a reduction of his observations. He gives as the results the following among other general conclusions :—The three primary colours in the spectrum are red, green, and blue ; by the mixture of these, colours chromatically identical with the other colours of the spectrum may be produced—the orange and yellow are equivalent to mixtures of red and green, which seems to put an end to the pretension of yellow to be considered a primary colour ; and the extreme ends of the spectrum (very feeble) are probably equal to mixtures of red and blue.

At a meeting of the French Academy of Sciences, during a conversation respecting the optical phenomena of the eclipse of July 18, M. Chevreul referred to the remarkable phenomena of Complementary Colours, and stated that he was then printing in the Society's *Memoirs* an account of his latest researches.

CRYSTALLIZATION AND POLARIZATION IN DECOMPOSED GLASS.

Sir D. Brewster has communicated to the British Association a "Notice respecting certain Phenomena of Crystallization and Polarization in Decomposed Glass." At the meeting of the Association held in Aberdeen, the author read a paper on the Decomposed Glass found at Nineveh, Rome, and other localities ;† but not then having any drawings to exhibit to the section, he found it difficult to convey an intelligible account of the structure and remarkable phenomena which the specimens exhibited both in common and polarized light. He now exhibited and explained very beautifully-executed coloured drawings and diagrams explanatory of these appearances and properties. In this paper he omitted all reference to those colourless specimens by which he had then shown that a bundle or pile of these transparent films act upon common and polarized light as negative uniaxal crystals, producing all the colours of polarized light, by the interference of two oppositely polarized pencils, one of which is the

---

* See *Year-Book of Facts*, 1860, p. 150.   † *Ibid.* p. 152.

transmitted light, the other a combination of all the pencils reflected from the anterior surfaces of the films. He then pointed out the difference between artificial glasses and naturally-formed cyrstals, like rock crystal. In the glasses the atoms are forced, by melting them at high temperatures, to unite by chemical affinity. In the others the particles have united by peculiar polar actions while crystallizing naturally. Hence, the atoms of crystals being simple and similarly united throughout the entire crystal, have no tendency to decompose or reunite in other forms at particular parts ; but the forces by which the earths, alkalies, and metals are composed, not being uniformly arranged as to the forces by which the different parts are held together, tend to separate and reunite in new or more natural crystalline relations in relation to particular points, lines, or surfaces in their mass.

Thus, the rock-crystal lens found by Mr. Layard at Nineveh was as perfect in its structure now as it was many thousand years ago, when in the form of a crystal, while the glass was found altered as in the specimens now shown ; and few bodies cease to exist with such grace and beauty as glass, when it surrenders itself to time and not to disease. In stables, where ammonia and other exhalations prevail, and in damp localities, or where acids or alkalies prevail in the soil, the process is more rapid, and it may frequently be broken between the fingers of an infant, sometimes presenting in the middle a plate of unaltered glass, to which the process has not extended ; but it is in dry localities, where Roman, Greek, and Assyrian glass has been found, that the process of decomposition is exceedingly interesting, and its results singularly beautiful. At one or more points in the surface of the glass the decomposition begins. It extends round that point in spherical surfaces, so that the first film is a minute hemispherical cup of exceeding thinness. Film after film is formed in a similar manner, till perhaps 20 or 30 are crowded into the 50th of an inch. They there resemble the section of a pearl (or of an onion), and as the films are still glass, the colours of thin plates are seen when we look down through their edges, which form the surface of the glass. These thin edges, however, being exposed to the elements, suffer decomposition. The particles of silex and the other ingredients now readily separate, and the decomposition proceeds downwards in films parallel to the surface of the glass ; the crystals of silex forming a white ring and the other ingredients rings of a different colour. Such is the process round one point, but the decomposition commences at several points ; generally these points lie in lines, so that the circles of decomposition meet one another and form sinuous lines. When there are only two points near, these circles of decomposition surround the two points, like rings round two knots in wood ; but when there are many points near, the curves unite and form sinuous lines. When the decomposition is uniform, and the little hemispheres have nearly the same depth, we can separate the upper film from the one below it ; the convexities of the one falling into the concavities of the others. The drawings of these were executed by

Miss King, now the Honourable Mrs. Ward. When the decomposition has gone regularly on round a single point, and there is no other change, there is a division of the glass into a number of hemispherical films within one another. The groups of films exhibit in the microscope circular cavities, which, under different circumstances, become elliptical and polygonal. M. Brame, of Paris, succeeded in rapidly producing this composition by immersing glass in a mixture of fluoride of calcium and concentrated sulphuric acid, or by exposing it to the vapour of fluohydric acid (*Comptes Rendus*, Nov. 2, 1852).

The author then proceeded with the diagrams, to explain the optical phenomena, grouping them into three chief varieties, but stating them to be so various and singular as to baffle description.

Many other optical circumstances connected with this variety were mentioned by the author and explained. In all these three varieties the films are pure glass, for they become colourless by a sufficient inclination of the plates, and also by introducing a drop of water or alcohol, which, when it evaporates, allows the original colours again to be recovered ; and although a film of the fluid separated each of the almost infinitesimal layers of the glass, yet they afterwards adhere as firmly as ever. If an oil or balsam be introduced, it slowly and unequally passes between the layers, so that the retreating colour is bounded by a stratum of the various tints which the film combines. But the author has often found between the true glass films beautiful circular crystals of silex, finely seen in polarized light. These are sometimes dendritic, and assume, round the black cross, foliated shapes. One form merits particular attention : around a minute speck of silex there is formed a circular band of equally minute crystalline specks, and at a greater distance a second circular band concentric with the first, consisting of still smaller siliceous particles hardly visible in the microscope. By what atomic forces does this central crystal group its attendant crystals around it ?

Mr. Stoney observed that Dr. Lloyd, at the Aberdeen meeting, had shown that the light from these specimens of decomposed glass, exhibited by Sir D. Brewster, was elliptically polarized, and that therefore they must behave like uniaxal crystals.

STATISTICS OF COLOUR-BLINDNESS.

Sir John Herschel observes :—"Dr. Wilson[*] gives it as the result of his inquiries, that one person in every eighteen is colour-blind in some marked degree, and that one in fifty-five confounds red with green. Were the average anything like this, it seems inconceivable that the existence of the phenomenon of colour-blindness, or dichromy, should not be one of vulgar notoriety, or that it should strike almost all uneducated persons, when told of it, as something approaching to absurdity. Nor can I think that in military operations (as, for instance, in the placing of men as sentinels at outposts),

* See *Year-Book of Facts*, pp. 150, 151.

the existence, on an average, of one soldier in every fifty-five unable to distinguish a scarlet coat from green grass would not issue in grave inconvenience, and ere this have forced itself into prominence by producing mischief. Among the circle of my own personal acquaintance I have only known two (though, of course, I have heard of and been placed in correspondence with several) ; and a neighbour of mine, who takes great delight in horticulture, and has a superb collection of exotic flowers, informs me that among the multitude of persons who have seen and admired it, he does not recollect having ever met with one who appeared incapable of appreciating the variety and richness of the tints, or insensible to the brilliancy of the numerous shades of red and scarlet. It may be, however, that the percentage is on the increase—certainly we *hear* of more cases than formerly ; but this probably arises from the fact of this, like many other subjects, being made more generally matter of conversation."—*Proceedings of the Royal Society.*

THE DICHROOSCOPE.

THIS apparatus, the invention of Prof. Dove, and described in Poggendorff's *Annalen,* is intended for the following purposes :—

1. To represent interferences, and spectra in different-coloured lights, both separately and combined.

2. To imitate the phenomena of dichroism both in the case in which the dichroitic crystals are viewed through a double-refracting arrangement, as, for example, Haidinger's dichroitic lens ; and also in the case of the phenomena produced when the dichroitic crystals themselves are used as analysers in a polarizing arrangement.

3. To combine elliptically, circularly, and rectilinearly polarized and unpolarized light, not in such a manner that the one is produced by the polarizing, and the other by the analysing arrangement, but so that they traverse the doubly refracting media simultaneously, and are then submitted to an analysing arrangement.

(For details, see the entire paper, translated in No. 134 of the *Philosophical Magazine.*)

THE CHROMOSCOPE.

MR. J. B. PERTH has sent to the British Association a specimen of the cut-out card by the rotation of which over a black ground in strong light, as sunlight, he could produce rings of various colours. There were also diagrams exhibited, painted so as to represent the several colours and tints of which the author had succeeded in causing the rings to appear. This communication gave rise to much conversation in the Section. Prof. Stevelly stated that Mr. Patterson, of Belfast, had commissioned him to mention at the first meeting of the British Association which he had the honour of being present at (Edinburgh, 1834), as an unexplained fact, that walking rapidly past high iron railings, while the country on the other side was covered with snow, and the sun shining brightly, the whole landscape suddenly assumed a reddish or crimson hue. His attention being thus arrested, he found that, by altering the speed at which he walked, the snow-clad country seemed to assume other colours. Sir D. Brewster referred to a paper which appeared in the *Philosophical Magazine* many years since, where colours such as those on the diagram were described as manifesting themselves under somewhat similar circumstances. The opinion of the members of the Section who joined in the conversation seemed to be universally, that the effect was due to the power of the retina to recover the power of noticing the several colours with different degrees of rapidity.

THE PSEUDO-DIASCOPE.

By means of this instrument an aperture transmitting light is made to produce on one eye an isolated impression, while the other eye is directed to an opaque body, such as the hand held before it. The image of the aperture is then found to be transposed, and its perception ceases to be assigned to the eye by which it is really seen, —the effect being that a perforation appears in the opaque body, through which the light seems to shine upon the eye by which this is viewed. The principle illustrated by this instrument, according to the author's view, is the essentially goniometrical and deductive nature of the visual act, whenever the distances of bodies are perceived, and their relative positions in space assigned.—*F. O. Ward; Proc. Lit. and Phil. Soc. Manchester.*

TO MEASURE DISTANCES.

Mr. PATRICK ADIE has described to the British Association an Instrument for Measuring Actual Distances. Prof. Stevelly stated that the Master of Trinity College, Cambridge, had, at the Southampton meeting of the British Association, explained a method similar in principle to this for observing the heights of the clouds. But from the difficulty experienced in getting a sheet of water for a reflector, both calm and at a sufficient distance below the observer to ensure sufficient accuracy, he (Prof. Stevelly) had been led to a modification of Dr. Whewell's method, by using mirrors in a way almost exactly the same as that of Mr. Adie ; but not nearly so neat in arrangement, nor admitting of such accuracy of observation as his instrument, which he hailed as affording, among many other uses, not only a means of observing the heights of clouds of different modifications, but also the distance from the observer of those lying off towards the horizon, a fact very difficult, under many circumstances, hitherto to determine, or even to estimate correctly.

SPECIFIC GRAVITY OF THE DIAMOND.

The specific gravity of this gem is generally stated in elementary works to range from 3·5 to 3·55 ; but these numbers do not represent the mean of recorded experiments, as will be seen by the following table :—

Diamond in Hunterian Museum, Glasgow .	3·53	Thomson.[*]
Specific gravity, as stated by Mohs . .	3·52	Mohs.[†]
Brazilian diamond	3·44 }	
Another variety of the same . . .	3·52 }	Brisson.[‡]
Mean specific gravity of a " beautiful collection }	3·48	Lowry.[§]
of diamonds" . . . . . }		
" Star of the south"	3·53 {	Dufrenoy and Halphin.[‖]
Borneo diamond	3·49	Grailich.[¶]
„ „ compact . . .	3·41 }	
	3·25 }	Rivot.[**]
Diamond used in Jacquelain's experiments .	3·33	Jacquelain.[††]
Specific gravity, as given by Henry . . .	3·55	Henry.[‡‡]
Well-crystallized Brazilian diamond, weighing }	3·48	Playfair.[§§]
0·5761 gramme, in the Edinburgh Museum . }		

Mean sp. gr. . ·   3·461

If we reject the second Borneo diamond of Rivot, which has too low a specific gravity, we have a mean sp. gr. of 3·48, which is the same number as that found by Wilson Lowry for the mean specific gravity of "his beautiful collection of crystallized diamonds" (Thomson's *Mineralogy*, vol. i. p. 46).

It is to be expected that the experimental determination of the specific gravity of diamonds should be rather above than below the truth ; for we are aware that they all leave a minute quantity of ash on burning, and that this ash, according to Petzhold, contains silica and iron.—*Dr. Lyon Playfair ; Proceedings of the Royal Society of Edinburgh.*

MICROSCOPIC VISION, AND NEW MICROSCOPE.

SIR DAVID BREWSTER has read to the British Association a paper on Microscopic Vision and a New Form of the Microscope. In this the worthy Principal again, after an interval of more than a quarter of a century, and notwithstanding all the disappointments which have intervened, recommends gems as material for lenses instead of glass. He objects even on the ground of truthfulness to object-glasses with large apertures, and sums up thus the other improvements which he suggests :—1. The first step, we conceive, is, to abandon large angular apertures, and to use object-glasses of moderate focal length, obtaining at the eye-glass any additional magnifying power that may be required. 2. In order to obtain a better illumination, either by light incident vertically or obliquely, a new form of the microscope would be advantageous. In place of directing the microscope to the object itself, placed as it now is almost touching the object-glass, let it be directed to an image of the object,

* Thomson's *Mineralogy*, vol. i.p. 46.
† Mohs' *Mineralogy*, vol. ii. p. 306.
‡ Brisson, as quoted by Böttger, *Specifische Gewicht.*, p. 32.
§ Lowry, as quoted in Thomson's *Mineralogy*, vol. i. p. 46.
‖ Dufrenoy, *Comptes Rendus*, vol. xl. p. 3.
¶ Grailich, *Bull. Geol.* [2], vol. xiii. p. 512.
** Rivot, *Ann. des Mines*, vol. xiv. p. 423.
†† Jacquelain, *Ann. de Ch. et Phys.* [2], vol. xx. p. 459.
‡‡ Henry's *Mineralogy*, vol. iv. p. 19.
§§ Experiment made for this paper.

formed by the thinnest achromatic lens, of such a focal length that the object may be an inch or more from the lens, and its image equal to, or greater or less than, the object. In this way the observer will be able to illuminate the object, whether opaque or transparent, and may subject it to any experiments he may desire to make upon it. It may thus be studied without a covering of glass, and when its parts are developed by immersion in a fluid. 3. The sources of error arising from the want of perfect polish and perfect homogeneity of the glass of which the lenses are composed, are, to some extent, hypothetical ; but there are reasons for believing— and these reasons corroborated by facts—that a body whose ingredients are united by fusion, and kept in a state of constraint from which they are striving to get free, cannot possess that homogeneity of structure, or that perfection of polish, which will allow the rays of light to be refracted and transmitted without injurious modification. If glass is to be used for the lenses of microscopes, long and careful annealing should be adopted, and the polishing process should be continued long after it appears perfect to the optician. Sir David believes that the time is not distant when transparent minerals, in which their elements are united in definite proportions, will be substituted for glass. Diamond, topaz, and rock-crystal are those which appear best suited for lenses. The white topaz of New Holland is particularly fitted for optical purposes, as its double refractions may be removed by cutting it in plates perpendicular to one of its optical axes. In rock crystal, the structure is, generally speaking, less perfect along the axis of double refraction than in any other direction, but this imperfection does not exist in topaz.

ANTIQUITY OF THE STEREOSCOPE.

At the meeting of the Photographic Society of Scotland, Sir David Brewster, President, has read a paper of historic interest, entitled, "Notice respecting the Invention of the Stereoscope in the Sixteenth Century, and of Binocular Drawings by Jacopo da Empoli, a Florentine artist." Sir David said that, inquiring into the history of the stereoscope, he found that its fundamental principle was known even to Euclid ; that it was distinctly described by Galen 1500 years ago ; and that Baptista Porta had, in 1599, given such a complete drawing of the two separate pictures as seen by each eye, and of the combined picture placed between them, in which we recognise not only the principle, but the construction of the stereoscope. Last summer, Dr. John Brown, while visiting the Musée Wicar at Lille, observed two drawings placed side by side, and perfectly similar. These drawings were by Jacopo Chimenti da Empoli, a painter of the Florentine school, who was born in 1554, and died in 1640. They represent the same object from points of view slightly different. That on the right hand is from a point of view slightly to the left of that on the left hand. By converging the optic axes, the pictures could be united so as to produce an image in relief, as easily and as perfectly as with an ordinary stereograph.

IMPROVEMENT OF THE STEREOSCOPE.

MR. A. CLAUDET has read to the British Association a paper "On the Means of Increasing the Angle of Binocular Instruments, in order to obtain a Stereoscopic Effect in proportion to their Magnifying Power." In a paper on the Stereoscope, which Mr. Claudet read before the Society of Arts in the year 1852, alluding to the reduction of the stereoscopic effect produced by opera-glasses on account of their magnifying power, he stated that, in order to redress that defect, it would be necessary to increase the angle of the two perspectives. This he proposed to do by adapting to the object-glasses two sets of reflecting prisms, which by the greater separation given to the two lines of perspectives, would reflect on the optic axes images taken at a greater angle than the angle of natural vision.

Such was the instrument that Mr. Claudet submitted to the British Association to prove, as he always endeavoured to demonstrate in various memoirs, that the binocular angle of stereoscopic pictures must be in proportion to the ultimate size of the pictures on the retina, larger than the natural angle when the images are magnified, and smaller when they are diminished; which, in fact, is nothing more than to give or restore to these images the natural angle at which the objects are seen when we approach them or recede from them. For magnifying or diminishing the size of objects is the same thing as approaching them or receding from them, and in these cases the angles of perspective cannot be the same. Mr. Claudet showed that, looking at the various rows of persons composing the audience, with the large ends of the opera-glass, all the various rows appeared too close to one another, that there was not between them the distance which separates them when we look with the eyes alone; and he showed also that, with the small end, the distance appeared considerably exaggerated. But, applying the sets of prisms to the opera-glass in order to increase the angle of the two perspectives, then looking at the audience as before, it appeared that the various rows of persons had between them the natural distance expected for the size of the image or for the reduction of the distance of the objects. By applying the two sets of prisms before the eyes without the opera-glass, it was observed, as was to be expected, that the stereoscopic effect was considerably exaggerated, because the binocular angle was increased without magnifying the objects. But looking with the two sets of prisms alone at distant objects, the exaggeration of perspective did not produce an unpleasant effect. It appeared as if we were looking at a small model of the objects brought near the observer. By the same reason, stereoscopic pictures of distant objects (avoiding to include in them near objects) can advantageously be taken at a larger angle than the natural angle, in order to give them the relief of which they are deprived as much when we look at them with the eyes, as when we look only with one eye; instead of being a defect, it seems that it is an improvement. In fact, the stereoscope gives us two eyes to see pictures of distant objects.

BINOCULAR VISION.

PROFESSOR W. B. ROGERS has described to the American Association some Experiments and Inferences in regard to Binocular Vision. In the theory of binocular vision expounded by Sir David Brewster, and maintained by Brücke, Prevost, and others, it is contended that no part of an object is seen single and distinctly but that to which the optic axes are for the moment directed, and that " the unity of the perception is obtained by the rapid survey which the eye takes of every part of the object." So that, according to this, our perception of an object in its solidity and relief is acquired not by a simple but by a cumulative process, in which the optic axes are converged successively upon every point of the object within view. Like conditions must obviously apply to the perception of the binocular resultant formed by the reverse of the twin pictures of a stereoscope. On this theory the conditions of binocular vision of a perspective line would be as follows :—1. The perception of the perspective line in the stereoscope would require the optic axes to be successively directed in such manner as to unite every pair of corresponding points of the two composite lines of the diagram,—or, which amounts to the same, they should be successively converged upon every point of the perspective resultant. 2. In cases of two intersecting lines appearing, instead of this single resultant, those lines should neither of them have a perspective position.

In an experimental discussion of the subject some years ago, Professor Rogers showed that the phenomena of the stereoscopic resultant do not necessarily conform to these conditions ; and that the perception of a perspective resultant line, or of a physical line, in the same attitude, does not require the successive convergence of the axes to every point. The truth of this position is proved by the fact that the resultant obtained by combining two inclined lines with or without a stereoscope, presents a perspective attitude, even when the component lines, instead of being united into one, are brought together to intersect at a small angle, each of the intersecting lines in this case appearing in relief. Professor Rogers described several experiments, in part new and in part modified repetitions of those already described by Professors Wheatstone and Dove, which offer decisive proof that such a successive combination of pictures, point by point, however it may enter into the complex process of vision, cannot be considered as an essential condition to the singleness and perspectiveness of the binocular perception.

One of these experiments is tried by holding a brilliant line in a perspective position at a convenient distance midway between the eyes, and regarding it for a few seconds so as to produce a lasting impression on the retina. On turning the eyes towards a blank wall or screen, the subjective impression will be seen projected against it and having the same perspective attitude as the original line. If, then, one eye be closed, the line will appear to subside into the surface of the screen, taking an inclined position corresponding to the optical projection of the original line as seen by the unclosed eye, and therefore corresponding to the position of the image formed in that eye. By opening and closing the eyes alternately, and finally directing both to the screen, we are able to see the two oblique lines corresponding to these projections, and their binocular resultant corresponding to the original object. For the success of this and the other experiments described by the Professor, the lines should be very strongly illuminated, and the observer should have some practice in experiments on subjective vision. But the following is a more simple proof that pictures successively impressed on the two eyes are sufficient for the stereoscopic effect :—Let a screen be made to vibrate or revolve somewhat rapidly between the eyes and the twin pictures of a stereoscope, so as alternately to expose and cover each, completely excluding the simultaneous vision of the two. The stereoscopic relief will be as apparent in these conditions as when the moving screen is withdrawn. Here there is no opportunity for the combination of pairs of corresponding points in the two diagrams by the simultaneous convergence of the optic axes through them: but at each moment the actual picture in the one eye and the retained impression in the other, form the elements of the perceptive resultant perceived. In repeating, with success, the curious experiments of Professor Dove, to obtain the stereoscopic effect by the momentary illumination of the electric flash, Professor Rogers found great advantage in using one of Ritchie's improved Ruhmkorff's coils, having a coated jar included in the outer circuit, the intensely brilliant spark of which can be made to throw its light upon the object viewed, in any direction or at any intervals that may be desired.

From the facts that the duration of an electric spark is less than one-millionth of a second (Wheatstone), and that we are able by a single flash of lightning to perceive the solidity and relief of an object to which the eyes are directed,—we may conclude that the perception of an object in its proper relief does not necessarily require the eyes to be converged upon every visible point of it in succession, and that the perception of the perceptive resultant, through binocular combination in a stereoscope or otherwise, may arise directly from the two pictures impressed, without the necessity of combining, pair by pair, all the corresponding points of the component lines or drawings. Nor is it necessary that the images of the corresponding points of the objects should fall on what are called corresponding points of the retina. The condition of single vision in this case seems to be simply this, that the picture in the two eyes shall be such and so placed as to be identical with the picture, which the real object would form, if placed at a given distance, and in a given attitude before the eyes.

Prof. Rogers has shown that the law of binocular vision is valuable in examining bank-notes. Put a genuine note in one compartment of a stereoscope, and a counterfeit note in the other, and every difference will be readily distinguished.

THE HUMAN EAR.

Mr. Toynbee, F.R.S., has communicated to the Royal Society a paper "On the Mode in which Sonorous Undulations are conducted from the Membrana Tympani to the Labyrinth, in the Human Ear."

The opinion usually entertained by physiologists is that two channels are requisite for the transmission of sonorous undulations from the membrana tympani to the labyrinth, viz., the air in the tympanic cavity which transmits the undulations to the membrane of the fenestra rotunda and the cochlea ; and secondly, the chain of ossicles which conduct them to the vestibule.

This opinion is, however, far from being universally received : thus, one writer on the physiology of hearing contends that "the integrity of one fenestra may suffice for the exercise of hearing ;" another expresses his conviction that "the transmission of sound cannot take place through the ossicula ;" while Sir John Herschel, in speaking of the ossicles, says, "they are so far from being essential to hearing, that when the tympanum is destroyed and the chain in consequence hangs loose, deafness does not follow."

The experiments and observations detailed in Mr. Toynbee's paper lead to the following conclusions :—

1. That the commonly received opinion in favour of the sonorous undulating passage to the vestibule through the chain of ossicles is correct.

2. That the stapes, when disconnected from the incus, can still conduct sonorous undulations to the vestibule from the air.

3. So far as our present experience extends, it appears that in the human ear sound always travels to the labyrinth through two media, viz., through the air in the tympanic cavity to the cochlea, and through one or more of the ossicles to the vestibule.

SENSITIVENESS OF THE HUMAN EAR TO THE PITCH OF MUSICAL NOTES.

M. F. FESSEL has obtained with the new Parisian Tuning-Fork the following results, which he has communicated to Poggendorff's *Annalen :—*

In tuning forks (says M. Fessel) I invariably pursue Scheibler's plan. The fork to be tuned, before having its vibrations compared with the seconds' pendulum, is, as is well known, tuned as far as possible by ear. My instrument and the seconds' pendulum happening on this occasion to be in different rooms for the sake of convenience, I naturally endeavoured to finish tuning my fork by ear only. In this, however, I found I could not succeed ; and having investigated all the circumstances with the greatest care, I was led to the following remarkable conclusion :—

I observed that a fork which I had tuned by holding it to my right ear while the standard was held to my left, when compared with the fork used for the exact pitch, made one vibration too many in the course of several seconds ; while a fork tuned by being held to my left ear while the standard was held to my right, vibrated less rapidly than the other. The fork in accurate pitch gave the lower note. Consequently, I hear all notes somewhat higher with my right ear than with my left.

I have since examined my musical friends, and I have not yet found one, even among part-musicians, whose ears are precisely alike in estimating the pitch of musical notes. By continued practice I am able to distinguish, by a simple experiment, with which ear any one hears the highest. In this experiment I have never yet failed. The person under examination holds a carefully tuned fork in each hand, and having sounded them simultaneously, he brings them successively the one to the right, the other to the left ear. I place my right ear at equal distances from both of his, my left being turned away and covered lightly with my hand.

In this position, that ear of the person under examination near which the fork is held which seems to me to have the highest pitch, hears all sounds higher than the other. If the tuning-forks are exchanged, precisely the same phenomenon results with respect both to the person under examination and to the listener. As far as my present experience extends, most people (here in Cologne) hear higher with the right ear than with the left.

These experiments are so striking that no one has hitherto attempted to dispute them. Indeed I had secured myself against contradiction, by always requesting the gentlemen whose hearing I tested to state their own opinions distinctly before I acquainted them with my explanation of the phenomenon. This precaution seemed to me to be necessary, since no one could blame a musician for resisting the imputation that he heard differently with different ears. In the end all were extremely astonished. I pass over the various

playful questions and remarks that have been made to me—
"Whether for the future, before beginning a concert, the hearers are
to be examined, and a place allotted to each accordingly, where he
may be able to hear with satisfaction?"—"Whether instrumentalists
are to be separated into two divisions, one of which is to use the
A right pitch, the other the A left?" &c. I content myself with
simply asserting the fact as I have found it.

The reason for this difference of hearing is probably that the
external passage of the ear is set in vibration, like a speaking-
trumpet, by the sounds that enter it, and that this vibration modifies
the pitch of the entering sound more or less according to the form of
the individual ear.

The supposition that the waves of sound, before impinging on
the tympanum, have to pass through a thin film which covers it,
is less probable, since such a film would of course be subject to
change from time to time, and thus the whole phenomenon might
be altered.

As may be supposed, I have not as yet been able to collect any
information on this subject.

If, in measuring the number of vibrations of musical notes, the
above circumstance has not been taken into account, some modest
doubt of the accuracy of the results may not be altogether unreasonable.—*Philosophical Magazine*, No. 136.

Professor Helmholtz, by a series of experiments, has been led to the
hypothesis that each narrow fibre of the auditory nerve is destined for
the perception of notes of a particular pitch, and is excited when the
note which strikes the ear corresponds in pitch to that of the elastic
formation in connexion with the fibre. According to this, the perception of different tones would realize itself through the simultaneous
excitation of the fibre which corresponds to the primary note, and of
certain others, corresponding to the incidental notes.—*Poggendorff's
Annalen*.

NEW SOUND-FIGURES FORMED BY DROPS OF A LIQUID.

IF a drinking-glass, or a funnel of about three inches diameter at
the edge, be filled with water, or alcohol, or ether, and a strong note
be made by drawing a violin-bow on the edge, a Sound-figure will be
formed on the surface of the liquid, consisting of nothing but drops
of liquid. If the vessel gives the fundamental note, the figure forms
a four-rayed star, the ends of which extend to the four nodal points;
but if the note which the vessel gives be the second higher, the star
will be six-rayed; and if the vessel gives still higher tones, other more
numerously rayed stars are produced.—*F. Melde; Poggendorff's
Annalen*.

VELOCITY OF THE SOUND OF THUNDER.

THE Rev. Mr. Earnshaw, in a paper on "A New Theoretical
Determination of the Velocity of Sound," concludes that it would
appear there is no other limit to the velocity with which a
violent sound is transmitted through the atmosphere, than that

which the possibility of supplying a sufficient degree of force in its agencies may oppose. Hence it is probable that there is no sound which is propagated faster than a thunder-clap, the genesis of which by the electric discharge being extremely violent and almost instantaneous, is accompanied by a large development of heat.

If the theory here advanced be true, the report of fire-arms should travel faster than the human voice; and the crash of thunder faster than the report of a cannon.

ACOUSTICS IN BUILDING.

A PAPER on Acoustics has been recently read at the Royal Institute of British Architects, by Mr. T. R. Smith. This gentleman, after referring to the experiments of M. Biot on the transmission of sound through a pipe 1000 yards long, through which a whisper was distinctly audible, and to the curious exception discovered by Mr. Scott Russell to the ordinary law of reflection of sound when the sonorous vibrations strike against a reflecting surface at an acute angle—maintained that in order to combine reflection and resonance in the construction of a building there should be an inclined surface above the head of the speaker, to reflect the sound down upon the audience; the walls should be covered with wood, and there should be a space above the ceiling and under the floor. But in thus assisting the transmission of sound great care should be taken to prevent echoes. To avoid echoes by reflection the head of the speaker should be near the ceiling, or a sounding-board should be placed above him, so that the sound may be propelled onward; and the surface of the walls should be broken by pillars or draperies, particularly at the end. The vibrations caused by resonance should also be prevented by draperies, or by breaking up the surface by projections. Mr. Smith considered a short parallelogram, with a semi-circular end, as the form best adapted for hearing; the speaker being advanced to a forward position among the audience. The most difficult of all buildings for hearing a speaker, he said, are parallelograms of four flat sides, and with a high flat ceiling. Mr. Scott Russell strongly enforced the necessity of breaking up the surface to prevent reverberation; and, alluding to the different effects of the transmission of sound in full and in empty rooms, he observed that the best possible means of making sounds distinctly audible in large rooms is to fill the walls with beads.

VISION AND SOUND.

PROF. STOKES, in a note to a paper in the *Philosophical Magazine*, No. 126, observes:—The remarkable phenomenon discovered by Foucault, and re-discovered and extended by Kirchhoff, that a body may be at the same time a source of light giving out rays of a definite refrangibility, and an absorbing medium extinguishing rays of that same refrangibility which traverse it, seems readily to admit of a dynamical illustration borrowed from sound.

We know that a stretched string which on being struck gives out a certain note (suppose its fundamental note) is capable of being thrown into the same state of vibration by aërial vibrations corresponding to the same note. Suppose now a portion of space to contain a great number of such stretched strings, forming thus the analogue of a "medium." It is evident that such a medium on being agitated would give out the note above mentioned; while on the other hand, if that note were sounded in air at a distance, the incident vibrations would throw the strings into vibration, and consequently would themselves be gradually extinguished, since otherwise there would be a creation of *vis viva*. The optical application of this illustration is too obvious to need comment.

PROGRESS OF PHYSIOLOGY.

LORD WROTTESLEY, as President of the late meeting of the British Association at Oxford, in his inaugural address, remarked :— " In the recent Progress of Physiology, I am informed that the feature perhaps most deserving of note on this occasion, is the more extended and successful application of chemistry, physics, and the other collateral sciences, to the study of the animal and vegetable economy. In proof, I refer to the great and steady advances which have, within the last few years, been made in the chemical history of nutrition, the statics and dynamics of the blood, the investigation of the physical phenomena of the senses, and the electricity of nerves and muscles. Even the velocity of the nerve-force itself has been submitted to measurement. Moreover, when it is now desired to apply the resources of geometry or analysis to the elucidation of the phenomena of life, or to obtain a mathematical expression of a physiological law, the first care of the investigator is to acquire precise experimental data on which to proceed, instead of setting out with vague assumptions, and ending with a parade of misdirected skill, such as brought discredit on the school of the mathematical physicians of the Newtonian period.

" But I cannot take leave of this department of knowledge without likewise alluding to the progress made in scrutinizing the animal and vegetable structure by means of the microscope—more particularly the intimate organization of the brain, spinal cord, and organs of the senses ; also to the extension, through means of well-directed experiment, of our knowledge of the functions of the nervous system, the course followed by sensorial impressions and motorial excitement in the spinal cord, and the influence excited by or through the nervous centres on the movements of the heart, blood-vessels, and viscera, and on the activity of the secreting organs—subjects of inquiry, which, it may be observed, are closely related to the question of the organic mechanism whereby our corporeal frame is influenced by various mental conditions."

THE PYRAMID OF NATURE.—ORGANIC FORCES.

PROF. LECONTE, of South Carolina College, closes an elaborate paper on the Correlation of Force, with these inferences :—

The most natural condition of matter is evidently that of chemical compounds, *i.e.*, the mineral kingdom. Matter separated from force would exist, of course, only as elementary matter or on the first plane; but united with force, it is thereby raised into the second plane, and continues to exist most naturally there. The third plane is supplied from the second, and the fourth from the third. Thus it is evident that the quantity of matter is greatest on the second, and least on the fourth plane. Thus nature may be likened to a pyramid, of which the mineral kingdom forms the base and the animal kingdom the apex. The absolute necessity of this arrangement on the principle of the conservation of force may be thus expressed. Matter, force, and energy are related to one another in physical and organic science somewhat in the same manner as matter, velocity, and momentum in mechanics. The whole energy remaining constant, the greater the intensity of the force (the elevation in the scale of existence) the less the quantity of matter. Thus necessarily results what I have called the Pyramid of Nature, upon which organic forces work upwards and physical and chemical forces downwards.

As the matter of organisms is not created by them, but is only so much matter withdrawn, borrowed, as it were, from the common fund of matter, to be restored at death; so also organic forces cannot be created by organisms, but must be regarded as so much force abstracted from the common fund of force, to be again restored, the whole of it, at death.[*] If, then, vital force is only transformed physical force, is it not possible, it may be asked, that physical forces may generate organisms *de novo?* Do not the views presented above support the doctrines of "equivocal generation" and of the original creation of species by physical forces? I answer that the question of the origination of species is left exactly where it was found and where it must always remain, viz., utterly beyond the limits of human science. But although we can never hope by the light of science to know how organisms originated, still all that we do know of the laws of the organic and inorganic world seem to negative the idea that physical or chemical forces acting upon inorganic matter can produce them. Vital force is transformed physical force: true, but the necessary medium of this transformation is an organized fabric; the necessary condition of the existence of vital force is therefore the previous existence of an organism. As the existence of physical forces cannot even be conceived without the previous existence of matter as its necessary substratum, so the existence of vital force is inconceivable without the previous existence of an organized structure as its necessary substratum. In the words of Dr. Carpenter: "It is the speciality of the material substratum thus furnishing the medium or instrument of the metamorphosis which establishes and must ever maintain a well-marked boundary between physical and vital forces. Starting with the abstract notion of force as emanating at once from the Divine will, we might say that this force operating through inorganic matter, manifests itself as electricity, magnetism, light, heat, chemical affinity, and mechanical motion; but that when directed through organized structures, it

* Carpenter, *Phil. Trans.*, 1850, p. 755.

effects the operations of growth, development, and chemico-vital transformations !"

CARDIAC INHIBITION.

DR. FOSTER has read to the British Association a paper on the Theory of Cardiac Inhibition. The author said that the snail's heart acted under direct stimulation by the interrupted current, as the heart of vertebrate animals does under stimulation of the pneumogastric ; and the study of the crab's heart seemed to show that the results of any stimulation of heart are very various according to the quantity of stimulus employed.

SACCHARINE FUNCTION OF THE LIVER.

DR. HARLEY has related to the Royal Society a number of experiments which he had performed in concert with Professor Sharpey ; the results of which experiments show that the animal as well as the vegetable kingdom possesses a sugar-forming power. The conclusions the author arrived at are in favour of the following generally received views upon this interesting subject :—1. Sugar is a normal constituent of healthy blood. 2. The portal blood of an animal fed on mixed diet contains sugar ; but that of a fasting animal, as well as of one fed solely on flesh, is devoid of saccharine matter. 3. The livers of healthy animals contain sugar irrespective of the kind of food. 4. The sugar found in the bodies of omnivorous animals is partly derived directly from their food, partly formed by their own livers. 5. The livers of carnivorous animals possess the power of forming a substance called glucogene ; which glucogene is, at least in part, transformed into sugar in the liver.

THE ÆSTHESIOMETER.

THIS is a small instrument invented by Dr. Sieveking, and made by Elliot Brothers, which is used for the purpose of aiding in the diagnosis of certain forms of nervous diseases. It is similar in form to an ordinary beam-compass, and its employment is based upon the principle that a diseased part of the body loses the power of distinguishing the distance between two points nearly close together. It is chiefly used in determining the progress of paralysis.

NEW EYE-SHADE—THE OCCHIOMBRA.

MR. JOSEPH CALKIN has patented a transparent Eye-Shade (*Occhiombra*), which promises to be a boon to those who suffer from impaired vision, or temporarily, from inflammation, or other irritating causes.

Its general appearance is that of the usual shade, but more symmetrical in its outline.

It consists of a very light wire framework, fitting with a spring closely round the forehead, just above the eyebrows ; and over the framework is extended an extremely fine transparent fabric of gauze or other material. A portion of the wire framework (almost invisible to the by-stander) rests upon the nose, passes close to the face under the eyes to the temples, supporting the fabric from the lower part of the shade, thus forming one large closed chamber for the eyes.

The fineness of the fabric will be found to protect the wearer from wind, dust, and sun, but allows of sufficient ventilation to keep the eyes perfectly cool; and a lengthened opening at the top of the shade (not observable when worn) provides for the escape of any heat that may be engendered by violent exercise—the want of which is felt in the ordinary shade.

The occhiombra can be placed and removed with the same ease as a pair of spectacles, and is so light as to be scarcely perceptible to the wearer, being in weight about half-an-ounce.

The fabric is sometimes doubled, to meet the requirements of those with weak or inflamed eyes, but is sufficiently transparent, in all cases, to enable the wearer to thread his way through any crowd with perfect comfort.

The occhiombra will be found of great service in protecting from wind and ashes those who travel by railroad. Travellers in India and Egypt, and Alpine excursionists, will find it of inestimable benefit—the first as a protection from sun and sand, and the latter from sleet, wind, and the painful glare from the snow. It also relieves the angler from wind and glare on the surface of the water; but it will be found of *especial* service to ladies, and those who visit the sea-side, protecting them from excessive wind and light, rendering it unnecessary for the former to wear a veil, and thus allowing free respiration of the pure sea air.

The occhiombra does not in any way interfere with the wearing of spectacles, and is manufactured in different colours, to meet the tastes of those who adopt it.

This new eye-shade is sold by Messrs. Weiss and Son, 62, Strand.

NEW SPIROMETER.

A NEW form of Spirometer has been exhibited to the British Association, by Dr. Lewis. The novel principle of the machine is the displacement of water by expired air, the amount of the latter being equivalent to the former. A graduated scale attached to the side of the instrument indicates the amount expired during an experiment.

Electrical Science.

INFLUENCE OF MAGNETIC FORCE ON THE ELECTRIC DISCHARGE.

PROFESSOR TYNDALL has exhibited at the Royal Institution a brilliant series of experiments illustrative of the constitution of the Electric Discharge and of the action of Magnetism upon it. The Report occupies nearly five pages of the printed proceedings of the Institution ; the following summary is from the *Mechanics' Magazine*. The substance of the discourse was derived from the researches of various philosophers, its form being regulated to suit the require‧ ments of the audience.

The influence of the transport of particles was first shown. The carbon terminals of a battery of 40 cells of Grove were brought within one-eighth of an inch of each other, and the spark from a Leyden jar was sent across this space. This spark bridged with carbon particles the gap which had previously existed in the circuit, and the brilliant electric light due to the passage of the battery current was immediately displayed.

The magnified image of the coal points of an electric lamp was next projected upon a white screen, and the distance to which they could be drawn apart, without interrupting the current, was noted. A button of pure silver was then introduced in place of the positive carbon, a luminous discharge four or five times the length of the former being thus obtained. The action of a magnet upon the splendid stream of green light obtained in the foregoing experiment was then exhibited, the light being bent hither and thither, according as the poles of the magnet changed their position : the discharge in some cases formed a magnificent green bow, which on the further approach of the magnet was torn asunder, and the passage of the current thereby interrupted.

A discharge from Ruhmkorff's coil was next sent through an attenuated medium ; and the glow, which surrounded the negative electrode, was referred to. An electric lamp was placed upon its back ; a horseshoe magnet was placed horizontally over its lens, and on the magnet a plate of glass ; a mirror inclined at an angle of 45° received the beam from the lamp, and projected it upon the screen. Iron filings were scattered on the glass, and the magnetic curves thus illuminated were magnified, and brought to clear definition upon the screen. The negative light above referred to arranges itself, according to Plücker, in a similar manner.

The rotation of an electric current round the pole of a magnet, discovered by Mr. Faraday in the Royal Institution, nearly forty years ago, was next shown ; and the rotation of a luminous current from an induction coil in an exhausted receiver by the same magnet was also exhibited, and both shown to obey the same laws.

Into a circuit of 20 cells a large coil of copper wire was introduced ; and when the current was interrupted, a bright spark, due to the passage of the extra current, was obtained. The brightness and loudness of the spark were augmented when a core of soft iron was placed within the coil. The disruption of the current took place between the poles of an electro-magnet; and when the latter was excited, an extraordinary augmentation of the loudness of the spark was noticed.

An experiment was next shown for the purpose of illustrating the important influence which the mode of breaking contact may have upon the efficacy of an induction coil.

The splendid effects obtained from the discharge of Ruhmkorff's coil through exhausted tubes were next referred to.

After a variety of other most beautiful experiments with a powerful battery of 400 of Grove's cells, lent by Mr. Gassiot, the discharge of the battery was finally sent through a tube, whose platinum wires were terminated by two small balls of carbon : a glow was first produced ; but on heating a portion of the tube containing a stick of caustic potash, the positive ball sent out a luminous protrusion, which subsequently detached itself from the ball ; the tube becoming instantly afterwards filled with the most brilliant strata. "There can be no doubt," said Dr. Tyndall on this point, "that the superior effulgence of the bands obtained with this tube is due to the character of its electrodes : *the bands are the transported matter of these electrodes.* May not this be the case with other electrodes ? There appears to be no uniform flow in nature ; we cannot get either air or water through an orifice in a uniform stream ; the friction against the orifice is overcome by starts, and the jet issues in pulsations. Let a lighted candle be quickly passed through the air, the flame will break itself into a beaded line in virtue of a similar intermittent action ; and it may be made to sing, so regular are the pulses produced by its passage. Analogy might lead us to suppose that the electricity overcomes the resistance at the surface of its electrode in a similar manner, escaping from it in tremors ; the matter which it carries along with it being broken up into strata, as a liquid vein is broken into drops."

THE ATLANTIC CABLE.

A REPORT on the state of the Atlantic Cable in Trinity Bay, dated St. John's (N.F.), July 3, 1860, has been received. It states :—

"After repeated attempts to raise the cable by grappelling, in order to test its electrical condition, and with a view to land it, we regret having to report that, although we have on many occasions been able to raise the bight, and so get on board at different times pieces of cable, in all amounting to about seven miles, we have invariably found it broken again a few miles off." The Report then details the proceedings from the 12th to the 30th June, on which day—"The cable was hooked at least three times, and probably more during the day, but broke before reaching the surface. At last a bight came on board, the cable at this spot being unusually good for about 30 yards ; the outer end was found to be broken about 200 yards off. About two miles of the inner end were recovered, when it parted again at a weak place where there was nothing but the gutta percha covered wire left ; this, however, was just able to bring the cable to the surface, when it snapped before it could be secured by a stopper. The point where we last grappelled this day was a little east of a straight line joining Tickle Point and Copper Island, in 140 fathoms water. Although mud is shown on the charts, there are most unquestionably rocks also, as was too plainly indicated by the state of the cable, rock weed, and sea animalcules adhering to and surrounding it in many places, showing that it had been suspended clear of the bottom.

"The recovered cable varied in condition very much, and what is most important is, that even those portions which came out of the black mud were so perished in numerous patches that the outer covering parted on board during the process of hauling in, and but for the dexterity and courage of the men in seizing hold of it beyond the break, where the iron wires stuck out like bunches of highly sharpened needle points, we should not have known so much of its condition. In a word, it was evidently sometimes embedded in mud, sometimes on small stones, sometimes half embedded, and sometimes wholly exposed over rocks, as was apparent from the condition of the outer covering. The iron wires in many places often appeared sound, but on minute inspection, were found eaten away and rotten; the sewing was also decayed. In some places the iron wires were coated with metallic copper, and much eaten, they having most probably rested upon copper ore, for there are veins of it in Trinity Bay. The gutta-percha and copper wire are, however, in as good condition as when laid down. The general ragged, precipitous, and rocky character of the surrounding land evidently extends below the surface of the water ; the unevenness of our soundings and condition of the cable indicate this plainly.

"We accordingly decided upon leaving the neighbourhood of Bull's Island altogether, as the cable in its present state at that part of the Bay will not repay the cost of recovery. We agreed simultaneously to attempt to raise the cable off Heart's Content, and ascertain its condition there, this being the most promising part of the Bay from the information we have been able to collect. Accordingly on the 1st of July we sailed to New Perlican, and grapnelled for the cable in a smooth sea. We hooked in 143 fathoms water in a straight line joining the north point of St. John's Harbour, and the south point of New Perlican, at a distance from the latter of about 6 nauts. The cable was during the day hooked at least four times—we believe more. It sometimes lifted off the ground before parting as much as 40 fathoms, sometimes only 15 ; in no instance did it come near the surface of the water. On two occasions the iron strands of the cable left most unmistakeable impressions on the grapnel, and iron rust, resembling that usually found on the cable, adhered to its claws. The bottom consisted of green mud and light-coloured clay, the latter very compact, and its consistency not much unlike the blue clay of London ; some parts of the bottom were of stone. Those portions of the recovered cable that were wrapped with tarred yarn were found, the tar and hemp having preserved the iron wires bright and free from rust. This will be further reported 'on when the pieces of recovered cable have been more closely examined. It is with deep regret we have to inform you that it has been necessary to abandon the cable."

The report is signed by Mr. Varley and Captain Kell.

INDICATIONS OF VACUA.

A PAPER "On Vacua, as Indicated by the Mercurial Syphon-gauge and the Electrical Discharge" has been read at the Royal Society, by Mr. J. P. Gassiot, F.R.S. The following is an abstract :—

That the varied condition of the stratified electrical discharge is due to the relative but always imperfect condition of the vacuum through which it is passed, is exemplified by the changes which take place in the form of the striæ while the potash is heated in a carbonic acid vacuum-tube. In order, if possible, to measure the pressure of the vapour, Mr. Gassiot had a carefully-prepared siphon mercurial gauge sealed into a tube 15 inches long, at an equal distance between the two wires. This tube was charged with carbonic acid. When exhausted by the air-pump and sealed, it showed a pressure indicated by about 0·5 inch difference in the level of the mercury ; the potash was then heated ; the mercury gradually fell until it became perfectly level. Dr. Andrews (*Philosophical Maga-*

zine, February, 1852) has shown that with a concentrated solution of caustic potassa, he obtained with carbonic acid a vacuum with the air-pump so perfect as to exercise no appreciable tension, as no difference in the level of the mercury in the siphon-gauge could be detected.   On trying the discharge in the vacuum-tube after the potash had cooled, Mr. Gassiot found it gave the cloud-like stratifications, with a slight reddish tinge ; consequently not only was the vacuum not perfect, as denoted by the form of stratifications, but in this tube the colour denotes that even a trace of the air remains, probably that portion in the narrow part of the siphon-gauge, which, from its position, was not displaced by the carbonic acid.

The potash was subsequently heated until the discharge was reduced to a wave line, with very narrow striæ ; in this state moisture is seen adhering to the sides of the tube ; but even in this condition the difference in the level of the mercury in the gauge did not ever vary more than ·05 inch.   As the potash cooled, the discharge altered through all the well-known phases of the striæ, the mercury again becoming quite level.   At first almost the slightest heat applied to the potash alters the form of the stratifications ; as the heating is repeated, longer application is necessary ; but it shows how sensibly the electrical discharge denotes the perfection of a vacuum, which cannot be detected by the ordinary method of mercurial siphon-gauge.

CONDUCTIVITY OF COPPER.

PROFESSOR WHEATSTONE has communicated to the Royal Society a paper prepared by MM. Matthiessen and Holzmann on the effect of the presence of metals and metalloids upon the Electric-Conductivity (or conducting power) of pure Copper.   After numerous experiments, and after studying the effects of sub-oxide of copper, phosphorus, arsenic, sulphur, carbon, tin, zinc, iron, lead, silver, gold, &c., on the conducting power of copper, the authors have come to the conclusion that "there is no alloy of copper which conducts electricity better than the pure metal."

NEW SECONDARY PILE OF GREAT POWER. BY M. G. PLANTÉ.

JACOBI has proposed the use of Secondary Electric Currents for telegraphic purposes, and Planté has suggested the substitution of electrodes of lead for those of platinum in these batteries.   A more extended study has convinced him of their use.   He states that a battery with electrodes of lead has 2½ times the electromotive force of one with electrodes of platinized platinum, and six times as great as that of one with ordinary platinum.   This great power arises from the powerful affinity which peroxide of lead has for hydrogen, a fact first noticed by De la Rive.   The secondary battery which he recommends has the following construction :—It consists of nine elements, presenting a total surface of ten square metres.   Each element is formed of two large lead plates, rolled into a spiral and separated by coarse cloth, and immersed in water acidulated with one-tenth sulphuric acid.·   The kind of current used to excite this battery depends on the manner in which the secondary couples are arranged. If they are arranged so as to give three elements of triple surface, five small Bunsen's cells, the zincs of which are immersed to a depth of seven centimetres, are sufficient to give, after a few minutes' action, a spark of extraordinary intensity when the current is closed. The apparatus plays, in fact, just the part of a condenser; for by its means the work performed by the battery, after the lapse of a certain time, may be collected in an instant. An idea of the intensity of the charge will be obtained by remembering that to produce a similar effect it would be necessary to arrange 300 Bunsen's elements of the ordinary size (13 centimetres in height), so as to form four or five elements of $3\frac{1}{2}$ square metres of surface, or three elements of still greater surface. If the secondary battery be arranged for intensity, the principal battery should be formed of a number of elements sufficient to overcome the inverse electromotive force developed. For nine secondary elements about fifteen Bunsen's cells should be taken, which might, however, be very small.

From the malleability of the metal of which it is formed, this battery is readily constructed; by taking the plates of lead sufficiently thin, a large surface may be placed in a small space. The nine elements used by Planté are placed in a box 36 centimetres square, filled with liquid once for all, and placed in closed jars; they may also be kept charged in a physical cabinet, and ready to be used whenever it is desired to procure, by means of a weak battery, powerful discharges of dynamic electricity.—*Comptes Rendus; Philos. Mag.*, No. 129.

APPLICATION OF ELECTRICAL DISCHARGES FROM THE INDUCTION COIL TO ILLUMINATION.

MR. GASSIOT proposes to take a carbonic-acid vacuum tube of about $\frac{1}{18}$th of an inch internal diameter, wound in the form of a flattened spiral. The wider ends of the tube, in which the platinum wires are sealed, are two inches in length and about half an inch in diameter; they are enclosed in a wooden case, so as to permit only the spiral to be exposed.

When the discharge from a Rubmkorff's induction apparatus is passed through the vacuum-tube, the spiral becomes intensely luminous, exhibiting a brilliant white light. Mr. Gassiot, who has exhibited the experiment to the Royal Society, caused the discharge from the induction coil to pass through two miles of copper wire; with the same coil excited so as to give a spark through air of one inch in length, he ascertained that the luminosity in the spiral was not reduced when the discharge passed through fourteen miles of No. 32 copper wire.

NEW KIND OF ELECTRIC CURRENT.

THE fifth number of Poggendorff's *Annalen* for 1859 contains an article of considerable length, the leading points in which are included in the following abstract:—

When pure water flows through a porous body, an electrical current is elicited—a fact established by experiments, says M. G. Quincke, may be stated concisely in these terms:—

Some thirty layers of thin silk stuff were placed over each other and attached over one tube of the apparatus; another tube was then adapted against the former, and the part separating them covered thickly with sealing-wax. Owing to the wide pores of the silk, considerably more water flowed through under equal pressure than when the clay plate was employed. The linen was used in the same manner.

The other substances were applied in the form of powder, in a glass tube of the diameter of the above tubes. The ends of these tubes, the length of which varied, according to the substance employed, from 20 to 45 millims., were ground flat, and over them were placed discs of the silk stuff spoken of, to prevent the flow of the fluid carrying away particles of the substance under examination. In the case of Bunsen's coal, the tube was closed with plates thereof.

Platina was made use of in the spongy form, iron as filings. The glass had been reduced to powder on an anvil. Ivory and the various kinds of wood were employed in the form of sawdust. It was endeavoured in vain to press water through a porous plate of wood, for the plate had to be luted in dry; and on becoming moist, even if cut perpendicular to the direction of the fibres, it warped so much that it broke the sealing-wax or the tube.

The direction of the electric current was not changed by adding acids or solutions of salts to the distilled water, but it was considerably weakened thereby.

MOVEMENTS OF ELECTRIC FLUID.

The Rev. T. Rankin has read to the British Association a paper "On the different Motions of Electric Fluid." The author, from several very striking and vividly-described thunder-storms and their permanent effects, concludes that sometimes the electric fluid moves downward, sometimes upward, and sometimes horizontally. On one occasion, some years since, about two o'clock, on a night on which it had thundered almost incessantly, a loud whizzing sound was heard to pass over the rectory-house, which he judged to be an aerolite; a tree in the direction it had passed was struck; and from the nature of the injury inflicted, the conclusion was drawn, that the motion of either the aerolite or of the electric fluid had been nearly horizontal.

ELECTRIC TARGETS.

An Electric Target has been brought into use by several Volunteer Rifle Companies, by means of which the necessity for a marker or signal-man being stationed near to the target, for the purpose of signalling by flags the portion struck by the projectile, is altogether dispensed with, the target itself conveying the information to the marksmen by means of electric signals.

The inventors of this improved target are Messrs. John Lang and Charles Chevalier, of the Submarine Telegraph Works, Birkenhead. The object of their invention is to enable a marksman to ascertain instantaneously, by means of self-acting electrical apparatus, the effect of his shot upon a target,—that is to say, to indicate upon the spot from whence a bullet is fired, or at any other convenient place, what part of the target has been struck by the bullet without the necessity for a marker near the target. In order to effect this, the target is made of several strong plates suspended from a suitably strong framing, and behind each plate are fixed insulated metallic points. Each plate or segment of which the target is composed is connected with one pole of a galvanic battery, and the points behind such plates or segments with the other pole, and at any convenient point of the circuit is placed a needle surrounded with a coil in such a manner that when any of the plates or segments of which the target is composed is struck by a bullet, it is caused to move backwards till it comes in contact with the points behind it, and thus forms electrical connexion, which, completing the circuit, causes the needle to be deflected. Each of the plates or segments being furnished with its special circuit and indicating needle, by inspecting these indicators is demonstrated which plate has been struck by the bullet, as only the needle belonging to that particular plate is deflected. But, instead of connecting each piece or portion of the target through a separate conducting wire with a separate needle or indicator, it is preferable for most purposes to reduce the number of conducting wires, and dials, and needles, and rely upon the changes and permutations which can be made or effected upon one dial with one needle, consistent with fewness of parts, simplicity of action, and the proper recording of the vibrations of the needle or pointer.—*Mechanics' Magazine.*

GUTTA-PERCHA AND INDIA-RUBBER.

A PAPER has been read to the British Association, "On the Character and Comparative Value of Gutta-Percha and India-rubber employed as Insulators for Subaqueous Telegraph Wires," by Mr. S. W. Silver. After pointing out some of the mistakes prevalent on the subject of the insulating properties of India-rubber, a comparison was made by the writer between the relative advantages and the insulating power of India-rubber and gutta-percha respectively. Insulation in the case of a submarine cable depends upon two causes or properties of the bodies used :—1. The specific non-conducting power of the substance ; 2. Its impermeability, by which the original insulating conditions may be maintained. The insulating power of gutta-percha is very high ; but, in the case of a submarine telegraph cable, its porosity renders it a very imperfect insulator in practice. India-rubber, with lower specific insulating properties (as would appear from experiments made in dry air), is, nevertheless, practically a far more efficient insulator, by reason of its complete impermeability, while in addition it possesses a lower inductive capacity. It was pointed out that impermeability is as important a question as specific non-conductibility in an insulator of such cables, and that even if a substance could be found insulating perfectly in dry air, it still might in practice be of questionable utility for submarine lines, owing to its porosity, as was the case with gutta-percha. There is now no difficulty in covering wires with India-rubber.

ELECTRICAL CONDITION OF THE EGG OF THE COMMON FOWL.

THE structure of the egg suggested to Dr. John Davy the idea of its exerting Electrical Action. This was confirmed on trial. Using a delicate galvanometer and a suitable apparatus, on plunging one wire into the white, and the other, insulated, except at the point of contact, into the yolk, the needle was deflected to the extent of 5°; and on changing the wires, the course of the needle was reversed. When the white and yolk were taken out of the shell, and the yolk immersed in the white, the effects on trial were similar; but not so when the two were well mixed; then no distinct effect was perceptible.

Indications also of chemical action were obtained on substituting for the galvanometer a mixture consisting of water, a little gelatinous starch, and a small quantity of iodide of potassium, especially when rendered very sensitive of change by the addition of a few drops of muriatic acid. In the instance of newly-laid eggs, the iodine liberated appeared at the pole connected with the white; on the contrary, in that of eggs which had been kept some time, it appeared at the pole connected with the yolk, answering in both to the copper in a single voltaic combination formed of copper and zinc.

The author, after describing the results obtained, declines speculating on them at present, merely remarking, that in the economy of the egg, and the changes to which it is subject, it can hardly be doubted that electro-chemical action must perform an important part, and that in the instance of the ovum generally, i.e., when composed of a white and of a yolk, or of substances in contact, of heterogeneous natures.

IMPROVED MAGNETO-ELECTRIC MACHINES.

MR. W. E. NEWTON has patented certain improvements in Magneto-electric Machines, relating—

1, to a novel construction of magnets, and consisting in constituting a wheel of magnets of a series of radial plates or bars connected at the inner ends by a continuous ring, thereby forming a compound magnet. Secondly, to a new combination of helices, which are so arranged that they may be readily adjusted to the magnets, and consisting in forming the spool heads elongated with holes through them, outside of the helix, for the passage of a bolt or spindle, by which they are secured to a ring or holding plate placed outside of the compound magnets, so that each helix can be swung around on the securing bolts or spindle into any position required, and then secured. Thirdly, to an arrangement of fixed bands or rings for receiving the induced electric impulses, and consisting in combining with rotating compound magnets one or more pairs of insulated rings of non-magnetic metal placed outside the circle of rotating magnets, and with which the terminal wires of the helices are to be connected, whereby the connection and disconnection can be readily made and changed, whether the machine be in motion or still. Fourthly, to what is termed a pole changer, that is to say, a mechanism for changing the direction of the currents which are delivered from and returned to the machine alternately in opposite directions, and cause them to pass to and through a conductor in one and the same direction as if induced by a battery. The details of the invention are voluminous. —*Mechanics' Magazine.*

HEATING AND TESTING OF TELEGRAPH CABLES.

MR. C. W. SIEMENS, in a letter to Professor Tyndall, in the *Philosophical Magazine*, describes how he has availed himself of a striking and most fortunate application of a well-known fact in electricity, that the resistance encountered by an electric current in passing through a wire, is augmented in proportion to the augmentation of temperature. Conversely, we can accurately infer the increase of temperature from the increase of resistance, and this is the principle which Mr. Siemens has so happily applied. He had charge of the Rangoon and Singapore telegraph cable, and was led by previous observation to surmise that a spontaneous generation of heat sometimes took place when large lengths of such cables are formed into coils. He was, therefore, anxious to keep himself acquainted with the temperature of the inner portions of his coil, but could not, of course, introduce ordinary thermometers there. He introduced, however, between the layers of the cable at regular intervals suitable coils of copper wire, the resistance of which for a long series of temperatures had been determined beforehand. The ends of these copper coils issued into the air, so that they could be connected at any time with a suitable apparatus for determining their resistance. Now, Mr. Siemens found that although the outer portion of the coil of cable had a temperature not sensibly higher than that of the air, the wires which he had placed within the coil showed a steady augmentation of resistance, from which he inferred that the cable was heating within. He waited until the augmented resistance indicated an increase of temperature from sixty to eighty-six degrees. Had he waited much longer, the cable would probably have been destroyed. Some of those to whom he communicated his conclusions regarded them for a time as the mere refinements of theory, but all their doubts were dissipated when a quantity of water, at a temperature of forty-two degrees, thrown upon the top of the cable, after passing through the inner portions of the coil, issued from the bottom with the temperature raised to seventy-two degrees.

The precise cause of this generation of heat has not, we believe, been yet determined. It may be due to some chemical action in the gutta-percha; but it may also be due to the gradual rusting of the iron which encases the cable. "Who can say (asks a writer in the *Saturday Review*) what injury was done to the gutta-percha covering of the Atlantic cable, through ignorance of the fact so opportunely observed in the case of that of Rangoon and Singapore?"

This cable has been tested by a process invented by Mr. W. Reid. During the manipulation of gutta-percha, a great quantity of air and water is liable to become mixed with it, and in marine cables, when covered with ropeyarn and iron wire, these faults have hitherto been detected only after submersion. By the plan of Mr. Reid, however, all such defects are alleged to be certain to be discovered. A coil of gutta-percha, from one mile to five, is placed in a strong cylinder that can be made air and water-tight. The first operation is to exhaust the cylinder; when a vacuum is formed, a column of water is allowed to rush in and fill up all the holes and crevices formerly filled with air. The cable is in this state tested with a delicate galvanometer and noted. A pressure is then applied equal to the pressure of a column of water the height of which is equal to the depth of the sea where the cable is intended to be laid, whether it be the Atlantic or any other. This is continued for a certain time, when the wire is again tested. On the pressure being removed, another testing takes place, and it is affirmed that if the smallest defect in the insulating medium, or mechanical injury, however minute and invisible to the naked eye, then exists, its detection is inevitable. The disease can accordingly be removed or repaired, and the manufacture proceeded with. Finally, it appears that the whole expense of the testing falls short of 5s. per cent. of the cost for making the cable.—*Times.*

ELECTRO-TELEGRAPHY.

At the *conversazione* of the Royal College of Physicians, Professor Wheatstone exhibited his *New Printing Telegraph*, so constructed that the message is sent by means of a perforated strip of paper, the holes in which, representing the letters, are made by means of a separate machine, worked by a finger-board. The advantage of this method is, that several persons can work at the finger-boards, and prepare several messages at once, and on the perforated paper being put into the telegraphing machine, it forwards the message at the rate of five hundred letters per minute, being about five times faster than by the present system. On its arrival at its destination the message is again pricked off on a paper tape, at the same rate, when it can be easily and rapidly read. Another advantage is, that the whole apparatus only occupies a few inches square, there being no battery required, as it is worked by magnetic electricity.

Professor Wheatstone also exhibited his *Universal and Military Telegraph*, especially adapted for rifle and field practice. This is a portable telegraphic apparatus, also worked by magnetic power. It is extremely light, being only six inches square, and is at all times in readiness for immediate use, without previous preparation. The communication in the field, or between the target and the gun, is maintained in the ordinary alphabetical language by the most simple means, so that any person who can read and spell is able to work it. The communicating wire is covered with rope, and is effectually protected from abrasion or pressure when lying on the ground, though of comparatively small thickness, and when not in use can be rolled on a drum. These telegraphs were used by the French in the late Italian war, and are now in use in various public offices. The one exhibited, although so small, forwarded messages to a distance of twenty miles, but by increasing the size of the magnet much greater power could be obtained.

Professor Hughes has produced a *Dial Electric Telegraph*, consisting of a train of wheels set in motion by a spring, and governed in its revolution by means of a vibrating spring. The dial revolves by means of friction, and whenever the keys upon which the letters of the alphabet are engraved are pressed down, the wheel is stopped and the electric circuit is closed. This attracts an armature of an electro-magnet at the distant instrument, which stops the dial by means of a catch ; thus the distant instrument imitates what is done upon the transmitting one. Any person can work this instrument without possessing any previous knowledge of such matters.

Among the improvements in *The Insulation of Electric Telegraph Conductors* is one by Mr. F. N. Gisborne, and is for suspended line wires. Mr. Gisborne's insulator consists of an enamelled cast-iron cap, with an enamelled wrought-iron screw-pin ; the interior of the cap being of a globular form, affords protection against the admission or accumulation of moisture. This insulator holds the main wire, upon a broad basis, without the assistance of any tie-wire or other fastening, and in such a manner that it cannot draw or slip ; each pole therefore sustains its own legitimate amount of weight and strain. It is readily attached to a pole or wall without any additional fastenings, and when attached remains perfectly firm in every particular.

New Instruments.—Mr. Thomas Allan, C.E., to whom we primarily owe the practical abandonment of heavy wire-bound submarine telegraph cables, has embodied these telegraphic improvements. The first relates to what are called pole-changers, or relays. A great difficulty with these has hitherto been the derangement caused by the action of the spark upon the delicate contact points of the relay. Now, this evil Mr. Allan has got rid of altogether, by combining an improved relay with an improved recording instrument, in such manner that the spark is not produced in the relay at all, but in the recording instrument, where it is of far less consequence. This improvement is attended by an immense advantage, for, now that the relay is relieved of the spark, the limit which has hitherto been practically placed upon the power of the local battery is removed. Of this fact Mr. Allan has availed himself in a most ingenious manner, by placing induction coils around the electro-magnets of the sending and receiving instruments, and so dispensing with the series of cells generally used for line currents, making the one primary current do the double work of recording its message and operating the successive distant relays, throughout the entire circuit. In the new recording instrument, every current makes a sign, as the relay does not require an opposite current to put it in position to print the next mark, as is generally done, nor does it need any spring or weight to bring it to a position in which the local circuit may be cut off; the printing magnet does that. This magnet also draws through the paper on which the message is to be received while (and only while) the signalling is continued. The new sending instrument, by Mr. Allan, is of a simi-

larly automatic character, all that is necessary being the mere putting of the message (that is, a perforated strip of paper) into the
machine.—*Mechanics' Magazine.*

Mr. Walter Hale has read to the British Association a paper
explanatory of a process for *Covering Submarine Wires with India-
rubber* for telegraphic purposes, and exhibited a model of his machine,
which effected the object by winding strips of leather, previously
moistened with naphtha, over the wire ; and the whole being afterwards subjected to a temperature of 140°. The wires thus covered
were protected with a plaited covering of hempen cord, into which
longitudinal steel wires were introduced for the purpose of giving
strength.

Messrs. Werner and C. W. Siemens then described their mode of
covering wires with India-rubber, and exhibited a very ingenious
machine for accomplishing this object. These gentlemen use no
solvent or heat whatever, but take advantage of the property which
India-rubber possesses of forming a perfect junction when newly-cut
surfaces are brought together under pressure. The core or wire,
with the ribbon of rubber applied to it longitudinally, is pushed
into an orifice, which serves as a guide to carry them into the
machine, so that the superfluous rubber is cut off by what may be
termed a revolving pair of scissors, formed by a disc of steel with a
sharp edge turning excentrically against a stationary plate; and
immediately, by means of two grooved wheels, the edges are pressed
together, and thus the wire becomes encased in a perfect tube of
India-rubber. As many additional tubes as may be desired can be
then put on. The machine is also applicable to the coating of wires
with what is known as Wray's Compound, a material of very high
insulating power, combined with very low inductive capacity.

PRIVATE TELEGRAPHS.

A PUBLIC Company has been formed, proposing to establish
Private Telegraphs in offices and elsewhere. For this purpose the
Company extend a rope, containing a great number of fine insulated
wires, over the streets and houses, and any one of those wires may
be rented. To render such arrangements practicable, it was essential,
in the first place, that the wire connexions should be effectually
made at a comparatively small cost. This object is attained by Mr.
Silver's process for insulating wires by coating them with India-
rubber. The wires are very much thinner than bell wires, and a
rope containing upwards of 30 of them properly insulated is barely
half-an-inch in diameter. The rope is fixed on poles at the tops of
the houses, about 200 yards apart, and it is said that the Company
have experienced no difficulty in obtaining the consent of the occupiers to have the poles fixed on their dwellings. This arrangement
is so economical that the Company offers to let out each wire at the
rent of 4*l.* per mile per annum. The instruments to be employed are
the magneto-electric telegraphs, invented by Professor Wheatstone,
its mechanism being slightly modified to adapt it to its new duties.

Chemical Science.

LORD WROTTESLEY, in his Presidential Address to the British Association, at Oxford, thus took a survey of the recent progress of Chemical Science :—

"In Chemistry I am informed that great activity has been displayed, especially in the organic department of the science. For several years past processes of substitution (or displacement of one element or organic group by another element or group more or less analogous) have been the main agents employed in investigation, and the results to which they have led have been truly wonderful; enabling the chemist to group together several compounds of comparatively simple constitution into others much more complex, and thus to imitate, up to a certain point, the phenomena which take place within the growing plant or animal. It is not indeed to be anticipated that the chemist should ever be able to produce by the operations of the laboratory the arrangement of the elements in the forms of the vegetable cell or the animal fibre; but he may hope to succeed in preparing some of the complex results of secretion or of chemical changes 'produced within the living organism,—changes which furnish definite crystallizable compounds, such as the formiates and the acetates, and which he has actually obtained by operations independent of the plant or the animal.

"Hofmann, in pursuing the chemical investigation of the remarkable compound which he has termed *Triethylphosphine*, has obtained some very singular compound ammonias. Triethylphosphine is a body which takes fire spontaneously when its vapour is mixed with oxygen, at a temperature a little above that of the body. It may be regarded as ammonia in which an atom of phosphorus has taken the place of nitrogen, and in which the place of each of the three atoms of hydrogen in ammonia is supplied by ethyl, the peculiar hydrocarbon of ordinary alcohol. From this singular base Hofmann has succeeded in procuring other coupled bases, which though they do not correspond to any of the natural alkalies of the vegetable kingdom, such as morphia, quinia, or strychnia, yet throw some light upon the mode in which complex bodies more or less resembling them have been formed.

"The power which nitrogen possesses of forming a connecting link between the groups of substances of comparatively simple constitution, has been remarkably exemplified by the discovery of a new class of amide acids by Griess, in which he has pointed out a new method, which admits of very general application, of producing complex bodies related to the group of acids, in some measure analogous to the Poly-ammonias of Hofmann.

"Turning to the practical applications of chemistry, we may refer to the beautiful dyes now extracted from aniline, an organic base formerly obtained as a chemical curiosity from the products of the distillation of coal-tar, but now manufactured by the hundredweight in consequence of the extensive demand for the beautiful colours known as Mauve, Magenta, and Solferino, which are prepared by the action of oxidizing agents, such as bichromate of potash, corrosive sublimate, and iodide of mercury upon aniline.

"Nor has the inorganic department of chemistry been deprived of its due share of important advances. Schönbein has continued his investigations upon ozone, and has added many new facts to our knowledge of this interesting substance ; and Andrews and Tait, by their elaborate investigations, have shown that ozone, whether admitted to be an allotropic modification of oxygen or not, is certainly much more dense than oxygen in its ordinary condition.

"In Metallurgy we may point to the investigations of Deville upon the platinum group of metals, which are especially worthy of remark on account of the practical manner in which he has turned to account the resources of the oxy-hydrogen blowpipe, as an agent which must soon be very generally adopted for the finer description of metallurgic operations at high temperatures. By using lime as the material of his crucibles, and as the support for the metals upon which he is operating, several very important practical advantages have been obtained. The material is sufficiently infusible to resist the intense heat employed ; it is a sufficiently bad conductor of heat to economize very perfectly the high temperature which is generated ; and it may be had sufficiently free from foreign admixture to prevent it from contaminating the metals upon which the operator is employed."

___

LIQUEFACTION OF GASES.

MM. Loir and Drion have described in the *Bulletin de la Société Chimique,* a method by which many of the Gases may be Liquefied in considerable quantities. It depends on the cold produced by the evaporation of volatile liquids, which was first used by M. Bussy in the liquefaction of ammoniacal gas.

In describing the liquefaction of a gas, authors have generally contented themselves with saying that it could be effected by a certain freezing mixture, which in many cases has a lower temperature than is absolutely necessary. Hence the liquefaction of gases is generally thought to be a more difficult operation than really is the case.

By blowing a dried current of air by means of a blowpipe bellows, through several tubes into about 7 ounces of ether, a temperature of −34° C. can be obtained : this temperature, which is reached in about four to five minutes, and can be kept pretty constant for fifteen to twenty minutes, is more than sufficient to liquefy a considerable quantity of *cyanogen gas.* By regulating the rapidity of the air-current, it was found that the temperature of liquefaction is −22°. By blowing slightly through an ordinary pair of bellows over the surface of the liquid gas it solidifies immediately.

By a similar arrangement a large quantity of *sulphurous acid* may be liquefied.

Chlorine cannot be liquefied by means of ether cooled to −34° C.; but when liquid sulphurous acid is substituted for ether in the foregoing experiment, considerable quantities of liquid chlorine may be obtained.

Ammonia may also be obtained in the liquid state by means of cooled sulphurous acid; the minimum temperature of which is −50°, while liquid ammonia boils at −35°·7.

When liquid ammonia is used as a cooling agent, by rapidly evaporating it under the air-pump in the presence of sulphuric acid, a temperature of −87° C. is attained; the limit of the lowering of the thermometer is determined by the total solidification of the ammonia. By this temperature Loir and Drion are able to liquefy carbonic acid under the atmospheric pressure. They have also prepared liquid carbonic acid by heating bicarbonate of soda placed in one of the branches of a sealed tube. On cooling, the carbonate of soda reabsorbs the carbonic acid gas.

The authors intend to investigate the physical and also chemical properties of the liquid gases prepared at these low temperatures; under these conditions the ordinary affinities are greatly modified. For instance, 20 cubic centimetres of liquid ammonia placed on a quantity of concentrated sulphuric acid, showed no action at first. Gradually an action was set up and the liquids combined, but with much less violence than might be expected.

The temperatures were measured in these observations by means of an absolute alcohol thermometer, the fixed points of which were determined by means of the temperature of melting ice, and of that of about two pounds of frozen mercury. The temperature of the latter was assumed to be −40° C. — *Philosophical Magazine*, No. 132.

OSMIUM.

PROFESSOR T. W. MALLET, in a paper communicated to *Silliman's Journal*, observes :—

The specific heat of Osmium, so far as its value as a physical character goes, opposes the introduction of this element into the arsenic group. It has been determined by Regnault = ·03063; multiplying now by the equivalent 97, we have the product 2·9711, thus placing osmium in the list of the elements (including the majority) for which the product of specific heat by atomic weight is nearly 3; while for phosphorus, arsenic, antimony, and bismuth, the product thus obtained is twice as great, or about 6. In this respect, however, osmium probably resembles nitrogen—the latter examined, as it necessarily is, in the gaseous form.

It is to be hoped that the conducting power for heat and electricity of compact osmium will soon be examined; nothing is as yet known of these characters.

Lastly, as regards the magnetic relations of the element: it is placed, with some doubt, by Faraday in the paramagnetic class; the metal and its protoxide were found to act feebly in this sense, while pure osmic acid is said to have shown itself clearly diamagnetic. The strongly diamagnetic character of phosphorus, antimony, and bismuth would render a re-examination of this point interesting. Arsenic, however, is said to be very feebly diamagnetic, and is placed by Faraday close to osmium in the list of metals examined, though on the opposite side of the line of magnetic neutrality or indifference.

Reviewing, now, the united physical and chemical characters of osmium, and comparing them with those of the generally recognised members of the "arsenic group," we are, I think, justified in concluding that here this curious metal should be placed in a natural arrangement of the elements ; while important distinctions seem to separate it from some, at least, of the platinum metals, with which it is usually associated and described.

ORGANO-METALLIC BODIES.

DR. FRANKLAND has read to the Chemical Society a paper "On the Organo-Metallic Bodies." He considers that all those bodies might be represented as derivatives of metallic oxides or chlorides, in which some, or all, of the oxygen or chlorine atoms were replaced by organic radicles. He remarked that, in many of these bodies, there are two distinct points of saturation, and that sometimes the higher, sometimes the lower, point is the most stable.

NEW FUSIBLE METAL.

DR. B. WOOD, of Nashville (U.S.), has patented an alloy composed of cadmium, tin, lead, and bismuth, which fuses at a temperature between 150° and 160° F. The contents of this Fusible Metal may be varied according to the other desired qualities of the alloy, viz., cadmium, one to two parts ; bismuth, seven to eight parts ; tin, two parts ; lead, four parts. It is recommended as being especially adapted for all light castings requiring a more fusible material than Rose's or Newton's "fusible metal," it having the advantage of fusing at more than 40° F. lower temperature than these alloys, and, owing to this property, may replace many castings heretofore made only with amalgams. Its fusing-point may be lowered to any extent by the addition of mercury, which may be employed, within certain limits, without materially impairing the tenacity of the metal. In a letter to the editors, dated Nashville, June 9th, 1860, Dr. Wood says :—

" One point in particular that strikes me as being worthy of note, is the remarkable degree in which cadmium possesses the property of promoting fusibility in these combinations. The alloy of one to two parts cadmium, two parts lead, and four parts tin is considerably more fusible than an alloy of one or two parts bismuth, two parts lead, and four parts tin ; and when the lead and tin are in larger proportion the effect is still more marked. It takes less cadmium to reduce the melting-point a certain number of degrees than it requires of bismuth, besides that the former does not impair the tenacity and malleability of the alloy, but increases its hardness and general strength.

" Bismuth has always held a pre-eminent rank among metals as a fluidifying agent in alloys. Its remarkable property of 'promoting fusibility' is specially noted in all our works on chemistry. But I do not find it intimated in any that cadmium ever manifests a similar property. The fact indeed appears to have been wholly overlooked—owing perhaps to the circumstance that as an alloy with certain metals cadmium does not promote fusibility.

"Cadmium promotes the fusibility of some metals, as copper, tin, lead, bismuth, while it does not promote the fusibility of others, as silver, antimony, mercury, &c. (*i.e.*, does not lower the melting-point beyond the mean). Its alloy with lead and tin in any proportion, and with silver and mercury within a certain limit, say, equal parts, and especially if two parts silver and one of cadmium or two parts cadmium and one of mercury are used, are tenacious and malleable, while its alloys with some malleable metals (gold, copper, platinum, &c.), and probably with all brittle metals, are ' brittle.'

"I notice a great discrepancy among authors as to the melting-point of this metal. It is usually put down the same as that of tin (412° F.). Brande (*Dict. of Science and Arts*) says it 'fuses and volatilizes at a temperature a little below that at which tin melts.' Daniell (according to the New American Cyclopædia) gives its melting-point at 360° F.; while Overman places it at 550°, and gives 600° as the temperature at which it volatilizes.

"The latter is doubtless the nearest the truth. The metal requires for its fusion a temperature too high for measurement by the mercurial thermometer; but from relative tests with other metals I should place its melting-point in round numbers at 600° F., as it melts and congeals nearly synchronously with lead, the melting-point of which is stated by different authorities as 594°, 600°, and 612° F. It volatilizes at a somewhat higher heat.

"I draw attention to these facts, believing that the metal possesses properties valuable to art and interesting in science, and that it merits more thorough investigation than appears to have been bestowed upon it."—Silliman's *American Journal*, September, 1860.

CARBONATE OF LEAD FROM LEADEN COFFINS.

MR. RICHARD V. TUSON, Lecturer on Chemistry at Charing Cross Hospital, states, in the *Philosophical Magazine*, No. 127:—

About twelve months ago an Order of Council was issued directing the coffins in the vaults of the church of St. Martin's-in-the-Fields to be transferred to the catacombs. A few days after the appearance of this order, my friend and colleague, Mr. Canton, in company with several other gentlemen, visited the vaults with the view of endeavouring to find the remains of the late celebrated surgeon, John Hunter, which were known to have been deposited there. The search proved successful, and Hunter's remains were subsequently reinterred in Westminster Abbey.

During his visit, Mr. Canton observed that many of the leaden coffins, although they retained their original shape, were, with the exception of an external and exceedingly thin plate or foil of metal, converted into an earthy-looking substance. Several pieces of this substance were removed from a coffin which, there is good reason for believing, had been in the vaults about eighty years. These were placed at my disposal; and although it was thought that they principally consisted of carbonate of lead, it was nevertheless considered, from the peculiarity of the circumstances under which the material was formed, that the results of its analysis might prove somewhat interesting.

The pieces of the substance referred to were about a quarter of an inch in thickness: they had a laminated structure, and possessed a fawnish or drab-white colour. Neither crystalline form nor metallic lead were detected even by the aid of the microscope. The material was tolerably brittle, and readily reduced to an impalpable powder.

On submitting it to quantitative analysis, the following were the results obtained :—

Moisture	0·10	
Organic matter and loss .	0·52	
Peroxide of iron .	1·94	
Protoxide of lead . .	82·29 } = { PbO, CO²	92·29
Carbonic acid . . .	15·13 } { + PbO	5·16

$$100·000$$

The results of the analysis of this substance, therefore, show that it chiefly consists of protocarbonate of lead with a small proportion of anhydrous protoxide of the same metal. The production of these compounds was doubtless mainly due to the moisture and carbonic acid evolved during the decay of the animal remains, acting, conjointly with the oxygen of the air, on the leaden coffins in which the bodies were placed.

The interesting points in connexion with this substance are, that it is anhydrous, that it contains but a small excess of oxide, and that it consequently differs in composition from any of the carbonates of lead hitherto described as being produced by the united action of air and water on metallic lead ; or by the influences concerned in the well-known Dutch method of manufacturing "white lead," and which it is believed approximate in character to those under which the material forming the subject of this communication was developed.

Lastly, it is most likely that the lead of the coffins was first converted into hydrated oxide, then into hydrated and basic carbonate, and finally into the anhydrous carbonate of the composition already given.

————

ON THE ALLEGED PRACTICE OF ARSENIC-EATING IN STYRIA.
BY DR. H. E. ROSCOE.

PROFESSOR ROSCOE being anxious to obtain further definite information respecting the extraordinary statements of Von Tschudi, quoted by Johnson in his *Chemistry of Common Life*, that persons in Styria are in the habit of regularly taking doses of arsenious acid, varying in quantity from two to five grains daily,—was supplied, through the kindness of his friend Professor Pebal, of Lemberg, with a series of letters written by seventeen medical men of Styria to the government medical inspector at Grätz, concerning the alleged practice. After reviewing the opinions of Dr. Taylor, Mr. Kesteven, and Mr. Heisch upon the subject, and having mentioned the results and conclusions arrived at by those who had previously interested themselves with the subject, Mr. Roscoe stated that all the letters received from the medical men in Styria agree in acknowledging the general prevalence of a belief that certain persons are in the habit of continually taking arsenic in quantities usually supposed sufficient to produce death. Many of the reporting medical men had no experience of the practice ; others describe certain cases of arsenic-eating which have not come under their personal notice, but which they have been told of by trustworthy people whose names are given ; whilst others, again, report upon cases which they themselves have observed. Professor Roscoe proceeded to bring forward, in the first place, evidence bearing upon the question—" Is or is not arsenious acid, or arsenic in any other form, well known to, and distributed amongst the people of Styria ?" He said that he had received 6 grms. of a white substance forwarded by Professor Gottlieb, of Grätz, accompanied by a certificate from the district judge of Knittelfeld, in Styria, stating that this substance was brought to him by a peasant woman, who told him that she had seen her farm-labourer eating it, and that she gave it up to justice to put a stop to so evil a practice. An accurate chemical analysis showed that the substance was pure arsenious acid. Extracts from many of the reports of the medical men were then read, all stating that arsenious acid, called "Hidrach" by the Styrian peasants, is well known and widely distributed in that country. The second question to which Mr. Roscoe sought to obtain an answer was, whether arsenic is or is not regularly taken by persons in Styria in quantities usually supposed to produce immediate death ?

The most narrowly examined, and therefore the most interesting, case of arsenic-eating, is one recorded by Dr. Schäfer. In presence of Dr. Knappe, of Oberzehring, a man thirty years of age, and in robust health, ate, on the 22nd of February, 1860, a piece of arsenious acid weighing 4½ grains, and on the 23rd another piece weighing 5½ grains. His urine was carefully examined, and shown to contain arsenic ; on the 24th he went away in his usual health. He informed Dr. Knappe that he was in the habit of taking the above quantities three or four times each week. A number of other cases, witnessed by the medical men themselves, of persons eating arsenic, were then detailed. Dr. Holler, of Hartberg, says that he and other persons, named in his report, guarantee that they are together acquainted with forty persons who eat arsenic ; and Dr. Forcher, of Grätz, gives a list of eleven people in his neighbourhood who indulge in the practice.

Professor Roscoe did not think it necessary to translate the reports *in extenso;* he gave extracts containing the portions immediately bearing upon the two questions at issue, and deposited authentic copies of the original reports with the society for the purpose of reference. He concluded that decisive evidence had, in his opinion, been brought forward, not only to prove that arsenic is well known and widely distributed in Styria, but that it is likewise regularly eaten—for what purpose he did not at the moment investigate—in quantities usually considered sufficient to produce immediate death.—*From the Proceedings of the Manchester Literary and Philosophical Society,* October 30, 1860.

ARSENIC IN COAL.

DR. R. ANGUS SMITH has given to the Manchester Literary and Philosophical Society a short account of his examination of Coal Pyrites for Arsenic. He stated that although the knowledge of the existence of arsenic in the iron pyrites found in coal may not be considered perfectly novel, it certainly does not seem to be known that arsenic is so widely disseminated as to form an ordinary constituent of the coals burnt in our towns ; and chemists of celebrity have held, and now hold, it to be absent there.   He had examined fifteen specimens of coal in Lancashire, and found arsenic in thirteen. He had also found it in a few others ; but Mr. Binney having promised a collection, properly arranged, the examination will then be made more complete.   Mr. Dugald Campbell had also lately found arsenic in coal pyrites ; this had a very direct bearing on our sanitary knowledge, as we must now be obliged to add arsenic to the number of impurities in the atmosphere of our large towns.   It is true that he had not actually obtained it from the atmosphere ; but when the pyrites is burnt the arsenic burns and is carried off along with the sulphur.   One or two coal brasses (as they are called) contained copper, a metal that is also to some extent volatilized, as may be readily observed wherever copper-soldering takes place.   Although an extremely small amount of copper is carried up from furnaces, it is not well entirely to ignore it.   The amount of arsenic, however, is probably not without considerable influence ; and we may probably learn the reason why some towns seem less affected than others by the burning of coals, by examining the amount of arsenic burnt as well as sulphur.—*Philosophical Magazine*, No. 134.

EFFECTS PRODUCED BY ARSENIOUS ACID.

PROFESSOR SCHMIDT and Dr. Stürzwage in Dorpat have made a series of experiments on the action of Arsenious Acid, when introduced into the circulation, on the oxidizing process in the body. The mode of experimenting consisted in determining the normal quantity of carbonic acid exhaled in an hour by certain animals (fowls, pigeons, and cats), and then administering to them arsenious acid, and again observing the quantity of gas exhaled in the same time. The apparatus consisted of a bell-jar, standing on a ground-glass plate, under which the animal was placed.   In the tubulure of the bell-jar were inserted two tubes, and a delicate thermometer.   One of these tubes communicated freely with the air, the other was connected with a series of tubes for the absorption of carbonic acid and water, and with an aspirator by which a regulated quantity of air could be drawn through the system.   Each experiment lasted about an hour, during which time about 30 to 35 litres of air were drawn through : the carbonic acid of this air was determined by a separate experiment, and allowed for.   The secretion of urea was determined in some cases : the determinations were made by Liebig's method.

From these experiments, Schmidt and Stürzwage conclude that arsenious acid introduced into the organism occasions a considerable diminution in the secretion of matter.   The phenomena are most observable in fowls ; but even in cats, which vomit after the injection, and are to be considered as starving, the diminution amounts to 20 per cent., even after eliminating the diminution caused by mere inanition. This fact explains the fattening of horses after the administration of small doses of arsenious acid, a fact well known to horse-dealers. That quantity of fat, and of albumen, which corresponds to the depression in the secretion of carbonic acid and urea, remains in the body ; and if the animal receive adequate nourishment, its weight increases.

CONTAMINATION OF WATER BY LEAD.

A LETTER having appeared in the *Times* from Professor Faraday, explaining a very simple mode of treating Water that was contaminated by receptacles of Lead in the neighbourhood of the sea (a matter of great interest at military posts), Sir John Burgoyne requested Dr. Faraday to favour him with a note on the subject, with the addition of any simple practical remedies, if such there were, for the presence of lead in water arising from other combinations. The following answer was returned by that eminent chemist :—

" Royal Institution.

" My dear Sir John,—I consider your request relating to the leaded water an honour, and in replying may add an observation or two to the original matter. The case at first was simply that of certain waters, which, having been collected from rain, by roofs, gutters, pipes, or cisterns of lead, were contaminated more or less with the metal. All water so obtained has not been found thus affected, and there is much difference and uncertainty about the mutual action of lead and water in different cases. When rain water falls upon surfaces of lead it is apt to act on them ; and the water thus contaminated, by standing exposed to air generally clears itself from the dissolved lead, the metal separating as a carbonated precipitate, and falling to the bottom. But when the sea spray has access to the leaded surfaces, the action of the rain water is such that the dissolved lead does not separate in this way, or if it does, only after a much longer time.* It is such water as this that I recommend to be treated with carbonate of lime. Enough whitening or levigated chalk is to be mixed with the fluid to make it of the consistency of good milk (though more will do no harm), and the whole is either to be filtered or to stand until clear. I have never yet found any sample of water poisoned as above, that was not freed from the lead by this process ; and from the actions that occur in the laboratory, I have no doubt, that if two or three pounds of such powdered chalk were put into a cistern, and stirred up occasionally after rain, it would keep the water free from lead. Now, my consideration was entirely confined to cases of the above kind, and to the service of the Trinity House. I might say much more to you about the modes of testing for lead in water, so as to discover its presence, and, within certain limits, its proportion, and also about the clearance of lead from all domestic waters by filtration, or otherwise ; but I have

---

* Professor Faraday, in his letter to the Editor of the *Times*, stated that "the salt of the sea spray, which often reaches the roofs of buildings, even when they are half-a-mile or more from the shore, causes the rain water to dissolve a portion of the lead, which is larger or smaller under different circumstances, and at times rises up to a quantity injurious to health, and poisonous."

M

always found that chemical practice was required to make such knowledge available, and that for that reason it was nearly useless in the hands of the public. When, too, a particular case becomes mixed up with the numerous cases that may be associated with it, I think it often disappears from view, and the whole are after a time forgotten. Hence, I prefer adhering to the case of adulteration arising from the joint action of salt water, or sea spray, and lead ; and I have the full confidence that if it arise at any of your military posts at home or abroad, no difficulty will be found in the effective application of the remedy.

"I am, my dear Sir John,
"Your very faithful servant,
"M. FARADAY.

"To Sir J. F. Burgoyne, &c., &c., &c."

POISONOUS METALS IN CHEESE.

PROFESSOR VOELCKER has stated to the British Association that he has detected both Copper and Zinc in Cheese. In some specimens copper, in others zinc, and in some both copper and zinc, were found. The description of cheese in which these Poisonous Metals were found was double-Gloucester cheese. Skimmed milk cheese, which was likewise examined for copper and zinc, did not contain any metallic impurity. Stilton and other varieties of cheese have not as yet been examined ; it must not therefore be inferred that cheese made in other districts than Gloucestershire contains poisonous metals. Inquiry in the dairy districts of Gloucestershire and Wiltshire has led to the discovery that in many dairies in these counties sulphate of copper, and sometimes sulphate of zinc, are employed in the making of cheese. The reasons for which these prejudicial salts are added to the cheese are variously stated. Some persons added sulphate of zinc with a view of giving new cheese the taste of old ; others employed sulphate of copper for the purpose of preventing the "heaving" of cheese. Dr. Voelcker also stated that he had found alum in Gloucester cheese, and mentioned that he had learnt that in some dairies alum was employed to effect a more complete separation of the caseine from the whey.

STRYCHNINE AND CURARE.

OUR readers may recollect that, in 1859, the Paris Academy of Sciences received an important communication from Dr. Vella, of Turin, on the successful application of the Curare or Woorali Poison to the cure of traumatic lock-jaw.[*] This was much too precious a discovery not to be immediately tried in France, but the attempts made at Paris and at Bordeaux were only successful in two cases out of seven, so that this remedy was soon abandoned, and Dr. Vella's success ascribed to good fortune rather than to the efficacy of the poison. But after the lapse of nearly a year, probably spent in making fresh experiments, we find Dr. Vella returns to the charge, and sends a new and highly interesting communication to the Academy of

[*] See the case detailed in the *Year-Book of Facts*, 1860, p. 109.

Sciences. As lock-jaw consists in an unnatural rigidity of the muscular system, which, with all its accompanying symptoms, may be artificially produced by strychnine, while the essential characteristic of the woorali poison is that of producing a relaxation of the muscular system, it will be easily understood that all Dr. Vella's researches tend towards establishing an antagonism existing between woorali and strychnine. For this purpose he has made 97 experiments, forming two different series, in the former of which animals poisoned with strychnine were cured by the inoculation of woorali into the blood, while in the latter a mixture of strychnine and woorali was injected into the veins, and found to be utterly innocuous. From these experiments, which it is unnecessary to describe more minutely, Dr. Vella concludes that woorali is the true physiological antidote to strychnine.—*Galignani.*

CAPTURE OF WHALES BY HYDROCYANIC ACID.

PROFESSOR CHRISTISON has published the result of some experiments suggested as long ago as 1831, by Messrs. W. and G. Young, of Leith, for the Capture of Whales by means of poison, the agent being Hydrocyanic or Prussic Acid. This subtle poison was contained in glass tubes, in quantity about two ounces. Among other difficulties one was to discharge the poison from the glass tubes at the right time. After various trials, the plan fixed upon was to attach firmly to each side of the harpoon, near the blade, one end of a strong copper wire, the other end of which passed obliquely over the tube, thereby securing it in its place; then throw an oblique hole in the shaft, close to the upper end of the tube, and finally to a bight in the rope, where it was firmly secured. By these means the rope could not be drawn tight, as it would when the harpoon attached to it struck the whale, without crushing the tubes; the poison would then enter the whale and death ensue. The Messrs. Young accordingly sent a quantity of tubes charged with the poison by one of their ships engaged in the Greenland fishery, and on meeting with a fine whale the harpoon was skilfully and deeply buried in its body; the leviathan immediately "sounded," or dived perpendicularly downwards, but in a very short time the rope relaxed, and the whale rose to the surface quite dead; but the men were so appalled by the terrific effect of the poisoned harpoon, that they declined to use any more of them. Subsequent experiments tend to convince the learned Professor that success will be established in this method of capturing whales.

ON CEMENTATION.

THE following experiments were undertaken by Caron, to ascertain the nature of the process of Cementation :—

An iron bar, completely surrounded by pieces of charcoal, was packed in a porcelain tube, which was placed in a reverberatory furnace, and heated to redness; while pure hydrogen, carbonic oxide, nitrogen, air, and carburetted hydrogen gases were passed through the tube in successive operations, each lasting two hours.   In none of these cases was there any true cementation.

With ammonia it was different : after two hours' heating, the bar was immediately tempered and hammered, and again tempered, and then exhibited a regular and beautiful cementation of $\frac{1}{10}$ inch in depth.   This was attributable to the action of ammonia on carbon, forming at this temperature cyanide of ammonium, which gives up carbon to the iron and forms steel.   A direct experiment was made, omitting the charcoal, and heating an iron bar placed in a porcelain tube to redness in a current of gaseous cyanide of ammonium. After two hours' heating, the bar was treated as before, and was found quite cemented, especially at the end nearest the place at which the gas entered.

It seemed probable that this property of cementation was not confined to cyanide of ammonium, but was shared by other alkaline cyanides ; the cementation by means of yellow prussiate of potash is probably of this kind.   To decide this point experimentally, the bar was placed in the tube surrounded by charcoal impregnated with carbonate of potass, and heated to redness in a current of air. Under these circumstances, as is well known, cyanide of potassium is formed.   After two hours the bar was found cemented in a magnificent manner to a depth of $\frac{1}{10}$ inch.   Soda, baryta, and strontia act in the same way, but this is not the case with lime.   This doubtless arises from the fact (which was proved by experiment) that it does not form cyanide of calcium when heated to redness in a current of cyanide of ammonium.

The action of the various receipts for cementation may be explained by the formation of cyanides.   It will be found that in all cases they contain the elements of the formation of alkaline cyanides.—*Comptes Rendus ; Philosophical Magazine*, No. 136.

ON THE DIFFERENCE IN SIZE OF MEDALS OF DIFFERENT METALS OBTAINED BY STAMPING, AND BY CASTING IN THE SAME MOULD. BY H. W. DOVE.

BAUDRIMONT has found (*Ann. de Chim. et de Phys.* vol. lx. p. 78) that wires of different metals drawn through the same press are not all of the same thickness ; for they are of different degrees of elasticity, and after being drawn through the press they expand to different amounts.   This expansion is proved by the fact that, with the exception of gold wire, no wire can be drawn through the same aperture through which it has been pressed.   Silver requires the least force, but the expansion caused by elasticity continues for several weeks.

It appeared probable that in stamping medals something similar would prevail, and that medals of different metals stamped in the same die would be different in size.   This is most readily seen in those medals in which the impression is symmetrically arranged in reference to the edge, as is the case with the medals of the French Exhibition, in which the coats of arms encircle the French eagle in the middle. One of those in silver, and one in bronze, were placed in the stereoscope, the eagle being fixed in the middle. After some time the stereoscopic combined medal was seen in the form of a hollow escutcheon, and of the colour of an alloy of the two metals. Evidently the reason of this lies in the nonius-like shifting of the individual lines of the impression. This result, which Prof. Dove has described (*Optische Studien*, p. 29), he has also obtained with large gold and silver medals which were kindly entrusted to him from the Royal Mint in Berlin. It was thought probable that medals obtained by casting would show the same thing, and this was found to be the case with tin, bismuth, and lead. The casts were very beautifully executed for him for this purpose by Professor Kiss. Hiero's crown led to the application of specific gravity to detect an adulteration ; the stereoscope is a new means.—*Poggendorff's Annalen ; Philos. Mag.*, No. 133.

LEAF-ALUMINIUM.

M. Degousse, a goldbeater in Paris, has succeeded in preparing Aluminium in fine plates like gold or silver. The operation of beating is effected in the usual manner, but it is necessary that the reheating be more frequent ; the fire of a chauffer is most suitable. Aluminium-leaf may replace silver in many cases ; its white, though less brilliant, is more durable.

Wöhler has the following remarks on Degousse's leaf-aluminium. It is readily combustible ; if held in the edge of a spirit-lamp flame, it takes fire and burns with great brilliancy. It is very thin ; a cubic inch only weighs a milligramme. If a leaf of it be pressed together, placed in a bulb and heated by means of a spirit-lamp in a current of oxygen, it burns instantaneously with a dazzling lightning-like appearance. The resultant alumina is fused, and as hard as corundum. Aluminium wire also burns in oxygen like iron ; but the combustion does not proceed far, for the next parts melt away before they have reached the temperature of combustion. Aluminium in the compact form does not decompose water, but the leaf, when placed in boiling water, decomposes a sufficient quantity to enable the hydrogen to be collected. The metal assumes at first a faint bronze surface colour. After several hours' boiling, the laminæ become partially translucent, that is, converted into alumina. If the residue be treated with hydrochloric acid, the unoxidized metal is dissolved, while the alumina remains undissolved.

RESEARCHES ON OZONE.

M. Le Roux states that if a platinum wire, not too large, be made incandescent by an electric current in such a manner that the ascending flow of hot air which has surrounded the wire comes into direct contact with the nostrils, an odour of Ozone is perceived. The experiment may be made in the following manner :—A very fine platinum wire ($\frac{1}{10}$th to $\frac{1}{15}$th of a millimetre) 20 centimetres long is taken ; it is formed in any shape, and supported in an almost horizontal position in any suitable manner. A glass funnel of 2 or 3 litres is placed over this, so that the air has sufficient access to the wire. As the neck of the funnel is usually too narrow, it is cut so as to leave an aperture 2 or 3 centimetres in diameter, on which is adjusted a glass chimney of a suitable length ; the object of which is to cool the gases heated by the wire. The wire is then made incandescent by means of twelve or fifteen Bunsen's cells. The gas issuing from the chimney is found to have the odour of ozone ; iodized starch-papers altered in a few minutes when placed over the chimney. In this case the air passing over the incandescent wire undergoes a peculiar modification by which it acquires the properties of ozone ; but whether this is effected by the electricity acting as a source of heat, or by its own proper action, must be reserved for further experiments.—*Comptes Rendus : Philos. Mag.*, No. 128.

Dr. T. Andrews, and Mr. P. Tait, of Belfast, have published in the *Philosophical Transactions* an account of their continued researches on Ozone, especially as to its volumetric relations ; to which is appended an account of the effects of the action of the electric discharge on hydrogen, nitrogen, cyanogen, and other gases. These gentlemen are still continuing their inquiries into the nature of ozone, which it is hoped will tend to throw more light on this mysterious substance.

FLUORESCENT SOLUTION FROM THE MANNA ASH.

STOKES has shown that several organic substances are capable of showing Fluorescence. Recently Prince Salm-Horstman has pointed out the fluorescence caused by *fraxine* extracted from *Fraxinus excelsior* (the common ash). Dufour states that a liquid endowed with beautiful fluorescent properties may be procured by means of the manna ash (*Fraxinus ornus*). By throwing into water some pieces of bark, there are immediately produced beautiful blue reflections, and in less than a minute there is a solution exhibiting the most beautiful fluorescence. The intensity of the effect surpasses that produced by sulphate of quinine. This solution, examined according to Stokes's methods, shows very well the characters of fluorescence, but it gives especially a marked coloration by the aid of the electrical light of Geissler. By taking one of Geissler's tubes, when the electrical current is surrounded by a liquid column, we obtain a shade of pure and intense blue. The facility and rapidity with which this solution can be obtained, without any chemical operation, and by the aid of a thin branch of *Fraxinus ornus*, render it useful for many experiments.

ACTION OF ALCOHOL, CHLOROFORM, ETC., ON THE NERVOUS SYSTEM.

THIS has been investigated by MM. Lallemand, Perrin, and Duroy, who have laid an account of their experiments before the French Academy of Sciences. They state their conviction that Alcohol, Chloroform, Ether, and Amylene act directly upon the Nervous System ; while carbonic acid and carbonic oxide act directly on the blood, which they modify, and thereby determine secondarily the phenomena of insensibility. This agrees with the opinion of M. Flourens, who stated long ago that in ordinary asphyxia the nervous system loses its power under the action of black blood (blood deprived of its oxygen); but in etherization the nervous system loses its power, at first, by the direct action of the single agent which determined it.—*Comptes Rendus.*

ON PETROL.

BUSSENIUS and Eisenstück have investigated a rock oil, which is obtained from some lias strata, near Hanover. The crude oil is distilled with high-pressure steam, and the oil which distils over is treated with sulphuric acid, which removes from it a peculiar bituminous smell. Thus purified, it comes into commerce; but the oil for this investigation Bussenius and Eisenstück took as it distils over with the steam, dried it, and submitted it to fractional distillation, and found it to be composed mostly of hydrocarbons, including a new hydrocarbon, which the authors named *Petrol*, but which they were not able to separate directly; but when the oil was treated with a mixture of sulphuric and nitric acids, a crystalline nitro-compound of this body was produced; the other hydrocarbons, of which the oil is mostly composed, are not altered, even by prolonged contact with this acid moisture. This nitro-compound was purified by repeated crystallizations from alcohol. The analysis of the substance showed it to be not quite pure, but probably to contain some of the nitro-compound of a higher hydrocarbon.

Petrol has the same composition as xylole (Cahours, Church), but, judging from the nature of its derivatives, it does not appear to be identical with it.—*Philos. Mag.*

COMBUSTION OF WET FUEL.

PROFESSOR SILLIMAN has read to the American Association a paper, showing not only how the Combustion of Wet Fuel is possible, but also how it may be accomplished with economical results. A furnace invented by a Mr. Thompson, in 1854, arrests the escaping products of combustion, and brings them back to consume themselves. This method shuts off the atmospheric air, and obtains the requisite oxygen from the steam.

GUN-COTTON.

A CORRESPONDENT writing to the *American Journal of Photography* makes the following statement in reference to the spontaneous combustion of Gun-cotton:—"While at work in my room, a spontaneous combustion of more than two ounces of gun-cotton took place in my trunk, with a loud report, filling the contents of the trunk with fire and smoke, which would have been destructive, had no one been present. I purchased the cotton some three months previous, and made good collodion from it, but laid it by to use another sample. About two weeks before the explosion I accidentally observed the bottle to contain a yellow vapour; and on removing the cork (which was much softened), strong acid fumes escaped. I put in a few drops of alcohol, which absorbed the vapours. I then sealed it, put it into the trunk again; but on looking at it again a day or two before it took fire, the yellow vapour had again collected: but as I had not heard of spontaneous combustion having ever taken place, I put it back, and the next thought of it was caused by the report, as above stated. What caused the cotton to ignite? Is this an isolated case? I have had other samples develope reddish-yellow vapours; and as it is good for nothing in that state, I have thus far destroyed it before it destroyed me." The Editor of the journal named, in corroboration of his Correspondent, states that he once purchased a bottle of gun-cotton prepared in Paris, which, as soon as the cork was removed, emitted fumes of nitric acid, and would, he believes, have ignited if it had not been at once plunged into water.

FIRE-DAMP IN COLLIERIES.

CAPTAIN E. B. HUNT has read to the American Association a paper upon the Explosions of Fire-damp in Collieries. He showed that the Davy-lamp had been proved to be unsafe when exposed to a current of gas. He recommends the substitution of coal-gas, manufactured at the surface and near the mouth of the mine, and forced down in pipes, with such gauze safeguards as may be necessary. The advantage of this would be the substitution of a system of lighting, under the care of a responsible person, for dangerous lamps in the hands of the careless and ignorant. Professor Rogers suggested that a very powerful Voltaic light might be used at some point, which, by a series of reflectors, should illuminate the mine. Both he and other gentlemen showed the great danger of employing illuminating gas; although Mr. Rockwell, of Norwich, who gave a variety of interesting information upon the subject of mines, showed that the system has been employed, under certain circumstances, in some parts of mines abroad.

GUANO.

WE derive the following items respecting this important manure from an interesting paper recently presented to the French Academy of Sciences by M. Boussingault. The deposits of Guano (*huano de pajoro*) extend from the 2nd to the 21st degree south latitude along the coast of Peru. Those which lie beyond these limits are much poorer in ammoniacal compounds than the former, and are not, therefore, equal to them in value. Guano is generally found deposited on small promontories or on cliffs; it fills up crevices, and is in general to be found in those places where the birds seek shelter. The rocks of this part of the coast consist of granite, gneiss, syenite, and porphoric syenite; the guano which covers them generally exists in horizontal layers; but sometimes the latter have a strong inclination, as at Chipana, for instance, where they are nearly vertical. The guano deposits are generally covered with an agglomeration of sand and saline substances, called *caliche*, which the labourers first remove before they begin their attack on the guano. In some places, as at Pabellon. de Pica and at Punta Grande, the deposits lie under a mass of sand descended from the neighbouring mountains ; and on this subject an observation made by M. F. de Rivero is extremely curious. At the places above mentioned the lowest guano deposits are covered with a stratum of old alluvial soil ; then comes another layer of guano, and then a stratum of modern alluvial soil. To understand the importance of this fact, our readers must keep in mind that the age of the modern alluvions does not extend beyond our historical times, while old alluvions date from the period immediately preceding that at which man first began to inhabit the earth ; so that the guanaes, or cormorants and other allied tribes of birds which deposit guano, must have existed thousands of years before man, seeing that the inferior layer of guano is several yards (sometimes from 15 to 20) in depth, and the old alluvial crust above it has a thickness of upwards of three yards.

To explain the immense accumulation of guano in these regions, M. Boussingault observes that there has been a combination of a variety of causes favourable both to its production and preservation. Among these causes must be reckoned a dry climate ; a ground presenting a vast number of chinks, fissures, and caverns, where the birds can rest, lay their eggs, and hatch them without being disturbed by the strong breezes from the south ; and then abundance of the food suited to them. Nowhere is fish so abundant as on this coast, where whole shoals of them are cast upon the shore even in fine weather. Antonio de Ulloa states that anchovies especially are in such abundance here as to defy description ; and he gives a good account of the manner in which their numbers are diminished by the myriads of guanaes which are seen sometimes flying in countless flocks, like clouds intercepting the sun's rays, and sometimes darting into the sea to catch their prey. According to M. Boussingault's calculation, 100 kilogrammes of guano contain the nitrogen of 600 kilogrammes of sea-fish ; and as the guano deposits, before they began to be worked, contained 378,000,000 of metrical quintals of guano, the birds must have consumed 2,268,000,000 of quintals of fish.—*Atlas Journal.*

FORMATION OF TARTARIC ACID FROM MILK-SUGAR.

LIEBIG gives a detailed description of the formation of Tartaric Acid by the oxidation of Milk-sugar by nitric acid. He discusses the mode of occurrence and constitution of tartaric acid, and several allied vegetable acids, and mentions an experiment in which he tried the action of aldehyde on cyanogen dissolved in water, in the expectation of effecting the synthesis of malic acid. It gave, however, an unexpected result. A flask containing about two quarts of water was saturated with cyanogen, about an ounce of aldehyde added, and the whole left in a cool place. The fluid remained clear and colourless ; but gradually a mass of white crusts separated at the bottom of the flask, which were found to be oxamide. The liquid, saturated for a second and third time with cyanogen, yielded fresh quantities of oxamide. On distilling the liquid some more oxamide separated, and it appeared as if the aldehyde had formed a combination with oxamide which was decomposed by boiling. The aldehyde which distilled over contained some acroleine. The mother-liquor, from which the oxamide had deposited, contained oxalate of ammonia.

The aldehyde in this experiment, either by its mere presence or by its co-operation, promotes the combination of cyanogen with water, to form, according as it combines with two or four equivalents of water, oxamide or oxalate of ammonia. The aldehyde acts as a sort of ferment; while any other affinity of the cyanogen, for the hydrogen or for the oxygen of the water, appears to be quite suppressed.—Liebig's *Annalen; Philos. Mag.*, No. 128.

PHOSPHATE OF LIME IN URINE.

DR. HASSALL has communicated to the Royal Society a paper "On the frequent occurrence of Phosphate of Lime in the crystalline form in Human Urine, and on its pathological importance."

The author concludes from his observations and investigations:—

First. That deposits of crystallized phosphate of lime are of frequent occurrence in human urine, much more so, indeed, than those of the amorphous or granular form of that phosphate.

Second. That the crystals present well-marked and highly characteristic forms, whereby the identification of this phosphate by means of the microscope is rendered easy and certain.

Third. That there is good reason to believe that deposits of phosphate of lime are of greater pathological importance than those of the phosphate of ammonia and magnesia.

CURE FOR HYDROPHOBIA.

THE *Presse Médicale Belge* states, on the authority of Father Legrand de la Liray, one of the oldest missionaries in Tonquin and Cochin China, that in those countries Hydrophobia is cured with complete success by boiling a handful of the leaves of Datura Stramonium, or Thorny Apple, in a litre of water, until reduced to one-half, and then administering the potion to the patient all at a time. A violent paroxysm of rage ensues, which lasts but a short time, and the patient is cured in the course of twenty-four hours. For the benefit of our readers we may state that the leaves of Stramonium are highly narcotic, and as such are recommended in asthma under the form of cigars, to be smoked as usual; but that the same leaves, taken in large quantities, whether in powder or under the form of a decoction, will produce temporary idiocy. As to its efficacy in confirmed hydrophobia it seems to be very earnestly recommended by Father Legrand, who declares he has tried it several times, and invariably with success. The great difficulty will of course consist in administering the remedy to the patient, which probably must be done by main force, with the aid of a horn; but on this subject the *Presse Médicale* is silent.

NEW SEDATIVE.

THE *Journal de Chimie Médicale* contains the following remarkable account of the discovery of a powerful Sedative in cases of neuralgia by Dr. Field :—Some time ago that gentleman was induced by a homœopath to put two drops of a solution, supposed to be diluted to the first degree, on his tongue, in order to try its effect. After the lapse of about three minutes he felt a sensation of constriction at the base of the neck, then violent singing in the ear, while his forehead became covered with abundant perspiration. He then was seized with uncontrollable fits of yawning, and remained senseless for several minutes ; his head fell back, his lower jaw sank down powerless, he became extremely pale, and for two minutes his pulse was silent. The homœopath, perceiving these symptoms, was terrified, thinking he had unconsciously committed a murder. Stimulants, however, brought Dr. Field to consciousness again, but he continued to feel a headache for half an hour after, with a sensation of pressure at the epigastrium, and general weakness. These symptoms disappeared in the course of that time. It was evident that the substance employed was a powerful poison, and that it had not been sufficiently diluted ; and it turned out to be nitrate of oxide of glycile, a substance obtained by treating glycerine at a low temperature with sulphuric or nitric acid. One drop, mixed with 99 drops of spirits of wine, constitutes the first dilution. Dr. Field was immediately struck with the idea that he had experienced the effects of what, in a much weaker dose, must be a useful sedative of the nervous system, while the homœopath was overjoyed at having discovered what he conceived to be a powerful agent.

SPECTRUM-ANALYSIS OF LONDON WATERS.

MM. A. AND F. DUPRÉ have analysed several London Waters by the recently-published method of Bunsen and Kirchoff, which adds two new constituents, lithium and strontium, to those already known.

If a small portion of the dry residue of any of the waters examined is brought into the flame of an apparatus, such as described in Bunsen and Kirchoff's paper (*Philosophical Magazine*, No. 131), the lines Li α and K α are seen with more or less distinctness as soon as the first glare of the sodium and calcium spectrum is somewhat diminished. After the Li, K, and Na have volatilized, the calcium lines come out with increased brilliancy ; and if the wire is now dipped into HCl and again brought into the flame, the lines Sr α and Sr γ are seen, as well as a very brilliant calcium spectrum. The strontium lines come out generally with greater brilliancy if the wire, before being moistened with HCl, is held for some time in a reducing flame, easily obtained by closing the air-holes of the Bunsen's burner. In some of the waters, especially the deep-well waters, the line Li α is somewhat masked by the bright sodium and calcium spectra : it is, however, in all cases seen with great distinctness if the residue of the water is treated with sulphuric acid and alcohol in the manner described by Bunsen and Kirchhoff under the head of lithium. The strontium lines may also be seen with great brilliancy on dissolving in hydrochloric acid some of the crust deposited in boilers and kettles, and bringing a drop of the solution into the flame of the apparatus. The shallow waters appear to be rather richer in Li and Sr than the deep-well waters; the presence of Li in the latter can, however, easily be demonstrated in an ounce or even in half an ounce of the water.

The following are the waters examined:—Thames water, taken at low and high tide, Westminster Bridge; also two samples as supplied by the Chelsea and Lambeth Water Companies. Water supplied by the New River Company; and water from the under-mentioned wells :—

Duck Island Well, St. James's Park .	}	Above the London
Pump H, Lincoln's Inn . . .	}	clay.
Burnett's Distillery, Vauxhall . .	}	From the sand above
Whitbread's Brewery, Chiswell-street .	}	the chalk.
Guy's Hospital well	}	
Trafalgar-square well	}	Chalk.

The above waters may be taken to represent the whole of the London supply, since, besides the specimens from the Thames and New River, others from the three principal water-bearing strata of London are included. -

To guard against all possible sources of fallacy, the waters were evaporated in platinum vessels, and all filtration avoided. It need scarcely be mentioned that the alcohol, HO, SO^3, and HCl used were free from lithium and strontium.—*Philosophical Magazine*, No. 134.

NEW DYE-COLOURS.

ABSTRUSE science has brought to light various substances, which have lately proved valuable accessories to the resources of the calico-printer. Thus (says Professor Crace Calvert, in a paper lately read by him to the Royal Institution) Dr. Prout, some thirty or forty years ago, made the curious discovery, that uric acid possessed the property of giving a beautiful red colour, when heated with nitric acid and then brought into contact with ammonia. The substance thus obtained was further examined by Messrs. Liebig and Wöhler, in a series of researches which have been considered as amongst the most important ever made in organic chemistry; and this substance they called *Murexide*. In the course of these investigations, they also discovered a white crystalline substance called Alloxan. For twenty years both these substances were only to be found in the laboratory; but in 1851 Dr. Saac observed that alloxan, when in contact with the hand, tinged it red. This led him to infer that alloxan might be employed to dye woollens red; and further experiments convinced him that if woollen cloths were prepared with per-oxide of tin, passed through a solution of alloxan and then submitted to a gentle heat, a most beautiful and delicate pink colour resulted. Subsequently murexide was employed and applied successfully by M. Depouilly, of Paris, to dyeing wool and silk, and to printing calicos, by the aid of oxide of lead and chloride of mercury as mordants ; but the great obstacle to its extensive use was the difficulty of obtaining uric acid in sufficient quantity for its manufacture. The idea soon occurred to chemists to extract it from guano ; and this is the curious source whence the chief supply of uric acid is obtained, and which enables printers to produce the colour called Tyrian purple.

Another example is adduced in the successive scientific discoveries which have led to the discovery of the recently popular colour, *Mauve*. Lichens, which have been the subject of extensive researches on the part of Robiquet, Heeren, Sir Robert Kane, Dr. Schunck, and especially of Dr. Stenhouse, have yielded to those chemists several new and colourless organic substances, which, under the influence of air and ammonia, give rise to most brilliant colours, and amongst these are orchil and litmus. Dr. Stenhouse, in a most elaborate paper, published by the Royal Society in 1848, pointed out two important facts : first, that the colour-giving acids could be easily extracted from the weed by macerating it in lime water, from which the colouring matters were easily separated by means of an acid ; and secondly, the properties of certain colouring acids, which gave M. Marnas, of Lyons, the key which enabled him to produce commercially from lichens a fast mauve and purple which, up to 1857, had been considered impossible of attainment.

The commercial production, by Mr. W. H. Perkin, of another purple at the same time is not less interesting. Some thirty or forty years ago, Dr. Runge obtained from coal-tar six substances ; amongst which was one called *Kyanol*, which substance was thoroughly examined by Dr. W. A. Hofmann, who proved it to be an organic alkaloid, and identical with a substance known by the name of aniline. Owing to the subsequent study of this substance by that eminent chemist, and the discovery that it yielded a beautiful purple colour when placed in contact with bleaching powder, his pupil, Mr. W. H. Perkin, was induced to make experiments, with a view to producing commercially a fast purple, in which he succeeded, and secured it by a patent in 1857. The process devised by this chemist is exceedingly simple. It consists in oxidizing aniline by means of bichromate of potash and sulphuric acid.

More recently Mr. Renard found a method of producing also from aniline, by means of chlorine compounds, a most splendid rose colour, called by him *Fuchsiacine ;* and, within the next few months, Mr. David Price also succeeded in producing from aniline, by the employment of peroxide of lead, either a fast purple or a pink, called by him Roseine, and a fast blue, according to the mode of operating. All these colours require special mordants to fix them on calicos or muslins ; Messrs. James Black and Co., and Messrs. Boyd and Hamel, of Glasgow, have fixed the last-mentioned colours by means of azotized principles, such as albumen, lactarine, &c.

The attention of dyers has within the past year been directed to some new tints which have been brought into the market. The colouring matter for these fine shades is extracted from gas-tar. The French call the colouring matter by the terms Magenta, or

Magent. Mr. Coleman's, which is somewhat different, is called Dianthine. The colouring matter, which is a liquid, is applicable in dyeing worsted, silk, and cotton. In the finer shades, as crimson and rose, cochineal, it is said, cannot approach it in brilliancy ; and even saffron yields a tint flat and thin compared with the new element. The shades range from a deep purple to a brilliant rose. The great object the dyers have now in view is to discover some mordant that shall perfect the process.

A new species of red dye more brilliant than any hitherto produced, and, above all, more solid than the best Chinese reds, has been discovered at Lyons. The colour is said to be particularly soft to the eye—something between scarlet and ponceau—the peculiar red beheld in the small garden-flower, the "blood of Adonis." It is already highly appreciated as "rouge sublime."

FLOWER-COLOURING.

Dr. George Lawson, in a paper read to the Royal Botanical Society of Edinburgh, says of Flower-colours :— "Our knowledge of the chemistry of these colouring matters is still very imperfect. Chlorophyll is not known in a state of purity, and the changes of colour which it undergoes, have been only partially explained. By Fremy and Cloez the colouring matters of flowers are referred to three distinct substances, two of which are yellow, while the other is of a blue or rose colour. The blue or rose colour is produced by a compound which has been termed *Cyanine*, the blue tint becoming red when exposed to the action of an acid. The yellow matter, which is insoluble in water, is termed *xanthine*, and that which is soluble has received the name of *xantheine*. These bodies, however, have not been isolated in a pure condition ; and some of the facts above recorded indicate at least a probability that three such bodies are insufficient to account for all the observed phenomena of flower-colouring."—*Edinb. New Philos. Journal.*

INFLUENCE OF SUN-LIGHT ON AMYLACEOUS SUBSTANCES.

Nièrce de Saint-Victor and Corvisart (*Comptes Rendus*) describe the following instances of the peculiar influence which the Sunlight exerts in modifying and changing Amylaceous Substances :—

If two 1 per cent. solutions of starch be prepared under the same circumstances, and if one of them be kept in the dark and the other exposed to the sunlight, the latter will be found to exert an action on the polarizing apparatus ; more dextrine and sugar have been formed. If very weak solutions be taken (about $\frac{1}{10000}$) and exposed to the sunlight for about eighteen hours, it will be found that the solution has lost the properties of the original amylum, and more resembles inuline.

Many substances, such as lactate or citrate of iron, and corrosive sublimate, limit or neutralize this action of the light ; while other substances, such as potassio-tartrate of iron, or nitrate of uranium, greatly increase it.

Dextrine and cane-sugar are unaffected by light.

There is a curious action on oxalic acid. If a 4 per cent. solution of the acid be mixed with a 1 per cent. solution of nitrate of uranium, and the mixture boiled for even a considerable length of time, *provided this is done in the dark*, no change takes place. But if the light, even of a clouded sky, have but a momentary action, a decomposition, evidenced by the disengagement of gas, at once sets in ; and if the mixture be placed in the sun, a quantity of carbonic oxide may be collected. That this action is due neither to the temperature nor to the free acid, is evident from the fact that at a temperature of zero, and with the employment of oxide of uranium, the same results are obtained.

Direct experiments have shown that animal starch (glycogenous substances) is more rapidly changed into sugar in the light than in the dark ; and remarkably enough, nitrate of uranium decreases instead of increases the action.

It is remarkable that animal starch in frogs' liver is not changed into sugar in winter, which is also the case with the vegetable starch.

This might explain why the sugar-forming substances which are so abundant in the membrane of the fœtus immediately disappear after birth.

It can scarcely be doubted that light plays a slow but very powerful part in effecting changes in the animal body ; and it is evident that a knowledge of the substances which accelerate or lessen this action is of great importance in medicine. The symptoms of diabetes, and the action which light has been observed to exert on scrofulous persons, may be adduced as cases in point.—*Philos. Mag.*

COMPOSITION OF THE PHOTOGRAPHIC IMAGE.

MR. JOHN SPILLER, F.C.S., of the War Department, has communicated to the *Philosophical Magazine*, No. 126, a paper, of which the following are the opening and closing passages :—

The composition and chemical nature of the Photographic Image, as produced by the action of light upon the chloride of silver, is even at the present moment, notwithstanding the numerous experiments recorded on the subject, one upon which authorities are divided. While there is abundant evidence to show that the darkening consequent on exposure to the sun's rays is a process of reduction accompanied with the evolution of chlorine, there are yet two opinions entertained as to the extent to which this reducing action ordinarily proceeds. In accordance with one hypothesis, the white or protochloride of silver ($Ag\,Cl$) is assumed to suffer the full decomposition into its elements, becoming, therefore, reduced to the state of metal ; while, according to a second view, the progress of this reducing action is limited to an intermediate stage, whereby a compound is produced containing less chlorine by one-half than the original substance, and to which the name and formula, subchloride of silver ($Ag^2\,Cl$), have been applied. As a contribution towards a fuller explanation of the chemical changes involved, I beg to submit the following results of a series of experiments, made at intervals of leisure during the summers of 1857, 1858, and 1859, which would appear strongly to favour the first-mentioned hypothesis.

*   *   *   *   *

Passing in review the results obtained in the foregoing experiments, it will probably be considered that the weight of evidence tends to show that the metal is the ordinary product of the chemical action of light upon chloride of silver ; and that the principal difficulty which has stood in the way of accepting this conclusion has in a great measure to be accounted for by the often varying shades of colour presented by the reduced metal, and more especially the transition observed at the moment of removing the unaltered portion of material by the application of the fixing agent. If in these several stages the change in physical condition be considered in its proper connexion, and due allowance be made for the very important influence known to be exercised over the light-reflecting capacity of these minutely divided particles by very slight modifications in their state of aggregation (quite irrespective of change in chemical constitution), there will then be no longer any difficulty in referring these results, with others of the same class (e. g., the several varieties of gold prepared and examined by Professor Faraday), to a series all of which are capable of similar explanation.

I subjoin, in the form of propositions, a statement of the results arrived at ; they appear to me to have been fully substantiated by the foregoing experimental considerations. And I will remark, in conclusion, that the hypothesis believed to be supported by the facts now communicated is in conformity with the previous results of Dr. Guthrie, MM. Girard and Davanne, and generally also with those of M. Van Monkhoven, and will consequently be to a certain extent opposed to the views advanced by Messrs. Hadow, Hardwich, Llewellen, and Maskelyne, in their joint report upon this subject recently presented to the meeting of the British Association.

Propositions.—1st. That chloride of silver, when decomposed by light, is separated into its elements.

2nd. That this change does not usually extend to the whole bulk of the material operated upon, on account of the opacity of the darkened product mechanically protecting a certain portion of unaltered chloride of silver from the action of the light.

3rd. That the degree and rapidity of reduction is influenced by the state of division of the particles, and by the presence of agents capable of absorbing the chlorine when liberated from its combination with silver.

PHOTOGRAPHY A CENTURY SINCE.

IN the *London Review*, Dec. 15, 1860, attention is called to a "foreshadowing" of the Photographic Art, in a book entitled *Giphantie à Babylone*, published in 1760 ; and in which the author, Tiphaigne de la Roche, relates the wonders which were revealed to

him in a vision by the chief of the genii of the elements. He there
recounts how the attendant genii had sought to fix the fleeting
images which were seen reflected in placid water, or painted on the
retina of the eye ; and, after some details, he describes how they at
last succeeded in discovering a subtle adhesive liquid quickly drying,
and capable, when poured on a flat surface, of fixing thereon, permanently, and in the twinkling of an eye, the images of whatever
natural scene was presented before it. Awaking from his vision,
Tiphaigne propounds three problems which had been suggested to
him by the genii, for the sagacity of mundane philosophers to un-
ravel : the nature of the glutinous liquid, the method of preparation
and best means of employing it, and the rationale of the action which
was exercised upon it by light. The account given by the genii (the
writer states) is almost, to its minute details, the present system of
collodion photography ; whilst Tiphaigne's three problems, important
as they have since become, are still very far from a satisfactory
settlement.

This is a very ingenious identification of a past speculation with
present fulfilment of which the amusing writer in the *London
Review* says :—" Never before, in modern ages, have we known so
clear an instance of a prophecy and its fulfilment." We cannot
agree with the writer to the full extent : he does not quote the *words*
of the author, which, in literary evidence, it is very important should
be done. That any one should *wish* for the fixing of a pleasing
image, in a mirror, or in water, the first natural mirror, is reasonable
enough, and far beyond the fantasies of a century since ; but the
how is a matter not so easily traceable. The Editor of the *Year-Book
of Facts* proposed *rolling* over a printer's form of type, instead
of beating with balls, long before the composition inking-rollers
were invented. The discovery of the process of making the *composition* for the rollers was the great secret, without which this important portion of printing machinery would, in all probability,
never have been perfected, We are too apt, in seeking the history
of discovery, to reason *a posteriori.* This tracing of collodion photography reminds us of the story of the magnetic correspondence in
the *Spectator,* which has been regarded as the foreshadowing of
electro-telegraphy.

_____

THE USES OF PHOTOGRAPHY.

UNDER this comprehensive title, the writer of an able paper in the
Mechanics' Magazine has grouped the more striking results obtained
by photographic agency, which far exceed even the sanguine anticipations of some one-and-twenty years since—the date of the birth of
this wonderful art.

A Photographic Recording Apparatus has been adopted for regis-
tering the meteorological indications of the instruments at the Royal
Observatory, Greenwich, with the greatest advantage. Since its
introduction, the staff of observers has been reduced in number, and
the fatiguing process of nocturnal observation has been altogether
superseded. The following is a description of the general principles

N

upon which this instrument is constructed, taken from the *Journal of the Photographic Society* :—

A pencil of light, brought to a focus by spherical or cylindrical lenses or reflectors, is so governed that its point or focus has a motion identical with, or bearing a known proportion to, the motion of part of the instrument which affords the indications to be registered. Thus, if the instrument be a magnetic needle, the axis of the lens or spectrum is made to coincide, or make a known or constant angle, with the needle, and therefore to participate in its movements. The focus of the pencil refracted or reflected receives a corresponding motion. If it be a column of mercury, as in the case of a barometer or thermometer, the direction of the pencil of light is varied, either by means of a float, which rises and falls with the mercurial column, or by transmitting the light through the tube, so as to produce the shadow of the column, in which case the movement of the shadow will be registered. The focus of the luminous pencil is made to fall upon a sheet of photographic paper; and if both it and the paper were stationary, a spot would be produced upon the paper at the place where the focus falls upon it. If, owing to the variation of the instrument whose indications are to be recorded, the focus of the luminous pencil moves, a line will be traced on the photographic paper, the length of which will bear a known relation to the variation of the instrument. Thus, if it be a magnetic needle, a variation of one degree east or west in its direction may impart a motion of an inch right or left to the focus of the luminous pencil, and a line of corresponding length would be traced upon the photographic paper. But by this means nothing would be recorded, except the extreme variation of the needle in a given time. An observer would still be necessary: and nothing would be accomplished more than is already attained by the self-registering thermometers, which show the maximum and minimum temperatures indicated during a given interval. The apparatus is, however, rendered perfect by rolling the photographic paper on a cylinder, which is moved by clockwork, so that a known length of the paper moves under the focus of the luminous pencil in a given time. When the focus of the pencil is stationary, a straight line is traced on the paper in a direction at right angles to the motion of the paper, and therefore parallel to the axis of the cylinder; but when the focus moves, as usually happens, to the right and left alternately, an undulating curve is traced upon the paper, the distances of the points of which from a known base line (also traced upon the paper) show not only the particular minute and second at which each change took place, but the actual state of the instrument at that moment.

The Editor of the same journal states that a beautiful apparatus, constructed for Kew Gardens, is the most reliable barometer ever yet invented. By means of a wire communicating with the atmosphere on the one hand, and a very delicate electrometer on the other hand, a silvered bead, placed at the end of a thread of glass as fine as a silkworm fibre (the glass thread being the most elastic of all substances), is carried to the right or to the left hand in the ratio of the amount of vitreous or resinous electricity. The bead reflecting a spot of light on to sensitive paper moved in the way before described, produces a permanent record of every change in the electrical condition of the atmosphere, day and night. As an elucidation of its use, the writer mentions a fact as gratifying as it will be astounding to many of our readers :—The day of the last celebration of Her Majesty's birthday was one of the succession of very numerous wet days with which it has lately pleased Providence to visit us. Upon that evening Professor Thomson, of Glasgow, was lecturing upon this electro-photographic apparatus at the Royal Institution. During the greater part of the lecture the rain was ominously pattering upon the roof of the theatre. At the conclusion of his lecture he proceeded to take an observation by the means of a wire passing through the roof of the theatre. He immediately procured a luminous pencil from the head projecting a bright spot of light, denoting about 45° of vitreous electricity ; upon which he observed that he was happy to state, for the information of those who were interested in the fact, that the rain had ceased, that there would be a fine evening, and a succession of very fine days. "From that moment, on that Friday evening, until the following Saturday week, we had not one drop of rain (says the writer) in London."

For military purposes, again, Photography has proved exceedingly useful. Captain Fowke, of the Royal Engineers, who has fitted out most of the parties of engineers that have taken photographic apparatus with them, invented a form of camera which is extremely portable, collapsing into a size that enabled it to be easily carried in a knapsack. The back of the camera is three or four times the size of the front. The sides can be detached from the front, but are hinged to the back in such a way as to allow them to fold one upon another flat upon the back. With a camera of this description, and with chemicals, &c., carried in boxes on pack-saddles, many photographs, which Captain Donelly exhibited, have been taken by sappers in Russia and Turkey ; and pictures by Sergeant Church, who accompanied Colonel Stanton when he went to verify the reports on the projected Honduras line of railway across the Isthmus of Panama. Others were done in India and at Singapore. Some were taken in China, and furnished Mr. Burford with the means for his Panorama. Others were taken by Sergeant Mack at Moscow, when he accompanied Lord Granville.

Photographs are found of great service in illustrating a report on a country, as they have been employed by Colonel Stanton ; and in this way they may be of service to a general commanding an army in the field. Photographs are also available in copying and multiplying plans,—as in the case of a plan, which was produced, of the position of the ships for landing the troops in the Crimea. Captain Donelly instances a number of photographs which were executed at Chatham, affording an admirable means of conveying descriptions of various operations (bridge-making and so on), giving perfect ideas of place. Photographs are likewise of great service in supplying engineers with a ready and rapid means of showing the state of works on a particular day.

_____

PHOTO-ZINCOGRAPHY. BY COLONEL SIR HENRY JAMES, R.E., DIRECTOR OF THE ORDNANCE SURVEY.

IN the Report of the Committee of which Sir R. Murchison was chairman, it is stated that the annual saving effected by my having introduced this (the photographic) method of reducing the Ordnance plans from the larger to the smaller scales, amounted in the year 1858 to 1615l. Since then we have so much reduced the cost of the photographs, that the saving which will be effected will amount to 35,000l. in the cost of the survey. Up to this period we have exclusively used the paper prepared with nitrate of silver for printing the number of copies required ; but we have made experiments with the printing paper prepared with the bichromate of potash, gum, and lamp-black, or any other pigment, called the Chromo-carbon process of printing.

The action of light on a coating of this composition produces the peculiar effect of rendering it insoluble in water, and consequently when a sheet of paper coated with it is placed in the printing frame under the collodion negative, the outline of the plan is rendered insoluble in water, and remains on the paper when all the remainder of the composition is washed away, and thus we have a "positive" plan in ink of any colour which may be required.

In comparing the reduced plans obtained by this process with those obtained by the use of paper prepared with the nitrate of silver, we obtain no advantage whatever, but, on the contrary, the prints are less clear and sharp in their outline.

But by a new mode of treatment of these chromo-carbon prints which has been introduced by Capt. A. de C. Scott, R.E., who has charge of this branch of the work, and Lance-Corporal Rider, R.E., who is a good photographer, and also possesses a considerable knowledge of chemistry, we can produce very sharp, clear lines. The ink of the print after being soaked in a saturated solution of caustic potash or soda becomes, so to speak, disintegrated, and is then in a state which enables us at once to rub down the print, and transfer the outline to the waxed surface of a copper-plate for the engraver. This promises to be of great importance to us, as after obtaining the photographed reductions of the maps we have hitherto been obliged to make tracings from them in ink, for the purpose of transferring the plan to the copper, the expense and delay of which will now be saved, whilst we run no risk of any error being made by the draughtsman.

We have also tried a method which is still more valuable, and by which the reduced print is in a state to be at once transferred to stone or zinc, from which any number of copies can be taken, as in ordinary lithographic or zincographic printing, or for transfer to the waxed surface of the copper-plates. To effect this, the paper after being washed over with the solution of the bichromate of potash and gum, and dried, is placed in the printing frame under the collodion negative, and after exposure to the light, the whole surface is coated over with lithographic ink, and a stream of hot water then poured over it; and as the portion which was exposed to the light is insoluble, whilst the composition in all other parts being soluble is easily washed off, we obtain at once the outline of the map in a state ready for being transferred either to stone, zinc, or the copper-plate, or we can take the photograph on the zinc at once.

This new method of printing from a negative is extremely simple and inexpensive, and promises to be of great use to us. Sheet 96, of Northumberland, has been transferred to the copper-plate from impressions taken by this process, and from the perfect manner in which we are able to transfer the impressions to zinc, we can, if required, print any number of faithful copies of the ancient records of the kingdom, such as *Doomsday Book*, the *Pipe Rolls*, &c., at a comparatively speaking very trifling cost. I have called this new method Photo-zincography, and anticipate that it will become very generally useful, not only to Government, but to the public at large, for producing perfectly accurate copies of documents of any kind.

A *fac-simile* of a manuscript of the time of Edward I., copied and printed at the Ordnance Survey Office, under the direction of Colonel Sir Henry James, by means of the photo-zincographic process, has been presented by the *Photographic News* to its readers.

———

ON THE SOLAR CAMERA.   BY A. CLAUDET.[*]

THE Solar Camera, invented by Woodward, is one of the most important improvements introduced in the art of photography since

———

[*] Read to the British Association at Oxford.

its discovery. By its means small negatives may produce pictures magnified to any extent ; a portrait taken on a collodion plate not larger than a visiting card can be increased, in the greatest perfection, to the size of nature ; views as small as those for the stereoscope can be also considerably enlarged.

The beautiful principle of Woodward's apparatus consists in his having decided the question of the position of the focus of the condenser, and in having placed it exactly on the front lens of the camera obscura.

As this principle had not yet been explained when the invention was exhibited before the Photographic Societies of London and Paris, and not even by the inventor himself in the specification of his patent, Mr. Claudet undertook, in the interest of the photographic art, to bring the subject before the British Association, and to demonstrate that the solar camera of Woodward has solved the most difficult problem of the optics of photography, and is capable of producing wonderful results. This problem consists in forming the image of the negative to be copied only by the centre of the object-glass reduced to the smallest aperture possible, without losing the least proportion of the light illuminating the negative.

The solar camera does not require any diaphragm to reduce the aperture of the lens, because every one of the points of the negative are visible only when they are defined on the image of the sun, and they are so (in that position exclusively), for the centre of the lens is the only point which sees the sun, while the various points of the negative which form the marginal zone of the lens are defined against the comparatively obscure parts of the sky surrounding the sun, are, as it were, invisible to that zone ; so that the image is produced only by the central rays, and not in the least degree by any other points of the lens, which are subject to spherical aberration. It is, in fact, a lens reduced to an aperture as small as is the image of the sun upon its surface, without the necessity of any diaphragm, and admitting the whole light of the sun after it has been condensed upon the various separate points of the negative. It is evident that from the centre of the lens the whole negative has for background the sun itself, and from the other points of the lens it has for background only the sky surrounding the sun, which fortunately has no effect in the formation of the image.

Such is the essential principle of Woodward's solar camera, which did not exist in that instrument when the focus of the condenser was not on the object-glass. This principle is truly marvellous, but it must be observed that the solar camera, precisely on account of the excellence of this principle, requires the greatest precision in its construction. For its delicate performances, it must be as perfect as an astronomical instrument, which, in fact, it is. The reflecting mirror should be plane, and with parallel surfaces, in order to reflect on the condenser an image of the sun without deformation ; and in order to keep the image always on the very centre of the object-glass, the only condition for the exclusion of the oblique rays, the mirror should be capable by its connexion with a heliostat of following the movements of the sun. The condenser itself should be achromatic;

in order to refract the image of the sun without dispersion, and to define more correctly the lines of the negative ; and a no less important condition for losing nothing of the photogenic rays would be, to have it formed with a glass perfectly homogeneous and colourless. With such improvements, the solar camera will become capable of producing results of the greatest beauty ; and, without any question, its introduction into the photographer's studio will mark a period of considerable improvement in the art.

Thus has Mr. Claudet shown that in order to obtain a perfectly good picture of any size from a small negative—in order to obtain a portrait, for instance, the size of life from a miniature the size of a visiting card—all that is necessary is to have recourse to Woodward's solar camera, provided it be accurately made, and so adjusted that the focus of the condensing lens fall exactly on the front lens of the camera obscura, neither behind it nor before it, as is common in the instruments as usually made.

MULTIPLICATION OF PHOTOGRAPHS BY STEAM.

A PAPER was read before the American Photographic Society on 13th August, 1860, by which it appears that twelve thousand photographs or stereographs an hour can now be produced from a single negative by means of condensed or focalized light and simple machinery worked by a crank. A sheet of ordinary paper, sensitized, was exhibited, containing 300 of these photographs. Mr. Charles Fontayne, of Cincinnati, Ohio, is the inventor of the process. The prepared or sensitized paper is simply passed, in a continuous sheet, before a negative, in a box, where condensed light is made to penetrate through the negative and impress its image upon the paper, which it does in ·03 of a second for each impression. The condensing lens is 7 inches in diameter. Thus, as it is said, "the illustrations for a book, having all the exquisite beauty and perfection of the photograph, may be turned out by the use of this machine with a rapidity wholly undreamed of either in plate-printing or in lithography." The cost of engraving, also, will of course be dispensed with. All sorts of drawings, too, may be thus multiplied, as well as actual objects photographed or stereographed, in cheap and endless profusion. The *Architects' Journal*, of New York, publishes a print thus produced from a rough sketch by the ordinary ammonio-nitrate process.

VITREOUS PHOTOGRAPHS.

AMONG the most admired things in the last Exhibition of the Society of Arts were specimens of Vitreous Photographs, produced by Mr. F. Joubert and Mr. John Wyard. These specimens are entirely novel, and in reference to the photographic art are likely to be of great importance, as they not only give to the photograph the permanence of any image which is produced in a glass or porcelain body, but also admit of a combination of a variety of colours in the production of photographic subjects. Among the specimens shown by Mr. Joubert are some monochrome photographs on earthenware tiles, manufactured by Messrs. Minton and Co.

PHOTOGRAPHY AND FLUORESCENCE.

PROFESSOR FARADAY has exhibited to the Royal Institution Photographs of fluorescent substances which had been prepared by Dr. J. H. Gladstone. He reminded the members present of experiments they had seen in that theatre showing that certain bodies, as bisulphate of quinine, emit a beautiful bluish light when they are exposed to the most refrangible rays of the spectrum, and are also phosphorescent. Several of these are white or colourless to look at under ordinary circumstances ; but it had occurred to Dr. Gladstone that on account of their lowering the refrangibility of the chemical rays they would perhaps not produce so great a photographic effect as other white substances. He had, therefore, drawn various devices in quinine salt, esculine from horse-chestnut bark, comenamate of potash, and other fluorescent substances on white paper, and had had the apparently white sheet photographed. The devices all came out dark, as was seen in the specimen exhibited ; and, more than that, on a sheet of paper coloured blue with cobalt were fixed letters cut out of white paper and steeped in the fluorescent solutions above mentioned. When this sheet was photographed the blue paper was found to have a much greater chemical effect than the white letters, which, therefore, appeared in the positive photograph dark on a light ground.—*Illustrated London News.*

THE NEOMONOSCOPE.

M. P. A. A. BEAU has patented a Neomonoscope, or apparatus for viewing photographic and other like pictures. This is constructed with one glass or several glasses superposed for the purpose of obtaining a similar effect to that derived from viewing pictures in or through a stereoscope. The monoscope is a pyramidal or conical-shaped case, with a part of one of the sides removed to admit light. The glass is fitted in the top of the apparatus, and, in some cases, flaps for forming when raised a dark chamber between the eye and the glass are added. The bottom of the apparatus is made to slide to admit of its being entirely removed in order to view transparent objects, or others apart from the apparatus itself. The sides of the apparatus are either made rigid or to fold.—*Mechanics' Magazine.*

PHOTOGRAPHIC OBSERVATION OF THE SOLAR ECLIPSE, JULY 18, 1860.

MR. JOHN SPILLER, F.C.S., has communicated to the *Philosophical Magazine*, No. 132, a description of the Photographic Representation of the Solar Disc, as it appeared from the station of the equatorial telescope of the Royal Artillery Institution, Woolwich, under the several phases of the particular Eclipse ; the successful termination of the day's labour resulting in the production of 23 photographic impressions of the phenomenon.

The telescope, with its portable stand provided with means of adjustment in altitude and azimuth, was, on the 18th of July, erected in the open air within the enclosures of the Royal Military Repository on Woolwich Common, and immediately contiguous to all the appliances of a well-furnished photographic laboratory. The object-glass, 4 inches in diameter, has a sidereal focus of 77 inches, and gives a representation of the sun's disc measuring, at this season of the year, ·7 inch in diameter. For photographic purposes the eye-piece was removed from the telescope and a small sliding-bodied camera adapted to the end of the tube; it was then easy to project upon the ground glass a perfectly defined image of the solar disc, using the means of adjustment which the camera afforded for the purpose of obtaining the best optical focus; and in this plane the prepared photographic surfaces were usually employed, for the chemical and visual foci had previously been ascertained to be very nearly coincident. The aperture of the object-glass was now stopped down until, with a diaphragm of ·25 inch, the exposure to the powerful action of direct sunlight was rendered manageable; and in order to secure an easy and sufficiently rapid means of opening and closing this small aperture, a card of about 6 inches square was provided, having cut out from its centre a narrow slit of about an eighth of an inch in diameter and nearly 2 inches in length. This, quickly moved by the hand in front of the diaphragm of the telescope lens, limited the period of exposure to a small fraction of a second, and besides made it possible to regulate the interval of time at the taking of each picture according to circumstances at the moment, which were occasionally varying, as light fleecy clouds passed over the face of the sun. Mr. Crookes, who took charge of this part of the apparatus, was provided with dark glasses, to enable him, by watching the sun, to select the proper moment and judge the length of time which each plate would require in its exposure; and he agrees with Mr. Spiller in preferring this system of operating to the use of a fixed mechanical contrivance for opening and closing the aperture of the lens.

By proceeding in the manner indicated, the observers endeavoured to restrict the photographic action to the representation of the sun's disc alone, and only in the first and second plates of the series was sufficient time allowed for the highly illuminated clouds around the sun to become imprinted in the camera; although faintly visible sometimes in the field of view of the telescope, their intensity was now so much lowered as not to be copied. It will be evident, also, from the foregoing description, that no clockwork mechanism was required for the purpose of making the apparatus follow the diurnal motion of the sun.

The glass plates on which the pictures were taken measured 2¾ inches by 3¼ inches, and were numbered at one corner by a scratching diamond; they were cleaned previously and arranged in their order of succession. The precise moment at which each plate received its exposure in the camera was registered immediately; Greenwich mean time being taken the same morning from the Woolwich Observatory, and kept by an ordinary good watch.

The collodion process seemed on all accounts the most available, and was that employed to furnish the negative pictures from which copies on paper have afterwards been printed ; and in order to guard against accidents, the silver baths, collodion, and the more important solutions were provided in duplicate, so that no difficulty was experienced in preparing the sensitive plates in rapid succession.

Mr. Spiller describes several of the photographs as exhibiting very clearly the position of the solar spots, and in many cases the lunar mountains are to be seen sharply defined against the bright face of the sun. A passing cloud rendered " the first contact" so perfectly invisible that no opportunity for opening the camera was presented ; but the plate representing the moment of maximum obscuration, and the phases both immediately preceding and following, are fortunately amongst the most successful of the photographic results ; and further, on comparing the present series with the disc of the sun taken at the period of the former eclipse, March 15, 1858, in precisely the same apparatus, the diminished size of the image consequent on the eccentricity of the earth's orbit is very strikingly exhibited.

NEW REMEDY.

THE effect of the perpetual inhalation of alcoholic beverages in the production of *delirium tremens* is well known. Short of this destructive effect, these beverages produce various derangements, commencing with an imperfect nutrition of the nervous system, and affecting more or less every other organ of the body. Of course the remedy for this state of things is abstinence from the stimulants producing the disease. But this is not alone sufficient. Repair of mischief done is necessary ; and Dr. Marcet has administered as a remedy the oxide of zinc, in a large number of cases, and with so uniformly beneficial an effect that there can be no doubt his experience is worthy the attention of the medical profession. This new remedy should, however, only be administered by medical skill.—See Dr. Marcet's pamphlet on the subject, published by Churchill, New Burlington-street.

Natural History.

ZOOLOGY.　•

ORIGIN OF SPECIES.

It was to the section D. (Zoology and Botany, including Physiology, a sub-section attached for the last-named subject) that the chief interest attached at the late meeting of the British Association, in consequence of the popularity at the present moment of discussion as to the Origin of Species. After a Report by Dr. Ogilvie, intimating the little that had been done, in consequence of the tempestuous weather and the early meeting of the Association, by the Dredging Committee for the North and East Coasts of Scotland, and a very interesting communication by the Rev. P. P. Carpenter, on the Progress of Natural Science in the United States and Canada, Dr. Daubeny led off in the great question of the day, by a paper on the Final Causes of the Sexuality of Plants, with particular reference to Mr. Darwin's work on the *Origin of Species by Natural Selection.*

Dr. Daubeny began by pointing out the identity between the two modes by which the multiplication of plants is brought about, the very same properties being imparted to the bud or to the graft as to the seed produced by the ordinary process of fecundation, and a new individual being in either instance equally produced. We are therefore led to speculate as to the final cause of the existence of sexual organs in plants, as well as in those lower animals which can be propagated by cuttings. One use, no doubt, may be the dissemination of the species ; for many plants, if propagated by buds alone, would be in a manner confined to a single spot. Another secondary use is the production of fruits which afford nourishment to animals. A third may be to minister to the gratification of the senses of man by the beauty of their forms and colours. But as these ends are only answered in a small proportion of cases, we must seek further for the uses of the organs in question ; and hence the author suggested that they might have been provided in order to prevent that uniformity in the aspect of Nature which would have prevailed if plants had been multiplied exclusively by buds. It is well known that a bud is a mere counterpart of the stock from whence it springs, so that we are always sure of obtaining the very same description of fruit by merely grafting a bud or cutting of a pear or apple tree upon another plant of the same species. On the other hand, the seed never produces an individual exactly like the plant from which it sprang ; and hence, by the union of the sexes in plants, some variation from the primitive type is sure to result. Dr. Daubeny remarked, that if we adopt in any degree the views of Mr. Darwin, with respect to the origin of species by natural selection, the creation of sexual organs in plants might be regarded as intended to promote this specific object. Whilst, however, he gave his assent to the Darwinian hypothesis, as likely to aid us in reducing the number of existing species, he wished not to be considered as advocating it to the extent to which the author seems disposed to carry it. He rather desired to recommend to naturalists the necessity of further inquiries, in order to fix the limits within which the doctrine proposed by Mr. Darwin may assist us in distinguishing varieties from species.

Professor Huxley deprecated any discussion on the general question of the truth of Mr. Darwin's theory. He felt that a general audience, in which sentiment would unduly interfere with intellect, was not the public before which such a discussion should be carried on. Dr. Daubeny had brought forth nothing new to demand or require remark. Mr. R. Dowden, of Cork, mentioned, first, two instances in which plants had been disseminated by seeds, which could not be effected by buds, first, in the introduction of *Senicio squalida*, by the late Rev. W. Hincks ; and, second, in the diffusion of chicory, in the vicinity of Cork, by the agency of its winged seeds. He related several anecdotes of a monkey, to show that however highly organized the Quadrumana might be, they were very inferior in intellectual qualities to the dog, the elephant, and other animals. He particularly referred to his monkey being fond of playing with a hammer ; but although he liked oysters as food, he never could teach him to break the oysters with his hammer as a means of indulging his appetite. Dr. Wright stated that a friend of his, who had gone out to report on the habits of the gorilla—the highest form of monkey —had observed that the female gorilla took its young to the sea- shore for the purpose of feeding them on oysters, which they broke with great facility.

. Professor Owen said that he wished to approach this subject in the spirit of the philosopher, and expressed his conviction that there were facts by which the public could come to some conclusion with regard to the probabilities of the truth of Mr. Darwin's theory. Whilst giving all praise to Mr. Darwin for the courage with which he had put forth his theory, he felt it must be tested by facts. As a contribution to the facts, by which the theory must be tested, he would refer to the structure of the highest Quadrumana as compared with man. Taking the brain of the gorilla, it presented more differences, as compared with the brain of man, than it did when compared with the brains of the very lowest and most problematical form of the Quadrumana. The differences in cerebral structure between the gorilla and man were immense. The posterior lobes of the cerebrum in man presented parts which were wholly absent in the gorilla. The same remarkable differences of structure were seen in other parts of the body; yet he would especially refer to the structure of the great toe in man, which was constructed to enable him to assume the upright position; whilst in the lower monkeys it was impossible, from the structure of their feet, that they should do so. He concluded by urging on the physiologist the necessity of experiment. The chemist, when in doubt, decided his questions by experiments ; and this was what is needed by the physiologist. Professor Huxley begged to be permitted to reply to Professor Owen. He denied altogether that the difference between the brain of the gorilla and man was so great as represented by Professor Owen, and appealed to the published dissections of Tiedemann and others. From the study of the structure of the brain of the Quadrumana, he maintained that the difference between man and the highest monkey was not so great as between the highest and the lowest monkey. He maintained also, with regard to the limbs, that there was more difference between the toeless monkeys and the gorilla than between the latter and man. He believed that the great feature which distinguished man from the monkey was the gift of speech.

This subject was resumed another day by a paper " on the Intellectual Development of Europe, considered with Reference to the Views of Mr. Darwin and others, that the Progression of Organisms is determined by Law," by Professor Draper, M.D., of New York. The object of this paper was to show that the advancement of man in civilization does not occur accidentally or in a fortuitous manner, but is determined by immutable law. The author introduced his subject by recalling proofs of the dominion of law in the three great lines of the manifestation of life. First, in the successive stages of development of every individual, from the earliest rudiment to maturity ; secondly, in the numberless organic forms now living contemporaneously with us, and constituting the animal series ; thirdly, in the orderly appearance of that grand succession which in the slow lapse of geological time has emerged, constituting the life of the earth, showing therefrom not only the evidences, but also proofs of the dominion of law over the world of life. In those three lines of life he established that the general principle is, to differentiate instinct from automatism, and then to differentiate intelligence from instinct. In man himself three distinct instrumental nervous mechanisms exist, and three distinct modes of life are perceptible, the automatic, the instinctive, the intelligent. They occur in an epochal order, from infancy through childhood to the more perfect state. Such holding good for the individual, it was then affirmed that it is physiologically impossible to separate the individual from the race, and that what holds good for the one holds good for the other too ; and hence that man is the archetype of society, and individual development the model of social progress, and that both are under the control of immutable law : that a parallel exists between individual and national life in this, that the production, life, and death of an organic particle in the person, answers to the production, life, and death of a person in the nation.

Turning from these purely physiological considerations to historical proof, and selecting the only European nation which thus far has offered a complete and completed intellectual life, Professor Draper showed that the characteristics of Greek mental development answer perfectly to those of individual life, presenting philosophically five well-marked ages or periods,—the first being closed by the opening of Egypt to the Ionians ; the second, including the Ionian, Pythagorean, and Eleatic philosophies, was ended by the criticisms of the Sophists ; the third, embracing the Socratic and Platonic philosophies, was ended by the doubts of the Sceptics ; the fourth, ushered in by the Macedonian expedition, and adorned by the splendid achievements of the Alexandrian school, degenerated into Neoplatonism and imbecility in the fifth, to which the hand of Rome put an end. From the solutions of the four great problems of Greek philosophy, given in each of these five stages of its life, he showed that it is possible to determine the law of the variation of Greek opinion, and to establish its analogy with that of the variations of opinion in individual life. Next, passing to the consideration of Europe in the aggregate, Professor Draper showed that it has already in part repeated these phases in its intellectual life. Its first period closes with the spread of the power of Republican Rome, the second with the foundation of Constantinople, the third with the Turkish invasion of Europe; we are living in the fourth. Detailed proofs of the correspondence of these periods to those of Greek life, and through them to those of individual life, are given in a work now printing on this subject, by the author, in America. Having established this conclusion, Professor Draper next briefly alluded to many collateral problems or inquiries. He showed that the advances of men are due to external and not to interior influences, and that in this respect a nation is like a seed, which can only develop when the conditions are favourable, and then only in a definite way; that the time for psychical change corresponds with that for physical, and that a nation cannot advance except its material condition be touched,—this having been the case throughout all Europe, as is manifested by the diminution of the blue-eyed races thereof; that all organisms, and even man, are dependent for their characteristics, continuance, and life, on the physical conditions under which they live; that the existing apparent invariability presented by the world of organization is the direct consequence of the physical equilibrium; but that if that should suffer modification, in an instant the fanciful doctrine of the immutability of species would be brought to its proper value. The organic world appears to be in repose because natural influences have reached an equilibrium. A marble may remain motionless for ever on a level table, but let the table be a little inclined, and the marble will quickly run off; and so it is with organisms in the world. From his work on Physiology, published in 1856, he gave his views in support of the doctrine of the transmutation of species; the transitional forms of the animal to the human type; the production of new ethnical elements, or nations; and the laws of their origin, duration, and death.

The announcement of this paper attracted an immense audience to the section, which met in the library of the New Museum. The discussion was commenced by the Rev. Mr. Cresswell, who denied that any parallel could be drawn between the intellectual progress of man and the physical development of the lower animals. So far from Professor Draper being correct with regard to the history of Greece, its masterpieces in literature—the *Iliad* and *Odyssey*—were produced during its national infancy. The theory of intellectual development proposed was directly opposed to the known facts of the history of man. Sir B. Brodie stated he could not subscribe to the hypothesis of

Mr. Darwin. His primordial germ had not been demonstrated to have existed. Man had a power of self-consciousness—a principle differing from anything found in the material world—and he did not see how this could originate in lower organisms. This power of man was identical with the Divine Intelligence ; and to suppose that this could originate with matter, involved the absurdity of supposing the source of Divine power dependent on the arrangement of matter. The Bishop of Oxford stated that the Darwinian theory, when tried by the principles of inductive science, broke down. The facts brought forward did not warrant the theory. The permanence of specific forms was a fact confirmed by all observation. The remains of animals, plants, and man, found in those earliest records of the human race, the Egyptian catacombs, all spoke of their identity with existing forms, and of the irresistible tendency of organized beings to assume an unalterable character. The line between man and the lower animals was distinct ; there was no tendency on the part of the lower animals to become the self-conscious intelligent being, man ; or in man to degenerate and lose the high characteristics of his mind and intelligence. All experiments had failed to show any tendency in one animal to assume the form of the other. In the great case of the pigeons, quoted by Mr. Darwin, he admitted that no sooner were these animals set free than they returned to their primitive type. Everywhere sterility attended hybridism, as was seen in the closely allied forms of the horse and the ass. Mr. Darwin's conclusions were an hypothesis, raised most unphilosophically to the dignity of a causal theory. He was glad to know that the greatest names in science were opposed to this theory, which he believed to be opposed to the interests of science and humanity. Professor Huxley defended Mr. Darwin's theory from the charge of its being merely an hypothesis. He said it was an explanation of phenomena in Natural History, as the undulating theory was of the phenomena of light. No one objected to that theory because an undulation of light had never been arrested and measured. Darwin's theory was an explanation of facts ; and his book was full of new facts, all bearing on his theory. Without asserting that every part of the theory had been confirmed, he maintained that it was the best explanation of the origin of species which had yet been offered. With regard to the psychological distinction between man and animals, man himself was once a monad—a mere atom ; and nobody could say at what moment in the history of his development he became consciously intelligent. The question was not so much one of a transmutation or transition of species, as of the production of forms which became permanent. Thus the short-legged sheep of America were not produced gradually, but originated in the birth of an original parent of the whole stock, which had been kept up by a rigid system of artificial selection.

Admiral Fitzroy regretted the publication of Mr. Darwin's book, and denied Professor Huxley's statement, that it was a logical arrangement of facts.

Dr. Beale pointed out some of the difficulties with which the

Darwinian theory had to deal, more especially those vital tendencies of allied species which seemed independent of all external agents. Mr. Lubbock expressed his willingness to accept the Darwinian hypothesis in the absence of any better. He would, however, express his conviction, that time was not an essential element in these changes. Time alone produced no change.

Dr. Hooker being called upon by the President to state his views of the botanical aspect of the question, observed that the Bishop of Oxford having asserted that all men of science were hostile to Mr. Darwin's hypothesis, whereas he himself was favourable to it, he could not presume to address the audience as a scientific authority. As, however, he had been asked for his opinion, he would briefly give it. In the first place, his lordship, in his eloquent address, had, as it appeared to him, completely misunderstood Mr. Darwin's hypothesis. His lordship intimated that this maintained the doctrine of the transmutation of existing species one into another, and had confounded this with that of the successive development of species by variation and natural selection. The first of these doctrines was so wholly opposed to the facts, reasonings, and results of Mr. Darwin's work, that he could not conceive how any one who had read it could make such a mistake—the whole book, indeed, being a protest against that doctrine. Then, again, with regard to the general phenomena of species, he understood his lordship to affirm that these did not present characters that should lead careful and philosophical naturalists to favour Mr. Darwin's views. To this assertion Dr. Hooker's experience of the vegetable kingdom was diametrically opposed. He considered that at least one-half of the known kinds of plants were disposable in groups, of which the species were connected by varying characters common to all in that group, and sensibly differing in some individuals only of each species ; so much so, that if each group be likened to a cobweb, and one species be supposed to stand in the centre of that web, its varying characters might be compared to the radiating and concentric threads, when the other species would be represented by the points of union of these ; in short, that the general characteristics of orders, genera, and species amongst plants differed in degrees only from those of varieties, and afforded the strongest countenance to Mr. Darwin's hypothesis. As regarded his own acceptation of Mr. Darwin's views, he expressly disavowed having adopted them as a creed. He knew no creeds in scientific matters. He had early begun the study of natural science under the idea that species were original creations ; and it should be steadily kept in view that this was merely another hypothesis, which in the abstract was neither more nor less entitled to acceptance than Mr. Darwin's ; neither was it, in the present state of science, capable of demonstration, and each must be tested by its power of explaining the mutual dependence of the phenomena of life. For many years he had held to the old hypothesis, having no better established one to adopt ; though the progress of botany had in the interim developed no new facts that favoured it, but a host of most suggestive objections to it. On the other hand, having fifteen years ago been privately made acquainted with Mr. Darwin's views, he had during that period applied these to botanical investigations of all kinds in the most distant parts of the globe, as well as to the study of the largest and most different floras at home. Now, then, that Mr. Darwin had published it, he had no hesitation in publicly adopting his hypothesis, as that which offers by far the most probable explanation of all the phenomena prescribed by the classification, distribution, structure, and development of plants in a state of nature and under cultivation; he should therefore continue to use this hypothesis as the best weapon for future research, holding himself ready to lay it down should a better be forthcoming, or should the now abandoned doctrine of original creations regain all it had lost in his experience.

The subject has been discussed with kindred interest in America.

The American Academy of Arts and Sciences reports the following summary of the argument of Professor Asa Gray, the distinguished botanist, who criticised in detail several of the positions taken at the preceding meeting by Mr. Lowell, Professor Bowen, and Professor Agassiz respectively; premising that he had no doubt that variation and natural selection would have to be admitted as operative in nature, but were probably inadequate to the work which they had been put to. Professor Gray maintained—

1. That varieties abundantly occur in nature, at least among plants, and that very few of them can be of hybrid origin; that hybridation gives rise to no new features, but only mingles, and, if continued, blends the characters of sorts before separate; and that a hybrid origin was entirely out of the question in species which had no congeners, or none in the country to which they were indigenous; yet that such species diverged into varieties as readily as any other. As to the general denial, 1, that there is any such thing as natural selection, and 2, that there is any variation in species for natural selection to act upon, he could not yet conceive how such denial was to be supported; but to answer its purpose it would have to be carried to the length of denying that the individuals of a species ever have anything which they did not inherit;—slight variations, accumulated by inheritance, being just what the theory in question made use of,—taking little or no account of more salient and abrupt variations, though instances of the latter kind could certainly be adduced.

2. In opposition to the view that such variations as cultivation or domestication so copiously affords are of no account in the discussion, and have no counterpart in nature, Professor Gray maintained, that the varieties of cultivation afforded direct evidence of the essential variability of species; that no domesticated plant had refused to vary; that those of recent introduction, such as Californian annuals, mostly began to sport very promptly, sometimes even in the first or second generation; man having done nothing more than to sow the seed here instead of in California, perhaps in no better soil. Here the variations were as natural as those of the wild plant in its native soil. Man produces no organic variation, but merely directs a power which he did not originate, and by selection and close breeding preserves the incipient variety which else would probably be lost, and gives it a choice opportunity to vary more. Consider, he remarked, how small the chance of the survival of any variety when originated in its native habitat, surrounded by its fellows,—when not one seed out of a hundred or a thousand ever comes to germinate, and not a moiety of these ever succeed in becoming a plant,—and when, of those that do grow up and blossom, the danger is imminent that the flowers may be fertilized by the pollen of some of its abundant neighbours of the unvaried type,—and it will be easy to understand why plants vary so promptly in our gardens, mostly raised from a small quantity of seeds to begin with, probably all from the same stock, where they are almost

sure to self-fertilize in the first generation,—where every desirable variation is watched for and cared for, and kept separate; and it may be confidently inferred that they vary in cultivation, at first, much as they would have varied in the wild state, if such favourable opportunity had there occurred. Continued cultivation under artificial selection would of course force some of these results to an extreme never reached in nature, giving to long-cultivated varieties a character of their own. Yet they may not deviate more widely from the wild type than do some of the wild varieties of many plants of wide geographical range. Moreover, Professor Gray maintained that there occur in nature the same kinds of variation as those to which we owe our improved fruits, &c.; that such originate not rarely in nature, and develope to a certain extent, enough to show the same cause operating in free as in controlled nature; enough to have shown the cultivator what he should take in hand; enough to render it likely that most of our cultivated species of fruit began their career of improvement before man took them in hand. Instances of such variations in the wild state were adduced from our hawthorns, especially *Cratægus tomentosa*, from our Wild Red Plum, Wild Cherries, and especially from our Wild Grapes and Hickories.

3. The view taken by Mr. Lowell, and especially by Professor Bowen, that the indefinitely long periods of time which the theory acquired and assumed was practically equivalent to infinity, and therefore rendered the theory "completely metaphysical in character," Professor Gray animadverted upon, mainly to remark that the theory in question would generally be regarded as too materialistic and physical, rather than too metaphysical in character; and that *à fortiori*, physical geology and physical astronomy would on the principle be metaphysical sciences.

4. Exceptions were taken against the assumption of such a wide distinction, or of any sharply drawn distinction at their confines, between the animal and the vegetable kingdoms, and especially against the view that instinct sharply defines the animal kingdom from the vegetable kingdom on the one hand, and from man on the other, and which denies to the higher brutes intelligence, and to man instinct.

5. Also, against the view that the psychical endowments of the brute animals, whether instinct or other, are invariable and unimproveable; and a variety of instances were adduced, as recorded in the works of Pritchard and of Isidore St. Hilaire, as well as some from personal observation, in which acquired habitudes or varied instincts were transmitted from the parents to their offspring. That such acquirements, once inherited, would be likely to continue heritable, was argued to be the natural consequence of the general law of inheritance, the most fundamental law in physiology; that it is actually so, Professor Gray insisted was well known to every breeder of domestic animals.

6. For decisive instances of the perpetuity by descent or fixity, under interbreeding, of altered structure, Professor Gray adduced Manx cats and Dorking fowls; and he alluded to well-known cases of six-digited people, and the like, transmitting the peculiarity to more than half of their children, and even grandchildren; showing that the salient peculiarity tended to be more transmissible than the normal state at the outset; so that, by breeding in and in, it was likely that *hexadactyles* could soon be made to come as true to the breed as Dorkings.

7. As to the charge that the theory in question denies permanence of type, Professor Gray remarked that, on the contrary, the theory not only admitted persistence of type, as the term is understood by all naturalists, but was actually built upon this admitted fact as one of its main foundations; that, indeed, one of the prominent advantages of this very theory was, that it accounted for this long persistence of type, which upon every other theory remained scientifically unaccounted for.

8. Finally, as to the charge that the hypothesis in question repudiated design or purpose in nature and the whole doctrine of final causes, Professor Gray urged:—1. That to maintain that a theory of the derivation of one species or sort of animal from another through secondary causes and natural agencies negatived design, seemed to concede that whatever in nature is accomplished through secondary causes is so much removed from the sphere of design, or that only that which is supernatural can be regarded or shown to be designed;—which no theist can admit. 2. That the establishment of this particular theory by scientific evidence would leave the doctrines of final cause, utility, special design, or whatever other teleological view, just where they were before its promulgation,

in all fundamental respects; that no new kind of difficulty comes in with this theory, *i.e.*, none with which the philosophical naturalist is not already familiar. It is merely the old problem as to how persistence of type and morphological conformity are to be reconciled with special design (with the advantage of offering the only scientific, though hypothetical, solution of the question), along with the wider philosophical question, as to what is the relation between orderly natural events and intelligent efficient cause, or Divine agency. In respect to which, we have only to adopt Professor Bowen's own philosophy of causation,—viz., "That the natural no less than the supernatural, the continuance no less than the creation of existence, the origin of an individual, as well as the origin of a species or a genus, can be explained only by the direct action of an intelligent cause,"— and all special difficulty in harmonizing a theory of the derivation of species with the doctrine of final causes will vanish.

At the Royal Institution, on Feb. 6, Professor Huxley (who at the Oxford meeting subsequently appeared as the champion of Mr. Darwin's theory) read a paper "On Species and Races, and their Origin." After some preliminary remarks, in the course of which the speaker expressed his obligation for the liberality with which Mr. Darwin had allowed him to have access to a large portion of the MSS. of his forthcoming work, the phenomena of species in general were considered—the horse being taken as a familiar example. The distinctions between this and other closely allied species, such as the asses and zebras, were considered, and they were shown to be of two kinds, structural or morphological, and functional or physiological. Under the former head were ranged the callosities on the inner side of the fore and hind limbs of the horse—its bushy tail, its peculiar larynx, its short ears, and broad hoofs: under the latter head, the fact that the offspring of the horse with any of the allied species is a hybrid, incapable of propagation with another mule, was particularly mentioned. Leaving open the question whether the physiological distinction just mentioned is, or is not, a universal character of species, it is indubitable that it obtains between many species, and therefore has to be accounted for by any theory of their origin. The species *Equus caballus*, thus separated from all others, is the centro round which a number of other remarkable phenomena are grouped. It is intimately allied in structure with three other members of the existing creation, the hyrax, the tapir, and the rhinoceros; and less strait, though still definite bonds of union connect it with every living thing. Going back in time, the horse can be traced into the Pliocene formation, and perhaps it existed earlier still; but in the newer Miocene of Germany it is replaced by the hippotherium, an animal very like a true equus, but having the two rudimental toes in each foot developed, though small. Further back in time, in the Eocene rocks, neither equus nor hippotherium has been met with, nor rhinoceros, tapirus, or hyrax; but instead of them, a singular animal, the palæotherium, which exhibits certain points of resemblance with each of the four existing genera, is found. The speaker pointed out that these resemblances did not justify us in considering the palæotherium as a more generalized type, any more than the resemblance of a father to his four sons justifies us in considering his as of a more generalized type than theirs. The geographical distribution of the equidæ was next considered, and the anomalies and difficulties it offers were pointed out ; and lastly the variations which horses offer in their feral and their domesticated condition, were discussed. The questions thus shown to be connected with the species horse, are offered by all species whatever; and the next point of the discourse was the consideration of the general character of the problem of the origin of species of which they form a part, and the necessary conditions of its solution. So far as the logic of the matter goes, it was proved that this problem is of exactly the same character as multitudes of other physical problems, such as the origin of glaciers, or the origin of strata of marble ; and a complete solution of it involves—1. The experimental determination of the conditions under which bodies having the characters of species are producible ; 2. The proof that such conditions are actually operative in nature. Any doctrine of the origin of species which satisfies these requirements must be regarded as a true theory of species ; while any which does not is, so far, defective, and must be regarded only as a hypothesis whose value is greater or less according to its approximation to this standard.

It is Mr. Darwin's peculiar merit to have apprehended these logical necessities, and to have endeavoured to comply with them. The pigeons called pouters, tumblers, fantails, &c., which the audience had an opportunity of examining, are in his view the result of so many long-continued experiments on the manufacture of species ; and he considers that causes essentially similar to those which have given rise to these birds are operative in nature now, and have in past times been the agents in producing all the species we know. If neither of these positions can be upset, Mr. Darwin's must be regarded as a true theory of species, as well based as any other physical theory ; they require, therefore, the most careful and searching criticism. After pointing out the remarkable differences in structure and habits between the carrier, pouter, fantail, tumbler, and the wild *Columba livia*, the speaker expressed his entire agreement with Mr. Darwin's conclusion, that all the former domesticated breeds had arisen from the last-named wild stock ; and on the following grounds—1. That all interbreed freely with one another. 2. That none of the domesticated breeds presents the slightest approximation to any wild species but *C. livia*, whose characteristic markings are at times exhibited by all. 3. That the known habits of the Indian variety of the rock pigeon (*C. intermedia*) render its domestication easily intelligible. 4. That existing varieties connect the extremest modifications of the domestic breeds by insensible links with *C. livia*. 5. That there is historical evidence of the divergence of existing breeds, *e.g.*, the tumbler, from forms less unlike *C. livia*.

Mr. Huxley then analysed the process of selection by which the domesticated breeds had been produced from the wild rock pigeon ; and he showed its possibility to depend upon two laws which hold good for all species, viz., 1. That every species tends to vary ; 2. That variations are capable of hereditary transmission. The second law is well understood ; but the speaker adverted to the miscomprehension which appears to prevail regarding the first, and showed that the variation of a species is by no means an adaptation to conditions in the sense in which that phrase is commonly used. Pigeon-fanciers, in fact, subject their pigeons to a complete uniformity of conditions; but while the similarly used feet, legs, skull, sacral vertebræ, tail feathers, oil gland, and crop undergo the most extraordinary modifications; on the other hand the wings, whose use is hardly ever permitted to the choice breeds, have hitherto shown no sign of diminution. Man has not as yet been able to determine a variation; he only favours those which arise spontaneously, *i.e.*, are determined by unknown conditions. It must be admitted that, by selection, a species may be made to give rise experimentally to excessively different modifications; and the next question is, Do causes adequate to exert selection exist in nature? On this point, the speaker referred his audience to Mr. Darwin's chapter on the struggle for existence, as affording ample satisfactory proof that such adequate natural causes do exist. There can be no question that just as man cherishes the varieties he wishes to preserve, and destroys those he does not care about; so nature (even if we consider the physical world as a mere mechanism) must tend to cherish those varieties which are better fitted to work harmoniously with the conditions she offers, and to destroy the rest. There seems to be no doubt, then, that modifications equivalent in extent to the four breeds of pigeons, might be developed from a species by natural causes; and therefore, if it can be shown that these breeds have all the characters which are ever found in species, Mr. Darwin's case would be complete. However, there is as yet no proof that, by selection, modifications having the physiological character of species (*i.e.*, whose offspring are incapable of propagation *inter se*) have ever been produced from a common stock. No doubt the numerous indirect arguments brought forward by Mr. Darwin to weaken the force of this objection are of great weight; no doubt it cannot be proved that all species give rise to hybrids infertile *inter se;* no doubt (so far as the speaker's private conviction went), a well-conducted series of experiments very probably would yield us derivatives from a common stock, whose offspring should be infertile *inter se;* but we must deal with facts as they stand, and at present it must be admitted that Mr. Darwin's theory does not account for all the phenomena exhibited by species; and, so far, falls short of being a satisfactory theory.

RECURRENT ANIMAL FORM.

Dr. Collingwood has read to the British Association a paper "On Recurrent Animal Form, and its Significance in Systematic Zoology." The object of this communication was to call attention to the frequent recurrence of similar forms in widely separated groups of the animal kingdom, similarities, therefore, which were unaccompanied by homologies of internal structure. These analogies of form had greatly influenced the progress of classification, by attracting the attention of systematizers while as yet structural homologies were imperfectly understood, and, as a consequence, many groups of animals had been temporarily located in a false position, such as bats and whales by the ancients, and the Polyzoa and Foraminifera in more modern times. These resemblances in form were illustrated generally by the classes of Vertebrata, and more especially by the various orders of Mammalia—the Invertebrata affording, however, many remarkable examples. Since no principle of gradation of form would sufficiently account for these analogies, the author had endeavoured to discover some other explanation, and had come to the conclusion, that the fact of deviations from typical form being accompanied by modifications of typical habits, afforded the desired clue. Examples of this were given, and the principle educed, that agreement of habit and economy in widely-separated groups is accompanied by similarity of form. This position was argued through simple cases to the more complex, and the conclusion arrived at, that where habits were known, the explanation sufficed; and it was only in the case of animals of low organization and obscure or unknown habits, that any serious difficulty arose in its application, so that our appreciation of the *rationale* of their similarity of form was in direct ratio to our knowledge of their habits and modes of life. In conclusion, by a comparison of the Polyzoa with the Polyps, it was shown that the economy of both was nearly identical, although they possessed scarcely anything in common except superficial characters, and this identity of habit was regarded as the explanation of their remarkable similarity of form.

PERSISTENT TYPES OF ANIMAL LIFE.

A DISCOURSE on this subject has been delivered at the Royal Institution, by Professor Huxley. He reminded his audience of what is meant by geological time, the forms of animal and vegetable life found in the lowest strata or layers of the earth's crust being considered to be earliest created. He stated that it was the growing conviction of geologists that the remarkable changes in the earth's crust are not due to violent rapid action, as supposed by early observers, but rather to the efficacy of gentle forces operating through very long periods of time, as seen now in the slow-floating ice of glaciers and the slow-growing coral reefs. He also considered that palæontologists had greatly exaggerated the number of animals viewed as extinct. After long investigation he concluded that of 120 ordinal types of animals only eight or nine types were extinct; and he added, on the authority of Dr. Joseph Hooker, the eminent botanist, that of the 200 ordinal types of plants not one was wanting. Professor Huxley exemplified his views from all departments of the animal kingdom—from the Polyzoa up to the Vertebrata—specimens of each being found in very low strata. He did not, therefore, believe that there was much greater difference between the earth's appearance in early geological times, and in our own, than there is now between the different regions of the globe. He remarked, in conclusion, that the little change in the persistent types of animal and vegetable life appeared to him to "indicate that each is but the result of an enormous series of antecedent changes of form, the whole of which are perhaps for ever hidden from us in the abyss of pre-geologic time."—*Illustrated London News.*

THE HUMAN COMPLEXION.

A COMMUNICATION has been made by M. Abbadie to the Professor of Natural History of the Museum of Paris (M. Quatrefages), declaring the Complexion of the Human Race to be entirely dependent on the mode of nourishment ; that he has beheld in Nubia whole races of negroes who, from the entire use of animal food, present as fine a carnation as the inhabitants of southern Europe. In Algeria it has long been the subject of remark that the butchers, generally negroes of Kalu, are as fair in complexion as the European settlers, although still preserving their woolly hair.

METHODS IN ZOOLOGY.

PROFESSOR AGASSIZ, in speaking to the American Association of Methods in Zoology, has said that the progress of natural science does not depend so much on our information as upon the methods in which this information is considered and combined. The results of our investigations are acceptable and satisfactorily proved when they stand the tests of criticism. Unhappily the devotees of natural history, still lingering upon the search for facts, have not yet been willing to submit their facts to the tests by which they should be judged. It is the great misfortune of American naturalists that there is so much upon this continent that has not yet been described ; all their efforts are directed to discoveries and descriptions, in the belief that in this way glory and fame are only to be obtained. There was a time when this plan was right ; now we want something more. We want to arrive at a clearer insight into the foundations of relationship. We must have the means of ascertaining whether our facts are worthy of preservation and record. In some departments of zoology the proper standard has already been obtained. Thus, since the investigations of Germans, transplanted into France and thence into England, there is nobody who does not understand that vertebrates are so different from other classes of animals, that there is no genetic connexion between them. He recalled the distinction between vertebrates and articulates, to show that their structural elements are entirely different. Professor Agassiz took up the Radiates, and illustrated upon the blackboard an exact system to which all animals, supposed to be radiates, may be referred as a test. He does not consider the mouth of radiates as corresponding to the mouth of other animals, but only an opening in the cavity of the body, no way analogous to the mouths of other animals. They are often called spheroidal, but they cannot be compared to a sphere because their centre of structure is not the centre of motion. He gives names to the two axes of the animals ; that around which the motion of the animal occurs is the actinal axis ; its main pole the actinal, and the opposite one the abactinal pole. The diameter in the direction of the motion he calls the cœliacal diameter, and that at right anglos to it the diacœliacal diameter. Hereafter we must not take the dictum of Mr. X. or Mr. Y., that "I hold this animal to be a radiate ;" but we will submit it to the test, and if it does not stand the test, we must throw it out.

ANIMAL MONSTROSITY.

MR. G. JEFFREYS has exhibited to the British Association several specimens of the common whelk (*Buccinum undatum*) having double opercula ; in one instance, a second or supplementary operculum being piled on the usual one ; and in the others, there being two separate opercula, instead of one, in each whelk. Mr. Jeffreys adverted briefly to the different kinds of Monstrosity which occur in animals and plants, and said he believed this to be the first case of a similar monstrosity in the Mollusca. He observed that the monstrosity under consideration appeared to be congenital, and not to have arisen from an accidental loss of the original organ, because in some of the specimens both opercula were cases of hypertrophy, and in the others of atrophy ; and he mentioned that all the specimens came from the same place (Sandgate, in Kent), showing a repetition, and perhaps an hereditary transmission, of the same abnormal phenomenon ; and he suggested that thus permanent varieties might in course of time be formed, and constitute what some naturalists would call "distinct species." He adduced, in support of this view, the case of a reversed monstrosity of the common garden snail (*Helix aspersa*), having been bred for many years in succession by the late M. D'Orbigny, in his garden at Rochelle, as well as many instances of a reversed form of almond whelk (*Fusus antiquus*) having occurred in the same localities on the coasts of England and Portugal, such being the normal form in the crag.

Professor Henslow remarked that this was an important communication, as it tended to elucidate the very interesting and difficult problem of the origin of species as treated by Mr. Darwin.

This, as well as the preceding paper, called forth remarks from several speakers on Mr. Darwin's hypothesis of the production of species by natural selection.

SOCIETY FOR THE ACCLIMATIZATION OF ANIMALS.

A SOCIETY for this purpose, upon a plan similar to that in Paris, has been formed in London. Its objects are :—1. The introduction, acclimatization, and domestication of all innoxious animals, birds, fishes, insects, and vegetables, whether useful or ornamental. 2. The perfection, propagation, and *hybridization* of races newly introduced or already domesticated. 3. The spread of indigenous animals, &c., from parts of the United Kingdom where they are already known, to other localities where they are not known. 4. The procuration, whether by purchase, gift, or exchange, of animals, &c., from British and foreign countries. 5. The transmission of animals, &c., from England to her colonies and foreign parts, in exchange for others sent thence to the Society. 6. The holding of periodical meetings, and the publication of reports and transactions for the purpose of spreading knowledge of acclimatization, and inquiry into the causes of success or failure. The Society have begun with small and carefully-conducted experiments. It is proposed that those members who happen to have facilities on their estates for experiments, and who are willing to aid the objects of the Society, should undertake the charge of such subjects for experiments as may be offered to them by the Society, periodically reporting progress to the Council. It will be the endeavour of the Society to attempt to acclimatize and cultivate those animals, birds, &c., which will be useful and suitable to the park, the moorland, the plain, the woodland, the farm, the poultry-yard, as well as those which will increase the resources of our sea-shores, rivers, ponds, and gardens. Hitherto the progress which the Society has made in obtaining encouragement has been very cheering. Miss Burdett Coutts has presented the fund with a donation of 500*l.*, together with a promise of subscription of 10*l.* annually for five years.

We quote the above from a report in the *Critic* of a lecture delivered by Mr. T. F. Buckland to the Society of Arts. If we remember rightly, the acclimatization of animals was one of the primary objects on the formation of the Zoological Society.

In the ably condensed "Scientific Intelligence" of the *Critic*, we find the following observations upon the paper by Mr. Buckland, who (the Editor observes) enumerated a large number of animals, birds, and fishes, which he thought would make desirable additions to the zoology of Great Britain; indeed, the bulk of his paper (with the exception of an historical account of the Société d'Acclimatation, now working with such success in Paris) consisted of an enumeration of these creatures, and a description of their qualities. The most part were what may be called game. The number of animals and birds capable of being extensively bred and sold (like the sheep or the turkey) is exceedingly small; and as for many of the creatures named (such as the black swan, the beaver, and the moose deer), we question very much whether they had not better be left out of the list altogether. One branch of Natural History was entirely omitted in Mr. Buckland's list, and that was the botanical. Now it appears from the labours of the French Society, that it is in this department that they have effected the most. The kangaroo and the ostrich have been great triumphs; but it is by the Sorgho and the *Dioscorea Batatas* that M. Geoffroy St. Hilaire and his coadjutors have added in the most effectual manner to the resources of their country. Both these already afford large and important crops. The Acclimatization Society formed in London already numbers among its members and patrons some of the first gentlemen in the country. The Society is, we hear, making arrangements to import several animals by way of experiment, and already we hear of an important pond fish (*Lucio perca*) as on its way hither. If the Society succeed in rearing and breeding from it, it is said that a very valuable edible fish will be added to the ponds of this country. Although the Society has not as yet got any garden or experimental farm for the conduct of its own experiments, we hear that many of its members have placed their parks and waters at the service of the managing committee. This is well ; but at the same time it will be better if they succeed in introducing one really valuable species, and spreading it over the length and breadth of the land, rather than waste and fritter away their means over a number of minor efforts. To bring Eland meat to the price of prime beef would be a greater achievement than the introduction of fifty new species of game. At the same time also, we hope that they will not continue to overlook the very great claims of the botanical kingdom.

THE ACCLIMATIZATION OF THE ALPACA AND LAMA

Is proceeding vigorously in France. M. Isidore G. St. Hilaire has reported to the French Academy of Sciences the recent arrival of thirty-three alpacas, nine lamas, and one Peruvian sheep ; the sole remains of a collection of 100 head brought from Peru and Bolivia by M. Roehn. The mortality was occasioned by the long and perilous journey by land and sea. M. St. Hilaire said that in less able hands the whole would most probably have perished. In 1765 Buffon recommended the enriching the Alps and Pyrenees with the lama and its congeners, saying, "I think that these animals would be an excellent acquisition for Europe, and would produce more real benefit than all the metal of the New World." In relation to this, M. St. Hilaire refers to the increasing numbers of these animals in France, England, Spain, Cuba, and Australia.

CHANGES IN EGGS.

DR. JOHN DAVY, in a paper "On the Albumen of the Newly-laid Egg," says :—"The albumen of the egg of the common fowl, newly laid, has properties differing in some particulars from those of the albumen of the stale egg. One of these, and that which is best known, is the milkiness which it exhibits when dressed for the table, provided the egg be not put into water of too high a temperature, and kept there unduly long. Another is seen in the manner of coagulating."

Dr. Davy then details experiments at various temperatures, and adds :—"These results seem to show that the white of the newly-laid egg is more readily affected by heat of a certain temperature than that of an egg exposed some time to the air, as indicated by the appearance of milkiness it exhibits, and yet that, within a certain range of temperature, the amount of coagulation or the degree of firmness is less.

"'That the difference of qualities which I have described is owing to exposure to, and the action of, atmospheric air, can hardly be doubted.* The proofs seem to be sufficiently clear. The newly-laid

---

* May not the disappearance of the curd which is seen in the salmon when dressed fresh from the sea, the clean fish of the angler, be owing to the same cause—viz., the absorption of oxygen on being kept exposed to the air, and the liquefaction of the curdy matter, a consequence of that absorption—a liquefaction similar to that which the fibrin of the blood undergoes from the action of oxygen ?

egg contains little or no air ; and if atmospheric air be excluded, its absorption prevented, as by lubricating the shell with oil or any oleaginous matter, the albumen retains for a considerable time the qualities of the newly-laid egg.   This is a fact well known to dealers in eggs.

"The exact time required for the change to take place, owing to the absorption of air, I cannot exactly say ; it varies, I believe, in some measure, according to the season—a shorter time in winter being required than in summer ; the egg, in the former season, owing to lower atmospheric temperature, contracting more in bulk, as regards its substance, than in the latter.   A very few days, as from five to six at furthest, seem to be sufficient.   In April I have observed the milkiness on the fourth, but not later.   On the contrary, if air be excluded, I do not know how long the quality of the newly-laid egg may not be preserved.   I have found an egg laid in the month of April, and then smeared with butter, hardly appreciably changed at the end of six months.

"Nor can I speak with any exactness respecting the amount of air, of oxygen absorbed, or of other alterations that may be effected in the composition of the egg by its action.   All that I have yet ascertained is, that with the absorption of oxygen in the instance of the stale egg, carbonic acid is formed, and ammonia, and the colour of the albumen is darkened, it becoming of a light brownish yellow, and at the same time acquiring a smell somewhat unpleasant, and a taste, as is well known, not agreeable.   The putrefactive process, I believe, does not take place, however long the egg may be kept, unless there be some admixture of the yolk and white."

Dr. Davy has extended his trials to the eggs of the duck, the turkey, and the guinea-fowl, with similar results.—*Abridged from the Edinburgh Philosophical Journal*, No. 22.

FLIGHT OF BIRDS.

Dr. John Davy, in a paper on the Specific Gravity of Birds, communicated to the *Edinburgh Philosophical Journal*, No. 22, says : "In conclusion, it may be remarked, that, judging from the foregoing results, the specific gravity of the body of birds is concerned but in a very subordinate manner with their aptitude for aërial locomotion.   That aptitude seems to depend on other circumstances, such as the great lightness of their feathers, owing to the air which they contain ; the little tendency of water to adhere to them, even when exposed to rain ; their form and arrangement, so admirably adapted for the purpose of impulse ; the high temperature of the body expanding the contained air ; and the immensely powerful muscles, the pectoral, belonging to the wings.   Is not the power of flight of each species in a great measure proportional to these conditions ?"

STOMACH OF THE FISH.

Dr. John Davy closes a paper "On the Stomach of the Fish,"

with these conclusions, deducible from his researches and observations :

"1. That the gastric juice, and probably the other fluids concerned in the function of digestion in fishes, are not secreted till the secreting organs are stimulated by the presence of food—a conclusion in harmony with a pretty general physiological law, and in accordance with what has been best ascertained respecting the gastric juice in other animals.

"2. The probability that the gastric fluid—a fluid with an acid reaction—is less potent in the instance of fishes as a solvent than the alkaline fluid of the *appendices pyloricæ;* and that even as regards the gastric fluid, its acidity is not essential to it, as its action does not appear to be arrested when it is neutralized by the presence of articles of food abounding in carbonate of lime.

"Lastly, as a corollary from the first, may it not be inferred that the migratory species of the salmonidæ, such as the salmon and sea trout, which attain their growth and become in high condition in the sea, there abundantly feeding and accumulating adipose matter, though not always abstaining in fresh water, which they enter for the purpose of breeding, are at least capable of long abstinence there without materially suffering? And may not this be owing to none of their secretions or excretions, with the exception of the milt of the male and the roe of the female, being of an exhausting kind ? And further, owing to the empty and collapsed state of the stomach and intestines, are they not, when captured, less subject to putrefaction, and thus better adapted to become the food of man ?"—See *Edinburgh New Philosophical Journal*, No. 22.

SALMON IN THE THAMES.

In the autumn of last year, two Salmon were taken in the Thames, off Erith. These fish had evidently entered the river (with others, doubtless, which have escaped capture) with the view of pushing up to the spawning-grounds. Salmon in the latter end of October are heavy in spawn, and, even in a well-stocked river, should not be taken. In the river they might have been most valuable, and have added in forming a small nucleus for breeding purposes. These fish might have spawned in the river, and probably would. It would have been two years before the fry would have required to come down again through the muddy pool to the sea. By that time the water might have been pure enough to allow them to do so safely ; and in all probability some hundreds of fine grilse would speedily have returned to gladden our eyes and re-stock our river ; and the salmon would once more have been naturalized in the Thames, without costing anyone one sixpence for spawn-boxes, watchers, &c., a process which, after all, too often forms but a doubtful experiment. Now, the Act of Parliament which regulates the close-seasons on the Thames, says that no one shall capture salmon after the 10th of September, nor before the 25th of January succeeding, under a penalty of 5*l.*, which penalty the captors of the above fish have clearly rendered themselves liable to. The fish, we hear, were sent.

as a present to the Queen's table.   We are sure, if Her Majesty
were aware of these facts that her good sense, as well as her veneration for law, would have led her to strongly discourage such a dis-
graceful and destructive act of poaching.—*From the Field.*

SALMON FISHERIES OF DEVON AND YORK.

It has lately been stated at Exeter, in evidence before the Salmon
Fisheries Commission, that, a century ago, a Salmon, weighing
30 lbs., had been purchased in the Exeter market for thirty pence;
that one fishery was let by the Corporation for 50l. a-year in 1601,
which was now valueless, and that a clause was inserted in appren-
tices' indentures to the effect that they should not be required to eat
salmon more than three times a week.   The present condition of the
fisheries is, however, totally different.   Very few salmon have been
caught in the Exe during the last few years, and scarcely any is
ever exposed for sale in the market.   The causes of this decay are
the use of illegal nets at the estuary of the river, by which large
quantities of young fish are destroyed; the construction of weirs,
which prevent the fish from going up to spawn—notwithstanding
that there are forty miles of the finest spawning beds ever seen—in
the upper part of the river; and to the fact that mills and gasworks
on the river let out deleterious matter into the water, which poisoned
the fish.   The remedies suggested are, that the Coastguardsmen of
Exeter should have the power to go on board fishing-vessels and
inspect the nets at the estuary of the Exe, and that the county
policemen have a similar power with regard to the upper part of the
river; that the police should also have power to enter the mills at
any time where illegal fishing was suspected; that the letting out of
poisonous matter into the river should be made a penal offence; and
that the fishing-season, instead of lasting from February to September, should commence on the 1st of May, and terminate on the
12th of September.   With regard to the Axe and the Otter—the
former of which was once a splendid salmon stream—similar reasons
for the almost total annihilation of fish which had taken place during
the last few years in these rivers were given by Mr. Pulman[*] and
the Rev. J. Gattey.

The Commission have also met at York, for the purpose of receiving evidence as to the state of the salmon fisheries in the Yorkshire rivers.   Sir W. Jardine stated that the Commissioners had
been out in Wales and the greater part of England for the last
nine weeks.   The result of their inquiries so far had led them to the
opinion that the diminution of salmon arose from their being locked
from the rivers by the numerous weirs or locks which had been
erected, and which kept them from ascending to their spawning
grounds in the tributaries which run into the larger streams.   He
then stated that the fisheries in Ireland, which had been in as advanced a state of decay as in this country, were now being made a

---

[*] Mr. Pulman, we should think, is fully competent to speak upon this subject, and his opinion is valuable, as every one who has read his admirable
volume upon the *Axe* must acknowledge.

great commercial resource ; and from this he argued that there was still hope for the resuscitation of the salmon fisheries in the streams of Yorkshire, which were among the best of the country, the area of drainage in the rivers of Yorkshire being, according to Professor Phillips, a good authority, 5836 square miles. A variety of evidence of owners and managers of salmon fisheries was then adduced, and went to show that the cause of the falling off in the quantity of salmon in the West Riding rivers arose principally from the erection of large numbers of manufactories on the banks of the streams, the waters from which were poisonous to the fish. In the North and East Ridings the cause of the falling off was said to be the locks and weirs, the improvements in the engines for catching, and the fearful havoc which had been and was being made among salmon by the use of traps and poaching. Some of the fishermen said that, a few years ago, they could have caught more in a day than they now got in a year. Various suggestions were thrown out with a view to remedy the present state of things, among which were an earlier compulsory closing of the rivers, the levying of a tax for their protection, and for the construction of salmon-ladders at all the weirs, and also a licence for angling and fishing.

FRESH-WATER FISH.

SEVERAL interesting letters have been addressed to the *Times*, in furtherance of Fish-breeding as a commercial object. The fish adapted for breeding-stock should be prolific, cheap to rear, of rapid growth, and good to eat, according to one correspondent, S. E., who says : —

" To begin with the worst—barbel are scarcely eatable, often unwholesome. Chub, dace, roach, and bream, when broiled within two hours of leaving the water, are tolerable, but within twelve hours the flesh becomes soft and tasteless. They are, therefore, not fit for the market. Perch make good water-souchy, but this is not a poor man's dish; moreover, they are slow of growth. Eels are brought from Holland cheaper than we can catch them here, except in the autumn ; besides which they are great destroyers of spawn. Carp require costly cookery, which at once puts the carp out of court as a trade fish. Mr. Boccius speaks highly of a German species, but it is not yet known here. Tench are good, but in this country not prolific, though De Huc describes them as easily and profitably cultivated in China. Probably our climate is too cold They might succeed, like the Chinese carp or goldfish, in ponds heated by the waste steam of our factories. The burbot is also good, but not prolific. Although not an angler's fish, and seldom taken by the net, it is never plentiful, and therefore not profitable. The char is excellent, but even in its most favourite haunt—Buttermere Lake—is by no means plentiful. Moreover, it seldom exceeds six or seven ounces in weight. The potted fish sold under this title are often small trout—a very good substitute. Pike are prolific and tolerable eating, but so voracious that they will only pay to keep where the better sorts will not thrive. In canals and meres they may be cultivated with profit.

" We have now narrowed the list to salmon, trout, and grayling—all excellent eating, prolific, and, from the size of their ova, easily bred artificially, by which process, I may here remark, about 90 per cent. of the ova become useful fish ; whereas by leaving this to the care of their natural parents about 90 per cent. are instantly devoured. The difficulties with salmon are that they must go annually to the sea to feed, and annually towards the river's head to spawn. Few persons possess the whole length of a salmon river ; the interests of the upper and lower proprietors become antagonistic, and so breeding ceases to pay. A Commission is now inquiring into this subject, and I sincerely hope they will devise some means reconciling the conflicting interests.

"In the meantime there is ample scope for all in trout and grayling, two of the best of British fishes, and possessing also this valuable quality, that the former is in season from March to August, and the latter from August to March, thus furnishing the table all the year round. To these, I think, the breeder should at present confine his attention. They require no feeding, and will grow in three years to between 15 and 16 inches in length, and 20 to 22 ounces in weight. This seems to be the most profitable age, as after that trout lives less upon flies and more upon fish, their own families not excepted, while grayling after this grow very slowly. The so-called Thames trout weigh much heavier for their length; one of 13¾ inches weighed 17 ounces, while a brook trout of the same length only weighs 13 ounces, and this difference increases as they grow older. These fish, however, seem to be merely emigrant brook trout under exceptional circumstances, and do not affect the general question. Occupiers of land through which clear streams run may breed large quantities of trout and grayling by merely separating rills, natural or artificial, from the main stream by fine gratings, digging a few holes in these watercourses for protection to the fish, and, after clearing out any resident fish, depositing vivified ova in the shallows. Nature will do the rest."

In a second letter S. E. says :—

"The arts of vivifying and hatching the ova require more space than the reasonable limits of this letter, for, to be practically useful, the description must be minute; but I am quite willing to give it. In the meantime, the inquirer may consult *Müller's Physiology; Boccius on Fish; Dr. Ransom on Ova*, in *Proceedings of the Royal Society*, vol. 7; *Carpenter's Physiology;* and the pages of the *Field*. The difficulties in procuring vivified ova are often misunderstood. The poacher can furnish dead spawn, as the salmon-roe fisher well knows; but artificial breeding requires all its processes to be deliberate and aboveboard. There is no indisposition in owners of streams to grant permission, but, if an open river, the water must be carefully watched for weeks beforehand, for the spawning-time may begin and end in a few days, and often, just when the watchers announce the fish to be ready, down comes a flood from the hills, and all is over for that year. In the operations for introducing the grayling into Scotland, in which I took an active part, this occurred in two out of five attempts, although we had every advantage, unlimited fish, eight miles of water, and intelligent keepers. The system of separate fenced-off rills gets rid of all this doubt and difficulty, and makes success certain. The old fish should be procured some months before the spawning time, and placed in what we may call rill No. 1. When ready they can be quietly removed, and as spawned deposited in rill No. 2. The process of artificial spawning, properly conducted, does not in the least injure the parent fish. The ova are now ready for placing in the gravel of rill No. 3, not in boxes but on the shallows, and all else is at the command of the breeder. Vivified ova are easily distinguished from addled eggs, as they are beautiful spheres, orange-coloured below (when placed in water) and semi transparent above, while each of the failures exhibits an opaque white spot. I would advise none but British fish or ova to be used at present."

Although we do not question the utility of Fish-breeding, we must not leave out of the question the facts that of the food generally in use, *fish contains the least nutriment, except vegetables.* It is disliked from being often eaten out of season, and after being too long or carelessly kept. Many of the varieties of fish are insipid and tasteless ("congealed water" they have been called), and to render them palatable, requires more time and acquaintance with cookery, than the middle or humbler classes can bestow upon them.

NEW CHAMELEON.

Mr. Andrew Murray has read to the Royal Physical Society, a notice of a New Species of Chameleon. This is a curiously-formed species of chameleon, brought from the interior of the Old Calabar district of West Africa, by one of the natives, to the Rev. Mr. Baillie, by whom it was presented to Mr. Murray. It is characterized by three salient horny processes on the head. Many lizards have singular spiny projections on all parts of the body ; but this very well marked species has not been hitherto recorded. In allusion to the prongs on the head, Mr. Murray named it *Chamœleon tricornis*.

BRITISH WELL SHRIMPS.

THE Rev. A. Hogan has exhibited to the British Association specimens of some remarkable additions not long since made to our British Crustacea. They consisted of two species of Nephargus (Fontanus and Kochianus), and the new genus, Crangonyx, with its single species Subterraneus of Spence Bate. These species have been described and figured in the volume of the *Natural History Review and Quarterly Journal of Science* for 1859. They are of great interest, as examples of a subterranean Fauna in England, analogous to that long known on the Continent and in America. The first established instance of the occurrence of Niphargi in England was Mr. Westwood's discovery at Maidenhead, Berkshire, of a well containing numbers of *N. aquileœ*. They have, more recently, been obtained from Corsham and Warminster, Wiltshire, and also from Ringwood, on the borders of the New Forest, Hampshire. *Crangonyx subterraneus* has occurred at the two latter places, but not at the first named. *Niphargus fontanus* is found at both Corsham and Ringwood, but with a difference in the shape of the gnathopoda and posterior ploopoda, amounting to a probably distinct variety, if not species. The form of the gnathopoda, or hands, is ,worthy of attention, being each armed with a moveable claw of large size, forming a prehensible organ of great power. *N. fontanus* is also possessed of small, yellow eyes, which distinguish it in a very marked way from the allied species (of the genus Gammarus) found on the Continent. Every member of the subterranean Fauna hitherto found has been destitute of eyesight. The movements of Niphargi, when kept in captivity, are interesting to observe ; but Mr. Hogan states that he has found great difficulty in preserving them alive. The longest period during which even the strongest specimen survived its capture was three weeks. The average temperature of the water in which Niphargus and Crangonyx are found is about 50° Fahr., and they seem to propagate in recently-formed wells as freely as in old ones. In no case have any species of this family been found, either in this country or abroad, in open wells or other than artificial ones,— pumps, in fact. They are found at all seasons of the year, but most abundantly towards the end of the autumn. The largest size known among the English species (that of *N. fontanus*) hardly exceeds half an inch. Mr. Hogan hoped that more extended observations would be made in Great Britain on this interesting family of Crustacea, as their economy and structure are as yet very imperfectly known, and an accurate examination would be sure to reward the investigator with results at least as interesting as those already obtained regarding their allies by continental naturalists. Mr. Westwood stated that it was curious to find this creature possessing the rudiments of eyes, for, in all other cases where creatures lived in the dark, they had no eyes at all. Mr. M'Andrew stated that he had described a species of Crustacea, dredged from a very great depth, that did not possess eyes.

TEREDINES, OR SHIP-WORMS.

MR. JEFFREYS has read to the British Association a paper on Teredines. He treated the matter first in a zoological point of view, and gave a short history of the genus Teredo, from the time of Aristotle and his pupil Theophrastus to the present time, especially noticing the elaborate monograph of Sellius, in 1733, on the Dutch Ship-worm; the valuable paper of Sir Everard Home and his pupil, Sir Benjamin Brodie, in 1806; and the physiological essays of Quatrefages, in 1849. He showed that the Teredo undergoes a series of metamorphoses; the eggs being developed in a sub-larval form after their exclusion from the ovary, and remaining in the mouth of the parent for some time. In its second phase (or that of proper larvæ), the fry are furnished with a pair of close-fitting oval valves, resembling those of a Cythere, as well as with cilia, a large foot, and distinct eyes, by means of which it swims freely and with great rapidity, or creeps, and afterwards selects its fixed habitation. The larval state continues for upwards of 100 hours, and during that period the fry are capable of traversing long distances, and thus becoming spread over comparatively wide areas. The metamorphosis is not, however (as Quatrefages asserts), complete; because the young shell, when fully developed, retains the larval valves.

He then discussed the different theories, as to the method by which the Teredo perforates wood, giving a preference to that of Sellius and Quatrefages, which may be termed the theory of "suction," aided by a constant maceration of the wood by water, which is introduced into the tube by the siphons. This process, according to Quatrefages, is effected by an organ which he calls the "capuchon céphalique," and which is provided with two pair of muscles of extraordinary strength. Mr. Jeffreys instanced, in illustration of his theory, the cases of the common limpet, as well as of many bivalve molluscs, *Echinus lividus*, and numerous annelids, which excavate rocks to a greater or less depth; and he cited the adage of "Gutta cavat lapidem non vi sed sæpe cadendo," in opposition to the mechanical theory. The Teredo bores either in the direction of the grain or across it, according to the kind of wood and the nature of the species; the *Teredo Norvagica* usually taking the former course: every kind of wood is indiscriminately attacked by it. The Teredines constitute a peaceful, though not a social community; and they have never been known to work into the tunnel of any neighbour. If they approach too near to each other, and cannot find space enough in any direction to continue their operations, they inclose the valves or anterior part of the body in a case, consisting of one or more hemispherical layers of shelly matter. Sellius supposed that the Teredo ate up the wood which it excavated, and had no other food; and, labouring under the idea that it could no longer subsist after being thus voluntarily shut up, he considered it to be the pink of chivalry and honour, in preferring to commit suicide rather than infringe on its neighbour. In this inclosed state, the valves often become so much altered in form, as well as in the relative proportion of their different parts, as not to be easily recognisable as belonging to the same species ; and one species (*T. divaricata*) was constituted from specimens of *T. Norvagica* which had been so deformed. The food of the Teredo consists of minute animalculæ, which are brought within the vortex of the inhalant siphon, and drawn into the stomach. The wood which has been excavated also undergoes a kind of digestion during its passage outwards through the long intestine. The animal has been proved by Laurent and other observers to be capable of renewing its shelly tube, and of repairing it in any part. It is stated by Quatrefages (and apparently with truth) that the sexes are separate, impregnation being effected in a similar mode to that which takes place among palm-trees and other diœcious plants. There appear to be only five or six males in one hundred individuals. The Teredo perforates and inhabits sound wood only, but an allied genus (Xylophaga) has been recently found to attack the submarine telegraph cable between this country and Gibraltar at a depth of from 60 to 70 fathoms, and to have made its way through a thick wrapper of cordage into the gutta-percha which covered the wire. The penetration was fortunately discovered in time, and was not deep enough to reach the wire. He gave several instances to show the rapidity of its perforating powers,—one of them having been supplied by Sir Leopold M‘Clintock while he was serving with the author's brother in the North Pacific.

Mr. Jeffreys then traced the geographical distribution of the Teredines, and showed that at least two species, which are now found living on our own shores, occurred in the post-pleistocene period ; and he inferred from the circumstance of one of these species having been found in fossil drift wood, that conditions similar to the present existed during that epoch. Some species inhabit fixed wood, and may be termed "littoral," while others are only found in floating wood, and appear to be "pelagic." Each geographical district has its own "littoral" species ; and the old notion of the ship-worm (which Linnæus justly called "*Calamitas Navium*") having been introduced into Europe from the Indies was contrary to fact as well as theory, because no "littoral" species belonging to tropical seas has ever been found living in the northern hemisphere, or *viœ versâ*. It is true that some species have been occasionally imported into this and other countries in ships' bottoms, and that others occur in wood which has been wafted thither by the Gulf and other oceanic currents ; but the fewer cases belong to littoral species, and never survive their removal, while the latter may be said to be almost cosmopolite.

Every species of Teredo has its own peculiar tube, valves, and pair of "pallets," the latter serving the office of opercula, and by their means the animal is able at will to completely close the en-

P

trance or mouth of the tube, and thus prevent the intrusion of crustacean and annelidan foes. The length of the tube is of course equal to that of the animal, which is attached to it by strong muscles in the palletal-ring, and varies in the different species from three inches, or even less, to as many feet. The internal entrance or throat of the tube is also distinguishable in each species by its peculiar transverse laminæ, and frequently a longitudinal siphonal ridge. Monstrosities not unfrequently occur in the valves and pallets ; and in one instance the pallet-stock is double, showing a partial redundancy of organs, as exemplified by the author with respect to the operculum of the common whelk. More than one species often inhabit the same piece of wood ; and want of sufficient care by naturalists in extracting the valves with their proper tubes and pallets may account in a great measure for the confusion which exists in public and private collections, and which has thence found its way into systematic works.

The Teredines have many natural enemies, both in life and after death. In the south of Italy, and on the North African coast, they are esteemed as human food. In Great Britain and Ireland, four species occur in fixed wood, and eleven others in drift wood, the latter being occasional visitants. Of these, no less than six have never yet been described, and two others are now, for the first time, noticed as British. The number of recorded exotic species only amounts to six more, making a total of twenty-one ; but it is probable that when the subject has been more investigated, a considerable addition will be made to this number. Mr. Jeffreys then explained the distribution of the littoral species on the shores of Great Britain and Ireland, and produced a synoptical list with descriptions of the new species. He believed all the Teredines were marine, except possibly Adanson's Senegal species, and one which had lately been found in the River Ganges, the water of which is fresh for about eighteen hours out of the twenty-four, and brackish during the rest of the day ; but as a well-known exception of the same kind occurs in a genus of marine shells (Arca), and the transition from fresh to brackish, and thence to salt water, is very gradual, such exceptions should not be regarded with suspicion or surprise. He concluded this part of the subject by exhibiting some drawings and specimens, and acknowledging his obligations to Dr. Lukis and other scientific friends. He next treated the subject in an economical point of view, and remarked that, although the French Government had issued two commissions at different times, and the Dutch Government had lately published the report of another commission, which was appointed to inquire into the mode of preventing the ravages of the Teredo in the ships and harbours of those countries, our own Government had done nothing. He alluded to the numerous and various remedies which had been proposed during the last two or three centuries, from time to time, some of which were very absurd ; but he considered, from a study of the creature's habits, that the most effectual preventive would be a silicious or mineral composition, like that which has been proposed by Professor Ansted for coating the decomposing stones of our new Houses of Parliament, or simply a thick coat of tar or paint, continually applied, which would not only destroy any adult ship-worms then living in the wood, but prevent the ingress of the fry. The Teredo never commences perforation except in the larval state.

A Committee of the Association has been formed, at the suggestion of Mr. Jeffreys, to inquire and report as to the best mode of preventing the ravages of Teredo and other animals in our ships and harbours.

Professor Van der Hoeven referred to the fact, that the ship-worm attacked ships more one season than another. In 1858 they committed great ravages on the ships of Holland, and a committee of the Dutch Academy of Sciences was appointed to investigate the subject.

Professor Verloren stated that the species which attacked the ships of Holland was *Teredo navalis;* but the species in Norway, France, and England, were sometimes different.

Sir W. Jardine expressed his surprise that the Government had not appointed a committee to investigate the subject.

Professor Huxley stated that probably the House of Commons had had too much experience of the utter inutility of attempting to stop a bore, to undertake the subject.

Dr. E. P. Wright exhibited some specimens of a new genus of Teredine, which he called *Halidaia.* It occurred near Feruckpore, in India, and inhabited perfectly fresh water. It was one of the largest species known, and the first which had been found in fresh water.

———

BORING OF THE PHOLADIDÆ.

MR. ALEXANDER BRYSON has read to the Royal Society of Edinburgh a communication referring to the various theories advanced to account for the Boring of the Pholadidæ in rocks.

The first hypothesis, which supposes that the molluscs perforate by means of the rotation of the valves acting as augers, he disproved by exhibiting old individuals of the *Pholas crispata* with the dentated costæ as sharp as in any young specimen. That these animals bore by silicious particles secreted by the foot, as suggested by Mr. Hancock, has been disproved by microscopic observation; and that currents of water set in motion by vibratile cilia, seemed also insufficient to account for the phenomenon.

Another theory supposes that an acid is secreted by the foot, capable of dissolving the rock. This the author showed was not tenable, as the strongest Nordhausen sulphuric acid fails to dissolve aluminous shales and Silurian slates; and also that any such acid secretion would act more readily on the valves themselves.

From many experiments on the cutting of hard silicious substances the author found that the softer the substance was in which the cutting material was impacted, the greater the amount of the work done. He was thus led to the conclusion that the pholadidæ bore with the strong muscular foot alone, and that they obtain the silica from the waves or the arenaceous rocks in which they are found; and hence there is no necessity for either an acid or silicious secretion. That the foot was the boring apparatus, and not the valves, he proved from a specimen of a Pholas hole in shale, where the pedal depression of the animal was distinctly seen.

He also exhibited a piece of glass bored to the depth of 1 50 of an inch, by means of the point of the finger and emery alone.

ANIMAL LIFE AT VAST DEPTHS IN THE SEA.

Dr. G. C. WALLICH, attached as naturalist to the *Bulldog*, equipped for the survey of the projected North Atlantic Telegraph route between Great Britain and America, has made a number of soundings, his main object being to determine the Depths to which Animal Life extends in the Sea, together with the limits and conditions essential to its maintenance.

As a general result, it may be stated that life exists in the sea at depths far exceeding those hitherto supposed to circumscribe it. The foraminifera are now proved to live at vast depths; they are minute animals, of one of the most simply organized families of the animal kingdom; and their calcareous shells constitute a large percentage of the oozy deposit brought up by soundings in the mid-Atlantic and elsewhere. Of these animals, the globigerinæ form a genus, and the point to be determined was, whether they were alive when first disturbed; for they could hardly be expected to show signs of life after the lapse of nearly an hour, during which time they had been brought from their normal medium, the pressure of which is estimated by tons, to an abnormal medium (the surface), in which the pressure is estimated by pounds. Direct evidence was wanting, owing to the bad weather; but after a laborious and continued examination of foraminifera, obtained from depths varying from 50 to nearly 2000 fathoms—that is, from 300 feet to nearly two miles and a half below the surface of the sea—the inferences are in favour of their vitality at the greatest depths as well as in shallow waters. Yet the number of specimens of globigerinæ taken from the deep oozy soundings in which the mass is extremely tenacious, showing the cell-contents entire, and in an apparently vital state, is small as compared with the much larger proportion in which the cells present no such character.

By far the most interesting discovery was made in sounding not quite midway between Cape Farewell and Rockhall, in 1260 fathoms. While the sounding-apparatus brought up an ample specimen of coarse, gritty-looking matter, consisting of about 95 per cent. of clean shells of globigerinæ, at the same time a number of starfishes, belonging to the genus ophiocoma, came up, adhering to the lowest 50 fathoms of the deep sea line, which must have rested on the bottom for a few minutes, so as to allow the starfishes to attach themselves to it. These continued to move about energetically for a quarter of an hour after they reached the surface. One very perfect specimen, which had fixed itself near the extreme end of the line, and was still convulsively grasping it with its long spinous arms, was secured *in situ* on the rope, and consigned to a bottle of spirits.

The great natural history fact of the Expedition is, that at a depth of two miles below the surface, where the pressure must amount, at least, to a ton and a half on the square inch, and where it is difficult to conceive that the most attenuated ray of light can penetrate, we capture a highly organized species of radiate animal, living, with its red and light pink tints as clear and brilliant as in its congeners which dwell in shallow and comparatively sunshiny waters. Where one form so highly organized has been met with, it is only reasonable to assume that other correlated forms may also exist. Hence we may look forward to the discovery of a new submarine fauna inhabiting the deeper zones of the ocean.

The law will eventually be found to hold good, according to Dr. Wallich, that "any marine animal, within the cellular structure of which air or any other gaseous fluid does not necessarily occur in a free state, and every portion of whose organization is permeable by fluids, either through capillary or endosmotic and exosmotic agency, may exist under the extraordinary pressure present at great depths."—See Dr. Wallich's *Notes*, together with "Observations on the Nature of the Sea-bed, as bearing on Submarine Telegraphy," published by Taylor and Francis.

STRUCTURE OF PEARL.

MR. ANDREW BRYSON has read to the Royal Physical Society a paper upon this interesting subject. We pass over the early history of Pearls, and come to that of the gems in our own time.

Mr. Bryson remarked that, though the French are now by far the most successful producers of artificial pearls, he had failed to obtain the slightest hint of the method employed, no paper having appeared, as far as he was aware, on the subject. The only notice of the formation of the *coques de perles* of the French which he had obtained was by Von Siebald, who has given, in his *Zeitschrift für Wissenschaftliche Zoologie*, a description of the process. It differs very little from that followed by the Chinese. A piece of nacre is sawn from a shell of the required form, and placed between the mantle and the shell of a nacle-producing mollusc; when sufficiently coated, it is filled with mastic, and a small plate of mother-of-pearl placed at the back. In regard to British pearls, the author stated that the first notice of the gem was by Tacitus, in his *Life of Agricola;* and that the pearls were the product of the fresh-water mussel of our rivers (*Unio margaritafera*) was very evident from the description that they were "not very orient, but pale and wan." To the theory advanced by Arnoldi in 1696, anew by Sir Everard Home in 1818, and also by Kellart in 1858, that pearls, or rather their nuclei, were due to the sterile ova of the molluscs which produced them, the author gave his decided opposition, as, from all the facts which he had observed, pearls were entirely due to a secretion from the mantle of the animal.

To illustrate the structure of pearls, Mr. Bryson exhibited a large

series of sections which he had prepared, and by which he showed
that by the microscope he could at once determine what shell had
produced them. He also explained the rationale of the iridescence
of mother-of-pearl,—a discovery due to Sir David Brewster, who
proved that it was due to the diffraction of the rays of light caused
by the out-cropping edges of the laminæ, and in some cases to the
minute plication of a single lamina. This phenomenon was also
shown by Barton's patent buttons, where the iridescence was produced by thousands of minute lines, so near each other as to require
a high magnifying power to resolve them. By taking an impression
with black wax under considerable pressure, the author succeeded in
obtaining the same iridescence as exhibited by the button itself.
This experiment Sir David Brewster had tried with success in 1815,
by taking an impression in wax from a mother-of-pearl button, and
by which he demonstrated the cause of the phenomenon.

The commercial value of pearls, the author stated, was still as
high as in the days of Cleopatra. A good Scotch pearl, with fine
lustre, of the size of a pea, fetches from 3l. to 4l. The famous
wager between Antony and Cleopatra gives us an insight into the
value of pearls. The two pearls which that luxurious Queen resolved to dissolve in vinegar, and serve up at the costly banquet,
were valued at ten millions of sesterces, about 76,000l. sterling. The
pearl in the possession of Mr. Hope, the largest of modern times, is
not worth a fourth of that sum. The weight of this pearl is 3oz. ;
it is 4½ inches in circumference, and 2 inches in length.

Notwithstanding the great value of the pearls, the shells of the
animals yield now a far more profitable return than the jewels. In
1856, the total value of the pearls imported into this country was
56,162l., whereas the imports of 2102 tons of mother-of-pearl shells
were valued at 76,544l. Mr. Bryson suggested that trials should be
made to produce artificial pearls from the Iridina, a nacreous shell,
having a much higher lustre than any hitherto found. It inhabits
the Nile and Senegal rivers.

NEW LEAF INSECT.

MR. ANDREW MURRAY has exhibited to the Royal Physical
Society a beautiful photograph of the underside of a Butterfly, in
every respect exactly like a dead leaf. He had received it from Dr.
William Traill, H.E.I.C., presently stationed at Russelcondah, in
the Madras Presidency. Dr. Traill, in transmitting the photograph,
writes :— " I wished to have sent you a curious insect, brought to
me as a Leaf Insect. In Singapore and the Straits, where a variety
of these singular forms are found, they are all allied to the Orthop-
tera, or the genera Mantis, Empusa, Phasma, &c. I am a good deal
accustomed to their various forms, but on this occasion I was completely taken in, and until the animal moved, I thought it a dea
leaf. To my surprise, I found it to be a butterfly ! When at rest,
its two anterior wings (which are slightly falcate at the tip) were
pushed forward in front of its head, so that a central line on them
exactly met a similar central line on the posterior wings, so as to

simulate the mid-rib of a leaf. The four wings so disposed presented the most exquisite resemblance to an autumnal leaf; and even the veining is represented with wonderful fidelity, especially if the animal is held two or three feet from the eye of the spectator. A remorseless rat one night carried off the insect, along with the pin on which it was impaled; but I had a few days before got a photograph of it made, which I now send you. It is, however, very far from giving a just idea of the original. The upper side of the wings were most brilliantly coloured, but I do not remember exactly what colours." Of course, these brilliant colours will only be seen when the insect is in motion; when at rest, and more exposed to danger, the folding back of the wings conceals them, and shows only this extraordinary resemblance to a leaf. The resemblance is every whit as great as that exhibited by the leaf insect proper (*Phyllium*), only being that of a dead leaf instead of a green one. The insect appears to be undescribed, and, from its powers of concealment, is no doubt rarely captured. Most butterflies have lines on the anterior and posterior wings, often both above and below, which become continuous when placed in juxtaposition; and there are several exotic species which have a line similar to the mid-rib of a leaf figured upon the under sides of the wings; but none hitherto described at all approach the present in its close resemblance to a leaf, both in shape, veining, and shading. It is impossible, from merely a photograph of its underside, to determine its genus; but from its falcate anterior and single-tailed posterior wings, it probably belongs to the same group of the *Nymphalidæ* as *Amathusia* and *Zeuxidia.*

ANTS IN NEW MEXICO.

MR. SAUNDERS has called the attention of the Entomological Society to a statement in Froebel's *Travels in Central America*, that certain species of Ants in New Mexico construct their nests exclusively of small stones, of one material, chosen by the insects from the various components of the sand of the steppes and deserts; in one part of the Colorado Desert their heaps were formed of small fragments of crystallized feldspar, and in another, imperfect crystals of red transparent garnets were the materials of which the ant-hills were built, and any quantity of them might there be obtained.

SHOOTING BUTTERFLIES.

MR. SAUNDERS has exhibited to the Entomological Society two injured specimens of *Papilio Antenor*, sent from Madagascar by Mr. Layard, and read a note on their capture by that gentleman, who stated that the insects were obtained by shooting with a gun, it being impossible, from their high and rapid flight, to get them by any other means.

GALL-FLIES.

MR. F. SMITH has read to the Entomological Society a paper "On *Cynips lignicola*, and *C. radicis*," in which he detailed his experiments in rearing some thousands of examples of these Gall-Flies, without the occurrence of a single male specimen, thereby confirming the observations previously made by M. Léon Dufour and others, and proving that no active male exists in this tribe of insects.

FERTILE WORKING BEES.

MR. TEGETMEIR has exhibited to the Entomological Society a portion of a bar-hive, containing Fertile Workers of the Common Honey-Bee, which had been produced by placing combs containing eggs and larvæ of workers only, in a hive which had been some time without a queen, and, consequently, contained no bread. No attempt had been made by the bees to produce a new queen from the workers' eggs; but when the latter were reared, the bees produced from them deposited eggs in the drone-cells only, from which drones were produced, and exhibited alive to the meeting. Mr. Tegetmeir observed, that Huber supposed these fertile workers were produced by the larvæ partaking of some of the food designed for the production of a queen, which had been deposited in the cells adjacent to the royal one. This supposition was, however, disproved in the present instance, as the hive contained no royal cell.

BOTANY.

COLOURING MATTER OF LEAVES.

M. FREMY has published an important investigation on the Green Colouring Matter of Leaves: this he has found to consist of a blue and yellow principle, which he has succeeded in isolating.

The colouring matter is contained in the green oil which is extracted by alcohol from leaves. This oil may provisionally be termed chlorophyll, but it contains several other substances which render the separation of the colouring matter difficult. The blue and yellow colouring principle have a different affinity for hydrate of alumina. When a strong alcoholic solution of chlorophyll was digested with hydrate of alumina, no alteration took place; but by adding a small quantity of water, a dark-green, almost blue precipitate was obtained, and the alcohol solution was of a yellow colour. When a considerable quantity of water was added, the precipitate had a colour like that of the ordinary colouring matter. Although this experiment effected some separation of the two colouring matters, the separation could not be carried further by its means.

Fremy next tried the action of different neutral solvents on the combination of alumina with the green colouring matter. He found that some, such as bisulphide of carbon, dissolved in preference the combination of yellow colouring matter and alumina; others, such as ether, alcohol, turpentine, dissolved out the green matter. By employing successively these different solvents, after the use of bisulphide of carbon, he succeeded in obtaining lakes of different shades, but was not able to carry the separation further.

The usual reducing agents, which change other colours, do not affect chlorophyll. But by the action of bases this body is converted into a yellow colour, which forms with alumina a beautiful yellow lake, soluble in neutral solvents, such as ether, alcohol, bisulphide of carbon. By acting on the solution of this body with acids, especially hydrochloric acid, it was transformed into the original green. Now, assuming that the green thus formed was composed of blue and yellow colouring matters, the point was to separate these two bodies at the moment of their formation. This must be done by the simultaneous use of solvents which act differently on the two colouring matters. Such a solvent is a mixture of hydrochloric acid and ether ; and it was used as follows :—

Two parts of ether and one part of hydrochloric acid, diluted with a little water, were shaken in a stoppered bottle for some time, so as to saturate the ether with hydrochloric acid. When the solution formed by the decolorization of the chlorophyll by bases was shaken with this solution, a remarkable change took place ; the ether retained the yellow matter, and the hydrochloric acid the blue colouring principle. The two colours were thus isolated ; but if now alcohol in excess was added, which dissolves both the yellow and green colouring matters and their solvents, the solution became of the original green tint.

To the yellow matter soluble in ether, Fremy gives the name *phylloxanthine*, and to the blue colouring matter the name *phyllocyanine*. To the other yellow body which results from the change of phyllocyanine, he gives the name *phylloxantheine*.

The blue and yellow colouring matters may be obtained directly from chlorophyll by adding the ether and acid mixture directly to the alcoholic extract of the leaves. The green first becomes brown, and is then resolved into phyllocyanine, which dissolves in the acid, and phylloxanthine, which dissolves in the ether. This interesting experiment may also be made directly with the leaves.

Fremy found that the yellow colouring matter formed in the young shoots is the same as that resulting from the decomposition of chlorophyll. It may be extracted by alcohol, and partially resolved into yellow and a little blue colour by means of hydrochloric acid and ether. Leaves which become yellow in autumn, then only contain phylloxanthine. —*Comptes Rendus ; Philos. Mag.*, No. 131.

RELATIONS OF PLANTS.

Mr. MAXWELL MASTERS has read at the Royal Institution a paper "On the Relation between the Abnormal and Normal Relations of Plants." The object of the lecturer was to show the difficulty, and in many cases the impossibility, of drawing any definite line between what is considered to be natural and what unnatural in plants. These difficulties depend on many circumstances, among which are— the very great powers of variation naturally possessed by plants ; the fact that a condition which is not unnatural or unusual in one species is the common condition in another ; that irregularity of growth is by no means an abnormal condition ; that a change may be abnormal in a physiological point of view, and may, nevertheless, be quite consistent with the assumed laws of morphology, &c. Nu-

merous illustrations of these points were given, and allusions made
to the great value of the study of the variations and malformations
in plants, as affording the basis on which the now generally-accepted
theory of vegetable morphology rests.   The lecturer concluded with
some remarks on the hypothesis of Mr. Darwin, and on the necessity
of employing the utmost caution in making use of arguments derived
from well-marked malformations, either for or against the doctrine.

THE WELLINGTONIA GIGANTEA.

MR. ANDREW MURRAY, in his *Notes on Californian Trees*, Part
II., says the first place where this (Californian) tree was found was
at a spot called the Calaveras Grove (more recently the Mammoth-
Tree Grove), near the head waters of the Stanislaus and San Antonio
rivers, in long. 120° 10′ W., lat. 38° N., and about 4590 feet above
the sea level.   There the number of trees still standing amounts to
92.   Two other localities are now known, one in Mariposa, and the
other in Fresno county.   The Mariposa grove contains about 400
trees, and the Fresno grove about 600.   The tree is also said to have
been met with in Carson Creek, a few miles to the north of Mammoth-
Tree Grove ; and Carrières stated that an officer of the French navy
brought cones identical with those obtained in California from a
latitude about ten degrees north of these localities, but the identity
of these cones with those of the *Wellingtonia* has been doubted.   It
is said also to have been met with in various other parts of the Sierra
Nevada ; but if so, it does not there attain the gigantic dimensions
of those in the groves above mentioned.

This tree is undoubtedly *the largest and most magnificent known on
the face of the earth*.   Its ally, the *Sequoia sempervirens*, is not far
short of it in size, but still stands a little in the background.   The
average dimensions of both trees when full grown are about 300 feet
in height and 90 feet in circumference.   We have great difficulty in
realizing this immense height, and to assist us we must have recourse
to other objects of comparison.   To an Edinburgh man we have a
very good one.   The Gas Company's great chimney, although built
in a hollow deep below Nelson's Monument, yet has its top 7 feet
higher.   Now it is only 329 feet high in all, including its pedestal,
which is 65 feet in height ; and one of these mammoth trees was
actually 450 feet high, or nearly a third higher than that tremendous
chimney.   And Lord Richard Grosvenor, in the number of the
Gardeners' Chronicle for 7th January, 1860, speaks of one he had just
seen as 116 feet in circumference, and 450 feet high.   It is taller
than St. Peter's, and little short of the height of the Pyramids.
That is, within 11 feet of the height of the spire of Strasburg Cathedral ; 26 feet higher than St. Peter's, at Rome ; 46 feet higher than
St. Paul's, London ; and 46 feet higher than twice the elevation of
the London Monument.

An attempt was made by certain American *savans* to appropriate
this tree for their great man by calling it *Washingtoniana*.   Mr.
Murray writes :—" Dr. Lindley is undeniably the first describer, and

the name given by him to the tree (*Wellingtonia gigantea*) has of course precedence over all others. Notwithstanding this, the Americans made a strong effort to change the name into one bearing reference to Washington. As Dr. Seemann tells us, 'they even commenced in their newspapers an agitation against the adoption of the name *Wellingtonia*, quite ignoring that the *savans* of their country bow to the same code of scientific laws which governs the conduct of their European brethren, and that no amount of popular clamour could cause the right of priority here at stake to be set aside. When, therefore,' says he, 'Dr. Winslow exhorted his countrymen in grandiloquent language to call the mammoth tree, if it be a *Taxodium*, *T. Washingtonium*; if a new genus, *Washingtonia Californica*; he simply proclaimed to all the world that he knew nothing whatever of the laws governing systematic botany.'" Thus, we see that the appropriation attempt turned out an unscientific bungle.

THE KOLA NUT.

A SPECIMEN of the Kola Nut from Sierra Leone (*Sterculia tomentosa*) has been exhibited to the Botanical Society of Edinburgh, which had been transmitted by Mr. Baillie from Mr. George Thomson. In the note accompanying the nut, Mr. Thomson says :—"It is held in great estimation by the natives in the neighbourhood of Sierra Leone, especially by the Mohammedans, who call it the 'blessed Kola,' and consider it to be the veritable forbidden fruit. In the interior of Africa it is scarce, and is so much prized that five Kolas are said to be equal to the price of a slave. I understand that it is much used as a substance for chewing, and is said to possess the property of keeping away the craving of hunger to such a degree, that a man can travel for many days without anything more than a single Kola. It will be observed how curiously the two halves of the bean lock into each other."

POISON OAK OF CALIFORNIA.

A PAPER has been received from Dr. C. A. Caulfield, of Monterey, and communicated by Mr. A. Murray, to the Royal Botanical Society of Edinburgh, thus describing this tree.

The "Poison Oak" is one of the greatest plagues of California. The plant is widely diffused, and numerous cases are constantly occurring in every district of persons suffering severely from its effects. Many antidotes and remedies have been published, though still there is a demand for more information on the subject. In the woods and thickets of California, as well as on the dry hill-sides, and in fact in every variety of locality, may be found a very poisonous shrub—the "poison oak" or "poison ivy," the *hiedra* of the Spanish people. The plant belongs to the natural order *Anacardiaccæ*, and is *Rhus varielobata* (Steud.) or *R. lobata* (Hook). It is very similar to the poison ivy of the Atlantic States, *R. Toxicodendron* (Linn.), both in its appearance and its poisonous qualities. This poison is the cause of a vast deal of misery and suffering in California, and there is scarcely ever a time in any little town or neighbourhood where there are not one or more persons suffering from cutaneous disease in consequence of coming in contact with the plant. The remedies in use for the effects of the poison oak are various, and some of them will cure the milder cases. Of all the common remedies, the warm solution of the sugar of lead has, within my experience, been productive of the best results. The water of ammonia, warm vinegar and water, the warm decoction of the leaves of *Rhamnus oleifolius* ("Yerba del oso" of the Californian Spanish), or even pure warm water, are sufficient sometimes to produce a cure. All these remedies are, of course, applied externally by way of washes to the parts affected.

But the only remedy found invariably successful as an antidote for this poison is an indigenous plant growing very abundantly in this vicinity (Monterey), and in other parts of the State. It is a tall, stout perennial, belongs to the composite family, and looks like a small sunflower.

ORDEAL BEAN OF CALABAR.

PROFESSOR BALFOUR, in a communication to the Royal Society of Edinburgh, on "the Various Plants used in Africa as Ordeal Poisons," has given an account of the introduction of the Calabar Ordeal Bean into Scotland, by the Rev. W. Waddell, and mentioned its peculiar poisonous qualities, as determined by Dr. Christison. To Dr. Hewan, and the Rev. Zerub Baillie, who are connected with the United Presbyterian Mission in Old Calabar, he was indebted for some observations on actual cases of poisoning in Africa. The Rev. W. C. Thomson, another missionary, was the first who procured flowering specimens of the plant. Some of these had been given to the author by Mr. Baillie, and from them, along with the legume and seeds, the characters of the plant had been drawn up. The plant belongs to the natural order Leguminosæ, sub-order Papilionaceæ, and tribe Phaseoleæ, and appears to be a new genus to which the name of *Physostigma* (φυσάεω, to inflate) has been given, from the peculiar inflated appearance of the stigma. To the species the name of *venenosum* has been given, in allusion to its poisonous qualities. The genus is nearly allied to Phaseolus, from which it differs in the stigma, and in the long, grooved hilum of the seed. In the last character it approaches Mucuna.

MUMMY WHEAT.

THE Rev. Professor Henslow has made to the British Association, some remarks on the growth of Wheat obtained from Mummies. He introduced his observations by reading a letter from Professor Wartmann, of Geneva, who had recently found that seeds might be exposed to a temperature of 198° below zero of Fahrenheit's scale, without losing the power of germination. Professor Henslow had himself exposed seeds to the temperature of boiling water, and they germinated. The question of how long seeds would retain their vitality was one of great interest; and a committee of this Association had reported on the subject, but they had not succeeded in making seeds grow which had been kept more than two centuries.

He then showed that all experiments recorded on the growth of
Mummy Wheat were fallacious, and especially noticed the case
which had been relied on so much, of the growth of mummy
wheat by the Rev. Mr. Tupper, from seeds supplied him by Sir
Gardner Wilkinson. The mummy wheat in this case was known to
have been removed in jars that had been used for storing recent
wheat. He then alluded to the raspberry seeds from the stomach of
a warrior, found in the neighbourhood of Corfe Castle, and stated
that the old seeds were actually exhibited at the Horticultural
Society on the same table with recent ones, so that they might
easily have been mixed. A discussion ensued, in which numerous
cases of the supposed antiquity of seeds were given, but no case
which could be said to afford experimental proof.

EFFECTS OF NARCOTIC AND IRRITANT GASES ON PLANTS.

MR. JOHN LIVINGSTON, in his paper which gained the prize in
the Botanical Class of the University of Edinburgh, after detailing
several experiments on Plants with sulphurous acid, hydrochloric
acid, chlorine, sulphuretted hydrogen, ammonia, nitrous oxide, carbonic oxide, and coal gas, remarks,—"It will be evident from the
preceding experiments, that gases divide themselves into two classes
as regards their action on plants—viz., into Narcotic and Irritant
Gases. This distinction, to whatever cause traceable, is as real in
the case of plants as in that of animals. When subjected to the
influence of a narcotic gas, the colour, it was observed, never became altered, and the plants looked as green and succulent at the
end of the experiment as at the beginning. Whenever the plant
began to droop, though removed to a forcing-bed and watered, in
no instance did it recover, but died down even more speedily than
it would have done if left to the continued action of the gas. In
one word, narcotic gases destroy the life of the plant. With irritant gases, on the other hand, the action is more of a local character.
The tips of the leaves first begin to be altered in colour, and the
discoloration rapidly spreads over the whole leaf, and, if continued
long enough, over the whole plant; but if removed before the stem has
been attacked by the gas, the plants always recover, with, however, the
loss of their leaves. In a short time they put out a new crop, and
seem in no way permanently injured; but, of course, if repeatedly subjected to an atmosphere of irritant gas, the plants were destroyed."

Geology and Mineralogy.

ANTIQUITY OF MAN.

LORD WROTTESLEY, in his inaugural address to the late meeting of the British Association at Oxford, thus referred to the above great geological question :—

"The bearing of some recent geological discoveries on the great question of the high Antiquity of Man was brought before your notice at your last meeting, at Aberdeen, by Sir Charles Lyell, in his opening address to the Geological Section. Since that time many French and English naturalists have visited the valley of the Somme in Picardy, and confirmed the opinion originally published by M. Boucher de Perthes, in 1847, and afterwards confirmed by Mr. Prestwich, Sir C. Lyell, and other geologists, from personal examination of that region. It appears that the position of the rude flint-implements, which are unequivocally of human workmanship, is such, at Abbeville and Amiens, as to show that they are as ancient as a great mass of gravel which fills the lower parts of the valley between those two cities, extending above and below them. This gravel is an ancient fluviatile alluvium, by no means confined to the lowest depressions (where extensive and deep peat-mosses now exist), but is sometimes also seen covering the slopes of the boundary hills of chalk at elevations of 80 or 100 feet above the level of the Somme. Changes, therefore, in the physical geography of the country, comprising both the filling up with sediment and drift, and the partial re-excavation of the valley, have happened since old river-beds were, at some former period, the receptacles of the worked flints. The number of these last, already computed at above 1400 in an area of fourteen miles in length, and half a mile in breadth, has afforded to a succession of visitors abundant opportunities of verifying the true geological position of the implements.

"The old alluvium, whether at higher or lower levels, consists not only of the coarse gravel with worked flints, above mentioned, but also of superimposed beds of sand and loam, in which are many fresh-water and land shells, for the most part entire, and of species now living in the same part of France. With the shells are found bones of the mammoth and an extinct rhinoceros, *R. tichorhinus*, an extinct species of deer, and fossil remains of the horse, ox, and other animals. These are met with in the overlying beds, and sometimes also in the gravel where the implements occur. At Menche-court, in the suburbs of Abbeville, a nearly entire skeleton of the Siberian rhinoceros is said to have been taken out about forty years ago, a fact affording an answer to the question often raised, as to whether the bones of the extinct mammalia could have been washed out of an older alluvium into a newer one, and so redeposited and mingled with the relics of human workmanship. Far fetched as was this hypothesis, I am informed that it would not, if granted, have seriously shaken the proof of the high antiquity of the human productions, for that proof is independent of organic evidence or fossil remains, and is based on physical data. As was stated to us last year by Sir C. Lyell, we should still have to allow time for great denudation of the chalk, and the removal from place to place, and the spreading out over the length and breadth of a large valley of heaps of chalk flints in beds from 10 to 15 feet in thickness, covered by loams and sands of equal thickness, these last often tranquilly deposited, all of which operations would require the supposition of a great lapse of time.

"That the mammalia Fauna, preserved under such circumstances, should be found to diverge from the type now established in the same region, is consistent with experience; but the fact of a foreign and extinct Fauna was not needed to indicate the great age of the gravel containing the worked flints.

"Another independent proof of the age of the same gravel and its associated fossiliferous loam is derived from the large deposits of peat above alluded to, in the Valley of the Somme, which contain not only monuments of the Roman, but also those of an older stone period, usually called Celtic. Bones, also, of the bear, of the species still inhabiting the Pyrenees, and of the beaver, and many large stumps of trees, not yet well examined by botanists, are found in the same peat, the oldest portion of which belongs to times far beyond those of tradition; yet distinguished geologists are of opinion that the growth of all the vegetable matter, and even the original scooping out of the hollows containing it, are events long posterior in date to the gravel with flint implements, nay, posterior even to the formation of the uppermost of the layers of loam with freshwater shells overlaying the gravel.

"The exploration of caverns, both in the British Isles and other parts of Europe, has in the last few years been prosecuted with renewed ardour and success, although the theoretical explanation of many of the phenomena brought to light seems as yet to baffle the skill of the ablest geologists. Dr. Falconer has given us an account of the remains of several hundred hippopotami, obtained from one cavern, near Palermo, in a locality where there is now no running water. The same palæontologist, aided by Colonel Wood, of Glamorganshire, has recently extracted from a single cave in the Gower peninsula of South Wales, a vast quantity of the antlers of a reindeer (perhaps of two species of reindeer), both allied to the living one. These fossils are most of them shed horns; and there have been already no less than 1100 of them dug out of the mud filling one cave.

"In the cave of Brixham, in Devonshire, and in another near Palermo, in Sicily, flint implements were observed by Dr. Falconer, associated in such a manner with the bones of extinct mammalia, as to lead him to infer that man must have co-existed with several lost species of quadrupeds; and M. de Vibraye has also this spring called attention to analogous conclusions, at which he has arrived by studying the position of a human jaw with teeth, accompanied by the remains of a mammoth, under the stalagmite of the Grotto d'Arcis, near Troyes, in France."

CO-EXISTENCE OF MAN WITH EXTINCT QUADRUPEDS.

THE following communication has been read to the Geological Society, "On the Co-existence of Man with certain Extinct Quadrupeds, proved by Fossil Bones, from various Pleistocene Deposits, bearing incisions made by sharp instruments." By M. E. Lartet, For. M. G. S.

The author, having for some time past made observations upon fossil bones exhibiting evident impressions of human agency, was requested by the President, who had examined the specimens indicated, to communicate the results of his researches to this Society.

The specimens referred to are :—1st, fragments of bones of *Aurochs* exhibiting very deep incisions, made apparently by an instrument having a waved edge ; 2ndly, a portion of a skull of *Megaceros Hibernicus*, bearing significant marks of the mutilation and flaying of a recently slain animal. These were obtained from the lowest layer in the cutting of the Canal de l'Ourcq, near Paris, and have been figured by Cuvier in his *Ossem. Foss.* Molars of *Elephas primigenius* found in the same deposit are figured by Cuvier, who states that they had not been rolled, but had been deposited in an original and not a *remanié* deposit. 3rdly. Among bones, with incisions, from the sands of Abbeville, are a large antler of an extinct stag (*Cervus Somenensis*) and several horns of the common red-deer. 4thly. Bones of *Rhinoceros tichorhinus* from Menchecourt, near Abbeville, where flints worked by human hands have been found. 5thly. Portions of horns of *Megaceros* from the British Isles. In reference to the remains of the gigantic deer, M. Lartet alludes to the Rev. J. G. Cumming's statement, that stone implements have been found in the Isle of Man embedded with remains of the *Megaceros*, and that hatchet-marks have been seen on an oak-tree in a submerged forest of possibly still older date. 6thly. Fragments of bone collected by M. Delesse from a deposit near Paris, and exhibiting evidence of having been sawn, not with a smooth metallic saw, but with such an instrument as the flint knives or splinters, with a sharp chisel-edge, found at Abbeville would supply.

If, says the author, the presence of worked flints in the gravel and sands of the Valley of the Somme have established with certainty the existence of man at the time when those very ancient deposits were formed, the traces of an intentional operation on the bones of *Rhinoceros, Aurochs, Megaceros, Cervus, Somenensis*, &c., supply equally the inductive demonstration of the contemporaneity of those species with the human race. M. Lartet points out that the Aurochs, though still existing, was contemporaneous with the *Elephas primigenius*, and that its remains occur in preglacial deposits ; and, indeed, that a great proportion of our living Mammifers have been contemporaneous with *E. primigenius* and *R. tichorhinus*, the first appearance of which in Western Europe must have been preceded by that of several of our still existing quadrupeds.

The author accepts M. d'Archiac's determination of the period of the separation of England from the Continent as having been anterior to the formation of the ancient alluvium or "loess," but subsequent to the great rolled gravel-deposits in which the flint hatchets of a primitive people are found. If M. E. de Beaumont's hypothesis of these gravels being due to the last dislocation of the Alps be accepted, the worked flints carried along with the erratic pebbles afford a proof of the existence of man at an epoch when Central Europe had not yet fully received its present geographical features.

The author also remarks, that there is good evidence of changes of level having occurred since man began to occupy Europe and the

British Isles, yet they have not amounted to catastrophes so general as to affect the regular succession of organized beings.

Lastly, M. Lartet announced that a flint hatchet and some flint knives had lately been discovered in company with remains of Elephant, Aurochs, Horse, and a feline animal, in the sands of the Parisian suburb of Grenelle, by M. Gosse, of Geneva.

FLINTS IN THE DRIFT.

AMONG the more striking communications of the past year upon this much-vexed question are the following : —

First is a letter from Professor Henslow, from Hitcham, in Suffolk. The writer having visited the celebrated gravel-pits at Abbeville and Amiens, details the evidence collected during his visit, and the inferences therefrom ; and in a second letter remarks having alluded to an opinion which has been promulgated, that the hatchets found in undisturbed gravels were of pre-Adamite origin, adding :—" M. de Perthes, the first observer of those which occur in the Valley of the Somme, considers them antediluvian. But geologists do not recognise this term in its vulgar acceptation. Many so-called diluvial gravels, in different districts, have been shown to be not contemporaneous in their formation. The terms pre-Adamite and antediluvial are scientifically objectionable. Unquestionable as are the merits of M. de Perthes in having got together a vast mass of evidence in proof of these hatchets being found in undisturbed gravel, no geologist can allow a considerable number of the flint objects he has obtained from the same beds to be the antediluvian relics which he regards them. They are mere '*lusus naturæ*,' common in flint. Certainly, a great and unexpected difficulty has been started by the occurrence of these hatchets in undisturbed gravels hitherto referred to a period prior to that in which we have supposed man to have been placed upon the earth. Is this difficulty to be removed by extending our received chronologies? or by concluding that certain extinct animals were coeval with man within the historic period? or may we conclude the hatchet-bearing gravels to have been formed within that period, but the extinction of the mammals to have occurred prior to that period, even though we find their remains in juxtaposition with the undoubted works of man ? The hatchets must have been entangled in the gravel, and the general configuration of the surface-soil must have been arranged before, perhaps long before, the Romans dug their graves at St.-Acheul. Suppose these graves to have been dug 1500 years ago, would another 1500 or 2000 years have sufficed for obliterating the superficial effects which a transient cataclysm may have produced along the Valley of the Somme ? How imperceptibly gradual the rise of an extensive district might be, and yet effect an elevation of several feet in two or three thousand years. A very slight depression now would cause the tide to flow considerably higher up the Valley of the Somme, and salt-water and fresh-water shells would be again mingled as they are said to have been found about Abbeville in the old deposits. Whenever these

Q

districts were (as all dry lands have been) at a lower level, banks of gravel may have obstructed the flow of the river, and a swampy lake district would have been the result. I am not aware whether marine shells have been found intermingled with freshwater so high up as Amiens."

In a P.S. Professor Henslow adds:—"In a communication just received from M. de Perthes, he considers I may possibly have attributed some of the apparent confusion at Moulins-Quignons, to the intermixture of different 'samples' of gravel from old workings which have been re-quarried; it being difficult (he says) in some cases to distinguish between these and the undisturbed parts in the pit. This remark, if just, cannot by any possibility be applied to the pits at St.-Acheul, where the intermixtures on which I have commented lie far below the Roman graves. I find I have been misunderstood in regard to what I have inferred, from supposing the partial or local confusion in these beds to have been due to some cataclysm like the bursting of a lake. I restricted such an event 'to that place,' and had no intention of ascribing the general arrangement of the gravel to a single debacle. These gravels occur over extensive areas in France and England, and from such descriptions as I have read, and from what I have myself seen of them, they all appear to be lacustrine, fluviatile,' and partially estuary deposits. I object to their being regarded as any evidence of a 'universal deluge.' I am induced to repeat the suggestion I made last year, when remarking on the Hoxne gravel in connexion with that at Stowmarket, viz., that these freshwater drifts may have been modified and partially re-arranged by a slight rise of the land throughout the whole of northern Europe, and within the period hitherto ascribed to the existence of man upon the earth! If such a supposition will not meet the facts, and a different conclusion shall be made palpable, we have only to be thankful that knowledge will have been increased. It is impossible to ignore the Bible in these investigations; but we have a right to expect that every link in the chain of evidence forged to contro'ert its *seeming* testimony should be most carefully scrutinized before its value as a holdfast can be admitted. We have cast off old prejudices erroneously deduced from the letter of the Scriptures, in regard to the age of the earth; but we cannot cast off our received opinions in regard to the time which man has inhabited the earth, without first feeling assured that these hatchet-bearing gravels must be several thousand years older than the Pyramids of Egypt."

ARROW-HEADS AND HORNS IN A CAVERN.

A COMMUNICATION has been read to the Geological Society, "On some Arrow-heads and other Instruments found with Horns of *Cervus megaceros* in a cavern in Languedoc." By M. E. Lartet, For. M.G.S.

In a cavern of the limestone at Massat, near Tarascon, in Languedoc (Department of the Ariège), examined by M. A. Fontan, the floor was found to consist of a blackish earth, with large rounded pebbles, among which were mixed, in great disorder, bones and horns of a Chamois, *Cervus pseudovirginianus*, *C. megaceros* and *Bos*, together with implements of stone and bone, to which MM. Isidore Geoffroy Saint-Hilaire and E. Lartet have referred in the *Comptes Rendus* of May 10, 1858.

M. E. Lartet, in his letter, has furnished drawings and descriptions of some barbed Arrow-heads of bone, some having indented grooves, probably for the appliance of poison ; also needles, and a flute-bevelled tool of bone, a splinter or knife of hard flint, and the horn of an Antelope hacked at the base, probably when the animal was flayed.

REMAINS OF MAN IN CAVES.

SIR GARDINER WILKINSON observes, in a letter, that "hasty conclusions should not be drawn respecting the contemporaneousness of Man with those Animals with whose Remains they are found in Caves. Sir Charles Lyell has already noticed the very pertinent fact that the human skulls are of the Caucasian variety, belonging, therefore, to one of those races which now inhabit Europe. The conclusion that, because their bones are deposited in the same cave, men and extinct animals must have lived at the same period, is as unnecessary as it is unreasonable ; and any one who has observed the process by which caverns and fissures in some parts of the world are filled with red cave-earth, similar to that found in many of our own limestone formations, will cease to feel surprised at the mixture of bones of extinct mammalia with those of man.

" It is evident that if those bones of animals had been first enclosed in the earth which formed a superficial coating of any limestone rock, and human remains had happened in after ages to be buried in the same earth, the bursting of a lake, or some other accident, might have brought upon it a body of water which, sinking into and disintegrating the substance of that earth (for the effect has not been that of a constant flow of water wearing by attrition the edges of rolled substances), would shift it from its original position, and by depositing the bones of animals and of men irregularly in some cave, would give them the appearance of having been contemporaneous. They may be contemporaneous in the cave, but not so as to the period when both were on the surface of this earth ; and the same remark applies to flints and other objects cut out or fashioned by man.

" In the bare limestone mountains of Egypt are many examples of caves filled with red earth, which, exposed to view by the fall of the cliffs, afford good illustrations of the manner in which the earth, once on the surface, has been washed, and is still sinking, into those caves, even in a country so little visited by rains ; and it is this red earth which tinges the stalagmitic deposits so generally found within them. It is true those caves (like many of our own) contain neither the bones of extinct animals nor of men—the Egyptians not having had the habit, common in Europe, of living, or burying bodies, on heights—but the process of the gradual washing of the red earth from the surface into the caves is the same, and I have often seen the residue on the fissures above them left there by a recent storm.

"Again, the fact of flint knives and chippings, in France, being found immediately on the chalk rock, is exactly what we might expect. These were originally on the surface, and, having been first washed off that surface, were necessarily deposited in the lowest position upon the rock; and the fossil remains, above which they had been placed by man, were then carried down, and deposited over the flints, some few of these which had been left behind becoming mixed with them. But any length of time may have elapsed between the original enclosure of the bones in the earth and the placing of the flints on its then unmoved surface: and they only became coeval as to the period when they were both deposited in their present position.

"I offer no theory; I judge merely from analogous facts, which any one can witness; and the conclusions to be obtained from them are, that the animals are of a primitive age long antecedent to the creation of man, and that the human bones found with them are of a comparatively recent period."

BONE CAVES IN GLAMORGANSHIRE.

A COMMUNICATION from Dr. Falconer has been read to the Geological Society, "On the Ossiferous Caves of the Peninsula of Gower, in Glamorganshire, South Wales;" with an appendix, on a Raised Beach in Mewslade Bay, and the occurrence of the Boulder-clay on Cefn-y-bryn, by Mr. J. Prestwich.

The object of this communication was to give a summary of researches made during the last three years by the author and Lieut.-Colonel E. R. Wood, F.G.S., the latter of whom has carefully explored, at his own charge, since 1848, some of the caves previously known, as well as several discovered by himself. The known bone-caves of Gower (of which Paviland, Spritsail Tor, and Bacon Hole have already supplied Dr. Buckland and others to some extent with materials for the history of the cave period) are in the carboniferous limestone; and, with the exception of that of Spritsail Tor, which is on the west coast of the peninsula, they all occur between the Mumbles and the Worm's Head. The most important are "Bacon Hole," "Minchin Hole," "Bosco's Den," "Bowen's Parlour," "Crow Hole," "Raven's Cliff Cavern," and, lastly, the well-known "Paviland Caves." Bone-caves at the Mumbles, in Caswell Bay, and in Oxwich Bay formerly existed; but the sea has destroyed them. One cavern named "Rain Tor," between Caswell Bay and the Mumbles, presumed to be ossiferous, remains unexplored.

Before proceeding to describe the bone-caves and their contents, the author briefly noticed a raised beach and talus of breccia, which Mr. Prestwich had lately traced for a mile along Mewslade Bay, westward of Paviland; and he pointed out their important relationship to the marine sands and overlying limestone-breccia found in several of the Gower Caves. Dr. Falconer also referred to Mr.

Prestwich's recent discovery of some patches of boulder-clay on the highland of Gower, and in Rhos Sili Bay.

We have not space for the details, but quote the author's conclusions :—

General remarks on the distribution of the mammalian remains in the different caverns were offered, and the special anomalies pointed out ; and, after a comparative review of the fauna of the Gower bone-caves in relation with that of other cave districts of England in particular, and of Europe in general, the author arrived at the following conclusions as being consistent with the existing state of our knowledge :—

1. That the Gower Caves have probably been filled up with their mammalian remains since the deposition of the Boulder-clay.

2. That there are no mammalian remains found elsewhere in the ossiferous caves in England and Wales referable to a fauna of a more ancient geological date.

3. That *Elephas (Loxodon) meridionalis* and *Rhinoceros Etruscus*, which occur in, and are characteristic of, the "Submarine Forest-bed" that immediately underlies the Boulder-clay on the Norfolk coast, have nowhere been met with in the British caverns.

4. That *Elephas antiquus* with *Rhinoceros hemitœchus*, and *E. primigenius* with *Rh. tichorhinus*, though respectively characterizing the earlier and later portions of one period, were probably contemporary animals; and that they certainly were companions of the Cave-Bears, Cave-Lions, Cave-Hyænas, &c., and of some at least of the existing mammalia.

BONE CAVES IN SICILY.

THERE has been read to the Geological Society, a "Notice of the Discovery of two Bone Caves in Northern Sicily," by Baron Anca de Mangalaviti, in a letter to Dr. Falconer.

One of the caves discovered by Baron Anca is at Monte Gallo, at the western extremity of the Bay of Palermo, the other near the village of Acque Dolci, at the foot of Monte San Fratello. These caves, especially the last, are very rich in bones, and contain large quantities of remains of carnivora, including jaw-bones with molars and canines. Bones belonging to animals of the following genera have been met with :—*Hippopotamus, Elephas, Equus, Bos, Cervus, Canis, Ursus, Hyæna, Felis,* and some smaller carnivores.

In these caves Baron Anca has found also a large quantity of flint implements, but only where remains of *Cervus* are abundant. Coprolites, also, both of carnivores and herbivores, were met with.

The author has also met with teeth of Carnivora in the Grotta dell' Olivella.

DIAMONDS.

MR. W. POLE, F.G.S., has communicated to *Macmillan's Magazine* a paper of a graceful character on Diamonds, illustrating in an attractive manner the economy and properties of this king of gems.

Some of the facts in this paper are worthy of quotation, as being little known.

Diamond cutting, in the present day, is almost exclusively done by Jews at Amsterdam, where large diamond mills have been established; and it is calculated that 10,000 out of the 28,000 persons of the Jewish persuasion living in that city are dependent directly or indirectly on this branch of industry.* One of the largest establishments is that of Messrs. Coster, in the Zwanenburg Straat, who use steam-power to drive their machines, and employ from 200 to 300 hands.

A curious substance has lately been found in the Brazilian mines, called "Carbonado," or amorphous diamond—a kind of intermediate grade between diamond and charcoal, combining the hardness of the former with the black unformed character of the latter. Close inspection shows curious traces of a passage between the two states; and it is thought further examination of this substance may lead to some better insight than we at present possess, as to the chemical nature of the change.

A very remarkable discovery has lately been made, that the chemical element *boron*, the base of the common substance borax, may, by a peculiar process, be obtained in transparent crystals which possess the high refractive power of the diamond, and a hardness as great, if not greater. At present, the crystals produced have been too small to be of commercial value; but it is quite possible that, hereafter, the discovery may prove to be of great importance.

GOLD FROM AUSTRALIA.

AT the International Statistical Congress, held in Somerset House, in July, there was presented a note "On the Gold Production of Australia, up to the End of the Year 1859," submitted by the Australian Delegates — which states that a very large portion of Australia Proper and of Tasmania and New Zealand is auriferous.

The officially recorded export of gold from New South Wales is inaccurate, owing to the indiscriminate addition for several years of large receipts of gold from Victoria to that which was produced in New South Wales. The escorts and posts conveyed in all, from 1851 to 1859 inclusive, 1,570,047 ounces, exclusive of 80,296 ounces conveyed from the Ovens gold-fields in Victoria, and therefore included in the estimate for that colony—314,009 ounces, brought down by other means, will make a total of 1,884,056 ounces. At 77s. per ounce, 7,253,616*l.* is the value of the total amount raised in New South Wales from the first discovery in 1851 to the end of the year 1859. But this is small compared with the corrected returns of the total yield of gold from Victoria to the end of 1859. This yield exceeds 21,000,000 ounces, of the value of nearly 94,000,000*l.* sterling. South Australia, in the last eight years, averages a produce of the value of only 160,000*l.* annually. Tasmania only 8000*l.* New Zealand, since 1857, has exported 35,000 ounces of the value of 140,000*l.* The value of the total quantity raised up to the end of 1859, was, in New South Wales, 7,253,616*l.*; in Victoria,

* The writer had lately the advantage of visiting the Amsterdam diamond works, along with Professor Tennant, one of our best English connoisseurs in precious stones, and to whose kindness he is indebted for much of the information in the present paper. See also Kluge's *Handbuch der Edelsteinkunde.*

93,810,212*l.* ; in South Australia, 160,000*l.* ; in Tasmania, 8000*l.* ; in New Zealand, 140,000*l.* ; total, 101,871,828*l.*

THE "WELCOME" GOLD NUGGET FROM BALLAARAT.

PROFESSOR TENNANT exhibited at the late meeting of the British Association at Oxford, the "Welcome" Gold-Nugget, found, June 11. 1858, at Bakery Hill, Ballaarat, Australia. The weight of the original nugget was 2166 ounces. It was melted Sept. 22, 1859, and yielded quartz, earthy matter, &c., 146½ oz. ; pure gold, 2019¾ oz. Value of the gold 8376*l.* 10s. 10d., being the largest gold-nugget known.

A gold-nugget was found in 1857 at Kingovver Diggings, 120 miles from Melbourne, which was called the "Blanche Barkly Nugget;" it was 2 feet 4 inches long, and 10 inches in its widest part, and weighed 1743 ounces ; it was melted August 4, 1858, and yielded gold to the value of 6905*l.* 12s. 9d. This nugget was exhibited several months at the Crystal Palace, Sydenham.—See *Notes on a Gold-Nugget from Australia, by Professor Tennant.*

GOLD IN VEINS.

DR. WILLIAM P. BLAKE has made to the American Association some remarks on the Distribution of Gold in Veins. His observations had shown him the fallacy of the common opinion that, if gold is found at one end of a quartz vein it extends through that vein. It follows a general vertical direction, and we should dig down for it instead of lengthwise. One gold mine in Georgia, when dug but 10 feet deep, yielded 10,000 dollars ; a single bushel of the blasted rock yielded 3000 dollars. He showed some remarkable nuggets from Georgia, quite equal in size and beauty to those from California and Australia. The nuggets came from the Nacoochee mines in Georgia, one of them weighing 387 pennyweights. There was also a quantity of coarse grain, 200 pennyweights, washed out of the soil on the summit of a high ridge. He argued that gold is of igneous origin.

GOLD IN NEW ZEALAND.

DR. HOCHSTETTER has delivered at Nelson, in New Zealand, a second lecture on the Mineral Products of that province. He states that the whole region of the eastern side of the Aorere Valley, rising from the river-bed towards the steep sides of the mountains, and occupying from the Clarke River towards the south, to the Parapara on the north, a superficial extent of about 40 English miles, is *a gold-field.* Throughout this whole district, on the foot of the range, we find a conglomerate deposited on the top of the slate rocks, reaching in some places to a thickness of 20 feet. Pieces of driftwood, changed into brown coal, indicate a probably tertiary age of this conglomerate formation. This is not only cut through by the deep gullies of the larger streams, but in some places washed by the more superficial action of occasional water, and so divided into parallel and rounded ridges, of which that portion of the district called the Quartz Ranges, is a characteristic example. This conglomerate formation must be regarded as the real gold-field, prepared in a gigantic manner by the hand of Nature from the detritus of the mountains, for the more detailed and minute operations of man. While the less extensive, but generally richer, river-diggings afford better prospect of gain to the individual digger, the dry diggings in the conglomerate will afford remunerative returns to associations of individuals who will work with a combination of labour and capital. The intelligent and energetic gold-digger, Mr. Washbourn, is the first person who has proved the value of the dry diggings in the Quartz Ranges, and has demonstrated the fact that gold exists in remunerative quantities in the conglomerate. We are indebted to Mr. Washbourn for the following interesting details. He writes :—" In the drives into the conglomerate of the Quartz Ranges, the average thickness of dirt washed is about two feet from the base rock ; and the gold produced from one cubic yard of such earth would be, as near as I can calculate, worth from twenty-five to thirty shillings. This includes large boulders ; so that a cubic yard of earth, as it goes through the sluice, is of course worth more, as the boulders form a large proportion of the whole. Where the earth is washed from the surface to the rock, the value per cubic yard is much less ; not worth more, perhaps, than from three shillings to six shillings per yard, and it would generally pay very well at that. With these data the following calculation may be made. We will reckon the superficial extent of the Aorere and Parapara gold-fields at thirty English square miles, the average thickness of the gold-bearing conglomerate at a very low rate at one yard, and the value of gold in one cubic yard at five shillings. Upon these data the value of the Aorere gold-field is 22,500,000l., or 750,000l. for one square mile."

Dr. Hochstetter adds, that he is confident that the mineral wealth of Nelson is enormous, and that vast mines of gold, copper, and coal, exist in the mountains.

TRIASSIC DRIFT.

A PAPER has been read to the British Association on the contents of three square yards of Triassic Drift near Frome, by C. Moore, of Bath. In order that it might receive a more careful examination than could be given on the spot, the whole of it, consisting of about three tons weight, was carted away to the residence of the author at Bath, a distance of twenty miles ; all of which has passed under his observation, with the following results :—The fish remains, which were the most abundant, were first noticed. Some idea might be formed of their numbers when he stated that of the genus Acrodus alone, including two species, he had extracted 45,000 teeth from the three square yards of earth under notice ; and that they were even more numerous than these numbers indicated, since he rejected all but the most perfect examples. Teeth of the Saurichthys of several species were also abundant ; and, next to them, teeth of the Hybodus, with occasional spines of the latter genus. Scales of Gyrolepis and Lepidotus were also numerous, and teeth showing the presence of several other genera of fishes. With the above were found a number of curious bodies, each of which was surmounted by a depressed, enamelled, thorn-like spine or tooth, in some cases with points as sharp as that of a coarse needle ; these the author supposed to be spinous scales, belonging to several new species of fish, allied to the Squaloraia, and that to the same genus were to be referred a number of hair-like spines, with flattened fluted sides, found in the same deposit.

There were also present specimens, hitherto supposed to be teeth, and for which Agassiz had created the genus Ctenoptychius, but which he was rather disposed to consider—like those previously referred to—to be the outer scales of a fish allied to the Squaloraia. It was remarked that, as the drift must have been transported from some distance, delicate organisms could scarcely have been expected ; but, notwithstanding, it contained some most minute fish-jaws and palates, of which the author had, either perfect or otherwise, 130 examples. These were from a quarter to the eighth of an inch in length, and within this small compass he possessed specimens with from thirty to forty teeth ; and in one palate he had succeeded in reckoning as many as seventy-four teeth in position, and there were spaces where sixteen more had disappeared, so that, in this tiny specimen, there were ninety teeth !

Of the order Reptilia there were probably eight or nine genera, consisting of detached teeth, scutes, vertebræ, and ribs, and articulated bones. Amongst these he had found the flat crushing teeth of the Placodus : a discovery of interest, for hitherto this reptile had only been found in the muschelkalk of Germany,—a zone of rocks hitherto wanting in this country, but which, in its Fauna, was represented by the above reptile. But by far the most important remains in the deposit were indications of the existence of triassic mammalia. Two little teeth of the Microlestes had some years before been found in Germany, and were the only traces of this high order in beds older than the Stonesfield slate. The author's minute researches had brought to light fifteen molar teeth, either identical with or allied to the Microlestes, and also five incisor teeth, evidently belonging to more than one species. A very small double-fanged tooth, not unlike the oolitic Spalacotherium, proved the presence of another genus ; and a fragment of a tooth, consisting of a single fang, with a small portion of the crown attached, a third genus, larger in size than the Microlestes. Three vertebræ, belonging to an animal smaller than any existing mammal, had also been found.

The author inferred that, if twenty-five teeth and vertebræ, belonging to three or four genera of Mammalia, were to be found within the space occupied by three square yards of earth, that portion of the globe which was then dry land, and from whence the material was in part derived, was probably inhabited at this early period of its history by many genera of Mammalia, and would serve to encourage a hope that this family might yet be found in beds of even a more remote age. A discussion followed, in which Sir C. Lyell, Professor Sedgwick, Dr. H. Falconer, and others took part, when the importance of the author's discoveries was recognised.

GEOLOGICAL PHENOMENON.

A PHENOMENON has occurred in Savoy, which is worthy of the notice of geologists. At Orcier, in the mountain-chain above Thonon, a part of the ground sank, and in its place a lake formed. The high 'chestnut-trees disappeared entirely, with the piece of ground on which they stood, and in their stead rose trunks of trees to the surface, which had evidently long been under water, and which must have belonged to a species of tree, not known about the country. At the same time a little brook has formed, that carries away the superfluous water of the lake.

THE GEOLOGY OF BOLIVIA, ETC.

A PAPER on the Geology of this country by Mr. D. Forbes has been read to the Geological Society. The great Bolivian plateau, with an average elevation of fourteen or fifteen thousand feet above the level of the sea, consists of great gravel plains composed of sand, saline formations, oolitic *débris*, volcanic tuff, and scoriæ, including an accumulation of clays, gravel, shingle, and boulders, immense at some places, being at La Paz more than 1600 feet thick. Freshwater ponds are found at a height of 14,000 feet. Silurian rocks (perhaps 15,000 feet thick) are well developed over an area of from 80,000 to 100,000 miles of mountain country, including the highest mountains of South America, and giving rise to the great river Amazon, &c. At the same meeting some remarks were made by Professor Huxley and Mr. J. Salt on some Bolivian fossils brought over by Mr. Forbes.

REMAINS OF THE MOA.

DR. HOCHSTETTER has been so fortunate as to obtain several excellent specimens of Moa bones, including a Moa skull, the most perfect yet found in New Zealand. These were found in caves in the Aorere Valley:—" The excitement of the Moa-diggers (Dr. H. writes), was great, and increased ; for the deeper they went below the stalagmite crusts covering the floor, the larger were the bones they found, and whole legs, from the hip-bone to the claws of the toes, were exposed. They dug and washed three days and three nights, and on the fourth 'day they returned in triumph to Collingwood, followed by two pack-bullocks loaded with Moa bones. I must confess that not only was it a cause of great excitement to the people of Collingwood, but also to myself, as the gigantic bones were laid before our view. A Maori bringing me two living kiwis from Rocky river, gave us an opportunity to compare the remains of the extinct species of the family with the living Apteryx. It gives me much pleasure to acknowledge the zeal and exertions of my countryman and friend, Haast, in adding such valuable specimens to the collections of the Novara Expedition. The observations of M. Haast, made during this search, throw a new light upon this great family of extinct birds. He found that, according to the depth so was the size of the remains, thus proving that the greater the antiquity the larger the species. The bones of *Dinornis grassus* and *ingens* (a bird standing the height of nine feet) were always found at a lower level than the bones of *Dinornis didiformis* (Owen), of only four feet high. I have the pleasure of showing you, here, a leg of *Dinornis grassus*. I have since had my collection of bones increased by various contributions from Messrs. Wells, Haycock and Ogg, and a nearly perfect specimen of *Dinornis ingens* presented by the Nelson Museum to the Imperial Geological Institution of Vienna. These gigantic birds belong to an era prior to the human race, to a post-tertiary period. And it is a remarkably incomprehensible fact of the creation, that whilst at the very same period in the old world, elephants, rhinoceroses, hippopotami ; in South America, gigantic sloths, and armadillos; in Australia, gigantic kangaroos, wombats, and dasyures were living ; the colossal forms of animal life were represented in New Zealand by gigantic birds, who walked the shores then untrod by the foot of any quadruped."

GEOLOGY OF THE VICINITY OF OXFORD.

PROFESSOR PHILLIPS has read to the British Association a paper, first calling attention to the value and extent of the collection of fossils acquired by the late Dr. Buckland in this locality ; and stating that, although the systematic arrangement of them was not completed, they might form some idea of their vast number by the fact that 50,000 of them had already passed through his hands. The Professor said that as the geologist would travel with deep interest those parts of this neighbourhood from which Dr. Buckland had made his collection of fossils, he would confine himself to those points. He then gave a general sketch, descriptive of the district round Oxford, commencing at the lias, and extending to the fresh-water sands at Shotover-hill. He admitted that it was a question whether the latter were of the age of the lower green sand or Wealden, and that it was open to discussion, but his own views inclined to the latter opinion. The Professor stated that at Stonesfield the bones of some enormous animals had been discovered, embedded in slate, and exhibited some fine and valuable specimens, including one of the foot-bones of the Megalosaurus, and an extreme claw of the foot of the Cetereosaurus, both of which gave indications that these creatures were partly terrestrial.—*Oxford University Herald.*

BLENHEIM IRON-ORE.

MR. E. HULL has read to the British Association a paper on the Blenheim Iron Ore, and the thickness of the formations below the Great Oolite at Stonesfield. The author showed that the economic importance of the liassic and oolitic iron-ores is yearly on the increase, owing to three causes—the expansion of the British iron trade, the local curtailment in the supply of clay iron-stone of the coal-measures, and the extension of the railway system, which has rendered available iron-ores far removed from the boundaries of the coal-fields, and which were almost unknown till within the last few years. From the mineral statistics of Great Britain, collected by Mr. Hunt, it appears that in 1857 the quantity of ore raised from the Cleveland,

Whittey, and Northamptonshire districts, reached the amount of nearly one and a half million of tons, or nearly one-tenth of the total quantity raised in Great Britain. It may safely be predicted that, ere long, Oxfordshire will also rank as an iron-producing county.

In a new geological map of the county of Oxford, exhibited to the Geological Section by Sir R. Murchison, the iron-ore in the Blenheim estate is clearly shown. Mr. Bull, who had taken part in the preparation of the map, described the geological features of the county as shown in the map. He particularly noticed the Blenheim iron-ore, which was of a very valuable character, and he had no doubt it would at some future day exercise a great influence upon the productions of this part of England.—*Oxford University Herald.*

FOSSILS OF THE LOWER ROCKS.

MR. ASH, who is known to Silurian geologists for his zeal in collecting fossils around Tremadoc, North Wales, has discovered remains of a Cheirurus (a species of trilobite) and Conularia (a pteropod mollusc) in association with *Agnostus pisiformis*, in the Lingula beds at Maentwrog Waterfalls, Caernarvonshire. This discovery takes the date of Cheirurus considerably lower down in the Lower Silurian scale than it had been previously fixed, although Murchison has already figured *Cheirurus clavifrons* among Lower Silurian trilobites. Conularia, too, is remarkable in this early age. The Lingula flags become more and more closely united with the Lower Silurian rocks, of which, as Murchison observes, "they form the true fossiliferous base."

FOSSIL VERTEBRÆ IN SOMERSET.

PROFESSOR OWEN has read to the Geological Society a paper "On some small Fossil Vertebræ from near Frome, Somersetshire." In this communication the author described three minute vertebræ discovered by Mr. Charles Moore, F.G.S., in an agglomerate occupying a fissure of the Carboniferous Limestone near Frome, in Somersetshire, in company with teeth of a small Mammal allied to the *Microlestes* of Plieninger. The vertebræ are stated to correspond in size with the teeth of *Microlestes;* but to have Reptilian characters, especially in their biconcave structure—a character common in Mesozoic Saurians, but rare in the existing genera. There appears to be but very slight grounds for supposing that such a character may have ever belonged to any Mammals, although some of the existing *Monotremata* have peculiar vertebral modifications somewhat resembling, in these respects, the structural features of Reptiles. In their large and anchylosed neutral arch, however, these little vertebræ present a mammalian character.

Remains also of small Saurians and Fishes occur in considerable numbers with the vertebræ in question, as well as the more rare mammalian teeth.

SUPPLY OF COAL.

M. DE CARNAL, a Prussian mining engineer, has prepared some general statistics of mining. He asserts that the quantity of Coal

raised throughout the world in 1857, amounted to 125 millions of
tons, worth 930 millions of francs. Prussia alone, he says, contains
enough coal to suffice for the consumption of the globe for nine centuries, taking as a measure that of 1857 ; while England, far from
being exhausted, as some Continental alarmists suppose, is able to
supply the world with coal for 4000 years.

SYNCHRONISM OF COAL-BEDS.

PROFESSOR C. H. HITCHCOCK has explained to the American
Association the Synchronism of the Coal-Beds in the Rhode Island
and Western United States Coal Basins, arguing from their fossil
remains, that they form a connecting link between the Appalachian
and Nova Scotian coals and those of the West.

Professor J. S. Newberry contended that the fossil remains did
not wholly show the synchronism of the coal measures. Professor
William B. Rogers said that in our early attempts to trace the continuity of single coal seams we are often led astray. Coal measures
may contain the same fossils, and yet not have been deposited at the
same time. Professor Agassiz took the same view, and said that it
was probable that our peat bogs of the north and cedar swamps of
the south may at one and the same time become coal-beds, and yet
their fossils would differ. So deposits formed at the same time, and
not far distant, may not contain a single identical fossil, and our old
method may therefore lead us to error. Again, the deposits of a
very long period may be of very small thickness. Thus the coral
beds of Florida, although but sixty or seventy feet thick, were probably begun before man was created ; and it may turn out that the
carboniferous epoch is really more than one, perhaps even ten cosmic
periods. He was satisfied that there is no better way of identifying
rocks than by the study of fossils, but the study of the geographical
distribution of animals on the present surface of the earth should
precede the attempt at classifying periods or strata by their fossils.

MANURES, ETC.

DR. LANKESTER, in his eighth lecture "On the Relations of the
Animal Kingdom to Man," dwells especially on the uses of bones
(recent and fossil) as Manures, and of gelatine and membranes. The
modes of nutrition of plants, and the history of the application of
manures (with especial reference to the labours of the great chemist
Liebig), were adverted to. The nature and sources of the first
mineral phosphates ; the nodules, formerly called coprolites (now
considered to be the ear-bones, &c., of fossil whales and sharks),
found in the green sand and red crag, and their mode of preparation
for agricultural purposes, were described. On the lecture-table were
placed specimens (from Mr. J. B. Lawes) of manufactured super-
phosphate of lime. The importance of the discovery of vast quantities of native phosphate of lime in Spain by Dr. Daubeny,
and by Mr. D. Forbes, in Sweden, as sources of wealth to those
countries, was specially noticed. The nature of gelatine, its
sources (from bones, skins, fish skins and fish sounds, and similar substances), and their manufacture into glue, size, jellies, and isinglass,

were next considered ; and the innutritious nature of gelatine, and the danger of confining diet to that substance, were pointed out. The lecture was concluded by an account of the manufacture of gold-beaters' skin, catgut, and silkworm-gut, from the membranes of the stomach of the sheep, &c.—*Illustrated London News.*

METAMORPHISM.

The production of crystalline rock forms the subject of an elaborate article in a recent Number of the *Annales des Mines*, by M. Daubrée, which contains an interesting account of his own experiments, and a *résumé* of the researches of other eminent mineralogists, with details of the artificial formation of precious stones, &c.

LOSS OF THE PRECIOUS METALS IN ASSAYING.

Mr. G. Makins (in the *Journal of the Chemical Society*) shows how small quantities of Gold and Silver are lost by volatilization in the flues, and by dissolution in the nitric acid employed. These small quantities, as he states, become important in the vast amounts which are passing through the hands of the assayer.

"SILVER SPRING" IN FLORIDA.

Professor John Le Conte has read to the American Association a paper on the Phenomena presented by the "Silver Spring" in Marion County, Florida. Although the optical phenomena of this spring had been greatly exaggerated, yet he found, on paying it a visit last December, that it was sufficiently wonderful. While it was reported to be 200 feet deep, a careful measurement showed it to be only 30 feet. On a clear and calm day, the view from the side of a boat is beautiful beyond description. Every feature of the bottom is as clear as if there were no water above it, but only the clear air. The bottom is thickly covered with luxuriant vegetable growth, developed by the large amount of sunlight which penetrates there. Objects beneath the surface of the water, viewed obliquely, appear surrounded by prismatic hues. The beholder seems to be looking down from some high point, upon a truly fairy scene. Large letters at the bottom can be read from the surface of the well as if they were in the open air. Small letters cannot be read so easily, because the surface is not entirely quiescent.

GROUND-ICE.

M. Engelhardt has repeated his experiments made in 1829, with a view to explain the formation of Ground-Ice.

In conclusion, the author attributes the formation of ground-ice to obstacles in the current, which, on the one hand, by the eddying motion, cause the water below 0° to sink to the bottom and cool the sides, and on the other hand, produce stationary parts in which the crystallizing power can exert its force. He observed the influence of these foreign bodies in a conduit at Zinsweiler. In 1829, ice formed at the bottom of the water in which there were large stones, trees, &c. The formation of ice was entirely prevented by removing these foreign bodies.—*Comptes Rendus.*

ERUPTION OF VESUVIUS.

THE Correspondent of the *Athenæum* writes, March 20 and 21 :—

"At 1 A.M. the mountain threw out fire and burning stones, at the same time uttering a loud noise, as of thunder. At the bottom of the crater several smoke holes have been formed, in which fire may be seen, and from which a noise continually issues. At the foot of the mountain three small craters were formed; 'and I counted this night,' says the guide, 'thirty-two currents of lava, one of which was full sixteen palms in width, and travelled rapidly in the direction of San Salvadore, whilst the others went towards the Piano della Ginestra. As I stood and looked, I saw the earth open and currents of lava issue.' All the proprietors of land in the direction of Torre del Greco are in a state of great apprehension, as their estates are threatened. 'On going up the mountain,' says the cautious and learned Cozzolino, 'take care of the smell of muriatic acid.'"

In the same journal of April 14, we find :—

"The eruption of Vesuvius continues and increases," writes a friend from Naples; "and during the last week the surface of the mountain has undergone great changes. On Friday night last the discharges were so loud and strong that the whole neighbourhood shook; and these were followed by a hissing sound, as of a rapidly flowing river. Looking into the crater, one sees a body of liquid fire; and on one occasion a tri-coloured jet was thrown up; so that it is generally expected that Commendatore Ajossa will send up a body of police to take note of and suppress this treasonable demonstration. The three colours—blue, violet, and black—were not, it is true, the Italian colours; but we do not stand to trifles here: number is as suspicious an element as colour. As these variegated circles of fire made their appearance, the crater shook with the violence of the effort. From the foot of the mountain a stream of water and of lava issued, and ran so rapidly, that in one hour it advanced a mile; its course was then slower, and always in the direction of Torre del Greco. Towards Resina the guides counted twenty currents; and in the midst of them had been formed a lake of fire, full forty feet in circumference. The appearance of the mountain from Naples is, of course, very striking."

In the journal of May 12 :—

"I send you the following report of the state of Vesuvius, which has just been brought in by the guide. The crater still sends out its thunders, followed by red-hot stones. At the bottom of it one sees a mass of fire, from which rise up fiery circles like carriage-wheels. The exhalations of muriatic acid are so strong that it is difficult to approach. At the foot of the mountain there are full a hundred currents of liquid lava, which have arrived at the 'Piano delle Ginestre.' At present the numerous craters are no longer visible; the whole ground seems to send forth lava, and the small proprietors are in great apprehension. The currents have been flowing over the old bed of 1794, when Torre del Greco was swept away, and the lava went half a mile into the sea."

NEW SEISMOMETER.

PROFESSOR CAVALLERI has constructed in the College at Monza a new Seismometer, for recording the shocks and convulsions to which the surface of our globe is subject; and Mr. R. Mallet has communicated to the *Philosophical Magazine*, No. 125, Professor Cavalleri's memoir upon seismology, in which he describes this new instrument.

Earthquake waves, says M. Cavalleri, as far as I can remember, in three distinct cases, which I have present to my mind, appeared very rapid and almost isochronous. Recalling these shocks, it does not appear to me far from the truth to assign about three undulations per second as the rate, at least in our Lombardy Plains. The instrument which I have constructed with this view will note the duration of these undulations, and consequently whether they are different in various countries and in different earthquakes.

We have not space to quote the details. The principle upon which the instrument is constructed is very simple. It consists of an arrangement of a large pendulum, an inclined bar, and a number of small pendulums, the latter terminating in sharp needles, which touch ashes placed beneath them, and upon which are left traces of the oscillations. Now, the instrument being capable of marking, 1st, the vertical altitude of the wave by the spiral pendulum ; 2nd, the horizontal undulation by the great pendulum ; 3rd, the time of the wave as marked by one or other of the small pendulums, we have all the elements necessary for calculating the intensity of the shock—lastly, it is clear that with these three elements we can make all possible theoretical inferences, and assign to each of the three its appropriate value in referring to the effects of an earthquake, whether on buildings, on plains, or on the sea, &c., in all of which one or other of the three mentioned powers will have a greater or less influence : it has been proved, for example, that with an equal degree of intensity, the vertical shock will do more damage than the horizontal. Thus we can note with these instruments —

1st. The moment at which the earthquake occurs.
2nd. The direction of the primary shock or earth-wave.
3rd. The general horizontal direction of the waves, their amplitude or length.
4th. The height of the vertical wave of shock, however complex the vertical and horizontal waves acting together may be.
5th. The resultant of both these elements, or the mixed shock itself.
6th. The inclination to the horizon of the mixed shock.
7th. The velocity and time of the wave.
8th. The total intensity of the wave, introducing into it the element of time as furnished by the pendulums.

If, then, as frequently happens, we also know the total duration of the earthquake, we may approximately infer its total intensity.

EARTHQUAKES IN NAPLES.

Mr. Robert Mallet, who, in 1859, undertook a journey to Naples, to study on the spot the results of the terribly disastrous Earthquake which occurred in that country, has prepared a voluminous document thereupon, in which the whole matter is discussed in its several bearings. He has reported from time to time to the British Association on the subject of Earthquakes generally, and from his last observations, can tell what was the primary direction of the shock, its subsequent variations, direction of emergence, and rate of movement. A competent observer, by going over the ground, would now be able to read off all these phenomena as from a book. Of all the directions in which a shock can travel, the horizontal is the most destructive. A shock or wave having risen to the surface, becomes more and more horizontal as it travels, and would throw down everything in its course, did it not become weaker with every furlong of distance. The shock that overthrew towns and villages in Naples had a movement of twenty feet a second : less than this suffices for destruction, for, according to Mr. Mallet, a horizontal wave travelling at four feet a second only would leave London a heap of bricks.—*Chambers's Journal.*

VELOCITY OF EARTHQUAKE SHOCKS.

MR. J. BROWN, in a communication to the British Association, proposes to estimate the velocity of Earthquake Shocks in the laterite of India, a clayey rock in a semi-pasty condition of perhaps the lowest degree of elasticity, reposing in some places on strata of sand and clay. Supposing the shock to have travelled from Quelon to Trevandrum, and taking the distance between these two places at thirty-seven miles, a velocity of propagation is obtained at between 470 and 530 feet per second, according to the time marked by different observers.

DESTRUCTIVE EARTHQUAKE IN THE STATE OF SALVADOR.

A LETTER from San Salvador of the 28th December, 1859, reports the occurrence of a fearful Earthquake on the night of the 8th of that month. It commenced about a quarter before nine, and continued for two minutes and 35 seconds. At Isalco the parish church was destroyed, except a portion of the naves and the sacristy. About 40 of the best houses and a number of smaller ones were destroyed; fortunately no lives were lost. During the night several other shocks of more or less severity and duration were felt. One of them, more violent than the others, completed the destruction of some buildings that had escaped the first shock. The shock was felt at Guatepeque, Opico, Apopa, Tepecoya, and other towns. At Tepecoya the church, cabildo, and several houses were destroyed. At Guatepeque the church and cabildo partially. Iaguaque suffered also, several houses were destroyed, and the church greatly injured. On the outskirts of the town great holes were opened, some over 100 yards wide. At Guayamoco houses were destroyed, and the church much damaged. At Panchimalco, houses injured, and large holes opened in the earth. San Martin and Comasagua, church and cabildo partly destroyed. Nanhuisalco suffered also, and soon after a destructive fire broke out which burnt over 200 houses,—thus, in a measure, destroying the whole place. On the night of the 10th, at 9.30, there were two more severe shocks. On both occasions the nights were very clear, but blowing a heavy norther until a short time before the shocks, when it fell calm, but again rose soon after the shocks. The Volcano of Izalco was, no doubt, the centre of vibration, as the shocks were felt all around, but most strongly in the N.E. direction, and for a distance of 150 miles, as far as known.

EARTHQUAKE IN CORNWALL.

AN Earthquake Shock through nearly all Cornwall, on the 13th January, 1860, at 10.32 p.m. (local time), during a squally and unusually dark night, appears to have been the severest recorded in this county. It was felt at great depths under ground, in several mines very distant from each other, although not in any of the mines of St. Just, on the west of Penzance. On the surface, however, in almost every locality, the persons who felt it were probably twenty times more numerous than those who experienced the shock of the 21st of October in the previous year.

EARTHQUAKE IN KENT.

A CORRESPONDENT of the *Athenæum* writes from River Hill, Seven-oaks:—"On September 3rd, at six or seven minutes past three in the afternoon, a smart shock, bearing all the characteristics of an earthquake, was felt over a district of several miles in extent, north, south, east, and west from this place. My information extends to Ightham, east; Tunbridge, south; Lullingstone, north; and Chip-stead, north-west. The statements of the different observers present the following variety. Persons on the ground floor in various houses thought that somebody was running about violently, or dragging the furniture about in the room overhead; or, in some cases, they imagined that some one had fallen down-stairs. The furniture in the different apartments, such as desks, tables, and beds, moved; and the inmates of different rooms ran out, imagining that something had happened in some other part of the house. In my own house, which is substantially built of stone, the impression produced on one of my sons was that some part of the house had fallen down. Another, up-stairs, with no room overhead, describes the sound as of a very heavily-laden waggon trotting past the front door; and he was at the same time conscious of a distinct motion from east to west, which appeared to throw him towards the window. In other houses in the neighbourhood, pictures suspended on the walls were seen to vibrate, the furniture was shaken, and curtain-rings rattled. In the neighbourhood of Ightham, a boy fishing felt the ground move under his feet, and saw, as he describes it, the rushes in the pond move. I myself had just driven off from the house in a two-wheeled dog-cart, and was not conscious of anything except what appeared to be a short and subdued clap of thunder; but some other persons, driving near the same spot at the same time, perceived the shock, which they at first attributed to an explosion at the Tunbridge powder-mills. I have no observation of the barometer for that day, but the sky to the south of this place, which commands a very extensive view, was densely overcast for two hours before and after the shock, and a very singular-looking mass of black vapour filled and obscured the valley. It was not like an ordinary thunder-storm, but formed a sort of wall of dark mist. Thunder was heard at a distance for some hours, but no rain fell here, nor was there here any loud thunder. I learned, however, that very heavy rain fell in detached storms at several places a few miles off, and the church at East Peckham appears to have been struck by lightning."

GEMS IN AUSTRALIA.

THE existence of Native Diamonds has been discovered in the black sand of the Ovens district, by an Irish miner, named O'Neill. Rubies and other gems of very small size had previously been found in the same deposit.—*Australian and New Zealand Gazette.*

Astronomical and Meteorological Phenomena.

THE ROYAL OBSERVATORY.

FROM the Annual Report to the Board of Visitors, presented on June 2, we select the following extracts :—

One of the most important departments in the Observatory is that of making Galvanic Communications. Under this head, Mr. Airy says :—"Our external galvanic communication has received a very important change. We had found for some time that our two underground wires leading to the Blackheath-gate of the Park, and there adapted to communicate either with one of the Admiralty wires (to the Admiralty, or to Woolwich, Chatham, Sheerness, Deal) or with one of the Submarine Company's wires (to the London Office, or to Calais or Ostend), had become practically useless. One of the four underground wires crossing Blackheath to the Lewisham Station of the North Kent Railway (there communicating by the London Bridge Station with Lothbury and with Deal) had shown signs of decay, but the others were very good ; but about the month of August last year the whole of the four wires failed. We have taken up parts and replaced them by new wire, but apparently the whole of the gutta-percha has perished. No special fault has been found, but every yard is faulty. I determined after this to trust no more to underground wires ; and having received the permission of the Right Honourable the First Commissioner of Parks and Public Works to extend wires at sufficient elevation above the Park—and having been met in my application to the London District Telegraph Company by the most liberal offer on their part—I have stretched seven wires in the open air from the top of the Octagon Room to the top of a house in George-street. From this point the wires are carried on in a similar manner to the following destinations :—one is the property of the London District Telegraph Company ; four are led to the Railway Station in Greenwich, whence, under the care of Charles V. Walker, Esq., they are continued on poles till they rejoin the continuation of the former North Kent lines at the railway junction (Mr. Walker is preparing arrangements for placing the wires in open air all the way to the London Bridge Station) ; two are led along the poles of the London District Telegraph Company to Deptford Broadway, where they meet the lines of the Submarine Company, and where they will communicate by turn-plate either with the Admiralty line or with the Submarine line, as formerly, at the Blackheath-gate of Greenwich park."

The peculiar object of interest at the annual visitation of this important establishment was the mounting of a new and magnificent Equatorial Telescope by the Astronomer Royal, Professor Airy, surpassing in magnitude any other in this country or in France, and nearly on a par with the celebrated instrument at Pulkowa, which has achieved much for the science, and is an instance of the munificence of the Russian Government. The size of the object-glass at the Royal Observatory is nearly thirteen inches diameter, and the length of the telescope appears to be about fourteen or fifteen feet. It is so nicely balanced on its axis as to be moveable vertically with the slightest touch, so that it can be elevated or depressed to the view of any object between the horizon and the zenith with such facility that it seems as if it moved self-supported in air, without the least friction on the supporting pivots.

The movement of the polar axis in longitude bearing the telescope upon it is a more difficult matter, and exhibits a variety of contrivances, by which the beautiful application of the telescope and the vast framing by which it is supported are carried round by a clock with the most perfect smoothness, so that in watching, through a microscope, the gradual onward movement of the minute scale not the slightest unevenness or irregularity in the movement can be perceived ; and this, considering that the whole apparatus set in motion by the clock weighs many tons, is a proof of great skill in contrivance, and great perfection in the workmanship. The connexion of the clock with the polar axis is not permanent, but is struck in or detached with perfect facility in an instant of time, so that the astronomer using the telescope directs it in equatorial or vertical motion with the most perfect command. If he desires to examine the object he has found, he attaches the telescope to the polar axis and brings the clock motion into operation almost in the same instant, which then moves the telescope equatorially in an opposite direction to the movement of the surface of the earth, so that the line of sight through it continues directed to that one object, whether it be the sun, the moon, any one of the planets or satellites, or any fixed star which the observer wants particularly to examine. Behind the object-glass are perceived minute cobweb lines, which enable the observer to measure with accuracy the movement inherent in the object he is examining, such as its revolution on its axis or the passage of a satellite across a planet.

The usual astronomical observations have been made during the past year, and their reduction and printing have been carried on with great regularity. The same may be said of the magnetical and meteorological observations, with the exception that the dipping-needles are still a source of anxiety. "The form which their anomalies appear to take (says Mr. Airy) is, that of a special or peculiar value of the dip given by each separate needle. With one of the 9-inch needles, the result always differs about a quarter of a degree from that of the others. I can see nothing in its mechanical construction to explain this, and I have been driven to the following conjecture. The theory of determination of dip rests on the assumption that, when the magnetism is reversed by double touch, the magnetic axis will be the same as before. Now it is conceivable that the magnetizable particles of steel may consist of two series, of which one is prepared to take one kind of magnetism and the other to take the other kind ; and that the axes of these two series may not be parallel. I am supported by Professor Faraday in the idea that this is not impossible ; and, if the conjecture have any foundation, we are never certain of having a dipping-needle free from special error."

The Report then refers to the rating of chronometers, the business of which had been very laborious during the past year. At one time there were about 210 chronometers in the Observatory.*

TOTAL ECLIPSE OF THE SUN, JULY 18, 1860.

THE most important observations of the Great Solar Eclipse of July 18, were obtained by the Expedition organized by the Astronomer Royal, who (says Mr. Warren De La Rue) took every opportunity, at successive meetings of the Astronomical Society, and by correspondence, to promote a complete series of observations of the eclipse. "As the result of the several discussions which were raised, the requisite observations became fairly taken up; moreover, as the astronomers who had charged themselves with them distributed themselves over a considerable extent of country, every possible contingency to ensure success was provided for. For the most part, the expedition was favoured with good weather on the day of the eclipse, and results were obtained which tend to throw considerable light upon, and possibly at once to set at rest, the question whether the luminous prominences and corona visible on the occasion of a total eclipse belong to the sun, or whether they are occasioned by the deflection and diffraction of the light of the sun's photosphere.

"As the most interest attaches to the few minutes of totality, I shall confine myself to the phenomena observed at and near this epoch.

"Some minutes before the totality I distinctly saw the whole of the lunar disc, and a luminous prominence on the east of the zenith. This was quite visible, while the sun's image was reflected by a glass surface fixed at an angle of 45°, in the eyepiece, and the intensity of its light consequently much diminished. The upper surface of the glass diagonal reflector I had, however, silvered to the extent of one-half, and, as I brought into action the silvered half just previous to totality, I perceived a large sheet of prominences on the east. A little to the east of the zenith a brilliant cloud, quite detached from the sun, and at some distance from the moon, came into view. This detached cloud did not escape the notice of other astronomers; the Astronomer Royal, and I believe others also, observed the cloud and prominences before the complete obscuration of the sun's disc; and Dr. Winnecke, who, with M. Struve and M. Oom, was at Pobes with the Astronomer Royal, saw them some minutes after the totality. The brilliancy of these prominences was wonderfully great, and far exceeded that of the corona. They were not uniform in tint, and, to my eye, they did not in general present a red or rose colour; two, however, had a decided but faint rose tint; much detail was visible in the protuberances both of light, shade, colour, and configuration. The side towards the sun was not brighter than the opposite side; but in some cases the more distant portions of the

* How Chronometers are rated in the Observatory is described in an able paper contributed to *Stories of Inventors and Discoverers.*

protuberances were fainter than the near portions ; it is not impro-
bable, therefore, that they consist of gaseous matter in an intense
state of incandescence.

"The surface of some of the eastern luminous prominences next to
the moon was, when first seen, very irregular, and far more so than
was attributable to mountains as seen in the profile on the moon's
edge. This irregular outline may, however, be explained by supposing these prominences to have been first seen floating like clouds
in a transparent atmosphere at some little distance from the sun's
surface, and consequently from the moon's edge—a supposition
which is supported by the fact, that one such prominence or luminous
cloud was seen distinctly detached, and at some distance from the
dark moon.

"As the moon glided over the sun's disc, the inner outline of the
prominences in the eastern hemisphere became less and less indented,
and at last they were bounded by the nearly even outline of the
moon's limb. As the eastern prominences became gradually covered,
a mountain-like peak, seen at first as a mere point in the north-west
quadrant, gradually grew in dimensions, then presented several
points, and at last resembled somewhat a colossal ship in full sail ;
and, extending from this through an arc of 60°, there came into
view in the north-west quadrant a long streak of luminous prominences, varying in breadth, and with a few points projecting outwards. This streak became very jagged in its inner outline as the
moon glided off from it just previous to the sun's re-appearance,
these luminous prominences presenting the same phenomena as those
on the eastern edge—that is, appearing like clouds floating in a
transparent atmosphere a little distance from the sun. This observation was also made by Professor G. Rumker.

"As the prominences which we see beyond the sun's limb on the
occasion of a total eclipse are merely such as are, from their situation, seen in profile, it is fair to presume that such prominences must
exist pretty generally diffused all over the sun's photosphere, and
that they must be at all times visible either as light or as dark
markings on the sun's disc. Whether they are the bright portions
or faculæ, or the darker portions (not the spots) of the sun's mottled
disc, or whether they may not in some cases appear more bright,
and in others less bright, than the general brightness of the sun's
disc, must still be a matter of conjecture. It is an interesting fact,
however, that on the 19th and 20th, a large mass of faculæ, surrounding a group of small spots, came round into view by the sun's
rotation, which must have occupied very nearly the position of the
brightest portion of a large streak of prominences on the south-
eastern quadrant. The prominences, in some cases, did not project
beyond the moon's limb to a greater extent than the thinnest line,
but in others the prominence reached a distance of 2'. The detached
cloud before mentioned, when first seen, was about half a minute
(14,000 miles) beyond the position occupied by the moon's dark
limb. It presented a double curvature on its northern side, both
curvatures being convex towards the north. It inclined in a curved

direction, at about an angle of 60° from a radius towards the east, and was a minute and a half (42,000 miles) long. As the moon glided onwards in her course, she approached it gradually, and at last touched the extreme point of this floating cloud, which glowed with all the brilliancy of one of our own terrestrial clouds at sunset. It presented a decided rose tint.

"At 72° from the north a protuberance, in shape reminding one of a boomerang, imprinted itself on a collodionized plate, although it was not visible to me in the telescope. The stem was 2 minutes long (56,000 miles) ; the point was bent towards the north, inclining downwards over towards the extremity of the detached cloud. It is a very curious circumstance that this protuberance imprinted itself distinctly, although it did not attract the eye directed especially to that locality. This may be accounted for on the supposition that it emitted a feeble purple light.

"My own observation, and those of others, furnish an additional proof that the luminous prominences retained a fixed position in regard to the sun, and that as successive portions of the moon passed before them, they did not change either their former appearance, except in so far that the moon, by passing over them, shut off one portion after another towards the east, while more was visible of those protuberances on the west ; and great protuberances came into view and were depicted in the second photograph. A more important inference, leading to the same physical conclusion, is, that the moon's disc distinctly slid between the upper and the lower prominences, by a quantity measurable on the photographs. This is confirmed by the Astronomer Royal's measures of angular position of the prominences.

"Just before and after the eclipse sun-pictures were made ; and during the progress of the eclipse 31 photographs were obtained, the times of which are carefully registered. These will serve hereafter to determine the path of the moon across the sun's disc and other data with considerable accuracy. The serrated edge of the moon is perfectly depicted in all the photographs, and in some of them one cusp of the sun may be seen blunted by the projections of a lunar mountain, while the other remains perfectly sharp. The indentations of the concave side of the luminous prominences, as seen in the photographs at the period of totality, are far greater than the well-marked profiles of the lunar mountains, shown in the photographs of the other places of the eclipse. The surface of the sun just bordering the moon's dark disc is brighter for a short distance than the other portions ; a phenomenon deserving of attention.

"With the Kew photoheliograph, the moon does not give the slightest trace of a picture with an exposure of one minute ; the pictures of the luminous prominences, which were procured in the same time, are over-exposed, and the corona has clearly depicted itself on both the plates ; the light of the corona is therefore more brilliant than that of the moon. When the second plate was placed in the telescope, the wind rose, and shook the observatory and telescope violently, and some of the brighter prominences have depicted themselves three times on the second plate ; thus showing how short a time was

really requisite to produce an image. Indeed, had it been possible
for me to have known beforehand how intense the light of the prominences really was, there would have been no difficulty in obtaining
the photographs in much less time ; and I do not doubt that four
might have been procured with an exposure of from twenty to thirty
seconds each.

"When the sun was reduced to a small crescent, the shadows of all
objects were depicted with great sharpness and blackness, reminding
one of the effects of illumination by the electric light ; the sky at
this period assumed an indigo tint, and the landscape was tinged
with a bronze hue. At the moment of totality the darkness was not
so intense but that I could proceed with my drawings without the
aid of a lamp I had at hand in case of necessity. The light of the
corona was silvery white, very bright close to the sun, and to my
eye extending about $\frac{8}{10}$ths of the moon's diameter beyond her limb.
The sky near the moon was of a deep indigo colour ; it passed through
a sepia tint into red, and a brilliant orange near the horizon. These
hues have been registered with great precision by M. Bonomi, who
had prepared himself by delineating the panorama several days previous to the eclipse. Mr. Joseph Beck, who had undertaken the
examination of the corona, has ascertained that its light gave strong
evidence of polarization. It is fair to assume from this observation
that the corona is due, to a great extent, to the illumination of an
atmosphere surrounding the sun. I did not attempt any exact
observation of the corona, but M. Oom, Professor Grant, and other
astronomers, have obtained good measurements of it.

"M. Oom, who was stationed on the Alto d'Urbaneja, near Pobes,
found by accurate measurements made by a comet-seeker, in which
a glass micrometer plate was fixed, that the corona consisted of a
bright ring 2' wide, then a fainter ring 3' wide ; beyond this there
was a great number of small rays, whose mean distance from the
faint ring was 2' ; the whole three rings extending, therefore, 7'
beyond the moon's edge. Besides the three rings there were five
rays, remarkable for their great length. The first was situate at the
position angle (reckoned from north towards east) 30°, its length
being 9', the second, at 90°, was 14' long. It consisted of several
beams, and had the appearance at the point of a star, as usually
drawn. The third beam was a very remarkable one ; it had somewhat the form of a sabre, the point bending over towards the east.
It extended 13' in a straight line from the position angle 155°, and
then, in a curved direction, 15' further ; the point bending over to
position angle 135°. The fourth ray reached 28' from the moon's
limb ; it being situate at position angle 227°. The fifth ray, situate
at 290°, was 10' long. M. Oom saw the moon distinctly between
five and six minutes after the totality. Baily's beads were not seen."

The British Government despatched the *Himalaya* steam-ship to
Santander, with several able astronomers, men of science, arts, &c.,
who made their observations at Rivabellosa, a village near Miranda
del Ebro.

The station selected was a threshing-floor, situated in latitude

42° 42′ north, and longitude 11′ 33″ west, at the height of 1572 feet above the mean level of the sea. The magnetic variation was found to be 20° 20′ mean west. The locality, being bounded by a beautiful panorama formed by the distant Pyrenean range, was well situated for observing the effect of the eclipse on the landscape. The more important object was to endeavour to obtain photographs of the various phases of the eclipse by means of the Kew photoheliograph. A very interesting account of the proceedings was communicated to the *Times* of August 9, by Mr. Warren De La Rue.*

The following records of effects produced upon animals and inanimate nature, are from the *London Review:*—

A Correspondent, writing from Santander, remarks:—

"The totality began at 2h. 58m. 24s., and lasted until 3h. 1m. 44s. At 3h. most of the thermometers laid upon the grass had fallen from 71 deg. 1 min. to 64 deg. 5 min., and there was a perceptible chill in the air, increased, perhaps, by the wind having veered almost due north at 2h. 9m. During the totality, the following phenomena were also observed:—At the moment in which darkness began to descend rapidly, consternation seemed to seize nature; pigeons flew about in clusters, confused and scared; poultry sought their roosts; my dog whined at my feet; small birds fluttered and twittered excitedly, as if a hawk was in view; a cow moaned loudly; and the dew gathered like sweat on the flowers as they drooped and closed their petals. But the most impressive moment was yet to come: as darkness descended, and the winds grew hushed, man and beast were struck dumb with awe."

Another Correspondent, from Tudela, states:—

"At 4 minutes past 3 an unearthly, ghastly glow, once seen never to be forgotten, covered the whole scene, and was most evident upon the gravelly ground at my feet. The light rapidly decreased; but with the exception of this glow, which was very conspicuous upon the clay hills, I could see no particular change of colour in the trees or landscape.

"At 5 minutes past 3 the western horizon was lost in darkness, and the conical hills to the north-north-west were invisible, while the clouds towards the east sent forth a bright glow of light, from the sun still shining on their fronts. At this moment bright waving lines of light flickered one after another over the ground parallel to my line of sight with the sun. On looking upward from these I found that the sun had already disappeared, and that I had missed the formation of the corona. The black circle of the moon was already surrounded by this crown of glory; two stars shone brightly a few degrees from the sun; and so magnificent was the spectacle above, so glorious the spectacle below, that I could not help looking for a few moments from the one to the other. A bright light, I think of a greenish-yellow colour, skirted the horizontal sky, and the banks of cumuli shone with a brilliant glow. The darkness was not intense; the light from the corona and the distant refractions far surpassed the brightest moonlight. It would have been easy to read the smallest type."

A Correspondent, from Fuente del Mar, observes, with respect to the rapid changes in colour upon the landscape, as well as the effect on animals, caused by the Eclipse:—

"Before totality commenced, the colours in the sky and on the hills were magnificent beyond all description; the clear sky in N. assumed a deep indigo colour, while in W. the horizon was pitch-black (like night). In the E. the clear sky was very pale blue, with orange and red, like sunrise, and the hills in

---

* See also "Photographic Observations of the Solar Eclipse," by Mr. John Spiller, in the Chemical Section of the present volume, pp. 199—201.

S. were very red; on the shadow sweeping across, the deep blue in N. changed like magic to pale sunrise tints of orange and red, while the sunrise appearance in E. had changed to indigo. The colours increased in brilliancy near the horizon, overhead the sky was leaden. Some white houses at a little distance were brought nearer, and assumed a warm yellow tint; the darkness was great; thermometers could not be read. The countenances of men were of a livid pink. The Spaniards lay down, and their children screamed with fear; fowls hastened to roost, ducks clustered together, pigeons dashed against the sides of the houses, flowers closed (*Hibiscus Africunus* as early as 2h. 5m.); at 2h. 52m. cocks began to crow (ceasing at 2h. 57m., and recommencing at 3h. 5m.). As darkness came on many butterflies which were seen about flew as if drunk, and at last disappeared; the air became very humid, so much so that the grass felt to one of the observers as if recently rained upon."

A Correspondent, from Tarragona, gives the following as the result of his observations :—

" At 1h. 42m., local time, the eclipse commenced, and it was curious to observe how rapidly the sun's rays lost their power, though the light did not at first sensibly diminish. At 1h. 47m. the thermometer (black bulb) marked 43 (centigrade), and from this it gradually went down to 10 at 2h. 57m., the centre of the eclipse. The sun was uncovered during the whole time, with the exception of a minute or so, five minutes before the totality. At about 2h. 56m. the last limb of the sun disappeared; but though the total eclipse was computed to last here for 3 minutes and 30 seconds, the time seemed too short to notice all the wonderful effects, and my attention was chiefly directed to the disc of the sun, which presented a magnificent spectacle. The instant the sun was shut out a most beautiful bright white corona appeared round the moon's circumference, which presented an orb of jet black, and, almost immediately, rose-coloured excrescences seemed to shoot out like small pyramids of fire from the rim of the sun. These were not constant, but seemed to keep changing; but this probably, was the effect of the moon's disc passing over them. Two on the sun's vertex were visible all the time, but one on the eastern limb soon disappeared, and was succeeded by one on the north-west limb of the sun, the most conspicuous of them all. The colour of the sky was a very deep blue, but not black, as it was clearly relieved against the moon's disc; and at least three or four stars were visible to the naked eye—Jupiter and Venus, the two nearest to the sun, shining almost as brightly as on a summer night."

In England the magnitude of the Eclipse may be judged from the following considerations :—If we consider the diameter of the sun to be represented by 100, then, at all those places situated on or near a line joining London and Liverpool, 83 parts of the diameter of the sun were obscured. At places situated near lines parallel to the above drawn through Dublin and Edinburgh respectively, 87 such parts were obscured on the former, and 79 on the latter; and at intermediate places the magnitude was intermediate. The greatest eclipse in the British Isles was therefore in Ireland, and the smallest in Norfolk. The point of the sun's border on which the moon first impinged, was situated on the right hand, and a little below a horizontal line drawn through his centre, and the last contact was a point on the left hand, or eastern border, above the horizontal line passing through his centre.

Although the phenomena of this Eclipse in England fell far short of those in the line of totality, yet it was the largest of any solar eclipse that will happen here till the 22nd day of December, in the year 1870; and the next and only large one in this century will be in the year 1887, on August 19th, which will be nearly total.— *London Review.*

COMETS.

Though the larger and brighter comets naturally excite most general public interest, and are really valuable to astronomers, as exhibiting appearances which tend to throw light on the internal structure of these bodies, and the nature of the forces which must be in operation to produce the extraordinary phenomena observed, yet some of the smaller telescopic comets are, perhaps, more interesting in a physical point of view. Thus the six periodical comets, the orbits of which have been determined with tolerable accuracy, and which return at stated intervals, are extremely useful, as being likely to disclose facts of which, but for them, we should possibly have ever remained ignorant. Thus, for example, when the comet of Encke, which performs its revolution in a period of a little more than three years, was observed at each return, it disclosed the important and unexpected fact, that its motion was continually accelerated. At each successive approach to the sun it arrives at its perihelion sooner and sooner; and there is no way of accounting for this so satisfactory as that of supposing that the space in which the planetary and cometary motions are performed is everywhere pervaded by a very rarefied atmosphere or ether, so thin as to exercise no perceptible effect on the movements of massive solid bodies like the planets, but substantial enough to exert a very important influence on more attenuated substances moving with great velocity. The effect of the resistance of the ether is to retard the tangential motion, and allow the attractive force of gravity to draw the body nearer to the sun, by which the dimensions of the orbit are continually contracted, and the velocity in it augmented. The final result will be that, after, the lapse of ages, this comet will fall into the sun; this body, a mere hazy cloud, continually flickering as it were like a celestial moth round the great luminary, is at some distant period destined to be mercilessly consumed. Now the discovery of this ether is deeply interesting as bearing on other important physical questions, such as the undulatory theory of light; and the probability of the future absorption of comets by the sun is important as connected with a very interesting speculation by Professor William Thomson, who has suggested that the heat and light of the sun may be from time to time replenished by the falling in and absorption of countless meteors which circulate round him; and here we have a cause revealed which may accelerate or produce such an event.—*Address of Lord Wrottesley, President of the British Association, Oxford*, 1860.

BAROMETERS FOR COAST STATIONS.

The Duke of Northumberland, as President of the Royal National Lifeboat Institution, in connexion with the Meteorological Society of London, has established, under the direction of Mr. Glaisher, F.R.S., and Mr. Sopwith, F.R.S., a complete series of Stations, not less than fourteen in number, furnished with Barometers. The primary object of the Duke (who generously contributes one moiety of the expense, the remaining funds being furnished by the Meteorological Society and by subscription) is the saving of life; but in associating the undertaking with the Meteorological Society and with gentlemen of eminence, he takes the best means of giving an important scientific value to these establishments, ensuring good instruments, and an efficient continuance of the observations.

The fourteen stations are,—one on each side of the Tweed at Berwick, one on Holy Island, the others respectively at North Sunderland, Beadnell, Newton, Craster, Boulmer, Alnmouth, Amble, Cresswell, Newbiggin, Cullercoats, and Tynemouth. At all these places the instruments are put in public view, either in the window of the establishment or outside the building, so that every one that will may have access to them at all times. A record of each day's fluctuations of the barometer is noted in dots on a ruled scale, and rules drawn successively day by day from one point to the other, so that thus a straight, or an irregular, or a curved line is drawn, which indicates at the first glance the states of the mercury for several previous days, thus adding to the efficacy of the indication given at the immediate time of observation. These diagrams are also publicly exposed; and a sailor looking at one sees what has been the tendency of the barometer. If he finds by the line drawn that the variation has been little, the dots being nearly horizontal, and the glass still steady, he knows that no change is probable. If, on the contrary, he finds the diagram exhibiting an ascending or descending curve, he knows that there has been a progressive rise or fall, and, comparing this with the actual state, he is enabled to judge whether fair or foul weather is to be expected, and, consequently, whether it will be prudent for him to put to sea or remain on shore.

Each station is furnished with a barometer, and a maximum and minimum thermometer, all of strong, plain, good workmanship; and the placing of the thermometer by the side of the barometer-index is a great improvement, as both can be read together. With them are issued very plain, intelligible printed directions for using them.

The Meteorological Observatories in the United Kingdom are exceedingly few, and every addition is a gain to science. One has already been established at Alnwick by his Grace, and two others at Allenheads and Bywell by Mr. W. B. Beaumont, M.P. A very efficient one has also been established at Osborne by his Royal Highness Prince Albert, and another at Holkham by the Earl of Leicester; but the total number of reliable observatories in the United Kingdom, we believe, in September last, fell considerably short of sixty.

We abridge the above from the *London Review*, in which journal especial attention is paid to Meteorology, and the progress of general science in connexion with the interests of the public.

SHIP STRUCK BY LIGHTNING.

LIEUTENANT LAPORTERIE has communicated to the Academy of Sciences an account of the effects of a stroke of Lightning experienced on board the *St. Louis*, man-of-war, in the roadstead of

Gaeta, on December 10. This account was accompanied by the platinum point of the lightning conductor which received the stroke, and a bit of melted copper from the rod of the same conductor. The storm of the 10th was chiefly confined to the north-west part of the heavens. At 1.30 P.M. the electric fluid struck the conductor of the mainmast, accompanied by a detonation equal to that of a discharge of artillery. A portion of the platinum point was melted, and the rest broken off from the rod. Curiously enough, the base of this platinum point, in the shape of a cone, had remained uninjured, with the screw by which it had been fixed by the rod; while the remaining extremity of the rod from where the screw had been snapped off, was melted! The conductors of the fore and mizenmasts had received no injury; but a sergeant, who was seated near the funnel of the engine, at a distance of 19 feet from the mainmast, felt such a violent shock that he thought he had been struck by some Sardinian projectile, which had fallen on board by accident. He thought that he felt blood trickling from the wound, and after being examined, could scarcely be persuaded that he had not been wounded. At the foot of the mainmast, a bluish flame, $2\frac{1}{2}$ feet in length, was noticed, but it immediately disappeared. The pocket-knife of one of the sailors was strongly magnetized, as were also some steel-pens in the officers' rooms.

SHOWER OF ICE.

CAPTAIN BLAKISTON, in a letter to General Sabine, which has been communicated to the Royal Society, dated H.M.S. *Simoon*, Singapore, 22nd of February, 1860, gives an interesting account of a Shower of Ice which fell upon the ship. He says:—"On the 14th of January, when two days out from the Cape of Good Hope, about 300 miles S.S.E. of it, in latitude 38° 53′ S., longitude 20° 45′ E., we encountered a heavy squall, with rain, at 10 A.M., lasting one hour, the wind shifting suddenly from east to north (true). During the squall there were three vivid flashes of lightning, one of which was very close to the ship, and at the same time a shower of ice fell, which lasted about three minutes. It was not hail, but irregular-shaped pieces of solid ice, of different dimensions, up to the size of half a brick. The squall was so heavy that the topsails were obliged to be let go. There appears to have been no previous indication of this squall, for the barometer at 6 P.M. on the two previous days had been at 30·00, the thermometer 70°. At 8 A.M. on the 14th the barometer marked 29·82, the thermometer 70°. At 10 A.M., the time of the squall, 29·86, the thermometer 70°; and at 1 P.M., when the weather had cleared, wind north (true) 29·76, thermometer 69°; after which it fell slowly and steadily during the remainder of the day and following night. As to the size of the pieces of ice which fell, two, which were weighed after having melted considerably, were $3\frac{1}{2}$ and 5 ounces respectively; while I had one piece given me, a good quarter of an hour after the squall, which would only just go into an ordinary tumbler; and one or two persons depose to having seen pieces the size of a brick. On examining the ship's sails afterwards they were found to be perforated in numerous places with small holes. A very thick glass cover to one of the compasses was broken. Although several persons were struck, and some knocked down on the deck, fortunately no one was seriously injured."

GREAT AURORAL DISPLAY IN 1859.

PROFESSOR ELIAS LOOMIS has read to the American Association a paper on this phenomenon, which is probably unsurpassed; and a greater amount of information has been collected about it than was ever before assembled. The details furnish materials for settling several important points. The first display was seen over about two-thirds of the globe, the second over the whole globe. Both conform to the general law, that the region of the greatest polar action is about 15° further south in the United States than in Western Europe. By a comparison of observations, it appears that the aurora of August 28 extended through a space from 530 to 40 miles above the earth's surface, and that of September 2, from 490 to 50 miles above. The illumination consisted chiefly of illumined paths parallel to the axis of the needle. The telegraph, and various tests and experiments in connexion with it, show that during the phenomena, electric currents were developed equal to the ordinary full strength of a Voltaic battery; or, in technical terms, to 200 cups of Grove's battery. This electricity must have been derived from the aurora, either by transfer or induction; if by transfer, the electricity is of the same character. Professor Loomis is compelled to admit that the auroral current is electricity; its colour is just the same as that of electricity passing through rarefied air. The aurora has a tendency to periodicity, or rather a displacement of the auroral region.

NEW PLANETS.

M. LEVERRIER has given to the Paris Academy of Sciences the positions of the new telescopic planet discovered at Washington by Mr. Ferguson, as follows:—

Mean T. Washington.	Rt. Ascension.	Declination.
Sept. 15. 0h. 39m. 14·2s.	23h. 4m. 37·3s.	—3deg. 22m. 56·8s.
„ 16. 8 29 50·9	23 3 46·1	—3 29 54·0

He further observed, that if the planets lately discovered were classified according to the order of their publication, M. Chacornac's planet would be the 59th, Mr. Ferguson's the 60th, and M. Goldschmidt's the 61st. He then informed the Academy that a 62nd planet, according to a letter from M. Encke, had been discovered at Berlin. M. Leverrier having communicated M. Chacornac's discovery to M. Encke at Berlin on the 14th ult., Dr. Forster and M. Lesser, being informed of the fact by him, immediately sought out the new planet, and found one near the place where it was to be, which, therefore, they took to be M. Chacornac's. But, on continuing their observations, they became aware that the elements of theirs did not coincide with those of the other, and consequently were forcibly led to the conclusion that their planet was a different one. The elements of this 62nd planet are :—Mean longitude, 13° 42' 58" ; anomaly—16° 24' 33" ; eccentricity, 10° 2' 22"; longitude of perihelion, 30° 9' 31" ; ditto of node, 126° 26' 59" ; inclination, 2° 11' 35" ; daily motion, 646·109" ; logarithm of the semi-axis major, 0·493134. The Minister of Public Instruction wrote to inform the Academy that M. Passot had sent a petition to the Emperor, praying that a commission might be appointed by the Academy to examine a paper already submitted to that body, "On the Law of the Variation of the Central Force in Planetary Movements," and to request the Academy to give his Excellency some information on the matter.

On the 24th of March, Dr. Luther discovered a new planet at the observatory of Bilk, near Düsseldorf ; it is the fifty-seventh of the small planets between Mars and Jupiter.

GREAT STORMS OF OCTOBER AND NOVEMBER, 1859.

REAR-ADMIRAL FITZROY has read to the Royal Society some Remarks on the Storms of October 25, 26, and November 1, 1859, from information obtained from lighthouses, observatories, and private observers.

The combined results of observations prove the storm of October 25 and 26 to have been a complete horizontal cyclone. Travelling bodily northward, the area of its sweep being scarcely 300 miles in diameter, its influence affected only the breadth of our islands (exclusive of the west of Ireland) and the coast of France.

While the central portion was advancing northward, not uniformly, but at an average rate of about 20 miles an hour, the actual velocity of the wind-circling (as against watch-hands) around a central "lull," was from 40 to nearly 80 miles an hour.

At places northward of its centre, the wind appeared to "back," or "retrograde," shifting from east through north-east, and north to north-west ; while at places eastward of its central passage, the apparent change occurring, was from east, through south-east, south, south-west, and west.

Our Channel squadron, not far from the Eddystone, experienced a rapid, indeed almost a sudden shift of the wind from south-east to north-west, being, at that time, in or near the central lull ; while, so near as Guernsey, the wind veered round by south, regularly without any lull. This sudden shift off the Eddystone occurred at about three (or soon after), and at nearly half-past five it took place near Reigate, westward of which the central lull passed.

From this south-eastern part of England, the central portion of the storm moved northward and eastward. Places on the east and north coasts of Scotland had strong easterly or northerly gales a day nearly later than the middle of England. When the *Royal Charter* was wrecked, Aberdeen and Banffshire were not disturbed by wind ; but when it blew hardest, from east to north, on that exposed coast, the storm had abated or almost ceased in the Channel and on the south coast of Ireland.

The storm of the 31st, and 1st of November, was similar in character ; but its central part passed just to the west of Ireland's south-west coast, and thence north-eastward.

Of both these gales the barometer and thermometer, besides other things, gave ample warning ; and telegraphic notice might have been given in sufficient time from the southern ports to those of the eastern and northern coasts of our islands.

At it is the north-west half of the cyclone (from north-east to south-west, true) which is influenced chiefly by the cold, dry, heavy, and positively electrified polar atmospheric current, and the south-west half that shows effects of equatorial streams of air—warm, moist, light, and negatively electrified ;—places over which one part of a cyclone passes are affected differently from others which are traversed by another part of the very same meteor, or atmospheric *eddy,* the eddy itself being caused by the meeting of very extensive bodies of air, moving in nearly, but not exactly opposite directions, one of which gradually overpowers, or combines with the other, after the rotation.

On the polar half of the cyclone, continually supplied from that side, the visible effect is a drying up and clearing of the air, with a rising barometer and falling thermometer ; while on the equatorial side, overpowering quantities of warm moist air, rushing from com-paratively inexhaustible tropical supplies, push towards the north-east as long as their impetus lasts (however originated), and are suc-cessively chilled, dried, and intermingled with the always resisting, though at first recoiling, polar current. After such struggles these two currents unite in a varying intermediate state and direction, one or other prevailing gradually.

Very plain and practical conclusions are deducible from these con-siderations :—

One, and the most important, is, that in a gale which seems likely to be near the central part of a storm, that should be (of course) avoided by a ship which has sea room ; a seaman, facing the wind, knows that the centre is on his right hand in the northern hemi-sphere, on his left in the southern ; he therefore is informed how to steer.

Another valuable result is that telegraphic communication can give notice of a storm's approach, to places then some hundred miles distant, and not otherwise forewarned.

ANTIQUITY OF "THE LAW OF STORMS."

Mr. HEELIS has communicated to the British Association a notice of an old work on the Origin and Nature of Wind, by R. Bohun, of New College, Oxon, published at Oxford in 1671, and which contains a statement of various points in the Law of Storms, such as their vortical motion, calm centre, change of currents, and action upon the barometer, twenty-seven years earlier than the earliest account hitherto noticed, which is that of Captain Langford, in the *Philosophical Transactions* for 1698.

COLOURED RAIN.

PROFESSOR CAMPANI, of Siena, in a letter to Professor Matteucci, states that on December 28th, about 7 A.M., in the north-western part of Siena, rain of reddish hue fell copiously for two hours ; a second red shower occurred at 11 A.M., and a third at 2 P.M. ; but that of the deepest red fell first. It was entirely confined to the north-western quarter of the town, and so nicely was the line drawn, that the cessation of the red colour was ascertained in one direction to be about 200 metres from the meteorological observatory, the pluviometer of which received Coloured Rain at exactly the same time. The temperature during the same interval varied between 8° and 10° Centigrade (40° and 50° Fahrenheit). The wind blew from the south-west at the beginning of the phenomenon, and afterwards changed to W.S.W. None of the rural population in the immediate vicinity of Siena remarked the occurrence, so that, most probably, the rain that fell round the town was quite colourless. The same phenomenon recurred in exactly the same quarter of the town on December 31, and again on January 1, the wind being W.N.W., and the temperature respectively 35° and 39° 42' Fahrenheit. Each time, however, the red colour diminished in depth, its greatest strength having at no time exceeded that of weak wine and water. Professor Campani considers that the colour must be owing to some solution, since the water has deposited no sediment. A similar phenomenon occurred in Wales in 1849 ; when a shower of rain, as red as blood, fell near the village of Bonvilstone, and extended thence in a westerly direction.—See *Year-Book of Facts*, 1850, p. 278.

GREAT STORM IN WILTSHIRE.

MR. G. A. ROWELL, of Oxford, Honorary Member of the Ashmolean Society, and until recently the obliging Assistant Under Keeper of the Ashmolean Museum, has read to the British Meteorological Society "A Lecture on the Storm in Wiltshire, which occurred on the 30th of December, 1859." This valuable contribution to meteorological science has been printed at the request of the Society. Mr. Rowell appears to have visited Calne, the locality of the storm, and to have spent three days in examining its effects, and to have since been assisted with many details on points of importance by persons resident upon the spot, where all classes were anxious to promote an investigation of the phenomena of the storm.

" Nearly all the accounts of the storm (says Mr. Rowell) describe it as a whirlwind. This may, in general, be considered a vague term, as storms are often described as whirlwinds, if of a violent character, and confined within narrow limits — without any consideration as to whether the wind moved in circles or not ; but in this case it was stated, that the effects of the storm gave full proof of its cycloidal character, and some of the writers stated the number of yards which they supposed the diameter of the cyclone to be. I very carefully examined the effects of the storm, over four miles of its track from the place of its commencement, within which space its principal effects were exhibited. I have also obtained information.

S

respecting it from every available quarter, and really can find no proof whatever of this storm being a cyclone, or of there having been any whirling of the wind whatever, further than the mere eddies, which all fluids in rapid motion would be liable to, when subject to such obstructions as the wind generally meets with in passing along the surface of the earth."

Mr. Rowell's lecture extended to nearly 50 pages, so that we can do little more than call our readers' attention to this very interesting record. At about a mile south of Calne, the storm is described as coming upon the villages in an instant, ushered in by a most vivid flash of lightning and an instantaneous clap of thunder, and attended by abundant rain and large hailstones.

"Indeed, so appalling was the whole scene, and in consequence men's senses seem to have been so paralysed with terror, that (strange to say), along the whole line of storm, where hundreds of trees were thrown down, scarcely a single individual saw or heard a tree fall, and nobody realized what was occurring till the hurricane had gone by. But in three minutes the storm had passed on, and then, when the frightened villagers emerged from their cottages, what a sight met the eye on all sides ! the largest trees torn up by the roots, upheaving tons of earth attached to them to a height of fourteen feet above the ground ; large branches snapped off and carried on many yards to where they fell; barns in ruins or prostrate on the ground ; ricks demolished, and the sheaves carried away; their own houses unroofed, and their gardens filled with straw, fallen chimneys, and tiles ; and all this havoc effected in three minutes of time !"

We cannot quote further details, except to point to Mr. Rowell's account of a waggon and hay being carried over a hedge during the storm, which must have been tossed nearly upright, and then carried onward by the direct force of the storm. (*See page 33 of the Lecture.*) Mr. Rowell attributes this phenomenon to " the sudden expansion of the air beneath the waggon, as the storm-cloud passed ;" and he then shows how this may have occurred.

Another violent effect was the storm seizing the heavy, substantial roof of a cattle-shed (53 feet by 16) and *lifting it off the walls which supported it in a solid mass*, although the thatch of the roof was *scarcely, if at all, damaged.* Mr. Rowell concludes :—

"I beg to observe that I have controverted the opinion that the storm in Wiltshire was a whirlwind, from a firm conviction that its phenomena must be otherwise accounted for, and with the hope of directing attention to phenomena in storms that are too often overlooked ; but I believe that a whirlwind may often result from causes similar to those to which I attribute this storm, as the rarefaction within a cloud, at a moderate elevation, may often produce a whirling of the air rushing onward and upward into the partial vacuum. I have controverted Mr. Espy's opinions on some points, but I believe the phenomena of the storm fully accords with his conclusions, ' that there is an inward motion of the air towards the centre of storms from all sides :' I only differ from that gentleman as to how such an effect is produced. The like remark will apply to my observations on Mr. Hopkins's views, as I believe he has, in his various papers on this subject, almost *proved* that the fall of rain is the principal cause of wind, although I have totally different views as to the reason why it is so."[*]

---

[*] Mr. Rowell is also the author of *An Essay on the Beneficent Distribution of the Sense of Pain* ; and of a very ingenious *Essay on the Cause of Rain and its allied Phenomena;* of both tracts, second editions have been printed. In the latter Essay, the ingenuity with which all the known phenomena of rain and storms are made to bear tribute to the author's theory, is very remarkable. Both works are sold by the Author, No. 3, Alfred-street, St. Giles's, Oxford.

METEOROLOGY OF 1860.

Results deduced from the Meteorological Register kept at the Royal Observatory, Greenwich, during the year 1860.

1860. Months.	Mean Reading of Barometer.	Temperature of Air.							Departure from average of 19 yrs.	Mean Temp. of the Dew Point.	Mean Tension of Vapour.	Weight of Vapour in a cubic ft. of Air.	Mean additional Weight required for saturation.	Mean Degree of Humidity, Saturation 1.00.	Mean Weight of a cubic foot of Air.	Relative proportion of Wind.				Mean Amount of Cloud. 0 to 10.	Rain.	
		Highest by Day.	Lower by Night.	Range in Month.	Mean of all Highest.	Mean of all Lowest.	Mean Daily Range.	Mean for Month.								N.	E.	S.	W.		No. of Days it fell.	Amount collected.
	In.	°	°	°	°	°	°	°	°	°	In.	Gr.	Gr.		Grs.					°		In.
Jan.	29·514	55·5	27·5	28·0	45·0	34·8	10·2	39·7	+1·5	36·2	·214	2·5	0·4	88	548	3	3	13	12	6·9	21	1·8
Feb.	29·857	53·5	23·2	30·3	42·5	30·1	12·4	42·5	-2·8	30·4	·170	2·0	0·4	80	559	11	4	6	8	6·5	13	1·1
March	29·655	59·5	23·5	36·0	49·2	35·0	14·2	41·1	-0·7	34·8	·202	2·4	0·6	78	549	5	2	6	18	7·5	18	1·9
April	29·796	65·0	28·2	36·8	53·7	35·6	18·1	42·9	-3·6	36·7	·218	2·5	0·7	79	549	10	8	5	7	7·0	13	1·0
May	29·746	76·5	32·5	44·0	65·5	44·6	20·9	53·8	+1·0	46·2	·313	3·5	1·1	75	536	1	7	7	16	6·5	14	3·9
June	29·613	74·0	43·5	30·5	65·0	48·5	16·5	54·8	-4·4	49·7	·357	4·0	0·9	82	532	2	1	13	13	7·9	23	5·8
July	29·843	75·0	41·6	33·4	69·2	50·1	19·1	57·6	-4·3	52·3	·393	4·4	0·9	83	534		4	7	23	8·3	10	2·8
Aug.	29·556	70·8	45·5	25·3	67·2	51·8	15·4	57·7	-3·8	52·5	·396	4·4	0·9	83	528		0	9	21	8·3	25	3·7
Sept.	29·761	69·7	45·7	24·0	63·4	45·8	17·6	53·4	-3·7	50·2	·364	4·1	0·5	88	537	7	5	8	10	7·4	17	3·1
Oct.	29·856	68·5	32·4	36·1	58·6	44·5	14·1	50·6	-0·9	47·6	·330	3·7	0·5	89	541		2	11	15	6·8	10	1·6
Nov.	29·696	55·3	28·5	26·8	46·7	35·3	11·4	40·8	-2·7	38·9	·237	2·7	0·3	93	550		13	5	5	7·9	11	2·5
Dec.	29·491	54·0	8·0	46·0	40·5	31·9	8·6	36·3	-4·0	33·5	·192	2·4	0·2	94	551	9	7	7	8	7·9	17	2·8
Means.	29·609	64·8	31·7	33·1	55·5	40·7	14·9	47·0	-2·4	42·4	·282	3·4	0·6	86	543	6	5	8	11	7·4	192 Sum	32·0 Sum

NOTE.—The sign + implies above, and the sign — below the average.

EXPLANATION.

The cistern of the barometer is about 159 feet above the level of the sea, and its readings are coincident with those of the Royal Society's flint-glass barometer. The observations are taken daily at 9 A.M., noon, 3 P.M., and 9 P.M.; the means of these readings are corrected for diurnal ranges by the application of Mr. Glaisher's corrections, as published in the *Philosophical Transactions*, Part I., 1848; and from the readings of the dry and wet bulb thermometers, thus corrected, the several hygrometrical deductions in columns 11, 12, 13, 14, 15, and 16, are calculated by means of Mr. Glaisher's Hygrometrical Tables. *Second Edition.*

The numbers in column 2 show the mean reading of the barometer every month, or the mean length of the column of mercury which balanced the whole weight of atmosphere of air and water; the numbers in col. 12 show the length of a column of mercury balanced by the water alone; and if the numbers in this column be subtracted from those in column 2, the result will be the length of a column of mercury balanced by the air alone, or that reading of the barometer which would have been, had no water been mixed with the air. [*Concluded on next page.*

The reading of the barometer was above its average value in February, April, July, and October; and in defect in the remaining months of the year.

The mean reading of the barometer for the year, at the level of the sea, was 29·879 inches.

The mean temperature of the air was above the average value of 89 years in January by $3\frac{1}{2}°$; March, by $\frac{1}{4}°$; May, by $1\frac{1}{4}°$; October, by $1\frac{1}{4}°$; and below, in February, by $2\frac{1}{2}°$; April, by $3°$; June, by $3\frac{1}{2}°$; July, by nearly $4°$; August and September, by $3°$; November, by $1\frac{1}{2}°$; and December, by $2\frac{3}{4}°$.

The mean high day temperature was above its average value in January, May, and October, and in defect in the remaining months of the year.

The mean low night temperature was above its average value in January, May, and October, and below in the remaining months of the year.

The temperature of the year 1860 was $2\cdot4°$ below the average value of the 20 preceding years. The highest temperature of the year was $76\cdot5°$ in May, and the lowest $8°$ in December; but in some parts of the country it went below zero, therefore the range of temperature exceeded $76°$.

The mean weight of a cubic foot of air was 548 grains in January, 532 grains in June, 551 grains in December; and the average for the year was 543 grains, exceeding the average value of the preceding nineteen years by 3 grains.

The mean temperature of the air for the year was $47°$; and that of the dew-point was $42\cdot4°$. The mean degree of humidity was 86, complete saturation being represented by 100. Rain fell on 192 days! the amount collected was 32 inches.

The warm period, which set in on December 24th, 1859, continued till January 24th, 1860. The excess of temperature on the 1st day of the year was 16°, that of the second was 11°, and of the third was 13°, whilst a fortnight previous the temperature was as much in defect; and from January 1st to the 24th, the average daily excess was 4°. On January 25th, a cold period set in, at first not severely, but became so afterwards, and continued, with a few exceptions, to May 8th. From May 9th to May 26th, the days were warm, and their mean temperatures were daily in excess of the averages to the amount of $5\frac{1}{2}°$. From May 27th till the middle of October the days were cold. During this interval the mean temperatures were in excess on 11 days only, the average excess being less than 1°, whilst on the remaining 130 days they were in defect, the average deficiency being 4°.

On October 22, a warm period set in, which continued till the 1st of November. The excess of temperature averaged $5\frac{1}{2}°$ in excess. On November 2nd, a cold period began, which continued till the 15th, the daily defect averaging $4\frac{1}{2}°$. From the 15th to the 26th, the temperature was alternately in excess and defect. On the 27th, the weather changed, and continued warm, with but few exceptions, to December 13, the temperature averaging $2\frac{1}{4}°$ daily in excess. On December 14, a cold period set in, at first not severely, but became so towards the latter end of the month; the average daily defect was $8\frac{1}{2}°$.

On December 24, the highest temperature reached was 28°; it fell to 16° at night, and to 8° by 7h. a.m. on the 25th; it then rose, by 9h. a.m., to 12°, and gradually to 30° by 10h. p.m., which was the highest temperature of the day. On the 26th, the temperature ranged between 26° and 35°; on the 27th, between 24° and 35°: on the 29th, between 24° and 35°: but on the morning of the 29th, it was as low as 7° at 7h. a.m.; at 9h. a.m., it was $14\frac{1}{2}°$; at 10h. a.m., $24\frac{1}{2}°$; an increase of no less than 10° taking place within one hour; the temperature then rose to 32° by midnight, and to 46° by 2h. p.m. on the 30th day, and a most rapid thaw set in.

The mean temperatures of December 24, 25, and 29, were $22\cdot4°$, $20\cdot2°$, and $23\cdot0°$ respectively. The previous instances in December of daily temperatures below 23° are as follows:—

1814, December	24,	the mean temperature was	20·9°.
1816, ,,	22,	,,	21·2°.
1819, ,,	11,	,,	20·9°.
1830, ,,	24,	,,	18·4°.
1830, ,,	25,	,,	18·6°.
1835, ,,	25,	,,	21·3°.
1835, ,,	26,	,,	22·3°.
1840, ,,	23,	,,	22·5°.
1855, ,,	21,	,,	20·2°.
1855, ,,	22,	,,	21·5°.
1859, ,,	19,	,,	22·4°.

So that in the year 1830, the 24th and 25th December were more remarkable for the severity of the cold, as shown in their mean temperatures, than in the present instance; but there is no instance of so low temperatures in December back to 1814, as those shown on Christmas-day and on the 29th day. The previous instances of low temperature in the neighbourhood of London are as follows, going backwards and confining myself to December :—

1855, December 19, the temperature was as low as 12°.		
1855, February 19,	„	11°.
1854, January 3,	„	13°.
1847, February 11,	„	13°.
1845, February 11,	„	minus 1½°.
1841, January 7,	„	13°.
1841, January 8,	„	14°.
1841, January 9,	„	4°.
1838, January 20,	„	minus 2¼°.
1830, December 25,	„	11°.

The low temperature of December 25 was general over the country, but more severe in some places than in others. The following are the readings by tested instruments made for the most part by Messrs. Negretti and Zambra, and examined before use by Mr. Glaisher, and spread over the country. They are arranged in order, starting from the place of highest temperature :—

	°		°		°
Helston	32·0	Alnwick	12·0	St. John's College	
Guernsey	30·0	Clifton	11·1	(Hurstpierpoint)...	3·0
Truro	26·0	Regent's Park...	10·9	Grantham	3·0
Ventnor	24·0	Battersea	10·5	Leeds...	3·0
Pembroke	22·0	Aldershott	10·0	Derby	2·0
Fairlight	20·0	Hartwell Rectory	10·0	Leyton	1·3
Osborne	19·0	Harrogate	9·5	Royston	1·1
Worthing...	18·0	Ben Rhydding...	8·5	Rose Hill (Oxford)...	1·0
Elgin	17·0	St. Paul's Parsonage	8·5	Gloucester	1·0
Little Bridy	16·2	Allenheads	8·3	Norwich	1·0
Liverpool	16·2	Greenwich	8·0	Sleaford	0·4
Stonyhurst	16·1	Lewisham	7·0	Holkham	0·0
Scarborough	16·0	North Shields	6·8	Belvoir Castle...	—1·0
Exeter	15·9	Camden Town	6·7	Wakefield	—2·0
Isle of Man	15·4	Bedford	6·0	Diss (Norfolk)...	—3·0
Petersfield	15·0	Lampeter	5·4	Manchester	—3·0
Barnstaple	13·5	Otley	5·0	York ...	—4·0
Exeter	13·5	Gt. Berkhampstead.	4·0	Nottingham	—8·0
Aspley	13·5	Cardington	3·6		
Whitehall	12·7	Bywell	3·5		

And if these be laid down on a map it will be found that the temperature on the south coast was about 20°; and it gradually became less proceeding northwards. It was about 7 in the neighbourhood of London. It was about 1°, in a line across the country from Gloucester, through Oxford to the east coast. It was below zero, between the latitudes 52° and 53¾°, from Wales to the east coast; and it was above zero at all places north of 54°; about 16° on both the east and west coasts, and of somewhat less temperature inland. It was 12° at Alnwick.

Obituary.

WILLIAM SPENCE, Entomologist, F.R.S., F.L.S., who, in conjunction with the Rev. Mr. Kirby, M.A., wrote the celebrated *Introduction to Entomology*, the seventh edition of which appeared in 1856: in the Appendix is reprinted, from Mr. Freeman's *Life of Mr. Kirby*, a sketch of the history of the friendship of the two authors for nearly half a century, and of the origin and progress of the *Introduction to Entomology*. The first volume of the work appeared in 1815; the third and concluding volume (the fourth) in 1826. It quickly became a standard authority, and has done more than any other work in diffusing a taste for Entomology throughout Great Britain.

COLONEL WILLIAM MARTIN LEAKE, Geographer.

GEORGE ROBERTS, of Lyme Regis. He wrote the *Social History of the People of the Southern Counties of England; and compiled a serviceable Geological Dictionary.

Dr. ROBERT BENTLEY TODD, late Professor of Physiology at King's College, and Physician to the Hospital. In conjunction with Dr. Grant, the Professor of Comparative Anatomy at University College, Dr. Todd commenced editing the *Cyclopædia of Anatomy and Physiology*, a gigantic work, which has only just reached its concluding part. Many of the articles were from his own pen. He also, afterwards, joined his distinguished pupil, Mr. Bowman, in the production of *The Physiological Anatomy of Man*. On the opening of King's College Hospital, which largely owed its existence to his exertions, Dr. Todd was appointed Physician and Professor of Clinical Medicine. Here, at the bedside of the patient, he applied his physiological knowledge to the explanation of the nature and the treatment of disease. A large number of his lectures has been reported in the medical journals, and a collection of these lectures, on Diseases of the Brain and Nervous System, and on other subjects, has been recently published. He also wrote a work in the early part of his career on *Gout, Rheumatic Fever, and Chronic Rheumatism of the Joints*. He was also a contributor to the *Transactions of the Medico-Chirurgical Society*, and of independent papers to the medical journals. Few men have filled a larger space in contemporary medical literature.—*Athenæum*, No. 1658.

Dr. EDWARD BEVAN, author of *The Honey Bee; its Natural History, Physiology, and Management*, 1827. This work at once attracted the attention of all engaged in the culture of bees, and has since gone through several editions. He also wrote a paper on the *Honey-Bee Communities*, which appeared in the first volume of the *Magazine of Zoology and Botany*. From the year 1819 he took up his residence at Hereford; and, as a proof of the esteem in which he was held, a local paper states that, on the occasion of a great flood in the Wye, in 1852, washing away all the Doctor's bee-hives and their inhabitants, a public subscription was raised, and a new apiary erected for him, free of all expense.

MRS. JAMESON, the accomplished writer on Art.

GEORGE SCHARF, artist.

ARTHUR SCHOPENHAUER, German philosopher.

Dr. THOMAS ALEXANDER, Director-General. His eminent services in the Crimea are thus sketched by a biographer in the *Times*:—"At the Alma his tenderness, his inexhaustible endurance, and noble devotion in the most terrible trial to which a surgeon, overwhelmed with calls on his utmost powers, and poorly provided with the means of relief, could be exposed, were especially remarkable. At Inkerman, for hour after hour, day after day, he toiled through scenes which those who have not witnessed a battlefield and the terrors of the hospital tents can never imagine or conceive, upheld by the noblest sense of duty; and many men now alive can bear witness to the heroic calm and skill which saved life and limb for them, and the prodigality of care he bestowed on others, regardless of everything but his sacred duties. In Lord Raglan's despatch he is described ' as deserving to be most honourably mentioned.' All through the winter he never left his post—nay, more, from the time he joined the Light Division till the British army quitted the shores of the Crimea he never was absent from his duty a single day." Dr. Alexander having been promoted to the rank of Local Inspector-General for service during the Russian war, he remained at home just one month and twenty-one days, when he was again ordered for service in Canada, as principal medical officer : after performing that duty for six months, Lord Panmure nominated him one of the Royal Commissioners to inquire into the sanitary state of the Army. He was also selected to draw up a new code of regulations for the management of barracks and hospitals ; and in 1858, he was appointed Director-General of the Army Medical Department, which appointment he held up to the day of his death.

SIR WILLIAM CHARLES ROSS, R.A., miniature painter to the Queen.

LIEUT.-COL. MURE, classical archæologist.

GILBERT M'NAB, of Jamaica, and one of the founders of the Botanical Society of Edinburgh. He was the first to introduce the *Victoria Regia* into Jamaica.

GEORGE RENNIE, F.R.S., who, in 1836, suggested to Mr. W. Ewart the Parliamentary Committee, which, besides inquiring into the state of the National Gallery, Royal Academy, and other institutions connected with the Arts, caused the immediate formation of Schools of Design. Together with the late Joseph Hume, he proposed and obtained the freest access to the public monuments of the Arts in St. Paul's, the National Gallery, the British Museum, and other depositories of the Fine Arts. When a member of the House of Commons, he first suggested, for the security of the public, that the Serpentine should be reduced to a uniform depth, and otherwise improved. If not the inventor, he was certainly the first to suggest to Sir W. Symonds (the then Surveyor of the Navy) the now widely-recognised advantages of watertight compartments in building ships. As Governor of the Falkland Islands, he raised them from a most abject condition to one of as great prosperity as the nature of the colony would admit.—*Athenæum (abridged)*, No. 1692.

GENERAL SIR THOMAS MAKDOUGALL BRISBANE, Bart., an active promoter of science, and who presided over the Royal Society of Edinburgh for twenty-seven years. It is related that Sir Thomas always carried a pocket sextant-chronometer and an artificial horizon, and by taking altitudes of the sun kept exact time. Besides performing his Government duties he erected an observatory at Paramatta, and supplied it with books, first-rate instruments, and two assistants from Europe, all at his own expense. The result of his observations at Paramatta, besides many valuable papers contributed to the Royal Society and the Astronomical Society, comprises the "Brisbane Catalogue of 7385 Stars of the Southern Hemisphere,"—a most important addition to astronomical knowledge ; and so highly esteemed were the results that the Home Government, on the representation of scientific men, gave instructions that the Paramatta Observatory should be kept up at the public expense. On Sir Thomas Brisbane's return to Scotland in 1826, he founded his celebrated astronomical observatory at Makerstoun ; and in 1841 he erected another observatory at the same place, for the purpose of making magnetical observations. The instruments supplied to both observatories were of the best and most costly nature. The sum paid for the clocks alone, in the magnetical observatory, was 1200 guineas. The work done has been excellent. From 1841 to 1846, magnetical and meteorological observations have been made every alternate hour, except in 1844 and 1845, when they were made every hour, day and night. Since 1846, nine observations have been made daily. The results have been published, and the Makerstoun Observatory has justly acquired the reputation of being one of the best magnetical and meteorological establishments in Scotland. Sir Thomas was, in 1810, elected a Fellow of the Royal Society ; and in 1828 he was awarded the Astronomical Society's gold medal. He was a Corresponding Member of the French Institute. The Universities of Oxford and Cambridge conferred upon him the degree of D.C.L., and in 1832 he succeeded Sir Walter Scott in the presidential chair of the Royal Society of Edinburgh, and retained that office during the rest of his life. During his presidency he founded two Gold Medals to be given annually as the reward of scientific merit, one by the Royal Society of Edinburgh, the other by the Society of Arts. The first of the former was presented in 1859, to Sir Thomas's fellow-countryman and fellow-soldier, Sir R. Murchison.—*Abridged from the Athenæum.*

LOUIS HERSENT, French painter.

PROFESSOR JAN GEEFS, of the Royal Academy at Antwerp, one of the most eminent Belgian sculptors.

GOTTHILF HEINRICH VON SCHUBERT, the natural philosopher.

GOODERICH, the American "Peter Parley," compiler of several pleasant books of science for the young.

THE REV. BADEN POWELL, Savilian Professor of Sanscrit at Oxford University. His first published work was *On Revelation and Science*, in 1833. His latest book was *The Order of Nature*, published in 1859. Between these dates he gave to the world a number of books, tracts, and articles on the religion of science and the science of religion,—the most noticeable of which were *The Connexion of Divine and Natural Truth* (1838),—*Tradition Unveiled* (1839), with its *Supplement* in the following year,—and *Christianity without Judaism* (1857). Mr. Powell was much engaged in controversy, and took an active part in the proceedings of the Society of Arts and of the Royal Institution. One of Professor Baden Powell's latest labours was his masterly paper "On the Study of the Evidences of Christianity," in the Oxford *Essays and Reviews*, the most striking work of its class published during the past year.

ALEXANDER GABRIEL DECAMPS, French painter.

RT. HON. JAMES WILSON, statist, and writer on political economy; founder of the *Economist* journal.

DUKE PAUL OF WURTEMBERG, for many years so well known as an indefatigable traveller in the service of science. His travels extended over nearly every part of the world; the result of his earlier journeys to Egypt, America, and Australia has been laid down in several works, and a series of letters to the Augsburg *Allgemeine Zeitung*. His latest travels, from 1849 to 1858, stretched over the whole continent of America (inclusive of California) and Australia. His castle, Mergentheim, near Stuttgart, contains, besides the many trophies from his travels, one of the largest ornithological collections in existence.

SALTER LIVESAY, M.D., F.L.S., Surgeon R.N., conchologist, microscopist, and artist.

JESSE HARTLEY, the engineer of the Liverpool Docks. Mr. Hartley, who was upwards of eighty years of age, was a native of the North Riding of Yorkshire, and after receiving an ordinary education, served his apprenticeship as a stonemason, and worked at the building of Borough-bridge. Subsequently, he succeeded his father as bridge-master in the district named, until his removal to Liverpool, on receiving the appointment of engineer to the Dock Committee. During the long period in which he held the responsible office of dock engineer in Liverpool, Mr. Hartley altered, or entirely constructed every dock belonging to the town. Besides this, he was employed as engineer for the Bolton and Manchester Railway and Canal; he was also consulting engineer for the Dee Bridge at Chester, the centring for which was considered a great triumph.

JELLINGER C. SYMONS, one of Her Majesty's Inspectors of Schools. The title of the various pamphlets, lectures, speeches, &c., and treatises on educational and social subjects which he published, fill upwards of six pages in the new catalogue of the British Museum. Mr. Symons is also known and remembered for a controversy which he carried on against Dr. Whewell respecting the revolution of the moon on its axis, and for an interesting essay on the authorship of *Junius*.

"Perhaps, with the single exception of Canon Moseley, of Bristol, there was no one whose name was more widely known than Mr. Symons in connexion with the great modern educational and reformatory movements. It must be acknowledged, however, that he was not so sound a mathematician as could have been desired. His letters on "the Rotation of the Moon," which appeared two or three years since, partly in the *Mechanics' Magazine*, and partly in the *Times*, must have astonished and pained every real mathematician."—*Mechanics' Magazine.*

DR. THOMAS FORSTER, the indefatigable meteorologist.

JOHN NARRIEN, Professor of Mathematics at Sandhurst.

DR. ROSCHER, the bold traveller, killed in his bed by a poisoned arrow, while in the western part of Zanzibar.

HAYMAN HORACE WILSON, Boden Professor of Sanscrit, and historian of India, one of our few really great Oriental scholars.

ANDREAS RETZIUS, the distinguished Swedish anatomist and ethnologist, Professor of Anatomy and Physiology at the Royal Caroline Institute, Stockholm. He was the son of Professor Retzius, of Lund, graduated in 1819, and soon after was attached as Anatomical Lecturer to the Veterinary Institution in Stockholm. He received the appointment which he held to the period of his decease, at the Caroline Institute, in 1830. He is the author of numerous anatomical and physiological monographs ; among which, the one descriptive of the Crania of Ancient Scandinavian Races, in which the attention of ethnologists is especially called to the modifications of the skull, defined by Professor Retzius as " dolichocephalic " and " brachycephalic," has, perhaps, made his name most generally known in scientific and literary circles in this country.

M. Retzius (it is stated in the *Athenæum*) died in the full pursuit of science. On his dying bed he made his observations on the progressing dissolution of his own body. " This struggle of death is hard," he said to those about him ; " but it is of the highest interest to note this wrestle between life and death : now the legs are dead ; now the muscles of the bowels cease their function ; the last struggle must be heavy, but for all that it is highly interesting." These were his last words.

SIR CHARLES BARRY, R.A., the architect of the New Houses of Parliament. His own preferences and tastes would have led him to adopt the Italian style of architecture for the New Palace of Westminster; but as the instructions to the competitors limited the choice of styles to Gothic or Elizabethan, he chose the former as the more suitable for such a building. From the moment he commenced his arduous undertaking, until the day of his death, a period extending over more than twenty-four years, this work occupied his thoughts night and day. The manner in which his professional services were requited by " a Government proverbially indifferent to the claims of Art," is a disgrace to the country, which the bare honour of knighthood can ill conceal. We sympathize in reading history with the ill-treatment of Sir Christopher Wren, and the cabal and controversy by which he was assailed ; but, in the present day, we have an equally glaring instance of meanness and injustice to merits of the highest order. Sir Charles Barry was elected a Royal Academician in 1842 ; he was also a Fellow of the Royal Institute of British Architects, a Fellow of the Royal Society, a Member of the Royal Commission for the Exhibition of 1851 ; and a member of many foreign academies, including those of Rome, Belgium, Prussia, Russia, Denmark, and Sweden.

CHARLES E. MAY, C.E., F.R.S., inventor of the compressed wooden fastening for railway chairs, and who constructed some of the most important astronomical instruments for the Greenwich Observatory.

ROBERT HUGHES, Assistant to the Engineer-in-Chief to the Admiralty (steam branch), where he aided to work out the great improvements which have taken place in machinery during the last fifteen years.

JOSEPH LOCKE, C.E., M.P., Engineer of the Grand Junction Railway, and the South Western line, " whence he accomplished the extension of the system to France ; where, in the construction of the Paris and Rouen, and Rouen and Havre lines, he introduced English capital, English workmen, and English contractors, and initiated the Continental Railway System. He was thus the first who promoted the establishment of the present rapid communication between the great commercial capital of Great Britain, and Paris, the fashionable metropolis of the Continent."—*Mechanics' Magazine*.

The main characteristic of Mr. Locke's genius as an engineer was his uniform adherence to the significance of financial results in the great works which he carried out. It was not that he feared engineering difficulties, for when they were inevitable he encountered and overcame them with skill ; as for instance in the works of the Manchester and Sheffield Railway. But his great anxiety, and which secured for him the confidence of a large body of capitalists, was to attain his object by avoiding difficult and expensive works, from a desire that all the works on which he engaged should be commercially successful. The abnegation of professional renown, arising from the construction of monumental works, whilst establishing his reputation as an economical engineer, induced him to turn to the locomotive engine, and to tax its powers (in which he had from the earliest period the greatest confidence) for overcoming steeper gradients than had hitherto been deemed compatible with economy and safety. In this he was very successful; and when viewed in conjunction with the previously-mentioned general features of his professional life, it must be conceded that the decease of Mr. Locke had caused a gap in the profession which will long be felt. Mr. Locke had acquired the confidence and esteem of a large circle of friends in the House of Commons.

HENRY BRADBURY, known by his beautiful system of "Nature printing," improvements in printing from surfaces, &c. (See *Year-Book of Facts*, 1860.)

ALFRED E. CHALON, R.A., portrait painter to Her Majesty. He was of Swiss extraction, and brother of John James Chalon, R.A.

DAVID JARDINE, writer on criminal law.

EBENEZER LANDELLS, engraver on wood, pupil of Bewick and Nicholson.

CAPTAIN MACONOCHIE, inventor of the Mark System of Prison Discipline, and the author of many tracts and papers on that subject.

ADAM THOMSON, the well-known watch-manufacturer, of New Bond-street, and author of a popular volume on *Time and Timekeepers*.

JOHN FINLAISON, actuary.

JOHN WHICHCORD, architect.

ALBERT SMITH, M.R.C.S., but more popularly known by his sketches of life and character.

CHARLES GOODYEAR, the inventor of the art of Vulcanizing India-rubber. Mr. Goodyear was born in New Haven, Dec. 29, 1800. The importance of vulcanization, its applicability to an indefinite and inexhaustible number of uses, its character of progressive development and perfectibility, were perceived by Mr. Goodyear in 1839; and with untiring perseverance to the last moment of his life he prosecuted the development of his invention. No less remarkable than his perseverance was the liberality with which Mr. Goodyear spent and applied the whole proceeds of his inventions and patents to the perfecting of the many forms and applications of the new material, Vulcanized India-rubber, which his inventive talent called into existence.

J. C. WELLS, a prominent architect of New York, on board an English steamer, bound for this country, of which Mr. Wells was a native. He died two hours before the vessel reached land. He designed several of the public buildings of New York, including Dr. Phillips's church on the Fifth Avenue. Various large stores, and a court-house at Wilkesbarre, Pennsylvania, also illustrate his skill. He held the office of treasurer in the American Institute of Architects.

THOMAS MOTLEY, C.E., of Washington. He was formerly of Bristol, and was the projector of the design of the wrought-iron arch bridge over the Avon from the rocks at Clifton, a model of which was exhibited many years ago. He went to America about seven years since, in hope of getting his plans adopted in that country.

JOSEPH MILLER, the well-known marine engineer, of Charlestown, South Carolina. He was a native of Carlisle, and when a young man went to Birmingham, where he served his apprenticeship at the celebrated Soho Foundry of Messrs. Boulton and Watt. He then became chief engineer at the Butterley Iron Works, and there commenced that career as a marine engine maker which, continued and extended under the names of "Barnes and Miller," and "Miller and Ravenhill," has given to his name a well-earned reputation. Undoubtedly, to him is to be ascribed an important share in those efforts at simplicity in design, elegance and lightness in proportion, and soundness of workmanship which have brought the marine engine to its present excellence. His firm worked extensively in the formation not only of our own steam fleet, but of those of many foreign Governments; and on the Thames, and between Dover and Calais, and on the Rhone and the Saone, the Danube and the Rhine, some of the earliest and most successful efforts at rapid steam navigation were made by vessels supplied with his engines. Mr. Miller was a Fellow of the Royal Society, and a man of elegant tastes. He bequeathed to the Institution of Civil Engineers the munificent sum of 5000*l.*—*Mechanics' Magazine.*

CHRISTIAN CHARLES BUNSEN, the profound scholar and historian of Ancient Egypt, and the learned annotator of the Bible. He did not live to complete more than three parts of "that grand enterprise," his revised *Bible for the People.* To such of our readers as wish to appreciate the labours of this learned man, we recommend Dr. Rowland Williams's able paper—" Bunsen's Biblical Researches," in the Oxford *Essays and Reviews,* pp. 50—93. "Bunsen's enduring glory," says Dr. Williams, " is neither to have paltered with his conscience, nor shrunk from the difficulties of the problem; but to have brought a vast erudition, in the light of a Christian conscience, to unroll tangled records, tracing frankly the Spirit of God elsewhere, but honouring chiefly the traditions of his Hebrew sanctuary. No living author's works could furnish so pregnant a text for a discourse on Biblical criticism. Passing over some specialities of Lutheranism, we may meet in the field of research which is common to scholars; while, even here, the sympathy which justifies respectful exposition, need not imply entire agreement.

* * * * * * * *

" If Protestant Europe is to escape those shadows of the twelfth century, which with ominous recurrence are closing around us, to Baron Bunsen will belong a foremost place among the champions of light and right. Any points, disputable or partially erroneous, which may be discovered in his many works, are as dust in the balance, compared with the mass of solid learning, and the elevating influence of a noble and Christian spirit. Those who have assailed his doubtful points are equally opposed to his strong ones. Our own testimony is, where we have been best able to follow him we have generally found most reason to agree with him. But our little survey has not traversed his vast field, nor our plummet sounded his depth."

JAMES FOGGO, painter and art-critic.

SIR CHARLES FELLOWS, the discoverer of the Xanthian Marbles, and one of the first adventurers to the summit of Mont Blanc. A narrative of his ascent was privately printed in 1827.

WILLIAM TASSIE, modeller, and collector of gems.

THOMAS, EARL OF DUNDONALD, " a renowned sailor-warrior, and an ambitious inventor." Since his retirement from naval service he had studied the science of naval warfare, and invented new projectiles and new methods of blowing up ships; and had published many valuable hints for the improvement of our steam navy. These will be found developed in the Autobiography of the Earl of Dundonald, which he just lived to complete. The fitful fever of his political life, and the coldness with which his bravery was acknowledged by an ungrateful country, or rather, persecuting administrations, are not our specialities. His merits as a scientific inventor were variously estimated. The Editor of the *Mechanics' Magazine,* in announcing his death, remarks: "Only last week, we made mention of him in terms which we do not wish to recal, but with less tenderness than we now feel in thinking of the grand old man who is no more. Thousands of inventors have outshone him; but no braver man or greater sailor ever lived, even in England." As to his bravery, and its insufficient rewards, there can be but one opinion. He was honoured with burial in Westminster Abbey; but, (to quote a homely proverb) to be treated with respect after death is but a poor recompense for being neglected while living.

GEORGE BAILEY, architect; Curator of the Soane Museum.

THE LATE SIR WILLIAM HAMILTON.

The following inscription has been put up in St. John's Chapel, Edinburgh: "In memory of Sir William Hamilton, Baronet, Professor of Logic and Metaphysics in the University of Edinburgh, who died 6th of May, 1856, aged 68 years. His aim was, by a pure philosophy, to teach that now we see through a glass darkly, now we know in part. His hope that in the life to come he should see face to face, and know even as also he is known." " It is not often," says the *Scotsman,* "that so much humility and truth meet over the grave of so much greatness."

GENERAL INDEX.

ARSENIC IN PAPER-HANGINGS.

WE quote the following well-attested instance from the *Chemical News :--*

A Mr. T. King, living at Highbury, had a little son three years and a-half old, and a daughter still younger. The breakfast-room was hung with green flock paper, and in this same room was a cupboard in which they kept toys and other things. A few days previously they cleared out this cupboard, and the little boy was noticed to put a piece of lace to be found there into his mouth and suck it. Not long after this he was sick, unable to eat, and speedily sunk into a semi-comatose condition, which was only broken occasionally by violent convulsions, and he died in about thirty-six hours. In the meantime his sister had been seized with similar symptoms; and as this was the second time they had been attacked simultaneously, it naturally occurred to the doctor that the cause of decease was not a natural one; he, therefore, sent portions of the body to Dr. Letheby, to be analyzed; and the result was, that he discovered arsenic in the stomach, the liver, and the evacuations. A piece of the green paper was also sent to him to be tested, and he found that one-third of its weight was arsenite of copper. An inquest was held on the body, and the verdict returned by the jury was, "That Clarence William King had been poisoned by the inhalation of arsenical fumes which had escaped from the green paper of a certain sitting-room." The fact is, Scheele's green, as the arsenite of copper is termed, is not only cheap, but produces a green of peculiar brilliancy. The public, for the most part, knowing nothing of the danger of covering their rooms with such paper, give it the preference over that of a duller tint; consequently there is a great demand for this paper, which, so long as it lasts, the manufacturer will continue to supply, utterly regardless of results.

---

* This excellent journal has been enlarged and otherwise improved, so as more efficiently to meet the requirements of a weekly chemical newspaper. We are glad to see the Royal Institution Lectures, by Faraday and others, at the Royal Institution, are to be reported in this improved series published by Griffin, Bohn, and Co., Stationers' Hall Court.

BANK OF DEPOSIT.

NATIONAL ASSURANCE AND INVESTMENT ASSOCIATION.

ESTABLISHED MAY, 1844.

EMPOWERED BY SPECIAL ACT OF PARLIAMENT.

CAPITAL STOCK, £100,000.

OBJECTS OF THE COMPANY.

THIS Company was established in 1844, for the purpose of opening to the public an easy and safe mode of Investment, with a high rate of Interest.

PLAN OF OPERATIONS.

The Bank of Deposit differs from ordinary Banks in the mode of employing Capital—money deposited with this Company being principally lent upon well-secured Life-Interests, Reversions in the Government Funds, or other property of undoubted value. This class of investment yields, it is well known, the greatest amount of profit, with ample security. Loans made by the Company are collaterally secured by policies of Assurance on the Lives of the Borrowers, or their nominees, effected at rates of premium which ensure the validity of the Policies against every possible contingency, secure adequate profit to the Company, and provide for the expenses of management.

ORDINARY DEPOSIT ACCOUNTS.

Accounts may be opened with sums of any amount, and increased from time to time, at the convenience of Depositors. A Stock Voucher, signed by two Directors, is given for each sum deposited.

WITHDRAWAL OF ORDINARY DEPOSITS.

In order that the permanent and profitable investments in which the funds are employed may not be unnecessarily disturbed, power is reserved to require six months' notice of withdrawal. It being, however, one of the principal objects of the Institution to unite a popular system of investment with the greatest possible accommodation to the public, the Board have power to dispense with notice, and to allow parties, in cases of necessity, to withdraw the whole or any portion of their Deposits on Special Application.

RATE AND PAYMENT OF INTEREST.

The Interest, which has never been less than Five per Cent. per Annum on Ordinary Deposits, is payable in January and July, on the amount standing in the name of the Depositor on the 30th June and 31st December, and for the convenience of parties residing at a distance, may be received at the Branch Offices, or remitted through Country Bankers.

SPECIAL DEPOSITS.

Deposits made by Special Agreement for fixed periods can be withdrawn without notice.

PETER MORRISON,

3, PALL MALL EAST, LONDON, S.W.   *Managing Director.*

Forms for opening accounts may be obtained at any of the Branches or Agencies, or will be sent, post free, on application.

W. KENT AND CO.'S

New and Beautifully Illustrated Works, &c.

In 4to, splendidly bound and gilt, cloth, 21s.; morocco, 31s. 6d.,

THE ART ALBUM. Fac-similes of Water-colour Drawings by George Cattermole, T. Sidney Cooper, A.R.A., Edwin Duncan, John Gilbert, William Hunt, R. P. Leitch, George H. Thomas, Mrs. Ward, Henry Warren, Edward H. Wehnert, Harrison Weir, and H. B. Willis.

*** This beautiful volume is a triumph of the printer's art, and should adorn every drawing-room table.

Small 4to, elaborately bound and gilt, in cloth, 15s.; morocco, 24s.

THREE GEMS in ONE SETTING, containing "THE POET'S SONG," by ALFRED TENNYSON; "FIELD FLOWERS," by THOMAS CAMPBELL; and the "PILGRIM FATHERS," by Mrs. HEMANS. Each page beautifully ornamented in Chromo-lithography, from designs by A. L. Bond.

*** This book, as its name implies, is a perfect gem. It needs but an inspection to make every lover of fine arts anxious to possess a copy.

Small 4to, handsomely bound, 7s. 6d.

HOUSEHOLD SONG. A Collection of Lyrical Pieces, selected from the works of Burns, Mallet, Hood, Milnes, Upton, Mackay, Rogers, Clarke, &c. With illustrations by Birket Foster, G. H. Thomas, L. Palmer, Solomon, J. Archer, A.R.A., Edmonston, Harrison Weir, &c.

A NEW BOOK FOR BOYS AND GIRLS.

Square 16mo, cloth gilt, 6s.

THE CAREWES: A Tale of the Civil Wars. By MARY GILLIES, Author of "The Voyage of the Constance." With 24 Illustrations, worked in tints, by Birket Foster.

Imperial 16mo, cloth gilt, 2s. 6d.; with coloured plates, 4s. 6d.

THE LORD'S PRAYER explained for CHILDREN, with a Preface, by the Rev. J. M. BELLEW, S.C.L.; and numerous Illustrations.

Now ready Vol. V., cloth, 4s.; with gilt edges, 4s. 6d.,

THE BOOK and its MISSIONS, containing a History of the progress of "The Book" all over the World, and details of the efforts of the Bible-women among the London Poor during the past year. All the back numbers of this Magazine are kept in print, and Vols. 1, 2, 3, and 4, bound in cloth, may also be had. Cases for binding the Numbers, 1s. each.

Eightieth Thousand, Fourteenth edition, limp cloth, 2s.; cloth boards, 2s. 6d.; with gilt edges, 3s.,

THE BOOK and its STORY. By L. N. R., Author of the "Missing Link," and Editor of "The Book and its Missions."

An edition printed on fine paper, suitable for a present, handsomely bound, 4s.

2

LONDON, FEBRUARY 1, 1861.

Just Published, with an Emblematic Frontispiece, 5s. cloth,

Mysteries

of

Life, Death, and Futurity;

ILLUSTRATED FROM THE BEST AND LATEST AUTHORITIES.

CONTENTS.

LIFE AND TIME.	THE CRUCIFIXION OF OUR LORD.
NATURE OF THE SOUL.	THE END OF THE WORLD.
SPIRITUAL LIFE.	MAN AFTER DEATH.
MENTAL OPERATIONS.	THE INTERMEDIATE STATE.
BELIEF AND SCEPTICISM.	THE GREAT RESURRECTION.
PREMATURE INTERMENT.	RECOGNITION OF THE BLESSED.
PHENOMENA OF DEATH.	THE DAY OF JUDGMENT.
SIN AND PUNISHMENT.	THE FUTURE STATES, ETC.

By HORACE WELBY.

Extract from the Preface.

"As the aim of the writer is to render his book acceptable to a large number of readers, he has endeavoured to make it attractive by the notes and comments of expositors of our own time, as well as from those sacred treasures of learning, and those studies of Scripture, which strongly reveal to us the relation of God to man. The most reverential regard for things sacred has been fostered throughout the work; and wherever the stores of classic thought and fancy have been resorted to for embellishment and illustration, these have been employed as subsidiary to the Spirit and the Truth."

LITERARY OPINIONS.

"It is a great deal to be able to say in favour of this book that we have discovered nothing in it which can offend or annoy a member of any Christian denomination; and that many of the quotations are not only valuable in themselves, but have been collected from sources not easily accessible to the general reader. Not a few of the chapters are, however, Mr. Welby's own composition, and these are, for the most part, thoughtfully and carefully written."—*From the Critic*, Jan. 5, 1861.

"The author and compiler of this work is evidently a largely-read and deeply-thinking man. For its plentiful suggestiveness alone it should meet with a kindly and grateful acceptance. It is a pleasant, dreamy, charming, startling little volume, every page of which sparkles like a gem in an antique setting."—*Weekly Dispatch*, Jan. 20, 1861.

"This book is the result of extensive reading, and careful noting : it is such a common-place book as some thoughtful divine or physician might have compiled, gathering together a vast variety of opinions and speculations, bearing on physiology, the phenomena of life, and the nature and future existence of the soul. With these are blended facts, anecdotes, personal traits of character, and well-grounded arguments, with the one guiding intention of strengthening the Christian's faith, with the thoughts and conclusions of the great and good of the earth. Mr. Horace Welby has brought together a mass of matter that might be sought in vain through the most extensive library; and we know of no work that so strongly compels reflection, and so well assists it."—*London Review*, Jan. 13, 1861.

"This closely-printed volume, with its thousand-and-one references to the works and opinions of our best and greatest writers, is not inferior, as an interesting literary curiosity, to the famous 'Anatomy of Melancholy.' In justice to Mr. Welby, we may add, that no religious scruples are likely to be outraged in his pages."—*Oriental Budget*, Jan. 1861.

Mysteries of Life, Death, and Futurity.

GENERAL CONTENTS.

GENERAL CONTENTS—Continued.

NEW WORK, BY THE EDITOR OF "THE YEAR-BOOK OF FACTS."

With Frontispiece and Vignette, 3s. 6d.

CURIOSITIES OF SCIENCE;

Second Series.

A BOOK FOR OLD AND YOUNG.

BY JOHN TIMBS, F.S.A.

CONTENTS :

* *The following are a few of the more characteristic Articles in this Work.*

KENT AND CO., PATERNOSTER ROW.

JUVENILE WORKS.

3